Anglo-Irish Modernism and the Maternal

Anglo-Irish Modernism and the Maternal

From Yeats to Joyce

Diane Stubbings

First published 2000 by
PALGRAVE
Houndmills, Basingstoke, Hampshire RG21 6XS and
175 Fifth Avenue, New York, N. Y. 10010
Companies and representatives throughout the world

PALGRAVE is the new global academic imprint of
St. Martin's Press LLC Scholarly and Reference Division and
Palgrave Publishers Ltd (formerly Macmillan Press Ltd).

ISBN 0–333–76026–3 hardback

This book is printed on paper suitable for recycling and
made from fully managed and sustained forest sources.

A catalogue record for this book is available
from the British Library.

Library of Congress Cataloging-in-Publication Data
Stubbings, Diane, 1961–
    Anglo-Irish modernism and the maternal : from Yeats to Joyce / Diane
    Stubbings.
        p. cm.
    Includes bibliographical references (p.) and index.
    ISBN 0–333–76026–3
    1. English literature—Irish authors—History and criticism. 2. Yeats,
    W. B. (William Butler), 1865–1939—Characters—Mothers. 3. English
    literature—20th century—History and criticism. 4. Joyce, James,
    1882–1941—Characters—Mothers. 5. Modernism (Literature)—Ireland.
    6. Motherhood in literature. 7. Mothers in literature. I. Title.
    PR8755 .S78 2000
    820'.9415—dc21
                                                            00–033354

10   9   8   7   6   5   4   3   2   1
        06   05   04   03   02   01   00

To
Mary Constance Ryan

Contents

Acknowledgements

For their kind permission to reproduce copyright material, my thanks to

The Board of Trinity College Dublin
The John M. Synge Trust
Colin Smythe Limited representing the Estate of the late C.D. Medley
The Estate of Sean O'Casey
Faber & Faber Ltd, publishers of the plays of Sean O'Casey

Many people have contributed, both personally and professionally, to the development and publication of this work, and I would like to take this opportunity to thank them for their advice, assistance, criticism and encouragement: my family, Dianne Naoum, Margaret Holyday, John Brennan, Ros Haynes, Mary Chan, Shirley Webster, Lis During, Declan Kiberd, Anna Gibbs, Roy Foster, Tony Gibbs, Julie Tapper, Warwick Gould, the Permissions Department of Faber & Faber, particularly Sally Robson and Suzanne Lee, and, from the publisher, Charmian Hearne, Ruth Willats and Eleanor Birne.

Special thanks to my mentor, Peter Kuch, who has nurtured this project from its earliest days.

And, finally, for the strength and the joy they give me, love and thanks to Michael, Jack and Darwin.

Part I
Introduction

1
Mother-Ireland Calls Me

Respect! I love my mother well enough, but I'm not going to delude myself because I had a mother.

George Moore, Mike Fletcher

You needn't teach me how to bring up children, I buried nine of them. Response from an Irish mother admonished for not feeding her children properly[1]

In a letter to Nora Barnacle, James Joyce writes of Ireland's call to him. It is a summons that Richard Rowan in *Exiles* also receives, 'called back to her now on the eve of her long awaited victory, to her whom in loneliness and exile [her children] have at last learned to love.'[2] It is a call that both artists seek to resist; yet for Joyce, coupled with this image of the mother seeking the return of her wayward son is that of the woman embracing the artist as mother to son, enabling him thereby to gain access to his own creativity. As Richard Rowan tells Bertha, he desires 'to be united with you in body and soul in utter nakedness', a coupling which, Joyce's letter to his own wife suggests, seeks to move beyond the intimacy of husband and wife to that of mother and child.[3] This conflation of the artist penetrating woman as mother, regressing through his union with her to those spaces wherein he himself might create, watched over by a prevenient mother-Ireland, captures both the artist's appropriation of maternal spaces and the burden exacted by a demanding nationalist icon. Joyce's complicated relationship with the maternal image is rehearsed throughout his work: in all, the struggle between mother and artist for that space where creativity is seeded and borne, where the artist may realize himself as artist, weaves through the text. It is a theme which develops progressively – hinted at in *Dubliners*, pivotal in *A Portrait of the Artist as a Young Man* and *Ulysses*, and flowing through *Finnegans Wake* – a development which mirrors, I argue, the shift in representation that characterizes modernism.

Joyce's privileged position within the modernist canon is undisputed, and he is one of a number of writers born in Ireland and engaging with Irish themes whose work contributed to and drew upon the modernist movement. In the Irish context, it is significant that the period which saw a radical shift in literary and artistic representation overlapped with a significant period of flux in society and politics: the Land Acts of the 1880s and 1890s which saw the redistribution of land and a shift in political power; the death of Charles Stewart Parnell in 1891; the Easter Rising of 1916 and the subsequent civil war; and the declaration of the Irish Free State in 1922. In the same period, the Irish Literary Renaissance – which saw the emergence of the Gaelic League, the Irish National Literary Society and the Irish Literary Theatre – flourished and abated. Further, Irish opposition to British imperialism was reinforced by the outbreak of the Boer War at the turn of the century and the Great War of 1914–18, a period which saw, Foster argues, the 'radicalization of Irish politics'.[4] It is within this confluence of modernism and political and social upheaval in Ireland that my exploration of the representation of the maternal is positioned.

A mother's place: the cultural context

The social and political function of the Irish mother in the nineteenth and early twentieth centuries is an area of historical research that has been largely subsumed by research into the role of women over the same period.[5] Where the mother-figure has been the focus of research, it is generally her familial function that has been explored, with her position within a broader cultural, social or political framework largely neglected. What has emerged is not so much an expression of the 'woman', but rather the reinforcement of the stereotypical figure, realized in terms of her relationship with male members of the family.[6]

Irish oral tradition proffers an image of the mother as a crucial figure in the politics and governance of ancient Ireland. Even so, as Wood warns, such a position within myth and legend does not necessarily '[reflect] the *actual* legal or social status of women'.[7] This tallies, according to Fyfe, with 'the general rule that there is an inverse relationship between the exaltation of *images* of women and their actual degree of *power*'.[8] The mythical mother was essentially a constructed figure, and during the nineteenth century that construct was subjected to the censorship and 'distortions [of] well-meaning Gaelic revivalists'.[9] Shifts in the Irish economy during the eighteenth and nineteenth centuries saw a concomitant social shift, with women, and particularly mothers, increasingly confined to a domestic role.[10] The same industrialization that confined women to the home saw a proliferation in goods designed to aid domestic work; however, the overall effect was an increase in housework due to increased expectations:

> The woman of the household should set the example of always sitting down to the table neatly dressed, and of having the room, whether it be the kitchen or any other room, where the meals are served in perfect order, and the table should be as temptingly set as possible... the home is, or ought to be, the woman's kingdom, and that she must rule it wisely, she must serve it well.[11]

No longer was the Irish mother merely expected to sweep the hearth and ensure that a 'stirabout' was simmering over the fire, though such an image was still romanticized as inherent to Gaelic tradition. It is just this image that O'Brien acutely satirizes in *The Poor Mouth (An Béal Bocht):*

> my mother was sensible, level-headed and well-fed; her like will not be there again. She spent her life cleaning out the house, sweeping cow-dung and pig-dung from in front of the door, churning butter and milking cows, weaving and carding wool and working the spinning-wheel, praying, cursing and setting big fires to boil a houseful of potatoes to stave off the day of famine.[12]

The subservience of women to the home and to the perceived needs of husbands and children was broadly accepted, and reinforced with each new generation. The burgeoning demands for women's rights, which occurred in Britain in the latter decades of the nineteenth century, did, however, see concomitant demands in Ireland. Even so, the women's movement in Ireland was undermined by a number of factors – social, religious and economic – not the least of which was the insistence of the Nationalists that women's rights must be set aside until Irish freedom was won.[13]

The confinement of the mother to the home was, in itself, not peculiar to Ireland. What was, however, of note was the degree to which the mother's role became caught up within Nationalist and religious discourses: such discourses, while seeming to offer the mother a privileged role in the liberation of Ireland – or her eternal rewards – did little more than tether her to private spaces and distance her from the source of genuine political power. She became a significant element in Irish resistance to British imperialism, resistance that took place on both political and cultural grounds;[14] the mother who failed in her indoctrination of Irish children to the Nationalist cause was represented as having a breast which was 'a poisoned fount'.[15] Abetting the Nationalist agenda was that of Irish Catholicism, which positioned the mother again in the home, defying the immorality and protestantism that threatened the hearth by bringing her children to baptism within the Catholic Church.[16] Howes refers to the 'twin images of chaste virgin and prolific mother'.[17] Similarly, Cairns and Richards argue that Catholicism was the 'cement' by which the 'ideological matrix of Nationalist discourse was held together'.[18] Both Catholic and Nationalist discourses insisted that familial mothers subjugate themselves to the 'cause'; at the same time mythical mothers – principally Cathleen ni Houlihan and the Blessed Virgin Mary – were privileged and venerated. It was this privileged space that was promised to the familial mother for her service, a space with no inherent power, all power reserved by and for those who constructed and disseminated the myths.

In his discourse 'The Glories of Mary for the Sake of Her Son', Cardinal Newman insisted that 'the glories of Mary are for the sake of Jesus; and that we praise and bless her as the first of creatures, that we may duly confess him as our sole Creator'.[19] He continued:

> Every church which is dedicated to her, every altar which is raised under her invocation, every image which represents her, every litany in her praise, every Hail Mary for her continual memory, does but remind us that there was One who, though He was all-blessed from all eternity, yet for the sake of sinners, 'did not shrink from the Virgin's womb'.[20]

Yet, despite the Cardinal's admonitions, the relationship between mother and child shifted such that the mother's suffering – as centred in the figure of the *Pietà* – tended to obscure the son's sacrifice: the very need to devote such a lengthy discourse to refuting Mary's entitlement to be worshipped in her own right suggests both the excess with which mariolatry was practised in Ireland and the disquiet with which such veneration was viewed by potential converts.[21] The same paradigm was evident in the relationship between Cathleen ni Houlihan and the sons who sacrificed themselves in her name: such sacrifices merely fed her cult, allowing 'her' to conscript more and more men (and women) into the fight to regain her 'four beautiful green fields'.[22] Cathleen was one of a number of figures from Irish myth and legend who were utilized for the cause. Brown notes that 'motifs' such as that of the sons of Ireland serving their mother through sacrifice 'were the fruit of the Literary Revival which had come to vigorous life when, from the 1880s onwards, scholars, poets, playwrights, historians and folklorists rescued much from the Gaelic past and reinterpreted that past in the interests of a raised national consciousness'.[23] 'If you want to interest [an Irishman] in Ireland,' Larry Doyle counsels in Shaw's *John Bull's Other Island*, 'youve [sic] got to call the unfortunate Ireland Kathleen ni Houlihan and pretend she's a little old woman.'[24]

The schism between familial mother and mythical mother was, superficially at least, a wide one: the familial mother must practise service and obeisance, while the mythical mother was potent, revered and to be served. Yet both constructions of the mother-figure served particular, though consummative, roles. The image of the 'good mother', subject to the needs of her family, bound the mother to the hearth and, more broadly, contained women according to the dictates of the patriarchy, while the mythical mother acted, as Joyce would suggest, as a siren, seducing men to service in the cause she personified.

Moving against tradition

Why the Anglo-Irish contribution to modernism – a contribution accurately described by McCormack as being 'disproportionate'[25] – should have proved so extensive and so profound is a question that has engaged a number of critics over recent years. In *From Burke to Beckett*, for example, McCormack seeks – not wholly successfully – to explicate Irish modernism through an examination of the 'Protestant Ascendancy', the particular nature of nineteenth-century Irish realism, and Yeats's construction of an Irish tradition. Arguments foregrounding British imperialism and its impact on Irish culture have, however, proved more fruitful. Deane contends that both an engagement with Nationalist discourse and the need to afford a previously unarticulated culture its own language spawned the creativity of the seminal Irish modernists – Moore, Synge, O'Casey, Yeats and Joyce.[26] Eagleton also draws a 'connection between colonial dissent and modernist achievement', arguing that the 'marginal nature of Irish realism is one reason why early twentieth-century Ireland was the only sector of the British Isles to witness an astonishingly rich outcrop of modernism'.[27] More recently, Kiberd, in *Inventing Ireland*, has drawn a specific link between Irish modernism and resistance to British imperialism – this resistance being rendered in the 'invention' of an Irish identity which would stand in opposition to that construction of 'Irishness' which reinforced the British imperialist enterprise.[28] However, the *need* to construct an alternative Irish identity or consciousness does not, in itself, explicate the *means* by which an imposed consciousness was resisted and its counter-consciousness represented. It is my contention that the unprecedented concentration of literary modernism in Ireland stems from both the prevalence of the mother-figure in the Irish cultural tradition and the constricting conditions that any relationship with that mother imposed. By representing her and, importantly, resisting her, it became possible to move beyond the constrictions of the cultural tradition and assert a subjectivity free of rigid discursive practices that were themselves an expression of British hegemony. The corresponding social and political upheavals facilitated this representation of the maternal as well as being a response to it.

In their survey of modernism, Bradbury and MacFarlane suggest that the final two decades of the nineteenth century are distinguished by their

> fascination with evolving consciousness: consciousness aesthetic, psychological and historical. And the preoccupation arises under the pressure of history, the push of modern times, that carry with them new evolutionary hopes and desires, and new underlying forces, psychic and social.[29]

The ironic rendering of cultural traditions, self-referentiality, the foregrounding of language and the 'overvaluation of the symbol'[30] were seminal techniques for realizing this evolution. Kristeva insists that, structurally, 'modern texts...perceive themselves as a production that cannot be reduced to representation.'[31] Often referred to as a 'crisis in representation', modernism saw both the rejection of inherited traditions and the assumption of alternative traditions. Further, the *fin-de-siècle* occasioned a desire to refigure what Kermode refers to as the 'sense of an ending',[32] to 'breakdown...teleology [and liberate]...art from the constraints imposed by the need to relate a moral anecdote or to vindicate a moral order'.[33] The social and historical ruptures of the early twentieth century – ruptures in which the inherited moral and cultural orders were further undermined – exacerbated the 'push of the modern', at once debilitating and propitious. The most notable of these ruptures were, of course, the First World War and, within Ireland, the Easter Rising.

It has been asserted by a number of feminist critics that modernism reflected a resurgence of literary patrilineage in the face of a strong women's voice,[34] yet the convergence of political, cultural and interpersonal crises which marked the modernist period emphasizes the attenuated focus of such arguments. In the Irish situation a conflation of profound social and political upheaval with peremptory discursive traditions established the context in which the modernist 'crisis of representation' was realized. Resistance to these traditions defines Irish modernism, and in that the mother-figure was central to these traditions, resistance to that mother-figure through her dismantlement and reconstruction in representation mirrors the artist's capacity to disrupt and reconstitute language.

In his 'Preface to Politicians', Shaw refers to 'the whole spirit of the neo-Gaelic movement, which is bent on creating a new Ireland after its own ideal'.[35] It was this 'discovery of Ireland's past and the Irish identity' which became the dominant 'literary trope' of the early Irish literary revival.[36] Lyons lists the influences of this 'small and closely-knit group' as 'theosophy, occultism and magic, Irish fairy-tales and folklore, the Celtic sagas, geography and politics',[37] while Kiberd cites the 'loose federation of personalities' – individuals who would in the course of history take up mantles as national poets, spiritualists, militant nationalists, politicians, Irish language authors and journalists – who would 'formulate a vision of their native country during a youthful sojourn in an imperial capital – and then return to implement it'.[38] Whatever the forces which bound them, the revival was to produce such disparate writers as George Moore, W.B. Yeats, J.M. Synge and, in its latter stages, Sean O'Casey. Importantly, there existed at the very roots of the revival a link to the traditions promoted within nationalist discourse, as well as elements which could, potentially, subvert those traditions. This fundamental disparity foreshadowed the conflicts which would beset the movement, particularly in its theatrical incarnation: whether English or Gaelic should have precedence; and to what extent literary considerations should be subjugated to political expedience.[39]

In theatrical terms, the inherited tradition was rich in melodrama and comic representations of the 'stage-Irishman', epitomized in Boucicault's *The Shaughraun*, and finding its modernist echo in the work of Sean O'Casey. *John Bull's Other Island*, with its 'uncompromising presentment of the real old Ireland', discloses the sham:

> when a thoroughly worthless Irishman comes to England, and finds the whole place full of romantic duffers like you, who will let him

loaf and drink and sponge and brag as long as he flatters your sense of moral superiority by playing the fool and degrading himself and his country, he soon learns the antics that take you in.[40]

Plays tended to 'advance a myth of Irish history which [was] both melodramatic and heroic',[41] and it was precisely this tendency that was resisted by those advocating a literary revival, with the figures of both the 'stage-Irishman' and the mythical hero – rendered as Cuchulain, Christy Mahon, Red Jim, Michael Byrne or Joxer Daly – appropriated to that cause. It was largely through the appropriation of these figures that dramatists such as Synge, O'Casey and Yeats were able to '[ground] their plays in a distinctive tradition of Irish drama, which they perpetuated and continued even as they renounced and transformed it'.[42] '[If] Ireland would not read literature,' Yeats asserted, 'it might listen to it', and the theatrical movement became yet another means of providing an opportunity for 'a new generation of critics and writers' – notably George Moore, Edward Martyn, Lady Gregory and Yeats himself – 'to denounce the propagandist verse and prose that had gone by the name of Irish literature'.[43]

The dramatic movement, Maxwell argues, '[developed] manners of presentation which [were] not discursive or sequential, which [moved] away from literal portrayal: towards, in short, modernist attitudes and methods'.[44] In the same way that writers such as Moore and Joyce absorbed the artistic movements suffusing literature in England and the Continent, writers working within the dramatic movement – principally Yeats, Synge and O'Casey – drew on symbolism, expressionism and other manifestations of modernism in the construction of their dramas. Pressures on the nature of representation were, therefore, emanating simultaneously from a number of sources: from the dictates of Nationalist and religious authorities as to what was morally and politically acceptable; from literary tradition in terms of the representation of Irish social, political and historical 'reality'; from shifts in aesthetics and artistic expression deriving from Europe and England; and from the desire to reject inherited and authorized traditions in order to realize an individual artistic subjectivity. What impact these pressures had on the representation of the mother-figure is the principal concern of this study.

A template for reading

The pre-oedipal relationship between mother and child – the relationship that exists prior to the intervention of a father – is posited by psychoanalytic theory to be one of fluid, inchoate forms, where child and mother are unable wholly to differentiate themselves from the other, and where their own sense of self is bound up inextricably with the identity of the other. This dyadic relationship is effected by the absence of the father. The inchoate sense of the pre-oedipal mother–child relationship, in terms of the child's inability to determine its own psychical self, is also reflected in the child's access to language, to the means of representation. Lacan, in his theory of the 'imaginary', and Kristeva in her 'semiotic', articulate the effect upon representation of a locus of signification where no bond exists between signifier and signified. The freedom of this fluid pool of forms and meanings allows the child to exist beyond symbolic and social structures; but this freedom carries with it the burden of the child's dependence on the mother and its inability to access speech or to determine the bounds of its self as subject.

The father's disruption of the mother–child bond is the means by which the child becomes subject to the laws and taboos of society. In return for his subjection to that societal authority, the child is afforded a name and a place within that society – the oedipal dynamic, 'properly' resolved, determines the child's access to processes of socialization and symbolization. These processes are, however, generally fixed, and the ability to challenge the social and symbolic orders becomes necessarily limited once the child moves within their purview. Therefore, in order to challenge representational practices, to shed new light on the 'signified' by shaking it free of its traditional 'signifier', psychoanalytic theory suggests that an individual must not only be first subject to that order by which signifier and signified have become bound, but also must have the means of subverting that rigidity by exploring those spaces where signified and signifier are no longer fixed. Kristeva and Lacan, in particular, argue that the individual may do this by accessing ruptures in the symbolic and social orders, ruptures that represent the emergence, if only briefly, of the repressed imaginary or semiotic into the symbolic. It is in this context that Kristeva theorizes a maternal space, the *chora* – a charged receptacle of motile signification which contains within itself the potential for the disruption of the socio-symbolic order.[45] Yet, significantly, this maternal space does not merely threaten the symbolic order – it provides a loose stitch in the symbolic fabric by which the individual may unravel, either in a controlled or uncontrolled manner, that society, or system of representation, to which they are subject. It is these symbolic disruptions that the Irish modernists were able to exploit.

Social and symbolic structures bind the mother by confining her to spaces in which she is rendered silent and powerless. Gauthier, drawing on Irigaray's theories, argues that the patriarchal cultural tradition affords women only two spaces – males or mothers. Ironically, to occupy the space of mother a woman has no alternative but to displace her own mother.[46] Yet, I argue, the mother is able to use this necessity to her own advantage, by ensuring that the woman who takes her place is of her own making: she ensures her own perpetuation by replicating herself in the daughter who will usurp her. Her service to the patriarchal cultural tradition continues unabated; the mother's place within the social and symbolic structures which uphold that tradition is undisturbed. This is one means by which the potency of the maternal is contained, and the threat to symbolic structures embodied in the semiotic is averted. What the cultural tradition represses in order to reinforce socio-symbolic structures is the 'phallic' mother, that mother who possesses the child and who, thereby, jeopardizes patrilineage. She is to be found on the margins of the socio-symbolic, present within birth, death, the *caoin*, song, music and madness, a perpetual threat to the linear narrative – structured around the father's authority – which the patriarchal cultural tradition seeks to impose. By 'writing' mothers who defy the spaces constructed for them by the patriarchal cultural tradition, by 'writing' mothers who exist at or beyond the borders of these socially and symbolically sanctioned spaces, the writer is able to access the underside of the symbolic order. For it is here that the nature of the structures reinforcing the cultural tradition become apparent and, therefore, vulnerable; and it is here that the resistance to, and refiguring of, the cultural tradition has its potential.

'To return to mother,' Sprengnether writes, 'is to die.'[47] The mother encapsulates birth and death, origin and ending. She initiates life, yet she embodies for the child the threat of subjective death – a death that comes from her refusal to relinquish the child and subjugate herself to the father's name. For, in seeking the mother who exists at the origin, who exists beyond the bounds of that subjectivity founded on the father's name, the child risks encountering the real mother, the 'phallic' mother, in whom the boundaries of self are dissolved. The 'phallic' mother may, however, be eluded through the construction of histories that contain the mother within a narrative that is generated by the subjective self and anchored in the social and symbolic structures determined by the father's name. In this she is diminished by the culturally constructed mother; even so, she will always exist as a ghost-like figure, lurking behind the construction, haunting the child and threatening the unravelling of subjectivity. Ultimately, it is the 'phallic' mother who must be encountered if the child is to rewrite the social and symbolic structures that bind him to the past, its discourses and its traditions. But she must first be recovered from cultural construction, and she must then be reconstituted in such a manner that the child is able to (re)assert his own subjectivity while she again comes to be positioned within the symbolic order.

This confluence of relational processes with broader social and representational practices affords a useful paradigm for reading the representation of the mother-figure in Irish modernism. In Kristeva's texts in particular, social and symbolic disruption are articulated in the context of an oedipal dynamic, and such arguments have provided the sub-text to my own study. In this, the mother-figure's function in relation to social and symbolic structures is exposed. Further, given the context – historical, social, political and literary – which provides the parameters of this study, such a reading illuminates not only the mother-figure as she is constructed by the Irish cultural tradition, but foregrounds the relationship between the artist (as son) and that construct.

*

To date, there has not been a comprehensive exploration of the representation of the mother-figure in Irish modernism, particularly in terms of any engagement between the mother-figure, literary traditions and the prevailing nationalist and religious discourses. In this, there is as much a gap in literary research as there is in historical and sociological accounts. One study of note is Innes's *Women and Nation in Irish Literature and Society, 1880–1935*, a text which provides a valuable insight into the social and political position of women in Ireland during a period which largely corresponds to that of modernism. Innes discusses at great length the figuration of women within the literature of the period, maintaining at all times a contextual perspective. Yet, as the title suggests, Innes's research encompasses women generally, and references to the mother-figure are peripheral rather than central to her research. While she does make some attempt to differentiate between women and mothers, given the scope of her work, it is a differentiation that is largely obscured by the broader picture. Further, Innes's work does not attempt to draw any links between the representation of the mother and modernism generally.

As with Innes's work, Anglo-Irish literary criticism has tended to examine the more expansive theme of the representation of women; and it is Yeats and Joyce who figure most prominently in such critiques, with the work of Moore, Synge and O'Casey not as extensively scrutinized. Most notable among these studies are those of: Kline, Cullingford, Howes and Keane in relation to Yeats; Cairns and Richards in relation to Synge; Henke and Unkeless, Cixous and Scott in relation to Joyce; and, for a general overview, Gallagher, Innes, and O'Brien Johnson and Cairns.[48] While the mother – as woman – is considered within these texts, she is rarely 'differentiated out' from women generally and so the analysis of her figuration is at best blurred and at worst confused. Where critics do devote a considerable proportion of their texts to the examination of the mother-figure, it is not uncommon for these analyses to drift into 'psychoanalysis' of the author on the basis of the texts. Kline, for example, argues that the 'symbolic place of woman was . . . the center of order in the life of an individual man or of a culture',[49] yet comes to this conclusion through a focus on Yeats's life and personality rather than on his texts. This tendency towards psychobiography is a common pitfall, seen at its most excessive in Webster, whose Freudian reading of Yeats concludes that '[in] dramatizing his ideal mother, Yeats also dramatized his disappointment in his real mother's lack of sympathy for him and her involvement with his siblings.'[50]

In Joyce criticism – where the texts often seem to be shrouded in canonical lore or, at least, received wisdom – the mother commonly is read as something of a sacred character and subsumed by the search (most notably in the soliloquies of Molly Bloom and Anna Livia Plurabelle) for an *écriture féminine* – a 'female mode of writing', an exposition of female desire. This is particularly evident in readings informed by feminist and psychoanalytic theories which are largely disengaged from the social and political context in which these women are realized. Here the mother is generally read as a nebulous archetype: an object of devotion; a 'spiritual and emotional protectress';[51] vessel of the word; receptacle of the seed of the imagination; or the 'connection between father and son'.[52] Henke concludes that 'for Joyce, woman is, first and foremost, a figure of motherhood'.[53] Further, 'woman emerges in Joyce's work as virgin or whore, madonna or temptress, but usually within a problematic context of maternity'.[54] The prevalence of these readings may be due, as Scott suggests, to Joyce 'writing' women who are predominantly archetypal and rarely 'complete deindividualized women'.[55] Yet this reintroduces the issue I raised with respect to historical research: the mother-figure within Irish society is primarily a 'type'; she does not exist within the cultural tradition as a 'deindividualized woman', and so cannot be rendered as such until the 'type' itself has been resisted through representation. Writers such as Joyce utilize the archetype in order to expose it; yet that exposure can only be read when the cultural context of the representation is taken into account. This is what so much of Joyce criticism fails to attempt.

The common tendency in Joyce criticism is to identify woman within a virgin–whore binarism or read her as embodying the (sacred) phallic mother, thus bearing the potential to both create and destroy.[56] In this, Joyce draws on the literary tradition of Ireland. O'Connor, in her survey of oral traditions, emphasizes the importance of this juxtaposition of life and death within representations of the mother which had as their common theme repentance and non-repentance.[57] In the late nineteenth century, such themes were taken up by writers such as Sheridan le Fanu and Bram Stoker;[58] therefore, that a life-and-death struggle between mother and child should manifest itself in the literature of Irish modernism – climaxing in the 'Circe' episode of *Ulysses* – should not, of itself, be unexpected. Yet, while Cullingford attributes such representations within the *fin-de-siècle* to male concerns regarding their ability to continue to oppress women in the face of a mounting women's rights movement,[59] I suggest they are more likely to reflect not only the literary traditions upon which the Irish modernists were building, but also the need to assert a subjectivity beyond that of service to mother-Church and mother-Ireland.

*

Within representations of the mother-figure in Anglo-Irish literature of the modernist period it is possible to trace the writers' response to, and in many cases resistance of, a sanctioned Irish cultural tradition. And, in that it was generally sons who were conditioned to respond, through self-sacrifice, to the mother-figure embedded within Nationalist and religious discourse, it is the response of male writers to these mother-figures that is my principal interest. In such representations, the life-and-death struggle identified by a number of critics is realized as a battle not simply for creative space, but for that space in which subversive creation has its fullest potential. In this, the mother-figure is not merely constructed by the patriarchal cultural tradition but formed and reified by the writers themselves in order to maximize their own access to those creative spaces which are, in essence, the domain of the mother. Inherent in these spaces is both the scope to bring within signification the indeterminacy and 'crisis in representation' that was central to modernism, and the opportunity to counter the mother-figure as constructed within Nationalist and religious discourses and, thereby, belie her efforts to confirm the artist-as-child within the cultural tradition those discourses promoted.

The study is divided into three principal parts: 'Social Spaces', which examines the mother-figure in her social context; 'On the Edge of Disorder', which delineates the mother-figure's function in disrupting social and symbolic structures; and 'Symbolic Spaces', which explores aspects of creativity, and the shifts in signification with which modernism generally is identified. The first part incorporates an examination of George Moore's work – particularly his positioning of the mother as 'procurator' of the child's subjectivity – and the early works of Yeats and Joyce. With respect to Joyce, I have included in this chapter reference to all his work except *Ulysses* and *Finnegans Wake*, and have identified the denial of the mother that is central to Joyce's notion of the child realizing his subjectivity. In dividing Yeats's work between *Responsibilities* and *The Wild Swans at Coole*, I have been guided by critics such as Ellmann, Kuch and Levine.[60] Further, I have confined myself to a study of Yeats's poetry, and here I identify a tendency towards displacement of the mother. In 'On the Edge of Disorder' I examine the principal dramatic and prose works of Synge and O'Casey, identifying Synge's use of the mother to disclose the means by which social and symbolic structures operate within society, and O'Casey's distancing of the mother from social and symbolic disruption. In 'Symbolic Spaces', again concentrating primarily on the poetry, I argue that Yeats's 'later' work unveiled the construction of the mother within society while at the same time reconstructing her in order to realize an artistic subjectivity. Complementing this is my examination of *Ulysses*, which emphasizes the crusade which must be undertaken against the representation of the mother, and the privileged position she has assumed in such representation, if the subjective self is to be afforded life.

Throughout the study I have included several inter-chapters which provide a sub-text to the overall argument. These chapters develop those contextual aspects that I have identified in this introduction, and traverse the considerations – social, political and theoretical – which have informed my reading. As such, they explore issues as they pertain to the examined writers generally, and closely relate to the three parts I have outlined above: 'Social Spaces' includes a discussion of the mother's social boundaries, and the interrelationship between the position of the mother and the position of martyr or saviour so often sought by the 'sons of Ireland'; 'On the Edge of Disorder' examines the mother's position at the origin of subjectivity and the potential for subversion that exists in maternal spaces, as well as the mother's function in social and symbolic 'revolution'; and 'Symbolic Spaces' begins with a specific delineation of the relationship between modernism and the maternal.

The study concludes with a brief excursion into *Finnegans Wake* and to that mother without beginning or end, who is source of both life and death, Anna Livia Plurabelle. What I seek to explicate are not merely developments in the representation of the mother over the period – and the degree to which Moore, Yeats, Synge, Joyce and O'Casey concur and differ in that representation – but the way in which the mother's representation is linked inextricably not only with the writers' responses to the mother-figures embedded within the Irish cultural tradition but also with the 'self' they wished to bear and define within their work. These writers, I suggest, did not deconstruct the mother-figure with the sole purpose of exposing the 'bricks and mortar' by which the cultural tradition was constructed, thereby to disempower the mother of her ability to entrap her sons within that tradition, though these were important effects of their work. In engaging with the mother-figure, they were able to appropriate the maternal, disclosing thereby a breach in the symbolic that not only could be exploited in refiguring those traditions in which the mother operated, but also could furnish their writing with that tenuous signification that characterizes the semiotic. To varying degrees, the deconstruction of the mother-figure allowed these writers to reconstruct her, and in her reconstituted face they were able to embed the image of their desired selves. And it is in this reflection of the face of the writer within the face of the mother (as constructed by the writer) that creativity and the potential to disrupt both cultural tradition and representation has, I argue, its source.

Part II
Social Spaces

Home and Hearth: the Mother's Social Boundaries

In her review of the work of Luce Irigaray, Grosz articulates the limitations placed upon the mother by society: 'As the silent unrecognised support...of culture, she must remain unacknowledged, confined to a pre-designated reproductive function. As mother, her material and economic possibilities are severely limited.'[1] These limitations are (re)enforced by the representations of the mother-figure inherent to that society, representations which are embedded in the symbolic order by which that society is determined. As Brennan states, the social context – or what she refers to as the 'paternal symbolic cultural tradition'[2] – is, in concert with the symbolic context, one of the central elements in establishing the mother's role in relation both to her children and to the 'father' or authority according to whose law those children must be raised. Any exploration of the representation of the mother-figure within a particular cultural tradition must be closely concerned with the social and political contexts from whose nodes the mother-figure is, as it were, suspended.

In the latter decades of the nineteenth century, the mother-figure was caught up in representations that bore the mark of the *fin-de-siècle*: she was largely synonymous with extremes of 'mothering', extremes that were realized in self-sacrifice or – more commonly – self-absorption. The mother either denied herself as woman or denied her child the life to which he was entitled. Yet what should not be lost sight of in any analysis of Anglo-Irish writing of this period, particularly that of Moore and Yeats, is the sense of a social ground that was shifting beneath the mother's feet. Moore refers to it as 'the inevitable decay which must precede an outburst of national energy',[3] a rumbling portent of social collapse that is evident in the infiltration of the mythical and mystical that Yeats chronicles, and in the pathos and impotence inherent to Dublin life as it is realized by Joyce. How the mother is used by the social order to mend these social fractures, and in what ways she is bound symbolically in order to shore up the 'paternal cultural tradition', are questions of central significance in unravelling the representation of the mother-figure within Anglo-Irish literature during the modernist period.

Angel in the house

In the Victorian period, the 'angel in the house' was the embodiment of all that was required of not merely mothers but women. She represented 'the essential character of Victorian love';[4] in her role as servant to the ideals of family the 'angel' was, more often than not, an icon of motherhood. Yet, as Auerbach argues, she was represented – whether within literature or other cultural discourses – as a figure not only of 'benediction' but also of 'captivity', one that is able to exist only within the confines of the family.[5] If she moves outside the family – or if she seeks to escape the boundaries society has marked out for her, for example as a doer of 'good works'[6] – not only her right to veneration, but also her existence – self-as-symbol – will dissipate. For the mother-angel there exists 'a conflict between the role of mother and that of political or civic being. Insofar as woman adopts the role of mother, her access to the public, social sphere is made difficult if not impossible.'[7]

Disturbances in the cultural consciousness during the nineteenth century could not help but impact on the mother's role. Within the English context – a context on which Anglo-Irish writers could not help but draw, but which, concomitantly, they sought to resist – the scientific work of Lyell and Darwin, as well as the vast social changes arising out of the Industrial Revolution, brought into question not only the relationship between humanity and the natural world, but seriously undermined the position at the centre of the (divine) universe that humanity had previously taken for itself. These effects were compounded in the later nineteenth century by women's demands for increased personal and political freedoms. Differentiation between the essential natures of male and female as a means of legitimizing a differentiation of sexual and cultural roles was utilized extensively to promote not only a specific patriarchy, but also the economic and political ideologies that the patriarchy espoused.[8] Further, sex differences became a means of differentiating between the public sphere 'where alienation was visible and inescapable, and the home, where there seemed to be no alienation at all'.[9] It became imperative on women within the home (almost invariably the mother) to protect the home and hearth from any encroachment of that same alienation. The irony was that the mother – through her privileged access to semiotic spaces wherein the symbolic became fragmented and the cultural bonds glueing signs in place were loosened – embodied that very alienation of self she was charged with repelling. It was for this reason that the mother's subjection to society – to her family, her husband and the symbols by which she was defined – was deemed to be essential if that society was to prosper.

Ireland in the nineteenth century – the social, political and cultural context in which Anglo-Irish modernism was nurtured – was a society undergoing profound shifts and threatened by extensive civil unrest. Disturbed within by struggles for land and power, undermined by extremes of poverty and emigration, it was subjected from without to the political and cultural imperialism of the British Empire. Resisting the colonizer, ensuring the viability of the home, and dispensing the codes of the burgeoning Nationalist and Catholic discourses were espoused as means of asserting an Irish identity. In all, the mother's fundamental role in realizing these goals was emphasized.

In addition to – and arising from – the internal economic and social upheaval which the Great Famine occasioned, the land agitations that erupted in the late 1870s reinforced the need to represent the home as an inviolable space.[10] Whether it was the peasants opposing evictions or the 'big house' ascendancy condemning the destruction of their homes, the inviolable hearth became a profound symbol of resistance. Already confined to that private sphere, anchored to her hearth and uniquely placed to socialize the child, it is perhaps not surprising that the mother was rendered as the symbolic source of resistance, nurturing her child with those codes – most notably Gaelic, Catholic, Irish – by which resistance could be realized. As such, she was utilized by both the Nationalists in their assault against British colonialism, and the Catholic Church in its defence of the moral codes which promoted its own ascendancy. The mother was to be bound in the home, and her role in society exclusively centred on her nurturing – literally and metaphorically – of the child. Any other role was forbidden her.

The mother locked into symbolic space

Grosz writes of the 'enormous investment' that is made in defining the woman's body, emphasizing that it is according to such definitions that the social space afforded to women is determined.[11] The maternal body

– theorized as active, powerful, abundant, phallic, embodying a potential for both denial of the social order and rupture in the symbolic fabric – must, therefore, require an even greater investment if it is to be suppressed and brought within the strictures of a cultural tradition that privileges the paternal. Ultimately, the maternal was contained by placing it on a pedestal from which it could not escape: it became bound up in symbolic nets which lauded the mother in terms of her access to love, morality and maternal instincts, but denied her a position as woman and equal within society. Social behaviour, as Poovey so perceptively argues, was, as a result, seen to reflect nature, thereby denying the degree to which 'nature' was constituted by social and cultural demands.[12]

The maternal instinct became an important means of confining the mother to the home. It was that same instinct which insisted her labour be directed towards emotional rather than economic ends. The mother was placed outside the economy and, as Sprengnether emphasizes in her discussion of Kristeva's 'Among Chinese Women', also placed outside 'knowledge and power' because of her 'marginal' position in relation to language.[13] The ultimate effect of this symbolization of the mother is that the semiotic is subordinated to the symbolic order; and it is, essentially, upon this specific subordination that social cohesion depends. Importantly, where this correlation between suppression of the semiotic and social cohesion leads is that a threat to one exists in any disturbance of the other. Where the semiotic refuses to be subjugated, the social order dissipates and meaning frays, an effect more often evident in its impact on the individual than on society as a whole. Alternatively, shifts in the social ground potentially allow a gap through which the semiotic may assert itself. It is under such circumstances that a fissure occurs in signification, and the potential exists for the establishment of new social and symbolic orders. And it is to avoid such fissures that the inherent order devotes so much of its energy to locking the mother within distinct social and symbolic spaces.

The devouring mother

In *The Interpretation of the Flesh*, Teresa Brennan persuasively argues that representation may be used as a means of 'castration', of disengaging the subject of that representation from power.[14] Representation not only locks the mother into a confined social and symbolic space, it does so in such a way as to insist on her participation in determining that space. Where the mother fails to 'participate', she is demonized, repressed, denied: she becomes the 'terrible' or destroying mother, a symbol where, according to Keane, 'masculine human consciousness [confronts] the unconscious, generally... symbolized as "maternal" and feminine'.[15] This propensity for destruction, Irigaray suggests, stems from the repression of sexuality that representations of the mother engender.[16] In a society where the mother is deemed to be not merely asexual but positively virginal, the destructive undercurrent of the mother-image would be particularly fierce indeed.[17]

'Matricide,' Kristeva writes, 'is our vital necessity, the *sine-qua-non* condition of our individuation.'[18] What then is the effect of a mother who cannot be killed, who is rejuvenated through the sacrifices she demands of her children, and who is perpetuated (and petrified) within the same symbolic system in which she is represented and into which she draws her children? She becomes, Kristeva argues, the 'death-bearing mother', bearing the guilt of the child who desires, but cannot realize, the mother's death: 'it is She who is death-bearing, therefore I do not kill myself in order to kill Her but I attack Her, harass Her, represent Her.'[19] This murder of the mother through representation compounds the trope of the destructive mother who has her source in the repressed sexuality of the woman. The extremes of the Irish cultural tradition – its strict moral demands, its veneration of a Virgin Mother, and its personification of nationhood in the trope of a mother who demands the sacrifice of her children that she may be sustained – define and are in turn defined by the rigid boundaries marking out the mother's realm. The potency of the trope of the destroying-mother in Anglo-Irish literature is, I argue, embedded in this same earth, fed by and (unconsciously) reacting to those same extremes.[20]

2
'A slut among nations': the Mother's Procurement of the Child in the Works of George Moore

Shortly after his return to Ireland in 1901, George Moore addressed a dinner given by T.P. Gill in honour of the new literary movement. Moore told the gathering that 'he felt. ...like a man who having deserted his mother in her poverty returned to her when she had become wealthy'.[1] A mere ten years later, Moore would desert that same mother, fearing that in the guise of Cathleen ni Houlihan she 'might over take me'. Mother-Ireland, as represented in *Hail and Farewell*, was no longer bounteous towards her children, but fatal: 'a fatal disease, fatal to Englishmen and doubly fatal to Irishmen'.[2] Freeing Ireland 'from the thrall of priestcraft and Catholicism', according to Seamus Deane, was one of four central tenets of Moore's literary endeavours.[3] However, the conjunction of Catholicism and mother-Ireland, which Moore witnessed and which he represents most coherently in the stories of *The Untilled Field* and in the autobiographical *Hail and Farewell*, made it inevitable that to extricate self or nation from the power of priest and pulpit, freeing Ireland and her children from the 'thrall' of the mother was equally necessary.

The good mother

Any discussion of the mother-figure in Moore's work must begin with the eponymous heroine of *Esther Waters*, the archetypal 'good mother' whose fall is redeemed when she delivers her son, Jackie, to that same society against which she has battled through the course of the novel. 'She was only conscious,' Moore writes, 'that she had accomplished her woman's work – she had brought him up to a man's estate; and that was her sufficient reward.'[4] Jackie's success is assured by Esther's subjugation of her own will, instincts and even moral codes to the greater demands of society. The individual reinforces society, its social and moral codes and its inherent order, through subjection to that society. The degree to which the social order and its codes are altered in this process depends to a significant extent on the manner in which the mother responds to the demands society places upon her, demands which seek to effect the disruption of the pre-oedipal bond and, thereby, establish the child within the existing social order. In *Esther Waters* that social order is primarily represented by the institution of the family, and it is, essentially, only the nominal head of that family – Will Latch – who succeeds in disturbing the bond between Esther and her son:

> What has the child got to do with you that you should come down ordering people about for? A nice sort of mean trick, and one that is just like you. You beg and pray of me to let you see the child, and when I do you come down here on the sly, and with the present of a suit of clothes and a toy boat you try to win his love away from his mother.[5]

The basis of the father's disturbance is material; what Will proffers to mother and son with his (comparative) wealth is the means to escape poverty and to enter into society through education, property and the establishment of a family. That Esther finally succumbs to Will's proposal reflects not merely her desire to see Jackie attain his 'estate' but the virility of the social order. And it is the renewal of this order which tempers the novel's resolution – the celebration, albeit subdued, of the survival of Esther and her son. Society's resistance to the affirmation of the individual is echoed in Esther's return at the close of the novel to the point where she began: physically and spiritually she has come almost full circle, and society has barely registered the struggle she made against it. Even so, the physical disorder that has overtaken 'Woodview', and the desolation of the environment in which Esther proudly greets Jackie's arrival, suggests the inherent decay of the society. It is against such decay that the reunited mother and child are so starkly foregrounded.

The 'good mother' is defined essentially in terms of her social function. In the Irish context, particularly within Nationalist and Catholic discourses, the 'good mother' was represented as breeding and raising the 'sons' who would ensure the rejuvenation of the nation and the perseverance of 'the cause'. In more generic terms, the 'good mother' is self-sacrificing, nurturing and wholly subject to the social order in which she is afforded her place; she sacrifices her own identity in order to subject herself to the family.[6] Esther Water's claim to the rubric cannot be questioned. Even so, in offering his audience a 'good mother' who is also the 'fallen woman', Moore confuses the archetype, and he achieves this by focusing on the effects rather than the causes of Esther's 'sin'. From the moment of her fall her own ethics are sacrificed, her own needs and exceptionally strong instincts subjected – but not for some abstract good, nor for the direct benefit of the social order. She reluctantly subjects herself to the demands society is making of her for one reason only – to ensure the survival of her son. This sacrifice of her own moral objectives in favour of a semblance of social propriety is seen most clearly in her choice of husband: the intemperate father is favoured over the sober evangelist.[7]

Esther's struggle against society takes place in a context wherein she is disdained, her own value determined solely on the basis of her ability to serve and service the needs of the higher echelons of the social order. A space exists for her within that social context only when she is able to offer her own milk to feed another mother's child. Even more disturbing, it is made clear to her that no space exists for her son, whose life is valued at no more than £5:

> when you hire a poor girl such as me to give the milk that belongs to another child, you think nothing of the poor deserted one. He is only a love-child, you say, and had better be dead and done with....It is all so hidden up that the meaning is not clear at first, but what it comes to is this, that fine folks like you pays the money, and [the baby-farmers and their like] gets rid of the poor little things. Change the milk a few times, a little neglect, and the poor servant-girl is spared the trouble of bringing up her baby and can make a handsome child of a rich woman's starveling.[8]

It is ironic that while Esther largely subdues her will to the greater purpose of securing her son's life, it is those same instincts which provide her with the inner strength to overcome the perpetual barriers that society places in the way of her singular goal. The society presented echoes with the battle for resources prevalent in Darwinian theory – and owes much to Moore's interest in naturalism: because of her class and status, society seeks to deny Esther the means of survival. At the same time, she fights to secure those resources which will sustain her son into the future.

The dynamic interrelationship of mother, child and social order is clearly evident in *Esther Waters*. The social order will embrace the child when the mother has proved herself worthy of her own place within that social order; and the relationship between the mother and society is mediated by her own social position, her moral standing, and the resources, physical or otherwise, to which she has access and which are valued within that society. Esther Waters, 'good mother' who, despite the odds, brings her child to his social 'estate' and who, in doing so, reinforces that estate, provides a useful benchmark against which Moore's other mother-figures may be assessed. For example, Mrs Ede, in *A Mummer's Wife*, is in no sense the 'good mother'. Despite her desire to submerge herself in her family – her invalid son, Ralph and her daughter-in-law, Kate – she is not subject to that family. Rather, she assumes a position of moral authority, proselytizing religious codes. She dominates the family, and the effect is a household which is at once rigid and enfeebling. When Ralph Ede attempts to assert his authority as the 'man of the house', the inevitable result is an exacerbation of his illness.[9] Kate's own inability to mother is directly related to the environment in which she herself has been 'mothered'. Blame, if such a word is appropriate, can be traced back to the stultifying moral environment engendered by Mrs Ede. Dick Lennox's arrival – bringing with it the powers of the imagination and the apparent romance of a life that has existed for Kate only in novels – foregrounds the fragilies of the Ede family unit, fragilities that had previously been veiled or denied. Kate's dilemma is to choose between the polarities represented by her mother-in-law's religious advocacy and the mummer's chaotic world of play and pretense. She can remain embalmed in one environment, or risk her life – physical and moral – beyond it. When she chooses, she chooses *against* her mother-in-law: '[Kate] was conscious that it suited her convenience to quarrel with her mother-in-law. She was tired of the life she was leading.'[10] She elopes with the mummer and embarks on a life untrammelled by moral restrictions, a life which she is ill-equipped to survive. She lacks Esther Water's instincts; she is 'without sufficient personal conscience to detach herself from the conventions in which she has been brought up'.[11] She is morally enfeebled, as her husband is physically enfeebled, a defect which is masked while she lives in the cloistered atmosphere of her mother-in-law's moral fortress. In this, a direct link is drawn between the mother's agency and the child's capacity to survive, a link which Moore would explore in a number of his later works, including *Esther Waters*.

The mother's martyrs

The theme of a dominant religious or moral authority – an authority procurated by the mother – that is unchallenged by any familial or social authority is one that Moore pursues throughout his work, and it is particularly prominent in works dealing with Ireland. In *A Drama in Muslin*, originally published in 1887, and the first of Moore's 'Irish' novels, the Land League agitations of the late 1870s and early 1880s are pitted against the social aspirations of Mrs Barton and the other mothers of the 'muslin martyrs'. For Mrs Barton the mission is clear: establish her daughters in marriages which will preserve the social order on which her wealth and position are based, and spurn the threat to that order – agitations of the Irish tenants for greater control of the land they work. The tension that exists between the preservation and destruction of the social hierarchy is reflected in the conflict between mother and daughter:

> '...Just look at the country-people, how sour and wicked they look – don't they, Alice?'
>
> 'Well, I don't know that they do, mamma,' said Alice, who had already begun to see something wrong in each big house being surrounded by a hundred small ones, all working to keep it in sloth and luxury.
>
> 'I don't know how it is, you always contradict me, and you seem to take pleasure in holding opinions that no one else does.'[12]

It is unfortunate that the novel is weakened by the occasional slackening of the theme of the land agitations while the plight of the young women in search of their place in society is explored. Even so, the sense of desperation to shore up the hierarchy is sustained throughout the novel:

> From the drawing-room window Mrs Barton watched, her little selfish soul racked with dividual doubt. On one side she saw her daughter's beautiful white face becoming the prize of a penniless officer; on the other she saw the pretty furniture, the luxurious idleness, the very silk dress on her back, being torn from them, and distributed among a crowd of Irish-speaking, pig-keeping peasants.[13]

Mrs Barton is, therefore, an active social agent, seeking to prevent both scenarios through the single act of engineering her daughter Olive's marriage to Lord Kilcarney. She operates in contrast to Mrs Scully – the eventual 'winner' in the marriage stakes – who 'sat apart, maintaining her solitary dignity'.[14] Alice – unsuited physically and emotionally to the demands of the marriage market, isolated from her environment and possessing, therefore, a rich insight into the social order (and dis-order) enveloping her family – becomes her mother's bane: 'She foresaw the trouble this plain girl would be to chaperon. The annoyance of having to find her partners would be great, and to have her dragging after her all through the Castle season would be intolerable.'[15]

As well as emphasizing the dire urgency of Mrs Barton's mission to have her daughters marry successfully, the social tensions are used to comment upon the respective desires of tenants and mothers. While Moore is not uncritical of the land agitations, he is more scathing with respect to the decrepit and tenuous nature of the social order for which Mrs Barton so assiduously works. It is significant that the novel con-cludes with neither 'side' victorious: the estate of the Marquis and his bride, Violet Scully, is unsustainable; Olive Barton is unable to secure a place as wife of 'riches, position and all that sort of thing'[16] and remains in a social limbo; and the tenants' rebellion has disintegrated.[17]

Structurally, Mrs Barton is central to the novel for without her the narrative would have nothing to propel it. She is the principal advocate and agitator for the social hierarchy; and, significantly, she is only able to act within the novel because of her husband's failure to act. In return for the peace of his studio, Mr Barton turns a blind eye to his wife's adulterous liaison with Lord Dungory and, in this, implicitly allows the codes and morals of the social order represented by that liaison to dominate the Barton household. He is marginalized, whether by choice or effect, and is unable thereby to exercise even a modicum of authority: 'He had been previously told that if he attempted any interference, his supply of paints, brushes, canvases and guitar-strings would be cut off.'[18] Mrs Barton, unhindered by a father's authority, works to establish at least one of her daughters in an appropriate place within the social order centred on Dublin castle. It is significant that her actions ulti-mately benefit neither her daughters nor herself.

Despite his obvious distaste for the mother's role in protracting the marriage market as seen in *A Drama in Muslin*, Moore reserves his most ardent criticism of the authorities with which mothers 'deal' for those transactions undertaken with religious authorities, principally the Catholic Church. This is particularly evident in *The Untilled Field*, the collection of short stories he wrote in the early years of his return to Ireland. In these stories there is a recurrent theme of the mother align-ing herself with religious authorities, most notably Catholic priests, an alignment which invariably works to the detriment of her children. As Moore makes clear, the mother's submission to the priest's authority is a vital element of the Church's jurisdiction; and the importance of the mother's submission lies not in her own acquiescence with Catholic orthodoxy, but in the instrumental role she plays as deputy, or agent, of that orthodoxy. Mothers, he elaborates in *Vale*, are essential if a voracious church is to be fed:

> [The] women of Ireland will come to me crying, Master, speak to us, for, at the bidding of our magicians, we have borne children long enough. May we escape from the burden of child-bearing without sin?[19]

Irish Catholicism, and the authority of the priest, is the 'culture' into which the child is indoctrinated; yet through the symbolism utilized in *The Untilled Field* – that of a crumbling, disintegrating church in urgent need of repair, and of a parish and country unable to furnish the means of repair – the inherent decay of Irish Catholicism is made explicit.[20] The tragedy implicit in the stories is that the disease is already endemic among Irish youth and that a cure, if one exists, is generations away. And while the role of the priests in engendering this disease and decay is consistently recognized by critics, the role of the mother remains largely unspoken.

In *Hail and Farewell*, Moore is adamant that the Irish imagination will not be liberated until the Catholic stranglehold is broken. 'Ireland,' he writes, 'will not forego her superstitions for the sake of literature, accursed superstitions that have lowered her in intelligence and made her a slut among nations.'[21] His use of the word 'slut' is pointed: his work suggests that the mother procures, or deals, with authorities – her children are bartered and her remuneration – whether consciously sought or not – is a privileged position within the social order. The nature of this transaction is emphasized in the account Moore gives in *Hail and Farewell* of the relationship between Edward Martyn and his mother:

> But by brooding on his words I understand them to mean that his mother imposed obedience upon him by appealing to his fear of God, and aggravating this fear by severe training in religious dogma. It is easy to do this; a little child's mind is so sensitive and so unprotected by reason that a stern mother is one of the great perils of birth... for from women's influence the son of man may not escape and it would seem that whoever avoids the wife falls into the arms of the mistress, and he who avoids the wife and the mistress becomes the mother's bond-slave.[22]

It is just this notion of the mother's 'bond-slave' that Moore represents in many of his fictional works. To survive, the child must break this bond and escape the pervasive influence of the mother. Ned Carmady in 'The Wild Goose' returns into exile, unable to tolerate that his son will be brought up according to the dictates of Catholicism, fodder to feed and perpetuate the Church. The son's destiny as a subject within the Church parallels the father's destiny as a child of the Irish nation; and in leaving Ireland, Ned is not merely escaping the bonds of mother-Church but mother-Ireland also:

> it was while writing *The wild goose* that it occurred to me for the first time that, it being impossible to enjoy independence of body and soul in Ireland, the thought of every brave-hearted boy is to cry, Now, off with my coat that I may earn five pounds to take me out of the country. Every race gets the religion it deserves.[23]

In Ireland, Ned Carmady must remain silent, unable to exert authority within his family, blocked by the Church from establishing his place within Nationalist discourse. He moves outside Ireland, to a place where, unfettered by Catholic censorship, he will be able to speak. Yet it is ironic that his efforts are bound to prove fruitless once he moves outside the mother's bounds, and Ireland, like his wife, takes her place on a pedestal, beautiful but inanimate. In order to speak, to effect change within Ireland, Moore suggests, Ned must encounter the fecund woman, the mother who will bear his child and advocate his word. It is not until *The Lake* that Moore finds any counter to this irony. It would have to wait until Yeats's and Joyce's explorations of their own creative processes for any solution to be found.

The need to escape Ireland in order to ensure life is also clearly seen in other stories in *The Untilled Field*, particularly those which detail the courtships of the Kavanaghs.[24] Through the machinations of the priest and several mothers, Kate is wedded to the 'good and foolish' Peter M'Shane, a man so enfeebled by his mother that he cannot even assert his conjugal rights without his mother's intervention: 'And Peter got to his feet and stumbled against the wall, and his mother had to help him towards the [bedroom] door. "Is it drunk I am, mother? Will you open the door for me?"'[25] Kate escapes to America the next day;[26] yet her true love, Pat Connex, having bowed to the unified will of mother and priest, seems destined to a life of paralysis: '[Kate] pressed [Pat] to answer her, and he told her he was waiting for the priest. His mother said he must marry, and the priest was coming to make up a marriage for him.

"Everything's mother's," [he said].'[27] Everything is mother's because the mother, in binding her son to the Church, has secured her own position. And this is the irony inherent in Moore's representation of the mother as she deals with the social and moral context in which she lives. The mother, particularly in the Irish context, is afforded a privileged social position; yet it is a position in return for which the social hierarchy makes significant demands. Her only value within society derives from the singular bond she shares with the child, a bond which uniquely positions her to bring the child within the realm of Catholicism, Nationalism or any of the other orthodoxies operating within her social context. Within Moore's *oeuvre*, the mother's dilemma is a relatively simple one: she can ignore the social, religious and political orthodoxies battling for her children and thereby risk her own position within the relevant social order; or she can procure her child for one or other of those orthodoxies and maintain the power she exerts as symbol. The mother may bring about her own demise, or she may secure a space for herself within the social order by ensnaring her child within that same order.

'The grey fear of having been born to die'

Drawing on memories of his own childhood, Moore, in *Hail and Farewell*, recalls a tale told to him by his mother:

> of a beggar woman who went about Ireland with four or five blind children, their eyes resembling the eyes of those who are born blind so closely that every oculist was deceived. But one day a child's crying attracted attention, and it was discovered that the mother had tied walnut shells over his eyes and in each shell was a beetle; the scratching of the beetle on the eyeball produced the appearance of natural blindness.... amusing disfigurements were the fashion, and high prices were paid for them.[28]

The tale encapsulates the function Moore reserves for most of his mother-figures: she manipulates her children for her own ends; she uses her children – literally and metaphorically – to sustain her own social position. The parameters of the child's own social and subjective position are, as a result, severely limited: two principal alternatives are available – escape from the mother; or, assumption of the space reserved by the mother, the result of which is enfeeblement or death. Rarely is the child allowed to thrive in their relationship with the mother; and, despite skirting the issue in his treatment of Kate Ede's demise and Esther Waters' motherhood, he persistently ignores the plight of the mother drained and weakened by her submergence in her child. It is as though, for Moore, the mother must play the villain.

The mother's motivation in her procurement of the child is painted as a desire to ensure self-perpetuation. Mrs Norton in *A Mere Accident*, and in the rewriting of that novel in *Celibates*, clearly manipulates her son's actions, promoting his marriage to a woman of her choice in order to perpetuate her own estate, a goal she is still pursuing in *Mike Fletcher*:

> Mrs Norton, in her own hard, cold way, loved her son, but in truth she thought more of the power of which he was the representative than of the man himself: the power to take himself a wife – a wife who would give an heir to Thornby Place. This was to be the achievement of Mrs Norton's life, and the difficulties that intervened were too absorbing for her to think much whether her son would find happiness in marriage.[29]

Mrs Barton too constructs her role in her daughters' lives in order to further her own cause: 'and then, out of the soul of the old coquette, arose, full-fledged, the chaperon, the satellite whose light and glory is dependent on that of the fixed star around which she invitingly revolves.'[30] Yet attendant on that role is the damage she will do to her daughters:

> But a woman is never vulnerable until she is bringing out her daughters....Until then the usual shafts directed against her virtue fall harmlessly on either side, but now they glance from the marriage buckler and strike the daughter in full heart.[31]

The mother seeks to perpetuate herself through a metonymic relationship with another woman. In John Norton's case, this woman is Kitty; and by marrying her John would produce, with his 'mother', the children who would carry on the family line. Mrs Barton similarly seeks to utilize the Dublin marriage-market, and her daughter's success in that market, to perpetuate and reinforce her own social and sexual position. 'Mother and daughter,' she tells Alice, 'should never hold different views; my children's interests are my interests – what interests have I now but theirs?'[32] In both cases, there is no familial father who will mediate between mother and child: John's father is dead, Mr Barton is marginalized from his family both physically and sexually.

Where a familial father does not exist to disrupt the bond between mother and child and, thereby, bring the child into society as subject, a space exists for the mother to 'deal' with another 'father', an alternative moral, social or political authority. This dynamic consistently corresponds with representations of the child as weak – physically and spiritually – or doomed. It is an effect of the mother's dealings with society that imagination is silenced and *esprit* dampened. It follows, therefore, that only by avoiding the mother will the child emerge with imagination and spirit intact. Alice Barton, in *A Drama in Muslin*, perceives in the death of May Gould's baby a portent of her own fate: 'The old, the terrible dream, the grey fear of having been born to die, without having lived, again possessed her, again laid hands upon her, held her with its cold, cruel and strangling fingers.'[33] She must escape her mother's reach if she is to thrive emotionally and spiritually; and she does so, creating within the suburbs of London 'new artistic impulses'.[34]

The misandrist Cecilia Cullen, in *A Drama in Muslin*, shares with her friend Alice Barton an essential alienation from the social environment dictated by the Anglo-Irish 'big houses' and the Dublin marriage-market. Labelled by many critics as distinctly lesbian, Cecilia's sexuality – whether or not it actually can be said to exist – is largely peripheral. Within the structure of the novel, Cecilia, defined by her severe emotional disfigurement, offers a contrast to Alice Barton – starting as they do from a similar isolated position but taking increasingly divergent paths in life – and, more significantly, throws light on the recurring mother–father–child dynamic:

> [Cecilia's] hatred of all that concerned sexual passion was consequent on her father's age and her mother's loathing for him during conception and pregnancy; and then, if it be considered that this transmitted hatred was planted and left to germinate in a misshapen body, it will be understood how a weird love of the spiritual, of the mythical, was the most inevitable psychical characteristic that a human being born under such circumstances would possess.[35]

Within this passage there is the sense of the child being squeezed or manipulated into a confined social or psychological space. Unable to escape in her own right, Cecilia takes refuge in a religious order, a space which is, according to Moore, as constricting and life-denying as the space the mother and society have created. Cecilia's disfigurement, he makes explicit, occurs principally through her mother's agency: it results from the mother's loathing of the father and her implicit unwillingness to subject herself to the father's authority. As bankrupt as that authority is shown to be, it is one which may have rescued Cecilia from her alienation, and her burgeoning irrationality, and allowed her a position within the social fabric. Refusing to consider a position within a social order determined by the sexual union of women and men, Cecilia succumbs to her intensely disturbed mental state, a state that is presented as the trace of her own mother's passionate hatred. That such disturbance directs her towards a life within the Catholic Church should, of course, be read as no coincidence.

Cecilia Cullen's fierce aversion to men, to the sexual congress by which, she insists, they demean women, is matched by the horror of the feminine evident in the misogynist, John Norton.[36] Summoned home by his mother, essentially to partake in that same sexual congress with a woman of his mother's choosing, John is repelled by his mother's realm, a world where boundaries and definition give way to soft, luxurious furniture and furnishings. He attempts physically to retreat by moving to a corner of the house;[37] and this physical retreat reflects his desire to make an emotional and psychical escape. Like Cecilia, though less committed, John accepts the rigid parameters of the self proffered by a religious order as the means of defeating his mother's unharnessed presence and vicarious sexual demands.

Healing the sexual wound

The late Victorian ethos against which Moore's early work struggled was that 'women were far more liable to the lapses of control that defined a character as "lost" or "ruined"....fallenness was predominantly defined in opposition to a masculine ideal of rational control and purposive action.'[38] It is a weakness of character, an inability to exert the control that not only society, but also one's own moral sense, demands, which is apparent in Moore's own representation of the fallen woman in *Esther Waters*: 'It is always a woman's fault.'[39] Yet Esther's fall, by the conclusion of the novel, has been redeemed. As Auerbach observes, Esther 'falls up', she 'rises through her fall above the life of her martyred mother and can boast at the end of her stolid typicality'.[40] However, what Auerbach and other critics fail to acknowledge is the degree to which Esther's maternity is instrumental in her social redemption. It is not merely that the 'good mother' obliterates the 'fallen woman', as Cave, for example, has argued:[41] predominantly, it is the abandonment of the sexual self, the assumption of virginity once child-bearing is completed, that allows the woman to take up the mantle of the Virgin

Mother. This is also apparent in *The Brook Kerith* where Moore indicates Mary has borne children other than Jesus, and where no suggestion is made as to the miracle of their conception.[42] Significantly, Jesus states quite explicitly Mary's agency as mother; yet he observes as part of his teaching that she is useless to him now that he has been brought to his estate.[43] In both cases, there is an inference that perfect mothering, mothering which brings the child to their social and symbolic estate, bestows virginity on the woman: perfect mothering belies sexuality. As Moore noted in *Ave*: 'The Virgin is always represented with a baby in her arms: motherhood is her constant occupation.'[44] Sexual mother is a contradiction in terms: where there is no mother, there can be no child.

There is no doubt that the 'fallen woman', or in broader terms the sexual woman, threatens the social order, and this threat stems from her defiance of the demand that she procure children for society. The 'fall' subverts that demand, and the woman may only be recovered when she succumbs to society by bringing her children to their social estate. The mother who refuses to succumb effectively kills her child. 'Agnes Lahens' offers such an example. Olive Lahens occupies the central space within the household, and her occupation of that space is dependent on her role as sexual creature – as woman rather than as mother. Her sexuality is acutely rendered in the 'red wound' of her mouth, and this wound becomes for Agnes a metonym for her mother.[45] Unable to accept the only space available to her in a household dominated by her mother's sexuality – that of another woman, playing the same sexual games – Agnes returns, permanently, to the convent: 'It is impossible for me to remain here, I cannot meet mother after what has happened.'[46]

What Olive Lahens represents is the mother whose sexuality allows no potential for the child to develop its own identity within the primal social and cultural organisation of the family. The sexual mother undermines the image of the 'angel in the house' because she refuses to submerge herself within the social demands exemplified by the familial order so lauded by the Victorians. She refuses to be subject to her family; and while contemporary readers may applaud her defiance of an archetype which would ensure her conformity to social (and exclusively patriarchal) demands, and welcome her subversion of the social and symbolic orders which constrain her, Moore does not represent the sexual mother in laudatory terms. While critics such as Watt argue that his subversion of the trope of the 'fallen woman' prevalent in Victorian fiction was a response to Victorian morals, it is not entirely apparent that Moore was able to sustain this subversion.[47] He was certainly sympathetic to the dilemma faced by the woman who was deeply aware of, and sought to express, her sexuality. Even so, he was unable completely to divorce himself from the sting of blame which society demanded be directed at these women. Of all mothers, it is the mother who asserts her own sexuality, who refuses to repress that sexuality, who ensures the ultimate demise of her children.

It is only in the 'fall' of May Gould in *A Drama in Muslin* that Moore paints a sympathetic portrait of the difficulty faced by the sexual woman in a society which refuses to recognize her:

> Every woman, or nearly every one, wants a husband and a home, and it is only natural she should, and if she doesn't get them the temptations she has to go through are something frightful, and if we make the slightest slip the whole world is down upon us.... We are told that we must marry a man with at least a thousand a year, or remain spinsters; well, I should like to know where the men are who have a thousand a year, and some of us can't remain spinsters.[48]

This failure of recognition passes over to the child, ensuring the child's death. In this respect, it could be argued that Moore attempts to divert blame for the child's death away from the mother and towards society: if social and moral authorities recognized the very real existence of women's sexuality rather than repressing it, then children such as those borne by May would survive. However, if this is the means by which Moore is seeking to question Victorian morals and subvert the trope of the 'fallen woman', he is far from successful. Had he sought to make this point, he could have made it far more strikingly if he had simply allowed a woman to bear healthy children while freely expressing her sexuality. That he did not reflects on both Moore and the society in which he was writing.[49]

'This flesh of her flesh...'

The mother–child bond, the 'calm of another life, the life of that other who wends his way while I remain henceforth like a framework',[50] is the seminal human relationship. It haunts all other interactions: the closed, mutually defining space where the self is fragmented and primed for (re)constitution will be reclaimed – or at least sought – in most subsequent (intimate) relationships. In terms of Moore's artistic development, particularly in the area of narrative technique, it is notable that his exploration of this bond remained largely at a level where the child has already been socialized within that order to which the mother herself is subject. Rarely is the pre-oedipal bond – the bond prior to the intervention of the 'father', of some moral or social law – examined. *Esther Waters* offers an exception: 'Her personal self seemed entirely withdrawn; she existed like an atmosphere about the babe and lay absorbed in this life of her life, this flesh of her flesh, unconscious of herself as a sponge in sea-water.'[51] What this passage ultimately foreshadows is a continual subjugation of Esther's own self to the needs of her child, a subjugation that cannot help but diminish Esther's own strength:

> She was now alone in a great wilderness with her child, for whom she would have to work for many, many years, and did not know how it would all end.... Her hair hung about her, her hands and wrists were shrunken, her flesh was soft and flabby, for suckling her child seemed to draw all strength from her, and her nervous depression increased from day to day, she being too weary and ill to think of the future.[52]

Esther Water's powerful instincts provide a stark contrast to those of Kate Ede in *A Mummer's Wife*. Kate belies Laura Forrest's determination that there exists 'in every woman [the instinct] to mother something'; Kate's natural instincts ('it was not without surprise that she caught herself wishing suddenly [the girls in the workroom] were her own children.... it was the first time a desire for motherhood had ever troubled her'[53]) have been blunted by both the mummer's life and the restricted life Kate led with her husband and mother-in-law. Defeated by 'the enmities of an unknown land',[54] Kate has neither the instinct nor the experience by which she may 'feed' her child: she is unable effectively to establish and sustain the pre-oedipal bond, and a profound gap separates mother from child:

> the child's cries were too weak; her mother lay in sleep beyond the reach of her wails, heart-breaking though they were. The little blankets were cast aside, and the struggle between life and death began: soft-roundedness fell into distortions; chubby knees were wrenched to and fro, muscles seemed to be torn, and a few minutes later little Kate, who had known of this world but a ray of moonlight, died – a glimpse of the moon was all that had been granted to her.[55]

While Kate's bond with her child lacks the intensity of that between Esther and her son, Moore does allow Kate to lose herself – if only momentarily – in the fragmentary and dissociated identity of her child.[56] Yet the child's access to subjectivity, its access to metaphorical life, is impeded by two significant barriers engendered by the mother. 'Kate was devoted to her child,' Moore writes, 'but the attention she gave it was unsustained, a desultory attention.'[57] But, more importantly, with the breakdown of her marriage and her alienation from the society in which she exists, Kate lacks the capacity for agency: she is unable to bring her child into subjectivity through her own subjection to a paternal authority. In such circumstances, the child's death is inevitable. Thereafter, Kate does not seem able to reconstitute her own identity from the pool that formed around her association with the infant child:

> a heedless nondescript – a something in a black shawl and a quasi-respectable bonnet, a slippery stepping stone between the low women who whispered and the workwomen who hurried home with the tin of evening beer in her hand. Like one held and guided by the power of a dream, she lost consciousness of all that was not of it.[58]

Her subjectivity remains dissolved, a dissolution exacerbated by her alcoholism. She barely exists and, inevitably, she too must die.

The level of intimacy between mother and child evident in *Esther Waters* is not explored again by Moore until *The Lake*, and it is not coincidental that *The Lake* also brings Moore closer to the work of his modernist successors that any other he wrote, before or after.[59] It is a shift which may be mapped in the increasing influence of Wagner and Dujardin on Moore's work, and the demise of early French conditioning. In Nora Glynn, Moore offers his most beautifully realized and psychologically adept exploration of the mother-figure; he utilizes the creation–destruction binarism traditionally associated with the mother in an innovative and life-enforcing manner. The novel's hero, Oliver Gogarty, willingly destroys and disintegrates himself through his relationship with the unwed mother, Nora Glynn. Yet, ultimately, he will use this relationship in order to facilitate his own rebirth and to establish his own myth of self-creation. As Malkan succinctly observes, Oliver Gogarty 'expresses his love [for Nora] in terms of immersion and reabsorption into a feminized version of nature, symbolized by his dive into the lake'.[60] The relationship between the priest, Gogarty, and the woman he has condemned from the pulpit for her immoral conduct is one that has its basis in the imagination and the spirit, and that develops through a series of letters to-and-fro that carry much of the novel's narrative. Through Nora – who throughout the novel refuses to subject herself to the moral dictates of either Church or society – Gogarty accesses an instinctual life that his vocation as a priest, and the binding authority of Catholic dogma, has denied him. 'There is ever a divorce,' he writes to her,

> between the world of sense and the world of spirit, and the question of how much love we may expend upon eternal things will always be a cause of perplexity to those who do not choose to abandon themselves to the general drift of sensual life. The question is as difficult as the cognate question of what are our duties towards others. And your letters raise all these questions.... A voice whispers, 'You could do very well with a little of her life, but you will not know any other but your present one.'[61]

It is by allowing himself to be absorbed into her life that his self, his identity, begins to disintegrate. 'I want to escape from myself,' he writes, 'and your letters enable me to do so.'[62] Nora embodies independence, a refusal to be bound, and it is in this that Gogarty bathes.[63] Released from the narrow constrictions of the Irish Catholic priesthood, and the word on which that priesthood is based – 'The Catholic Church had come to the end of its thread; the spool seemed pretty well empty, and he sat down that he might think better what the new faith might be'[64] – he discovers a new world in her, a world of unleashed spirit and imagination. And through a relationship with this mother that echoes the pre-oedipal bond, the facility exists for Gogarty to take a part of this world into himself. Gogarty finds new (self-)definition in her, and acquires the instincts and impulses that will enable him to endure in the new life he is about to enter.[65] Something of a rarity among the mother-figures Moore represents, Nora Glynn has no desire to perpetuate either herself or a paternal authority through her relationship with Gogarty. Rather, she nurtures him vicariously, and equips him, imaginatively and spiritually, for a new life.

Having abandoned his priestly self, Gogarty swims into the lake, leaving behind his clerical garb in the anticipation that 'Father Gogarty' will be seen to have drowned. Finding the lake's far shore – not without difficulty – he emerges into exile and into a desired life of 'letters' where he may create a new word, a new language of sorts, by which the old, constricting, dogmatic word may be diminished.

The metaphor of rebirth inherent in *The Lake* is embellished through the symbol of the lake itself, a symbol that is explicitly linked with Nora.[66] Gogarty's final swim across the lake, his priestly 'coat' discarded, becomes a succinct metaphor for the entire novel.[67] What that final swim mirrors is the relationship Gogarty has shared with Nora Glynn, one wherein he comes to lay aside the dogmas and practices of the Church, immerses himself in the dark and formless life of the lake, and struggles ashore to find a new self, one which will discover something of its own form in the image of the mother – Nora Glynn – who facilitated the transition.

New language, new religion

Rarely is mother-Ireland explicitly present, though she is, I suspect, extensively sublimated, in Moore's fiction.[68] One exception is 'The Wild Goose', where Ellen Carmady assumes the role of metaphorical as well as literal mother. Her advocacy for the Catholic Church, her subjection to Catholic dogma rather than to her husband's will, becomes the antecedent to the phenomenon of the Irish exile. The parallel is directly drawn: 'I don't think I should have cared for you, Ned if you hadn't loved Ireland.'[69] She reiterates the association as their marriage begins to crumble: 'Of course, if you thought that any other woman would tempt you and that you would be unfaithful to me and to Ireland, dear – .'[70] The point is made again when he leaves her: 'For five years you have been devoted to Ireland, and now you and Ireland are separated like two ships.' Ned answers simply, highlighting the interaction between Ireland, mother and Catholicism: 'Yes, like two ships. Ireland is still going Romewards and Rome is not my way.'[71]

Moore makes clear in his autobiographical writing that he considered the Catholic religion as practised in Ireland to be totally incompatible with the flourishing of the Irish imagination anticipated by those who championed the revival of the Gaelic language. While he was more than sympathetic to arguments for a Gaelic revival – 'just as a man has to change his coat when it becomes threadbare, a nation has to change its language if it is to produce a new literature'[72] – he argued that a new language was of no use without a new religion.[73] The means by which these objectives could be achieved was not always evident. At times he believed that the new language must come first. 'But,' AE asked, 'what use will her language be to Ireland if she is not granted the right to think?' Moore answered, 'The filing of theological fetters will be the task for the next generation.'[74] 'The Wild Goose' deals with this very dilemma, suggesting, in the confused dynamic of Ned, Ellen and Church – or father, mother-Ireland and Catholicism – precisely why Ireland remains shackled.

In arguing that a new language must precede a new religion, Moore was averring to the importance of establishing a new symbolic order as a means of defeating a stagnant social authority. To escape from the Church – to diminish its power – one must first escape from – or discard as one would a coat – the language through which the Church asserts its authority, the language which the mother speaks on the Church's behalf. It is a lesson which Oliver Gogarty, in *The Lake*, learns through the course of the novel.

In *Hail and Farewell*, the wasteland of the English language is explicitly stated: 'a language wearied with child-bearing',[75] a sentiment which would later echo through the 'Oxen of the Sun' episode of *Ulysses*. The metaphor of mothers fatigued through the labour of child-bearing also is used to elucidate the Church's 'spell' over, and employment of, the women of Ireland. The entanglement of language and religion was explicitly realized, as was the importance of establishing new versions of both if Ireland was to truly flourish. Yet Moore was unable to determine the means of establishing either; and the reason for this, I argue, is his lack of insight into his own creative processes. 'A man of letters,' he notes in *Salve*, '...plays with his ideas as a mother with her child.'[76] Creativity is constructed as a mother engaging with her child; yet it is a child full-formed, beyond infancy, established in the world. Rarely does Moore encounter his creativity as mother and child within the pre-oedipal bond: formless, inchoate, mutually fragmented and mutually defined.[77] There is almost the sense that Moore's own understanding of his place in literary history depended on his not being seen to question the sources of his creative capacity, merely to play with it and direct it, much as a maiden-aunt would. Even *Confessions of a Young Man*, which chronicles Moore's progress from art to literature, does not see Moore interrogating his creative urge. Rather, he uses this text, as with other autobiographical writings, as a canvas to construct himself as writer and man of letters.[78] The creative spirit was something beyond the self, something that Moore would pursue externally – embodied in Shelley, Wagner, Balzac, even Mrs Braddon – rather than discover as an essence within himself.[79]

*

Moore's representation of the mother-figure reached its epitome in *The Lake*. The mother as vessel, in whom the child might both destroy and then (re)create its self, set the parameters by which both a new religion and a new language might be established. However, Moore, even in his later novels employing the technique of 'imaginative reverie', was unable to harness this trope. Preoccupied with the constant reiteration and reconstruction of himself as literary figure, he may not have even realized the potential for re-creation that he had captured in the relationship between dissatisfied priest and willing, unbound mother. In the end, neither religion nor language was troubled by his presence. And perhaps the reason why he failed to meet his objective of liberating Ireland from Catholicism and priestcraft, through the establishment of a 'new language', stems from his inability to deal with the trope of the destroying mother. This trope dominates Moore's work, and despite his desire to challenge the Victorian moral ethos, his representation of the mother as a figure bestowing death and enfeeblement on her children continually undermined his efforts to do so. It is for this same reason – this inability to move beyond the mother who betrays and destroys to the mother who simultaneously facilitates disintegration and renewal – that, I argue, Moore stands outside modernism. Moore touched the latter in Nora Glynn but, examined over the entire body of his work, he was never able to confront and defeat that destroying, devouring mother who had chased him from Ireland.[80] In terms of his efforts to extricate himself from his literary influences and challenge the literary context in which he worked during the first half of his writing life, this was perhaps his greatest limitation.

3
Eve's Curse No More: Yeats's Displacement of the Mother, 1889–1914

For Yeats, the mother-figure affords a means by which he might explore both the nature of myth and his own creative processes. What he discovers is not only the mother's place at the generation of myth, but her (re)figuration as myth. And it is as myth that she is transformed and absorbed by patriarchal history.

Like his (modernist) contemporaries, Yeats's interaction with inherited myths and traditions was an increasingly troubled one.[1] In Yeats's case, the inherited structures of Christianity, scientific rationalism and the British cultural and political hegemony were pitted against more 'ancient traditions' deriving from esoteric spirituality and Irish legends and fables. Kuch has suggested that the 'ancient traditions were important to Yeats for a number of reasons': they engendered a 'coherent faith'; they served as a barrier against the 'corrosive and debilitating fragmentation of European sensibility'; and they enabled him to access an 'Irish identity'.[2] Within these ancient traditions, therefore, there existed the means by which Yeats could resist his immediate cultural inheritance. Further, through both the recovery of ancient heroes and legends – Cuchulain, Red Hanrahan, Fergus, Cathleen ni Houlihan – and the refiguring of inherited orders – Christian, historical, political – the symbology of inherited traditions (and the affects associated with that symbology) were not only made available for appropriation, but the means by which the inherited order functioned was disclosed. Yeats's representation of the mother-figure was caught up in this process of resistance, appropriation and disclosure.

Yet what is most notable about Yeats's representation of the mother-figure in his early work is her absence. The *Autobiographies* pay her only fleeting attention, a treatment that is particularly remarkable in *Reveries over Childhood and Youth*; in 'The Stolen Child', the picture of the hearth, despite its warmth and peace, does not include the mother. Apart from Moll Magee (who foreshadows 'old Madge' in 'The Friends of His Youth') and Emer (drawn from myth and functioning to effect Cuchulain's tragedy), Yeats does not engage significantly with mother-figures until the 1904 volume *In the Seven Woods*. Here he utilizes her to explore themes of 'labour' and creativity – 'Adam's Curse' – and to 'laud' a Nationalist mother-figure who has been robed in the symbols of the Catholic Madonna – 'Red Hanrahan's Song About Ireland', a poem which creates a tension between disparate constructions of the mother similar to that achieved in 'The Unappeasable Host'. Even so, it is not until *Responsibilities* that these themes – which would continue to figure in Yeats's later work – are developed, and Yeats's engagement with the mother-figure within his poetry actually initiated.

It is difficult to account for this delay, particularly given Yeats's inter-action with traditions in which the mother was a prominent construct. Of course, within his dramatic works, and to a lesser extent his prose, the mother was often a central character. Mothers figured in the plays *The Countess Cathleen*, *The Land of Heart's Desire* and *Cathleen ni Houlihan*, the early novels *John Sherman* and *The Speckled Bird*, and in stories such as 'The Twisting of the Rope', 'Our Lady of the Hills' and 'The Adoration of the Magi'; however, the mother was largely confined to social roles, a factor reflecting the nature and style of the plays and prose Yeats was writing at that time. While these social roles allowed some room for the exploration of the symbolic parameters of the mother's function, it was not until his dramatic writing became more symbolist in its structure and techniques that Yeats effectively could extend this exploration. Even so, it is clear that he was unable readily to transfer these figures (whose bounds – within his imagination at any rate – remained largely social) into his poetry.

It is possible to speculate as to the reason for the mother-figure's absence from the poetry, though very often such speculation leads to spurious conclusions about the poet's relationship with his mother. It may be that the poet needed to mask the mother-figure or deny her in order to access an Irish tradition that privileged a 'mythical' patrilineage, one that included not only Cuchulain but 'Davis, Mangan, Ferguson' (from whom the writer would later seek pardon for his 'barren passion'). It may be that Yeats needed to develop the technical tools that would facilitate his representation of the mother in the more figurative and symbolic terms that his poetry required. Or it may be that it was not until Yeats – through his own relationship with women – began to explore the construction of women, and the male response to those constructions, that the figure of the mother and the way that she operated within Nationalist and Catholic discourses became more accessible to him. Certainly, as Toomey elaborates, it was during this period that Yeats was confronted with Maud Gonne's revelation that she herself had borne children: 'although Yeats was patently intimidated by Maud Gonne in her new guise as sexual being and mother, it was this which he had to integrate when he returned to poetry.'[3]

Developments in Yeats's representation of the mother-figure up to *Responsibilities* chart a transition from social to symbolic renderings of the mother and the maternal. What this transition indicates is that Yeats's engagement with the mother-figure facilitated his exploration of mythical structures and mythical traditions, particularly the investment in those structures and traditions made by both mother-figures and the patriarchy. Yet, as Moynahan warns, Yeats's work needs to be rigorously interrogated to discover to what extent he was merely utilizing those symbols and myths which existed within the cultural traditions upon which he drew, and to what extent he himself was constructing those myths in order to articulate his own sense of self, and the place of that self within a broader literary, inter-personal, and political world.[4] Within the context of the representation of the mother-figure, it is this interaction between cultural tradition and the writer that this chapter aims to illuminate.

Cathleen ni Houlihan

In *Cathleen ni Houlihan* Yeats exposes something of the function of myth, particularly in the Irish context – the play serves, therefore, as a useful introduction to the poetry. Here, tension is established between the preservation and perpetuation of the family, and the threat to the nation that is being played out beyond the threshold. This tension is realized in the character of Michael Gillane, who must choose between the Old Woman, through whom the nation will be reborn, and the bride, who is to take his mother's place in the home – 'Leave me alone now till I ready the house for the woman that is to come into it'[5] – thus rejuvenating, both materially and symbolically, the family. However, underlying this drama of Michael Gillane's divided loyalties is a subtext in which not family and nation, but literal and mythical, compete.

Michael Gillane responds to the Old Woman's tale of suffering; yet what is most remarkable about this tale is that it is not the Old

Woman who actually tells it. Rather, she creates the space wherein a narrative of her suffering may be constructed. Initially, she holds her story close to herself, merely responding to the probes the Gillane family direct towards her, and disguising in song the death entailed in her cause. And it is in this way that she is able to empty her words of their meaning, their import: they become ambiguous, and the family, imbuing them with literal rather than mythical meaning, is kept off-guard and vulnerable:

> OLD WOMAN: But when the trouble is on me I must be talking to my friends.... Too many strangers in the house.... My land that was taken from me.... My four beautiful green fields.[6]

It is only the audience, from its critical distance, who may – potentially – read her words in metaphorical terms.[7] Within the context of the play, within the context of the representational structures employed in the play, the Gillanes have access to no other system of signification (the existence of omens having already been dismissed by Bridget Gillane[8]) than that which reads the woman's words literally. Each of the characters responds, according to type, to the literal figure before them. It is left to the audience to read the mythical system the Old Woman represents. What the Old Woman indicates, in her simple guise and her simple speech, is that access to myth, absorption by myth, is facilitated through the utilization of literal, social or historical figures with whom there already exists some emotional or psychical bond. Barthes refers to the 'form [which] is empty but present, its meaning absent but full',[9] and this is precisely what the Old Woman's words entail. Cullingford has noted the importance of the woman-figure in drawing men into mythical structures: 'Only the love of a woman is a strong enough metaphor for the love of country: a love that leads, in both "September 1913" and "Easter 1916" to death.'[10] I argue that the mother-figure, bearing both the frailty of womanhood and the impress of the intense pre-oedipal relationship she shared with her children, is an even more potent metaphor.

Michael, as will Stephen Dedalus, seeks the mother in whom his own subjectivity is prefigured: the self he desires is, essentially, one defined by a romantic heroism. It is a subjectivity that Bridget Gillane, locked into the family and desiring to see her son locked within that same structure, is unable to offer – this is her failure. Into this space of a 'desired mother', therefore, the mythical mother, Cathleen ni Houlihan, is able to step:

OLD WOMAN: They shall be remembered for ever,
They shall be alive for ever,
    . . .

BRIDGET: . . . Look here, Michael, at the wedding clothes. Such grand clothes as these are! You have a right to fit them on now; it would be a pity tomorrow if they did not fit.[11]

Both mothers seek to draw Michael, not so much towards themselves, but towards that order or that ongoing narrative in which they would have him play a part. The choice of mother and, thereby, the choice of that socio-symbolic order each mother is charged with defending and perpetuating, is determined finally by the subjectivity the child seeks.

Shifting meaning, exacting response

In 'The Ballad of Moll Magee', Moll Magee shifts signification simply through the construction of her story, a story in which she does not act but is acted upon. Through the revelation of her accidental killing of her child, and the continuous suffering this predicates, the meaning of the coupling 'me/Magee' – which is present in rhymes employed in the first and last stanzas – shifts dramatically in the course of the poem. The mother's dilemma is used to facilitate this shift in meaning and, as a result, there is a shift in the reading of the woman who 'owns' the ballad. The poem thus introduces a theme which Yeats will explore extensively in his later work, that of the dues to be paid by the child to the suffering mother: the child or, in this case, 'reader' is drawn into the mother's suffering and responds to the demands embodied within that suffering. In Moll Magee's case, the reader is asked to offer pity;[12] however, the suffering of other mothers, including Cathleen ni Houlihan, demands a more exacting response.

The figure of Cathleen ni Houlihan is utilized to facilitate a similar change in signification in 'Red Hanrahan's Song About Ireland'. That Red Hanrahan's song is both about Cathleen and the catastrophes overwhelming the land sets up an immediate association between the nation and its mythical personification. Cathleen functions within the poem as passive centre, as point of supplication and submission, and as place of refuge; and in this, as Cullingford notes, Yeats draws heavily on the iconography of the Virgin Mary of Catholic tradition.[13] As Foster emphasizes, Yeats underwent a period of 'hectic and fervent mariolatry' which marked the 'rejection of his Protestant background and wish to identify with "the people"'.[14] Here, Yeats's appropriation of the iconography serves to subvert Catholic discourse while promoting that of the Nationalists. The structure of the poem – three stanzas each presenting an antithetical scenario – highlights the centrality 'of Cathleen, the daughter of Houlihan' as the bridge from danger to safety, from disorder to order. She enables the passage of the people from one state to another: she does not carry them, she merely provides the conditions under which such passage may occur. She is still; she does not act. And it is this stillness, this failure to act, which allows the figure of Cathleen to be loaded with the redemptive and restorative powers required by a people seeking those symbolic structures which may afford their suffering some meaning. She becomes the overvalorized 'good mother', drawing her children to her and demanding from them service worthy of her suffering.[15]

In 'Two Years Later', Yeats writes: 'Suffer as your mother suffered / Be as broken in the end.'[16] The mother's suffering tempers the child's joy: the child is either fated to repeat her mother's life, or to pay dues to the mother who has borne her. Having utilized both the tropes of destroying-mother – recall Emer in 'Cuchulain's Fight with the Sea' – and suffering-mother in his early work, it is with the demands of the suffering mother that Yeats, like Joyce, becomes most concerned. For it is the myth of the suffering mother that most readily 'locks up' the responses, and therefore the personal, social and symbolic freedoms, of the 'child'.

'My mother dandled me and sang'

In 'A Song from "The Player Queen"', the mother weaves a story and draws the child into a mythical system which will ensure her own greatness. The mother constructs a place for the child as Queen by enveloping her within a narrative framework in which such a place exists. Yet as the structure of the poem makes clear, it is purely by the mother's volition that these symbols are positioned about the child; and, as Ellmann notes, they are symbols which are wholly 'independent of life or fact'.[17] It is the mother who sings the song; it is the mother who makes the golden cradle and pulls the threads which make the golden gown.[18] The dream which the child articulates as mystical and mysterious is represented as having been manufactured by the mother. For in elevating her child's life, the mother acts to afford meaning to her own. The absent father both fosters the confirmation of the child into a symbolic structure of the mother's choosing, and implicitly motivates the mother to seek meaning for the suffering his desertion has occasioned:

'He went away', my mother sang,
'When I was brought to bed',
And all the while her needle pulled
The gold and silver thread.[19]

The myth the mother constructs excludes the physical father; it does not name him. However, it does embrace an alternative father, a father derived from mythical symbols, and whose lineage the daughter is conditioned to perpetuate. Within the poem, the child's conception is represented in mystical terms, a conception more in keeping with the mythical structures the mother is building than 'traditional' social or symbolic structures.

However, the mother's role in constructing the parameters within which the child's subjectivity may be realized is an implicit threat to patrilineage, particularly that patrilineage sanctioned by the cultural tradition. The mother must serve the cultural tradition as she weaves her tales if a patriarchal history is to be perpetuated, and the tension between the mother and patriarchy that such a dynamic occasions is a consistent theme in Yeats's later work. More often than not, as in 'A Song from "The Player Queen"', the patriarchal history is one which fosters the generation and continuation of a mythical or symbolic authority. Johnsen argues that: 'Patriarchal culture is founded on rejecting a matriarchy it will never know, which perhaps never existed in the form we imagine, except as a patriarchal nightmare.'[20] Indeed, by using the mother-figure solely as the means by which a patriarchal culture or symbolism is expressed, the power of the mother is effectively undermined. She is displaced through that expression.

History, replete with the father, is evident in 'The Magi', written over a decade later. Here the mother-figure is absent, the events of Bethlehem rendered simply as 'The uncontrollable mystery on the bestial floor'.[21] 'The Magi' not only canvasses the dissatisfaction of seekers after salvation – here represented as the Magi – with the consequences of the birth they have witnessed and venerated; but, more importantly, the poem captures the Magi within an eternal cycle: the Magi come again to that birth, come again to that death which, Ellmann notes, sees 'their miraculous God [die] as a human being'.[22] Not recognizing the significance of Calvary, they return to the initiatory moment, seeking again 'The uncontrollable mystery' they first witnessed. The cycle of history in which they find themselves has been closed by their own dissatisfaction, their own misunderstanding of the finale, and their lack of recognition of the myth of rebirth or resurrection by which the cycle would gape open. Yet, in terms of the mother-figure, she only is present within the poem through knowledge of the myth which the reader brings to the poem. While she is central to the 'uncontrollable mystery', to have named her would have challenged the myth of the ineffable father with that of a powerful mother-myth, and it is in this respect that the poem differs significantly from Yeats's earlier story, 'The Adoration of the Magi'.[23]

The mother's function in transmitting the father's history is represented as encompassing more than merely being vessel to the father's seed. The success of the transmission implicitly depends on the purity or worth of the vessel into which the seed is poured. In 'Cuchulain's Fight with the Sea' and *On Baile's Strand*, it is clear that the mother, through her assertion of her own position, has tainted Cuchulain's seed: the patriarchal line is, thereby, debased. The eponymous heroine in *Deirdre* must, within the play, be seen to warrant her place as the King's favourite. Further, she must be constructed in terms which allow her fate to be seen in a truly tragic light. Such a construction affords her no mother.[24] The mystery of her birth accords with the place she must occupy within the play, and the destiny she must bear. Similarly, the mother is absented in the earlier poem 'The Sorrow of Love':

> A girl arose that had red mournful lips
> . . .
> Doomed like Odysseus and the labouring ships
> And proud as Priam murdered with his peers;[25]

The girl facilitates the transposition of perception, of representation. Yet, in doing so, she is permitted to carry only the father's mythical history. The mother's absence – emphasized in the repetition of 'arose' – ensures that the father's history is both untainted and unchallenged.

What Yeats's early work begins to explore is the construction of mythical and historical narratives, the degree to which the mother is implicated in the construction of these narratives, and how the mother is used and discarded in order to ensure the proliferation of a narrative of the father's lineage. The suggestion is that the mother-figure envelops her child in a narrative which will ensure her access to a desired space, a space in which she herself may be mythologized, but, importantly, a space that distances her from the 'real' world. For Yeats, therefore, she acquiesces in her own representation; and, in doing so, she subjects her own history to the father's in order to secure for herself a privileged –

though very often silent – position within that same history. Representation is not something thrust upon the mother, but rather, for Yeats, a shawl in which she chooses to wrap herself.[26]

'I have no child, I have nothing but a book'

'To Ireland in the Coming Times', the final poem in *The Rose*, emphasizes the gap between Ireland as geographical, social or political entity and Ireland as symbol. Further, the poem illuminates the means by which this gap, and the symbology of Ireland, is perpetuated. The rhymes of the poets and the measure of mother-Ireland's[27] dance feed off each other, each sustaining the other's place in a burgeoning myth. That there is a sense of foreboding in the poem's conclusion – a conclusion which reiterates the self-perpetuating qualities of myth while echoing and personalizing the earlier '*Man ever journeys on with them*' – needs to be recognized. To 'know how my heart went with them / After the red-rose-bordered hem'[28] posits a future of thwarted desire; an endless march into an unknown governed only by mythical structures, and in pursuit of an ideal which can never be fully represented or realized. 'Man ever journeys' beyond the moderating effects of more sober 'realities'. What the poem suggests is that myth is not merely devised by the poet. Rather, it is myth itself which bears the poet into that symbolic structure wherein he seeks to exist. For Yeats such structures were those of the 'Young Ireland' poets, Irish legend and fables, and mysticism. Once 'born' into that structure, the poet's own verses, through their utilization of the same symbolic structure, reinforce the myth. The myth, chosen by historical necessity, 'transforms history into nature' and makes 'contingency appear eternal'.[29]

Mother-Ireland is a metaphor on which Yeats draws heavily in his early work. She is manifest in *Cathleen ni Houlihan*, 'Red Hanrahan's Song About Ireland' and 'To Ireland in the Coming Times'. In 'Into the Twilight', from *The Wind Among the Reeds*, Yeats writes that:

> Your mother Eire is always young,
> Dew ever shining and twilight grey.[30]

Mother-Ireland functions in this poem much as she does in 'Red Hanrahan's Song About Ireland'. She counters age and fatigue; she offers more than hope and more than love. Yet at the heart of the poem is a tension that undermines its optimistic surface. The poem is embedded with correlates of hope and despair, and while a first reading may see 'mother

Eire' as balm to that despair, there is implicit within the poem the reading that 'mother Eire's' youth is predicated upon the decay and despair that exists around her. The grey despair of Ireland is her 'fountain of youth': the greyer her context becomes, the brighter will she shine. Suffering, not merely her own, but that which she takes on herself from her 'children' or the context in which she exists, fills her with meaning. In this, Yeats does not merely, as Kearney asserts, '[offer] the myth of Mother Ireland as spiritual or symbolic compensation for the colonial calamities of historical reality'.[31] Rather, he offers the myth to be read ironically.

Yeats's use of maternal metaphors, however, was not limited to constructions of the mother-Ireland trope. In 'Pardon, old fathers . . . ', the introductory poem to *Responsibilities*, the maternal metaphor is utilized in the context of his own creativity. A generational narrative addressed to a 'silent and fierce old man' forms the backbone of the poem. However, its particular interest lies in that the speaker, in making his address, identifies himself with the female side of generation. The speaker refers to himself not as impotent, but as barren:

> Pardon that for a barren passion's sake,
> Although I have come close of forty-nine,
> I have no child, I have nothing but a book,
> Nothing but that to prove your blood and mine.[32]

By thus positioning himself, the speaker suggests that he has failed the father in failing to produce the child through whom the generational line will be continued. The mother-figure becomes the means of exploring both the generation and perpetuation of symbolic structures, most particularly the structure of myth; and in assuming for himself the mother's role in relation to his work, Yeats was uniquely placed both to disrupt and to reconstruct existing symbolic orders. To explore fully the dynamics of symbolic structures, Yeats needed to exploit the border between order and disorder, a feat in which he would, in many respects, be surpassed by Synge.

Cullingford, in her discussion of a later volume, *Michael Robartes and the Dancer*, identifies the relationship between poet, 'mother' and creation as one where the mother participates in creativity but is excluded from bearing the 'child'. [33] However, the extent to which these same dynamics are evident in Yeats's earlier work is questionable. Webster, alternatively, links the growth of the child in the womb with the creation of the poem: they are analogous events in that they are both ultimately destructive. The object is, according to Webster, necessarily devoured in the course of creating the poem.[34] There is, I agree, an aspect of destruction in Yeats's use of the maternal metaphor; yet it is the means of representation which is disintegrated. The destruction of the object is apparent due merely to the disintegration of the symbolic structures by which it is held in place. As I have argued, the mother often is represented as the means by which the father's history or myth is transmitted. By degrees, she is diminished in the process of creation, allowing the myth of the father to reign unchallenged by any alternative history. Where she is explicitly present within the myth, she is charged with the task of ensuring that the child of the mother–father union is not tainted with either her flesh or her own history. It is into this space that Yeats began to insinuate himself as poet.

In Yeats's earliest work, creation tends to be represented relative to the male. The Countess in *The Countess Cathleen* highlights this point:

> For surely He does not forsake the world,
> But stands before it modelling in the clay
> And moulding there His image.[35]

Here Yeats has done little more than appropriate a Judaeo-Christian myth of creation; and within this myth, there is no place for the mother. For to allow her a place would detract from the divinity of creation upon which the myth depends. The mother is similarly absent in the more modest 'creation' represented in 'A Cradle Song'. A simple lullaby, the poem focuses not so much on the babe in the cradle, as the father standing before it. The mother is absent, both literally and figuratively, while the father gazes into the cradle and offers his gentle words. 'A Cradle Song' turns on the father's recognition that the advent of the grown child necessitates the complete loss of the infant before him: 'I shall miss you / When you have grown.'[36] That the child functions within the poem as both physical entity and metaphorical 'new life' places the speaker's words within the context of creator and creation, a context that silences, displaces the mother, while the father is centred.

It is in 'The Song of the Old Mother' that Yeats begins to move towards a maternal space. The central thread of the poem emanates from the mother's creation of life with her first breath upon the fire; and there is a sense of the poem moving not merely through the mother's day, but through motherhood itself. It is not until the penultimate line that the mother is actually rendered as old. This leaves open the reading that the 'old mother' has herself aged with the day. What the poem also suggests is that the song is not merely that of the 'old mother' but of the poet himself. The poem moves from first life to death:

> Till the seed of the fire flicker and grow;
> ...
> And the seed of the fire gets feeble and cold.[37]

It suggests an interdependency between mother and child, and, perhaps, between poet and poem. It is an interdependency which sees the child in ease and idleness while the 'mother's' life, like the fire, dies from her toil.

The life-draining effects of creativity are canvassed again in 'Adam's Curse'. Here the speech is explicitly of poetry:

> I said, 'A line will take us hours maybe;
> Yet if it does not seem a moment's thought,
> Our stitching and unstitching has been naught.[38]

Appearing in *In the Seven Woods*, a volume marked by its ironic rendering of the idealization of woman, an idealization that Yeats himself had utilized extensively in earlier volumes, the poem is one of many which evinces the underside of the pedestal on which woman is placed. 'Adam's Curse' is structured as a dialogue, its rhythm languid and pensive. The conversation is recalled through the prism of the speaker's memories, and its reconstruction is entirely dependent on the purpose of the speaker. While the poem ostensibly addresses the work of the poet and the decline of love, there is an ambiguity of meaning within the poem, which turns on the use of the word 'labour'. The poet's creative process, having been set above the travails of the general populace, is contrasted with the 'work' of woman:

> 'To be born woman is to know –
> Although they do not talk of it at school –
> That we must labour to be beautiful.'[39]

Beauty derives not merely from cosmetic effort but, more insidiously, from the production of children, from motherhood:

> I said, 'It's certain there is no fine thing
> Since Adam's fall but needs much labouring.'[40]

The reader is thus invited to view the poet's craft in the light of a maternal metaphor. The reference to Adam's fall – and the title of the poem – further demands that readers bring to the poem their knowledge of the creation myth surrounding Adam and Eve. It is important to recall that the banishment from Eden brings curses on both of the primordial parents: Adam is cursed to toil for food; Eve is cursed to bring forth children in pain. While the poem addresses the burden of creative labour, Eve, whose 'curse' is more relevant to the poem than Adam's, is excluded. The burden of labour is transferred exclusively to the male: it is 'Adam's curse'. Within the context of the poem, the woman's words are not addressed directly by the speaker. Rather, they become the means by which the speaker strengthens his own argument. Talk of poetry turns to thoughts of dying love; yet the function of the maternal metaphor, which lies beneath the surface of the poem, in facilitating this process is not entirely clear. However, it is worth noting that the maternal metaphor, whose presence is encapsulated in the use of the word 'labour', facilitates the exclusion of Eve, of woman, from the creation myth. This exclusion follows directly upon the woman's articulation within the poem of her own labour, an articulation which may have necessitated the speaker's action in reframing the Eden myth, and dismissing the threat to his own sense of creativity that the 'real' mother poses. What the speaker perceives as the 'weary-hearted' passion between man and woman may be associated with Eve's exclusion: the speaker's position relative to the woman has been refigured, and in this there is a faint parallel with the refiguring of the relationship between Eve and Adam.

In terms of the displacement of the mother-figure, Yeats's most interesting text within this period is undoubtedly 'The Dolls'. Here the reader is permitted to see the displacement actually effected. Almost fable-like in its telling, the poem establishes a conflict between the creations of the father and the creation of the mother. Carriker refers to this conflict as embodying 'the anguish of the mother, the father's emotional distance from the event, and the distress that the child's birth has caused the family – the disruption of the symbolic order'.[41] Yet the conflict is more fundamental than this. The conflict centres on the creative powers of father and mother, and is resolved only when the mother subjects herself to the father, subordinating her own power and, thereby, elevating his. An interesting aspect of the poem is that it is neither father nor mother who initiates the conflict. Rather, it is the creations themselves which are, essentially, antagonistic, and it is this antagonism which is transferred to the relationship between man and woman: 'The doll-maker's wife is aware / Her husband has heard the wretch.'[42] It is at this point that the doll-maker's wife capitulates:

> 'My dear, my dear, O dear,
> It was an accident.'[43]

It is on this capitulation that the poem concludes. The mother relinquishes responsibility for the child she has borne, and creative power shifts to her husband. It is ironic that, in a sense, her deference to her husband only serves to accentuate the fundamental difference in their 'creations' and the mockery that the child implicitly makes of the doll-maker's dolls. It is through 'The Dolls' that Yeats acts to defuse his own role in displacing the mother by representing her own surrender to the paternal metaphor.

It is this process of displacing the mother that is one of the most significant developments in Yeats's representation of the mother-figure in this period. Even so, it is a process that is far from complete: while Yeats has displaced the mother, or at least diminished her role, he has not yet completely occupied (vacant) maternal spaces. The extent to which Yeats, in his later work, assumes the maternal metaphor, the extent to which he confronts the social and symbolic limitations inherent to the mother's function of ensuring the pre-eminence of the patriarchy and patrilineage, and the uses he makes of the maternal metaphor to modify or resist mythical and symbolic structures will be explored further in the subsequent chapter, 'Playing Her Part Too Well'.

Mothers and Martyrs

...however picturesque his mother may be as she sits crooning songs of hatred against her betrayer, a young nationality...must find something lacking in a mental and spiritual attitude so uncompromisingly negative.

John Eglinton[1]

And since woman has been subjected as Mother, she will be cherished and respected first of all as Mother.

Simone de Beauvoir, The Second Sex

Charles died a martyr; he died as Christ died, hounded to death by those who should have stood by him.

Parnell's mother[2]

'Parnell's fall,' James Joyce wrote, 'came in the midst of [political] events like lightning from a clear sky.'[3] The myth of Parnell 'was to echo through Irish literature and politics with a passion that has not even yet entirely died away'.[4] At the heart of the myth is the great man, a saviour, being torn down by the mob. Eye-witness accounts of his funeral in 1891 paint the scene in apocalyptic terms, befitting a man who has moved beyond simple humanity and now wears the martyr's cloak: 'I state a fact – it was witnessed by thousands. While his followers were committing Charles Parnell's remains to the earth, the sky was bright with strange lights and flames.'[5] Joyce read into Parnell's fall the image of Christ betrayed, torn to pieces not by the English but by the Irish themselves.[6] Yeats, who would himself take up these myths in his poetry, marks Parnell's fall and death as a point of change in Anglo-Irish literature, as the moment from which the transition to 'the modern' may be traced.[7] Yeats's assessment of the emergence of 'the modern' in Ireland – an assessment which is both espoused and refuted by critics[8] – may be as much a function of the Parnell myth itself as a considered reading of Anglo-Irish literary history.

As Deane argues, Parnell's fall embodied a literary trope in itself:[9] the hero betrayed, and the guilt of the mob, are extensively explored by Yeats, Joyce and O'Casey, and has one of its most ironic renderings in Synge's *The Playboy of the Western World*. A powerful trope, drawing as its does on Christian myth, it has not merely been absorbed within literature, it has become overlaid on Irish history. As Kearney has noted:

> The IRA's ideology is *sacrificial* to the degree that it invokes, explicitly or otherwise, a 'sacred' tradition of death and renewal which provides justification for present acts of suffering by realigning them with recurring paradigms of the past and thus affording these acts a certain timeless and redemptive quality.[10]

The trope can be read at its most florid and romantic in the poetry of Padraic Pearse, poems which both glorify sacrifice and hallow the mother for whom the sacrifice is to be made. Poems such as 'I am Ireland' and 'The Rebel' emphasize a correlation between the representation of the mother-figure and the representation of her 'son'. It is a correlation noted by Kristeva, who claims that 'it is likely that all beliefs in resurrections are rooted in mythologies marked by the strong dominance of a mother goddess'.[11] What is implied is that the 'son's' *self*-representation is dependent on representations of the mother prevalent within the cultural context. Yet what the work of Yeats, Moore and Joyce tends to suggest is that the mother plays a pivotal role in her own representation. That Pearse's mother should request him to compose his overwrought poem 'The Mother',[12] and that Parnell's mother should decry her son's death by asserting his place as a new Christ, suggest the affinity between 'real' mothers and those mother-figures articulated within the literature. For what both Pearse's and Parnell's mothers are effecting is their own space as the mother of a martyr, a space that Christian iconography has deemed to be worthy of praise and adulation. The mother uses her son's sacrifice to enact her own self-representation. It is not merely the child who reads their identity in the mirror that is the mother's face, but the mother who reads, and embellishes, her own identity in the face of her child.

Whose face in the mirror?

The space of 'mother of the martyr' is one of the few in which mothers are able to assume any power. It is ironic that, as de Beauvoir argues, the mother can assume this position only by subjecting herself to the patriarchal cultural tradition by which that space is constructed: 'As servant, woman is entitled to the most splendid deification.'[13] The interdependence of the mother's (self-)representation and the child's (self-)representation has its source in what Lacan terms the 'mirror-stage'. What the child sees in the mirror that is, more often than not, his mother's face is an image in which the fragmented self appears to coalesce, albeit tenuously; yet, significantly, it is an image in which the child essentially 'misrecognizes' its self. What the child perceives as fact is, in effect, a fiction: 'By clinging to the reference-point of him who looks at him in a mirror, the subject sees appearing, not his ego ideal, but his ideal ego, that point at which he desires to gratify himself in himself.'[14] Yet while the fragmented child is theorized within psychoanalytic discourse as finding coalescence in the mirror, that same discourse fails to articulate fully the degree to which the mother similarly 'misrecognizes' her self, and constructs her own image from the shards that the paternal cultural tradition offers to her as she gazes into the face of the child.[15]

Tropes of motherhood and martyrdom are heavily interdependent, an interdependence that has its paradigm in the pre-oedipal mother–child dyad. Therefore, the child staring into the mirror of its mother's face accesses not only the mother sanctioned by the symbolic order, but that more dangerous mother, that 'figure of subversion', whose potency resides in that which the symbolic order represses.[16] Equally, I argue, the mother reflected back in the face of her child has a rare opportunity to read not only the figure prescribed by patriarchal culture, but also her own – for want of a better term – phallic figure, through whom representation may be disrupted and reconstructed. It is in this potential for disruption of the symbolic that the mother's true power lies. Yet, ultimately, she acquiesces to a position of spurious deification where her power is contained within representation. It is an irony evident in Moore's work, and one which will haunt Stephen Dedalus in particular: the potential of the child's subjectivity resides in the pre-oedipal mother, and to realize a desired subjectivity the child must search for the pre-oedipal mother who bears that potential. Even so, the pre-oedipal mother must be sacrificed if that same subjectivity is to be attained; she is sacrificed in the working out of the Oedipus complex, a process which hinges on the 'realization' of castration. I am inclined, along with critics such as Irigaray, Ian and Sprengnether, to read this castration in terms other than the mere lopping off of the phallus. Rather, I read 'castration' as the severing of the mother's access to the capacity to subvert the symbolic order. That is, castration is effected in the split of the mother–child dyad; a split – enforced through representation – in that relationship in which the mother has access to the a-symbolic order she embodies. It is not the child-as-phallus that the mother loses when the dyad is severed; rather, it is her access to the semiotic, to that which is reflected to her in the mutually defining mirror that stands between mother and child.

The face of the Virgin, the face of the nation

Jane Gallop, in her essay 'The American Other', emphasizes that within the metaphor of the mirror there exists both the semiotic image which threatens subversion and the mirror's frame or structure which insists that the image itself must be denied.[17] The metaphor of the mirror does, of course, appear frequently in Anglo-Irish literature during the modernist period. Both Wilde and Joyce utilized it, as did Yeats in his schism of self and anti-self. Whether it was art, Ireland or the blurred self coming into focus in its face, the mirror offered a nexus between the actual and the possible, cohesion and disruption. The use made of the mirror image by these writers differs widely; however, my particular concern is where mirror and mother are juxtaposed. The rich mother-images embedded within Irish culture – mother-Ireland and the Blessed Virgin – which may have been reflected back at coalescing subjectivities, and the potential impact on those subjectivities, is an issue which cannot be divorced from the frame in which those mother-images were held. As Kristeva argues with respect to the power of the Virgin – a power which extends to mother-Ireland – she exists beyond language, she '[occupies] the tremendous territory hither and yon of the parentheses of language'. Even so, she is subject to the 'word' that the Church has mythologized as 'the beginning'.[18] While the child may find its subjectivity in its opposition to the mother, that subjectivity, when found in the mother's image, must always be bound by that same frame, within that same symbolic order. It is against this dilemma that many of the characters within the texts struggle.

Marina Warner, in her comprehensive study of the cult of the Virgin Mary, argues that '[in] motherhood Mary was glorified, and through her prostration before her child, became more glorious for her humility.'[19] Innes refers to the 'cult of humility' that mariolatry and its icons reinforced in the Irish context.[20] Yet what mariolatry seeds within a culture is not merely the underside of the worshipped woman – the woman degraded as slut and whore – but a space for the child as the sacrificial victim who will immortalize the mother's suffering. It is a space into which mother-Ireland also draws her children.[21] De Beauvoir is one critic who theorizes this link between the venerated mother and the victim child:

> the *mater dolorosa* forges from her sufferings a weapon that she uses sadistically; her displays of resignation give rise to guilt feelings in the child which often last a lifetime; they are still more harmful than her displays of aggression.[22]

Kearney, writing with specific reference to the Irish context, argues that the colonialism to which Ireland was subject compounded with mariolatry and *bean si* tradition to evoke a potent myth of the motherland,[23] a myth that links inextricably the child's sacrifice in response to the mother's suffering and the renewal or rebirth that will result from that sacrifice.

The point which must be made is the profound impact Catholic and Nationalist myths – defining as they do the face of the mother – have on the subjectivity of the child whose self is reflected from, and developed in response to, that same face. However, the child, gazing upon that face, is distracted from the potentiality for subversion that rests in the (phallic) mother by the frame in which she – and in which he too when he looks in that mirror – is bound. In the profound suffering that the mother reflects, the child is drawn – through guilt – into a position that demands sacrifice. The mother, thereby, creates the space for the martyr. And the martyr, concomitantly, creates the space where the mother may be venerated for the suffering she endures. It is an eternal cycle of life and death, and one from which Anglo-Irish literature of the modernist period seeks first to escape and then to appropriate in the subversion of symbolic structures. Where this cycle is complicated in the Irish context – in the representations of the mother-figure that authors such as Joyce and O'Casey create – is that the mother is not only heavily implicated in the proliferation of these structures, she also effectively blocks the child's 'resurrection' by encroaching, herself, on that space reserved for her martyred children. The defeat of the mother, while maintaining access to the maternal spaces that facilitate creativity, is the dilemma with which both the authors and their creations must contend.

4
Denying the Mother: Escaping Confirmation in Family and Father in the Work of James Joyce, 1907–14

In one of the most commonly quoted passages in Anglo-Irish literature, Stephen Dedalus records in his diary: 'Welcome, O life! I go to encounter for the millionth time the reality of experience and to forge in the smithy of my soul the uncreated conscience of my race.' What few critics include is the image of the mother with which the diary entry begins: 'Mother is putting my new secondhand clothes in order,' Stephen writes. 'She prays now, she says, that I may learn in my own life and away from home and friends what the heart is and what it feels. Amen. So be it.'[1] The presence of Mrs Dedalus in the diary entry of 26 April, that entry in which Stephen states most succinctly the aesthetic ideal for which he is reaching, clearly signals just how far he is from breaking finally with his mother. Her implicit participation in his departure, her packing of his suitcase, and her words, afford her a control over his actions and goals that she would not possess had he insisted on her absence, had he acted alone. Whether it is Stephen or Mrs Dedalus or even both who refuse to forgo the mother–child bond is not entirely clear; but it is, I suggest, this failure to sever effectively the pre-oedipal link which will haunt Stephen throughout *Ulysses*, and effectively block his ability to realize his artistic objectives.[2]

The mother's acquiescence in the child's movement beyond her realm has here the effect of consolidating the link between mother and child, and Stephen Dedalus's departure from Ireland is not the first example within Anglo-Irish literature of the 'exile' who, in a sense, bears the mother with him. In George Moore's 'The Wild Goose', one of the stories from the 1903 volume *The Untilled Field*, Ned Carmady also leaves Ireland in search of a freedom of expression Ireland has denied him. It is his wife, Ellen, representative of both mother-Church and mother-Ireland, who articulates the step that he has long felt inevitable, but which he has not himself taken. Leaving Ireland, he tells himself that 'distance would bring a closer and more intimate appreciation of her',[3] 'her' referring not merely to his wife, but to Ireland itself. Leaving the mother will enhance her image, because he takes her with him in her ideal aspect.

Joyce's indebtedness to Moore is discussed extensively by critics.[4] McCarthy, in one of the most useful surveys of the 'Moore–Joyce nexus', argues that the similarities between the work of the two men are as much a matter of influence as they are of a shared disdain for the paralysing effects of Irish society: 'parochialism, prudery, the influence of a conservative priesthood, the ignorance of the average Irishman.'[5] Nowhere are these parallels more apparent than in the exile – the flight – from Ireland of Ned Carmady and Stephen Dedalus. The association of birds with metaphorical flight is, no doubt, archetypal; however, it is an association extensively utilized by Moore. Moore applies the image of the tame bird in a cage to both Kate Ede in *A Mummer's Wife* and Wilfred Owens in *Celibate Lives*. In *The Lake*, Oliver Gogarty sees in the flight of birds the omen that directs his own escape from the fetters of Irish Catholicism:

> I know that belief in signs and omens and prognostics can be laughed at; nothing is more ridiculous than the belief that man's fate is governed by the flight of birds, yet men have believed in bird augury from the beginning of the world.[6]

Joyce is reputed to be one of those who did laugh at Oliver Gogarty's musings; yet as McCarthy notes 'it seems likely that in 1906 Joyce was seriously biased against a book in which Moore had solved some of the artistic problems that Joyce was failing to solve in his autobiographical novel, *Stephen Hero*.'[7] Even so, it is in Moore's 'The Wild Goose' that, I argue, Stephen's flight is most precisely foreshadowed. Interestingly, this is one line of influence that few critics have traced; however, the confluence of birds, flight and nets – the net image having been developed by Moore early in the story when Ned and his soon-to-be wife seek to trap a legendary, yet previously untrappable, trout – has very definite echoes in Joyce's *Portrait*. Ned Carmady, like Oliver Gogarty, looks to the sea-birds for guidance as he seeks a resolution to his dilemma, a dilemma which is represented by Moore in terms of the nets – woven by Ireland and Catholicism – into which Carmady feels he, like the

trout, is swimming. Carmady's thoughts as he gazes over the sea resonate in Stephen Dedalus's words to Davin:

> The soul . . . has a slow, dark birth, more mysterious than the birth of
> the body. When the soul of a man is born in this country there are
> nets flung at it to hold it back from flight. You talk to me of nation-
> ality, language, religion. I shall try to fly those nets.[8]

What is of particular note is that the mother-figure plays a prominent
role in all these instances. In Moore's work she tends to personify the
cage wherein the 'bird' is trapped. This is how she operates in *A Mummer's Wife, Celibate Lives* and 'The Wild Goose.' Yet, in *The Lake*, the
mother-figure establishes the conditions under which that cage may be
breached. Nora Glynn is an important variation on the mother-figure in
this respect, in that she is more aligned with the pre-oedipal mother,
that mother who, rather than imposing on the child the subjectivity
demanded by the patriarchal cultural tradition, prefigures the subjectivity the child desires. It is this aspect of the mother that Joyce will
develop to effect Stephen Dedalus's escape.

The ways in which Joyce draws on, and develops, the work of his
predecessors and contemporaries in his representation of the mother-
figure is one focus of this chapter. While his debt to European literature
– classical, romantic and modern – cannot be ignored – and, as *Stephen
Hero* and his critical writings indicate, it was to a large extent his 'Euro-
peanism' which set him in conflict with Irish Nationalism – it is the
degree to which he worked within and subverted Anglo-Irish representational practices that is my particular interest. Moore and Yeats were
the most notable writers engaging with this tradition at the time Joyce
began to write. In the first decades of the new century, as Costello
argues, Irish literature was flourishing and the arrival of George Moore
served as a 'realistic' antidote to the 'strain of literature associated with
Yeats [which] was idealistic and romantic in tendency.'[9] It was during
these same years that Joyce was first realizing his vocation. Yet it was
predominantly Moore's, rather than Yeats's, legacy that Joyce absorbed,
transformed and sought to discard. For while Yeats's influence cannot be
ignored, it is Moore, both in terms of the genre in which he had his
greatest success, and his determination to expose the hypocrisy of Irish
Catholicism and liberate Irish language and art, who is Joyce's natural
precursor. The representation of the mother-figure, particularly the
social, political and symbolic contexts within which she is constructed,
offers a useful means of tracing the extent of such influence, and how

the 'gravitational pull' exerted by individual writers within the Anglo-Irish tradition may have operated. Joyce, whose own radical stylistic developments are mirrored in his representation of the mother-figure, offers between *Dubliners* and *A Portrait of the Artist as a Young Man* a rapid shift in the construction of the mother-figure, transforming her from a social to a symbolic presence. In this he very quickly outruns Moore's plodding later work, and pre-empts Yeats who, in his second great creative burst, beginning with *The Wild Swans at Coole*, began to explore the same territory.

Patriarchal fictions: the covert rule of the mother

In *Dubliners* the mother is curiously absent in the stories of childhood and – except for 'Eveline' – in the stories of youth. Ironically, her presence is felt primarily in the stories of adulthood and public life, both spheres in which she should, by rights, be largely invisible. In one of these stories, 'A Mother', Mrs Kearney's efforts to secure the terms of her daughter's contract within the public space of the Nationalist Eire-Abu society lead to her condemnation by the society and her daughter's artistic ruin. Mrs Kearney is a good wife who has married not as a result of a passionate liaison, but rather to silence her friends. She married a man who would 'wear well', 'a model father' who, it is implied, does not challenge her dominance of the household.[10] As described by Joyce, the patriarchy is a fiction, a sheen veiling the matriarchy that operates at a covert level. Yet in order to operate effectively the matriarchy must maintain its covert nature. Miller argues that Mrs Kearney is acting 'to avoid the paralysis that the other characters succumb to';[11] however, I argue that Mrs Kearney's error lies in that, having been invited to utilize her skills within the public sphere, she merely forgets her place.[12] Her organization and control of events becomes overt, and she is undone.

The story of 'A Mother' opens with the delineation of Mrs Kearney's role in the organization of the concert: 'but in the end it was Mrs Kearney who arranged everything.' She is represented in contrast to Hoppy Holohan 'with his hands and pockets full of dirty pieces of paper.'[13] Even so, while Mrs Kearney's endeavours ensure the concerts go ahead, it is important to bear in mind the setting in which she works with Mr Holohan, particularly where the contract with the society is finalized:

> She brought him into the drawing-room, made him sit down and brought out the decanter and the silver biscuit-barrel. She entered heart and soul into the details of the enterprise, advised and dissuaded:

and finally a contract was drawn up by which Kathleen was to receive eight guineas for her services as accompanist at the four grand concerts.... She was invariably friendly and advising – homely, in fact.[14]

In this passage, a cogent metaphor of the mother's role is offered: within her home she agrees to terms which will secure her child's services to a father-figure. Mrs Kearney acts to ensure her daughter's place within the Gaelic revival which she, mistakenly, perceives Mr Holohan and the Eire-Abu society to represent; yet the pitiful nature of the father-figure Mrs Kearney chooses (an implicit criticism of Yeats and others who spawned and promoted 'the revival') does not auger well for the contract. Even so, in securing that contract, she forgoes her right to act any further on her child's behalf. Kathleen has been 'confirmed' in the society of the Eire-Abu, a confirmation which requires both her and her mother's subjection. Mrs Kearney does not merely step outside that 'private' space in which she may wield her limited, yet overt, authority – she attempts to assert her will where her will is not recognized. She errs in that she has made a contract with a society that is torpid and disorganized. Further, having made that contract, she refuses to abide by it. While the Eire-Abu society has broken the letter of the law, the pact Mrs Kearney implicitly made with them as a metaphoric 'father' should have overridden any common law. That she does not acknowledge this fact is the cause of her downfall.

In 'A Mother', Joyce does not merely articulate the boundaries within which the mother is confined, but explores the effect of her breach of those boundaries, particularly her humiliation within public spaces, a humiliation effected by a ridiculous and disorganized patriarchy. More acute than Moore in his portrayal of social stagnation and the inertia of sexual, political and religious conservatism, Joyce reveals a reigning patriarchy which is impotent, and a pervasively potent matriarchy which is denied any measure of social authority. This contradiction is the weight that Irish society bears, impeding its progress. For it is this very contradiction which occasions the gap wherein Catholic and Nationalist discourses may exert their own authorities and assert their own orders. The mother's function in the process whereby the familial father's authority is impoverished, affording to mother and child an exaggerated reliance on alternative authorities, particularly Catholic orthodoxy, is frequently explored in Joyce's fiction, and the dynamics of the family provide an important clue to the source of the nets which bind the artistic spirit.

Father and child, father as child

When Stephen Dedalus, in *A Portrait of the Artist as a Young Man*, suffers homesickness, it is for his mother that he longs.[15] She offers comfort, shelter and certainty in an otherwise disorienting world; yet she is silent and unnamed. Her only voice is the music to which her son dances. She is 'nice', but she must not cry. She is veiled, but unveils herself to kiss her son.[16] She is 'thinly clad', frugal and patient, and tries to maintain the peace, balancing her subservience to her husband with her subservience to her faith.[17] She is centred in the home; she is rarely represented beyond it. And nowhere more than in the disastrous Christmas dinner in the Dedalus household is her expected function within society more precisely rendered. While critics have noted Mrs Dedalus's role as mediator in the argument over Parnell and the Church, her role in the confirmation of her son – within the family and within the Church – has not been as readily acknowledged. It is within the ritual of the Dedalus Christmas that Stephen's mother brings him to both his familial and his spiritual fathers – to Christmas dinner and to Catholic mass.[18] Mrs Dedalus perpetuates the tradition of father to son; she is stalwart of the social and symbolic orders which dictate her place and which she, in turn, serves. Stephen, in partaking Christmas dinner outside the nursery, takes his first steps in the severance of his bond with his mother, bypassing her as his source of sustenance and nurture. He dines on a discourse of politics and religion; and he is borne towards his subjectivity on the day that Christ himself was born. Yet the conversation that day – a day celebrating the birth of a king – turns on the fate of another martyr, Charles Stewart Parnell, 'My dead king'.[19] Parnell's sacrifice, his position within myth as victim, provides a template that Stephen will, in later years, seek to make his own.

Despite the efforts of Mrs Dedalus to quell the Christmas day argument, to silence both Dante and her husband for the sake of her son – 'you should not speak that way before Stephen. It's not right' – Stephen 'felt the glow rise to his own cheek as the spoken words thrilled him.'[20] He is both confused and excited by the unravelling of order and civility, and, perhaps, he senses his mother's ambivalence in offering him as subject to his father's authority. Tension is established between allegiances to the Church and to Ireland, allegiances that, as observed in both his father and in Dante, had once been complementary.[21] The argument touches on issues central to Irish sensibility: sacrifice, destruction, religious authority, nationalism, national pride and fidelity. Yet Mrs Dedalus's position on any of these matters remains unclear, unstated. She chides her husband and Dante in turn, but it is evident that she does so not from any conviction of her own, but in order to maintain peace, and, principally, in order to protect her son from the subversion of religious authority that Simon Dedalus's accusations against the Church threaten.

In my discussion of George Moore's representation of the mother-figure, I noted that the father was often either absent or marginalized, and that the mother mediated between the child and conservative authorities, generally nationalist or religious, though in Moore's case the protection of the social *status quo* was also an important consideration. Mrs Dedalus enacts a similar role; yet it is not certain in the early stages of the novel whether Simon Dedalus will take his place as the central authority within the family, or whether he will be marginalized in favour of the Church. The potential for either outcome exists within the context of the Christmas dinner. Yet Simon Dedalus's authority is foreclosed stealthily over the course of the novel: the family moves and Stephen comes to understand something of his father's 'troubles'; Stephen uses his prize-money to provide, briefly, for his family, usurping his father's place; the 'breakwater of order' Stephen had sought within the 'commonwealth' of his family – the commonwealth symbolically held together by his father – disintegrates, highlighting his own 'futile isolation ... divided ... from mother and brother and sister.'[22] Material and social considerations, though present in the early stages of the schism between Stephen and his father, do not effect the breach. Ultimately, it is effected by the impotence of his father's narrative to evoke the images Stephen discovers anchored in a single word carved into a desk: what is, in effect, the defeat of the 'phallus' by a '*Foetus*', an actuality by an alternative potential.[23] *A Portrait*, as Ellmann notes, begins with Simon Dedalus:[24] the father offers the narrative in which Stephen is defined: 'His father told him that story: ... He was baby tuckoo.'[25] It is a narrative embedded in language, and contrasts with the music and elusive sensuousness his mother offers. Yet while the second chapter opens with Stephen's bonding with the male lineage – his immersion in the athletics so closely associated with the nationalist movement[26] – by the close of the chapter, Simon Dedalus is effectively marginalized and powerless, and Stephen has commenced his search for a new father.[27]

The failure of the father to be positioned as authority is a consistent theme in Joyce's early work and, like Mrs Dedalus, other mother-figures effect – whether actively or passively – the subversion of the father's position. Joyce suggests that this stems from both the mother's equivocation in her own subjection to the father's will, and the impotence of the father in asserting authority. The depressing dynamics of the Irish urban family – and its chronic inability to meet the ideal espoused by Catholicism – is exposed throughout *Dubliners*. In 'Eveline', the mother is associated with happiness and protection, her absence with the threat of violence.[28] In 'Grace', Mrs Kernan

> made beef-tea for [her husband] and scolded him roundly. She accepted his frequent intemperance as part of the climate, healed him dutifully whenever he was sick and always tried to make him eat a breakfast. There were worse husbands. He had never been violent since the boys had grown up.[29]

Within the home she suffers, and sometimes tempers, the father's excesses. Yet, for the most part, mothers in Joyce's Dublin tend not only their children but their husbands also, a role which explains their prominence in the stories of adulthood and public life. There is a distinct correlation between the violence and drunkenness into which fathers descend and the infantilization of the father by the mother, a correlation which is not presented as a simple matter of cause and effect, but rather a cycle from which both mothers and fathers are unable to escape. The cycle serves no purpose within the family; it does, however, serve an important purpose in bringing the child to the Church. This is, as Kristeva suggests, the way the mother participates in culture, 'not by giving birth to her children, but merely by preparing them for baptism.'[30] I prefer to read the mother's role in Joyce's work as one of bringing the child to confirmation – which marks not merely the absolution of original sin but full acceptance into the faith – and, as 'Grace' indicates, that child may be either infant or father. It is the mother who disciplines father and child; it is she who nourishes and nurtures. But only within the home.

While Joyce presents the infantilization of the father as merely one element in a stagnant cycle, he does tend to lean towards structures which emphasize the mother's role in suppressing the father's authority. There is, therefore, a sense of blame in his representation of the mother-figure's function within that process which sees the father emasculated and irrelevant in the eyes of his children, and the concomitant elevation of her own place within the family. 'A Little Cloud' is a pertinent example. Here, the 'infant hope' of Chandler's imagination is set against the child of his marriage.[31] Unlike Bertha, in *Exiles*, Chandler's wife, Annie, does not vicariously nurture the imaginative life within her husband. In fact, just as Polly Mooney has done with Bob Doran,

Annie has so pinioned Little Chandler within marriage that every infant hope is bound to be stillborn. Chandler reads the effects of his marriage in the room around him.[32] In Chandler's survey of the furniture and furnishings of his home, Joyce suggests the staleness and coldness of the marriage, and a wife within whom there is no hint of the sensuality of life: 'He looked coldly into the eyes of the photograph and they answered coldly.... They repelled him and defied him: there was no passion in them, no rapture.'[33] That the eyes in the photograph defy him is important in establishing the mother's eminence within the sphere of their home, as is Chandler's helplessness in the face of the infant's wailing. In fact, Chandler cowers from his wife and fears her. When she returns from the store, Annie Chandler is confronted with two despairing infants: the 'prisoner of life' so bound that he will never be able 'to express the melancholy of his soul in verse', and her frightened, screaming son.[34] In their despair, father and son are, symbolically, united. Yet within the imagery of the text it is mother and child who, as Cixous notes, 'are framed by a circle of light, from which Little Chandler withdraws.'[35] It is the son who receives the mother's comfort. It is the child who is 'My little man! My little mannie!... Mamma's little lamb of the world!', while Chandler takes the position of the disgraced child: 'Little Chandler felt his cheeks suffused with shame and he stood back out of the lamplight. He listened while the paroxysm of the child's sobbing grew less and less; and tears of remorse started to his eyes.'[36] This episode suggests the readiness with which father and child reverse their roles within a home dominated by the mother's will: the ground on which the man stands within the home is liable to shift once wife becomes mother. As has been suggested by a number of critics, Annie Chandler's reference to her child as 'mamma's little lamb of the world' associates the child with Christ. Of more significance, I argue, is that this reference brings Chandler's family into stark contrast with the Christian family upon whom the Catholic ideal is based. The association between the child and Christ implies an association between Annie and the Virgin Mary, and another between Little Chandler and Joseph, the foster-father whose authority dissipates as the myth of the Virgin birth is disseminated.

The 'mothering' that Little Chandler's infant hope requires is suggested in *Exiles*. Echoing Joyce's own letters to his wife, Richard Rowan seeks in Bertha access to the pre-oedipal spaces which will feed his creativity: 'To hold you by no bonds, even of love, to be united with you in body and soul in utter nakedness – for this I longed.'[37] It is, Joyce suggests, the mother's denial of her own sensuality which precludes the 'child's' access to the fount of creativity which the mother alone possesses. Joyce's recognition and articulation of these structures goes some way to explaining the development in his construction of the mother-figure, particularly the metaphorical mother, between *Dubliners* and *A Portrait*.

'Eve yielded ... '

In 'Grace', Mrs Kernan refers fondly to the anniversary of her 'wedding' but not her 'marriage': she had 'after three weeks ... found a wife's life irksome and, later on, when she was beginning to find it unbearable, she had become a mother. The part of mother presented to her no insuperable difficulties.'[38] There is a suggestion in 'wife' of sexual duties which are not inherent to 'mother'; there is also a suggestion of authority in the mother's role that would not have been afforded to a wife. In both *Dubliners* and *A Portrait*, sexuality is rarely attributed to mothers. Unlike Moore's work, where sexuality in the mother-figure effected the death or enfeeblement of the child, in Joyce's early work sexuality is inevitably sublimated to the mothering role.[39] This is evident, for example, in 'The Boarding House', where Polly's sexuality is used to establish her own motherhood, thereby re-establishing herself in her mother's place.[40] Polly is described as a 'little perverse madonna', a role that is matched by Mrs Mooney's perversion of the mother's silent, passive role: it is through her silence that Mrs Mooney lures Bob Doran into her trap.[41] Mother and daughter are complicit in compromising Mr Doran, covertly working to drag him into a 'family', thereby ensuring his paralysis and degradation:

> [Mrs Mooney] had been made awkward by her not wishing to receive the news in too cavalier a fashion or to seem to have connived, and Polly had been made awkward not merely because allusions of that kind always made her awkward, but also because she did not wish it to be thought that in her wise innocence she had divined the intention behind her mother's tolerance.[42]

Mrs Mooney, who ironically has been awarded the care of her children by the priest, has the moral upper-hand: 'She was sure she would win. To begin with she had the weight of social opinion on her side: she was an outraged mother.'[43] Sexuality, Joyce suggests, is the bait that drags men into the debilitating family cycle that will see them emasculated and infantilized. Yet it is possible to surmise on the basis of the pattern established in *Dubliners* that, having caught her quarry, Polly Mooney will become as asexual as her own mother: Bob Doran will no longer have access to the woman. She will be 'mother', and he must relate to her as child. Sexuality as the bait which entraps men is a central trope within Catholic discourse, as the sermon delivered in *A Portrait* emphasizes.[44] Yet, in *Dubliners*, Joyce suggests that sexuality itself is not the danger: it is the effect of succumbing to that sexuality, of offering the woman the seed by which she will become mother, that establishes the conditions for the male to become not so much father – with all the authority that title entails – but child.

The rich yet silent symbol

In his notes to *Exiles*, Joyce exposes the 'infallible practical instinct' of the Italian Catholic Church, an instinct which is instrumental in the Church's discovery of 'the rich possibilities of the figure of the Madonna.' For him, the figure of the Madonna provides a potent symbol: she is the mother able to draw within her ambit the son who previously 'had neither wife nor mistress nor sister and would scarcely have been associated with his mother.'[45] Through the image of the Madonna, the son is bound inextricably to the mother: bound not as man, but as child. Further, the Catholic Madonna afforded an image which illuminated the mutual dependence of mother and Church in Catholic Ireland: the mother serves the Church by delivering the child and, in return, she receives the honour and position reserved for her in Catholic discourse.

The mother's submission to the Church, and her delivery of her children to the social and symbolic orders emanating from the Church's authority, were common themes in Moore's work and are particularly prevalent in Joyce. Often, for Joyce, the role of the mother in securing the child's place within the range of the Church's orthodoxy is an elusive one, a mere hint of mediation which lingers like a 'peaceful odour' and undermines competing authorities. Something of the subtlety of the mother's role is suggested in 'An Encounter'. The narrative of the Wild West is interrupted momentarily: 'His parents went to eight-o'clock mass every morning in Gardiner street and the peaceful odour of Mrs Dillon was prevalent in the hall of the house.' Shortly after, the narrator notes that: 'Everyone was incredulous when it was reported that [Joe Dillon] had a vocation for the priesthood.'[46] Less subtle, but still covert, are Mrs Kernan's efforts to submit her husband – a husband she mothers – to the will of the Church. Unlike other mothers in Joyce, she has a pragmatic rather than a devout faith. It is the symbolism of the Church, its myths, and the peace it claims to bring which occasions her respect: the Church offers the meaning and order lacking in her relationship with her husband.[47] The rich symbolism of the Church – and of other myth and fables embedded in the Irish cultural tradition – counters the paucity, colourlessness and incoherence of their own families. There is a sense of these mothers finding in the Church an authority for which they yearn, and which their husbands, and society in general, are unable to provide. It is just such strength, the certainty of its promise for the future, that Mrs Dedalus seeks for her son.

In *Stephen Hero*, Mrs Daedalus explicitly mediates between her son and the Church. While Stephen berates the priests for '[encouraging] the study of Irish that their flocks may be more safely protected from the wolves of disbelief... [withdrawing] the people into a past of literal, implicit faith,' his mother is 'probably pleased [that he is learning Irish] for she thought that the superintendence of the priests and the society of harmless enthusiasts might succeed in influencing her son in the right direction.'[48] Stephen's mother acts as agent for the Church in much the same manner as I have argued mothers in George Moore's work were prone to act: to submit to the Church and, by their submission, to ensure the child's confirmation into the Catholic orthodoxy. Stephen's sister's confirmation had already been achieved: 'She had acquiesced in the religion of her mother; she had accepted everything that had been proposed to her. If she lived she had exactly the temper for a Catholic wife of limited intelligence and of pious docility.'[49] Yet, significantly, Joyce draws on one of his epiphanies to have Isabel die as a result of 'some matter coming away from the hole in [her]... stomach', her umbilical link with her mother.[50] The pathos of Mrs Daedalus's innocent, uncertain and terrified response is left to linger. The inference is that not only is the mother not fully aware of the significance of the link between herself and her child – or what she has sacrificed in allowing the Church to effect its castration – but, that link broken, the Church to which Isabel is dedicated is unable to sustain her life:

> The wasted body that lay before him had existed by sufferance; the spirit that dwelt therein had literally never dared to live and had not learned anything by an abstention which it had not willed for itself. She had not been anything herself and for that reason had not attached anything to herself or herself to anything.[51]

There is nothing capable of replacing the pre-oedipal link.

Stephen Daedalus perceives his mother's mediation between himself and the Church as '[setting] the shadow of the clergyman between her nature and his.'[52] His mother pleads directly with Stephen to fulfil his Easter duties, and he uses his discussion with her to define his own sense of self, much as he uses the mirror on her dressing-table in *A Portrait*. His discussion with his mother is 'his latest conflict with orthodoxy' and he is ruthless in his probing and prodding at her faith. Significantly, there is a suggestion that Mrs Daedalus sees Stephen's rebellion as her own failure: 'I never thought I would see the day a child of mine would lose the faith. God knows I didn't. I did my best for you in the right way.' However, she persists with her aim to confirm him and her family: 'I'll burn every one of those books. I won't have them in the house to corrupt anyone else.'[53]

In *A Portrait*, Stephen Dedalus is drawn to the Church by the rich iconography of the Virgin Mary; and his flirtation with the priesthood is as much an attempt to envelop himself in the 'secret knowledge and secret power'[54] inherent to the symbolism of the Church as it is to discover a subjectivity within that order. When the vibrancy of the Virgin's shrine begins to fade, Stephen loses his faith. His mother, not understanding the nature of his earlier devotion, aims to win him back to the Church. The episode of the Easter duties is repeated in *A Portrait*, but Stephen's conversation with his mother is discarded, and the reader learns of his mother's pleas only through Stephen's conversation with Cranly. Cranly links the stoicism and suffering of the mother with the measure of sacrifice her children owe to her on account of that suffering, and this may account for Joyce's decision effectively to silence Mrs Dedalus in *A Portrait*. For, relative to her counterpart in *Stephen Hero*, who is both intellectually curious and able to challenge, or at least meet, her son on a verbal level, Mrs Dedalus is silent. This shift in the representation of the mother is significant in that *Stephen Hero* offers a mother who is allowed to yearn for a life beyond the family. Mrs Daedalus tends towards being the 'new woman' in a few brief moments of the narrative. In her conversation with Stephen about Ibsen she reveals a keen intellectual curiosity, doused by marriage but not yet extinct.[55] In *A Portrait*, however, she regresses to type. It is this regression into silence and suffering that serves to focus more acutely Stephen's own experience.[56] In her silence, Mrs Dedalus becomes an incarnation of the suffering, passive Madonna; and in representing her thus, Stephen is allowed greater scope to take up his place as the Christ-like redeemer, and victim, of his people. The quiet intensity of her suffering taxes Stephen's devotion more than is the case in *Stephen*

Hero, ensuring that his rebellion is both more dramatic and more compelling.

Stephen's conversation with Cranly is important in that the mother's role in assuring her child's place within the Church is explicitly stated. In a sense, the question which has burdened Stephen since his time at Clongowes – 'Do you kiss your mother?' – is again put to him. Throughout the novel, he knows neither the meaning of the question nor its answer. 'I tried to love God,' Stephen explains. 'It seems now I failed. It is very difficult. I tried to unite my will with the will of God instant by instant. In that I did not always fail. I could perhaps do that still.'[57] Cranly persists in drawing Stephen's service to the Church – and implicitly his love of God – back to the service of his mother. The mother's suffering on behalf of the child dictates, according to Cranly, just such service, bonding the child to the mother's will:

> Whatever else is unsure in this stinking dunghill of a world a mother's love is not. Your mother brings you into the world, carries you first in her body. What do we know about what she feels? But whatever she feels, it, at least, must be real. It must be.[58]

However, Stephen's bond with his mother had already begun to slip: he no longer defines himself in a reflection of her 'face' – her world and, in one specific instance, the mirror on her dressing-table – but in his opposition to her:

> her mistrust pricked him more keenly than his father's pride and he thought coldly how he had watched the faith which was fading down in his soul ageing and strengthening in her eyes. A dim antagonism gathered force within him and darkened his mind as a cloud against her disloyalty.[59]

Though in this instant he becomes 'dutiful towards her again', it is 'a first noiseless sundering of their lives', and it foreshadows his inability to do as he suspects Cranly would do, to 'shield [women] with a resolute arm and bow his mind to them.'[60]

In his essay 'A Portrait of the Artist', Joyce's speaker, having left the Church, affirms his intention to 'reunite the children of the spirit' whose treasons were 'social limitations, inherited apathy, an adoring mother, the Christian fable.'[61] It is for this same purpose that Stephen Dedalus departs Ireland. The Church's complicity in Ireland's paralysis is argued within the body of Joyce's work, and just as Moore had offered the dilapidated village church as a symbol of the ruin and stagnation into which Irish mothers were baptizing their children, so too Joyce embeds his disdain of the Church in the images he presents, images significantly harsher than Moore's. In 'The Dead', the Church discards the women for which it has no use; in 'Grace', it preaches a sermon that will do little to alter Mr Kernan's wayward life; in 'Counterparts', it calls Mrs Farrington to service, exposing her son to his father's cruelty; and it implicitly sanctions Mrs Mooney's entrapment of Mr Doran. In *Stephen Hero*, Stephen ridicules his friends' faith in 'Mother Church', only to be challenged by Madden: 'We remain true to the Church because it is our national Church, the Church our people have suffered for and would suffer for again.'[62] Stephen recognizes the power of the Church, but is none the less ardent in his belief that the Church maintains this power by stupefying the nation.[63] Ultimately, Stephen will not submit. In 'A Portrait of the Artist' it is a simple *Nego*.[64] In *Stephen Hero*, he refuses to pledge allegiance to either the Catholic Church, Nationalism or the 'mother-country', declaring that his only loyalty is to his 'bodily liberty ... [and] my own mind.'[65] In *A Portrait*, he says: 'I will not serve', a statement which immediately links him to Satan (as presented in the sermon heard during his school-days), the 'poison of eloquence' poured into the ear of Eve, and his final rebellion from 'God the Father' and the authority that name carries.[66] And with each negation, as Cranly reminds him, he also negates his mother, her own service of the Church and, in rejecting the almost singular purpose of her life, that life itself.

While mother-Ireland may be 'the old sow that eats her farrow',[67] it is, Joyce suggests, the symbolism of the Madonna which presents the most distinct danger to the aesthetic spirit. The mother-figure inherent to Irish Nationalism comes a poor second. In *A Portrait*, it is the Virgin Mary who, almost succeeding where Mrs Dedalus has failed, drags Stephen towards the nets 'flung' by the Catholic Church 'to hold [him] back from flight', an entrapment no less insidious than that enacted by Mrs Mooney.[68] Henke refers to the Virgin Mother as a 'Dublin coquette' but this, and her contention that it is 'Stephen's ambition throughout the novel to "deflower" the Blessed Virgin', overstates the sexual nature of Stephen's attraction to her cult (though it may not overstate the sexual nature of the lure).[69] The child seeks to please the Virgin Mother: 'Tomorrow and every day after I hope I shall bring you some virtue as an offering for I know you will be pleased with me if I do.'[70] Her name is, as 'Counterparts' suggests, a talisman. She brings light into the dark cathedral. She is pervasive and loving, 'saying, I am susceptible of change, an imaginative influence in the hearts of my children. ... Years and years I loved you when you lay in my womb.'[71] It is this 'imagina-tive influence' which threatens Stephen Dedalus: 'The glories of Mary held his soul captive.'[72] Stephen's devotion is not sexual; it is romantic, almost pre-Raphaelite. He imagines being her knight, her priest, her servant. She, in turn, will restore him to purity and bless his union with E—C—. He is attracted to her as symbol, drawn by the rich, sym-bolic potential of the Church embodied within her. Yet his 'call' to her priesthood, as articulated by the priest, highlights her essential power-lessness. It is the 'chill and order' of the life to which she has, through her lush image, enticed him that ultimately repels Stephen, a rejection which parallels Joyce's own rejection of not so much the 'Virgin's love' but rather of a 'father church, harsh, repressive, maculine.'[73] As Stephen leaves the Jesuit college, he 'turned his eyes coldly for an instant towards the faded blue shrine of the Blessed Virgin.'[74] She has been drained of her light, her imagery, and is no longer a threat. His search for the maternal source wherein he will find the 'foetus' of his aesthetic self must continue.

Finding the pre-oedipal mother

When the young Stephen Dedalus writes his poem to E—C— it is to his mother that he turns for reassurance: 'After this the letters L.D.S. were written at the foot of the page and, having hidden the book, he went into his mother's bedroom and gazed at his face for a long time in the mirror of her dressingtable.'[75] It is in that space where the mother's own face is reflected that he seeks definition. The verses and his mother are symbolically linked, and his Byronic intent, tempered by the habitual rendering of Jesuit mottoes, foreshadows the conflict to come between religion and his imagination. For, as Stephen comes to understand in the course of *A Portrait*, the image of himself reflected in his mother's 'mirror' is one that binds him, first and foremost, to the Church. It is this image of the mother which he must resist.

What Stephen seeks is a subjectivity that neither his father nor the Church represents; yet he cannot access his desired subjectivity through his mother, for she acts for the Church and the status quo. Joyce's work insists that the child must break from the familial mother, the social mother, and find instead a symbolic mother who embodies a potential for subjectivity beyond that offered by Irish society: to find the desired father the child must first find the mother within whom that father exists, albeit in a diffuse and incoherent form.[76] It is the (uncon-scious) realization of this necessity which, I believe, affords the word 'foetus' – scratched into a desk and observed by Stephen during an excursion to Cork with his father – its potency. For it competes directly with the paternal history, the subjective potential, which Simon Dedalus represents and which, ultimately, fails to satisfy him.[77] What the foetus will become depends, ultimately, on the mother who bears it; yet, 'the unsubstantial image which his soul so constantly beheld'[78] was to be found in neither the mother who would confirm him in the Church, nor the father who would have him bound within the same cycle of debt, failure and alcoholic debilitation into which he himself was locked.

Towards the conclusion of the fourth chapter of *A Portrait* – having sensed a 'first sundering' from his literal mother – Stephen has his first real insight into the nature of the symbolic father he seeks. He looks to the mythical father whose name he bears, and flight becomes the organizing principle of the symbolic order to which he is willing to submit:

> a prophecy of the end he had been born to serve and had been following through the mists of childhood and boyhood, a symbol of the artist forging anew in his workshop out of the sluggish matter of the earth a new soaring impalpable imperishable being?[79]

It is not until the final stages of the novel that the full significance of this insight becomes apparent. The image of his mother's face – that same image to which he turned having written his first poem to E—C— – presents itself; yet in the wake of his second poem to E—C—, and the desired subjectivity that can only realize itself through the mythical father Daedalus, the mother's image – and thereby his own self-image – is transformed:

> The inhuman clamour soothed his ears in which his mother's sobs and reproaches murmured insistently and the dark frail quivering bodies wheeling and fluttering and swerving round an airy temple of the tenuous sky soothed his eyes which still saw *the image of his mother's face.* . . . A soft liquid joy flowed through the words where the soft long vowels hurtled noiselessly and fell away, lapping and flowing back . . . and he felt that the augury he had sought in the wheeling darting birds and in the pale space of the sky above him had come forth from his heart like a bird from a turret, quietly and swiftly.[80]

He banishes (if not finally) his literal mother, and in the wash and flux of the metaphorical mother's chaotic embodiment of flight, music, silence and floating, unanchored words, Stephen seeks to veil his (actual) mother's face and, thereby, that (socially sanctioned) self formed in May Dedalus's image. In this, he touches the metaphorical father who will enable him to flee Ireland's nets. Yet where Oliver Gogarty in Moore's *The Lake* appeared to have succeeded in his 'rebirth', in completely discarding his identity as priest, Stephen's desired self is not wholly born. He is unable to realize fully the image of the metaphorical mother and, therefore, unable to recognize in her 'face' the first coalescence of his artistic subjectivity. Ultimately, what Stephen accesses in this episode is little more than a potential. The realization – or otherwise – of that potential is not contained within the pages of *A Portrait*, and diary entries with which the novel closes, while indicating that Stephen has found a place from which he may speak, nevertheless suggest that his occupation of that space is, at best, tenuous.

Bearing the word

For Stephen Dedalus, the power to create is inextricably linked with the power of flight. Beyond the nets of Ireland, his aesthetic spirit may be released and his creativity realized. And it is in the figure of the mother, particularly the Madonna, that Stephen recognizes the paradigm that will facilitate his creativity: the icon of the Annunciation; the Virgin touched by a divine seed. To fulfil his creative goals, Stephen acknowledges, he must subjugate himself to the spark of the imagination as the Virgin at the Annunciation subjugates herself to the seed of God. It is not enough to identify with the mother; he must become the mother. As Kristeva argues in 'Stabat Mater', 'the most intense revelation of God . . . is given only to a person who assumes himself as "maternal" ';[81] and Stephen's revelation is that, as creative artist, he, himself, is able to bear the 'word':

> his soul took up again her burden of pieties, masses and prayers and sacraments and mortifications, and only then for the first time since he had brooded on the great mystery of love did he feel within him a warm movement like that of some newly born life or virtue of the soul itself.[82]

The important aspect of this utilization of the figure of the Blessed Virgin is that, in his complete identification with the mother, the artist subsumes her and, thereby, disarms her. Again, this subsumption of the mother is something that Stephen Dedalus will never wholly achieve.

As Joyce indicated in 'A Little Cloud', the 'infant hope' of creativity is easily doused by the mother, by an inability to defy her and dominate her. Yet, in *Exiles*, a confused exploration of the creative process, Richard, like Stephen, seeks the creative spirit through his own death and resurrection, his own martyrdom and victimhood: 'To be forever a shameful creature and to build up my soul again out of the ruins of its shame.'[83] This shift in the construction of the mother's role in the artist's realization of his creativity is an important one, and echoes, as well as extends, Moore's own construction. Yet, unlike Moore, Joyce encounters the creative work in its foetal state. Further, he insists – and Bertha [Rowan] and Nora [Joyce] are the seminal examples of this – that the artist must not merely encounter, immerse himself in, and displace the mother, but he must attain a union with her that is, if not literally, then symbolically, sexual.

The call of the dead

Both Gabriel Conroy in 'The Dead' and Richard Rowan in *Exiles* are unable to shake themselves free of their dead mother's grasp, a dilemma Stephen Dedalus will himself face in *Ulysses*. As Leonard notes, Gabriel is unable to let go of his mother's disapproval:[84] 'A shadow passed over his face as he remembered her sullen opposition to his marriage. Some slighting phrases she had used still rankled in his memory.'[85] What *Exiles* highlights is the embellished power of the mother who is no longer bound by social and familial borders: 'I fought against her spirit while she lived to the bitter end. It fights against me still.'[86] In death, the mother's suffering is eternal, impossible to assuage, and the guilt the child must bear – a guilt which binds the child irrevocably to her and which demands acquiescence – is equally eternal. With her death, Richard Rowan is bound to his mother – and Ireland – as he never has been before. In the final moments of the play, Richard refers to the 'deep, deep wound of doubt in my soul...a deep wound of doubt which can never be healed.'[87] It is a wound which signifies not only his blocked creativity, but a disruption in the relationship with both his mother and his country to which his creativity is linked. The wound is suggestive of the 'castration' that comes of the severing of the mother–child bond, a bond which Richard Rowan impotently seeks to restore through his writing. Yet the wound can only be healed through total immersion in the mother – 'The old mother. It is her spirit I need'[88] – a mother he is unable to access without also confronting her demands for the service of God and country. Like Moore, Joyce has few answers to the threat of the destroying mother. He suggests escape through exile, yet it is an escape that is never wholly effective, particularly when the mother, idealized in death and defined by her suffering, calls to the child, demanding what she had been denied in life.

The mother's power in death comes, Joyce suggests, from her unresolved suffering. From this space the mother acts, not to disrupt the social order, but to draw her child further within the same social and cultural tradition which has disempowered and destroyed her. As Stephen Dedalus will learn, the child's attempt to move beyond the stasis inherent to Irish society – a stasis in which the mother seeks to have the child confirmed – is profoundly intimidated by the hand that reaches from beyond the grave. The dead mother, Joyce suggests, has a power not afforded to her in private spaces, and one that is much more prodigious than that which she exercises within the home. This is particularly evident in the *Dubliners* story, 'Eveline', where the dead mother functions within the text in a manner that will later be developed in *Ulysses*. Eveline's escape with Frank is undermined by her promise to her dying mother. Leonard argues that Eveline is trying to resurrect her relationship with her mother, and her dilemma is whether to repeat her mother's life or to flee.[89] Certainly, there is a correlation between the mother's resurrection – occasioned by associations and memories – and Eveline's intention to break her contract. But whether this resurrection is of Eveline's volition is not apparent. However, in meeting her dead mother again, Eveline has, in a sense, the opportunity to reconsider the contract which has bound her in service to the home. Clearly, Eveline's instinct is to escape; yet to do so would be to place herself in an environment where she has no identity, where she does not exist. The portrait of her life presented through her reveries fixes her sense of self: for Eveline, escape equates with disintegration. The narrative containing her own identity is very much that which bears the mark of her mother: she exists within her mother's life and subjection, and her contract with her mother binds her to the perpetuation of that life, 'her promise to keep the home together as long as she could.'[90] Ultimately, Eveline chooses order, identity and duty, reading in Frank's offer a life wherein the only self she knows would be completely overwhelmed: 'All the seas of the world tumbled about her heart. He was drawing her into them: he would drown her. She gripped with both hands at the iron railing.'[91] She grips with both hands at the contract she has made through her mother with society. Her mother's madness, a fate Eveline will almost certainly share, accentuates the irony with which the futility and stagnation of Dublin society is rendered: the mother, perpetrator of the lifeless repetition of the social order, becomes, inevitably, its victim.

*

Though Joyce would shudder at the suggestion, there are shades of Stephen Dedalus in Ned Carmady, Alice Barton, Oliver Gogarty, and even the persona Moore adopted in the autobiographical *Hail and Farewell*. The urgency of escape from Ireland in order to feed the creative spirit, and the inevitable link between this escape and the mother – whether she be dominant, destructive, the source of rebirth or the paradigm of creativity – is a common construction in both writers. Yet Joyce carries the construction much further than Moore was able to take it. This may be due to Moore's distance from his own creative essence, and Joyce's intense immersion in the maternal space – a heavily sensual space – in which he believed his creativity had its source. It may be, as Joyce astutely observed, that 'from *Celibates* and later novels [it is plain] that Mr Moore is beginning to draw upon his literary account.'[92] Or it may be, as McCarthy argues, that Joyce observed, and learned from, both his predecessor's solutions to structural problems, and his mistakes. The artist's role, as signalled by Joyce in *A Portrait of the Artist as a Young Man*, is a privileged one, in that it allows access to the semiotic while remaining anchored in the symbolic. This is embodied in Stephen's epiphany on the beach – the fusion of the mother with flight – and his appropriation of the image of the Annunciation. The boundaries between the symbolic and the pre-symbolic are breached through the artist's realization of his creativity as a bond between mother and child. And, with each bringing forth of a creation, there is the potential for a new symbolic order to be acknowledged.

As Kristeva suggests, representation can only be subversive when it is freed from 'God',[93] from authority. Joyce frees representation not only from God-the-father, but from the mother who would confirm and confine the artist in the realm that bears (the Catholic) God's name. In works such as *Dubliners*, he portrays the mother's role in this confirmation: she is implicated in the smothering of the life of the imagination. In *Exiles*, he argues that to leave the mother – whether actual or metaphorical – is not sufficient if the artist is to escape the nets into which she would see her children drawn. The artist must die and be reborn: he must re-create himself through the auspices of a symbolic mother in whom there exists the locus of the aesthetic subjectivity he seeks. Conversely, the artist must also negate the mother by becoming mother to his own creation, a delicate balance of relations with the mother-figure which Stephen Dedalus does not fully accomplish. Stephen Dedalus recognizes that, in becoming himself 'mother', he bears the potential to subvert the symbolic order, to reshape it and redefine it, such that it may, in fact, alleviate and revitalize a debilitating and stagnant society. Only by fully accessing the semiotic, and its potential to disrupt the symbolic order, may Stephen create what has heretofore remained uncreated; and as mother to that creation he may ensure that, to para-phrase Kristeva, he does not include the child within the social and symbolic norms which he has repudiated for his own sake. He must break the 'chain of generations' which is holding the conscience of Ireland captive.[94]

The potential to achieve all this – to realize fully his creativity – is what Stephen Dedalus bears with him as he sails from Ireland. Whether Stephen realizes this potential, the reader will need to look to *Ulysses* to determine.

Part III
On the Edge of Disorder

Origin, Space, Opposition: Constructing, Containing and Privileging the Maternal

The narrative of Yeats's *Reveries over Childhood and Youth* has its origin in an inchoate space. Here associations are tenuous and symbolization is unstable:

> My first memories are fragmentary and isolated and contemporaneous, as though one remembered some first moments of the Seven Days. It seems as if time had not yet been created, for all thoughts are connected with emotion and place without sequence.[1]

There is no definite sense of beginning; no initial moment has been constructed by the author, and the narrative itself is threatened by the frayed point in time from which it is drawn. It is not coincidental that the mother within this narrative, Yeats's mother, is absented from the speaker's beginning, and that her absence is marked throughout the *Reveries*. She does not make her first appearance until the final paragraphs of Chapter IV, her image linked with the mystical tale of a 'banshee crying.'[2] She is rarely brought into the narrative on her own account, but rather as a memory associated with various incidents, places and moments that the speaker revisits – the earth, Sligo, tales told by the fisherman's wife:

> When I think of her, I almost always see her talking over a cup of tea in the kitchen with our servant, the fisherman's wife, on the only themes outside our house that seemed of interest – the fishing people of Howth, or the pilots and fishing people of Rosses Point.[3]

She is present within the narrative almost as a ghost is present. Ultimately, she is subsumed by Yeats's efforts to position himself within a paternal lineage. *Reveries*, Foster notes, 'is about [Yeats] in 1914, not between the ages of one and twenty.'[4] The past is constructed in order to fulfil present ambitions, and the mother is absorbed into Yeats's construction of, not merely his own fledgling artistic subjectivity, but also Irish history.[5] Yet, because Yeats, at the age of twenty, is still unclear of the subjectivity to which he aspires, the construction of the mother-figure in whom that subjectivity is prefigured must remain equally elusive, sketched with just sufficient definition to allow Yeats to subsume something of her emotions: 'I longed for a sod of earth from some field I knew, something of Sligo to hold in my hand....it was our mother, who would have thought its display a vulgarity, who kept alive that love.'[6] Because the origin of the narrative does not gel about her presence, and because there is no space from which the father is able to displace her and assert his own history, the narrative perambulates over the years of the speaker's childhood and youth, its direction and boundaries set by nothing more than arbitrary lines of association by which people, events and places are embedded within memory. They are not drawn within a constructed history that is the father's, and grafted to that line of narrative in order both to enhance the father's history and secure a subjectivity that has its basis in the father's name.

Origin

In her analysis of the Madonna paintings of Bellini, Julia Kristeva refers to the mother-figure as a filter, 'a thoroughfare, a threshold where "nature" confronts "culture"'.[7] Positioned on the cusp between the semiotic and the symbolic, the mother occupies that space where subjectivity moves towards affirmation and, equally, where subjectivity begins to recede. The mother saturates that space which, according to Kristeva, would otherwise remain void, absorbing subjectivity almost as a black hole absorbs light, 'a permanent threat against ... [subjective] stability.'[8] The mother's presence fills this void not in any real or literal sense, but because the mother's body, an 'undifferentiated space',[9] allows the child to construct an origin which will mask the void. The separation from the mother, mythologized in the umbilical split that castrates the mother, frees the child, allowing him to assume the father's history and to move within the social and symbolic structures that are founded on the father's name.

The mother stands – veiled – at the origin of the individual's history, that narrative of self by which the individual constructs a place within the father's social and symbolic structures. As such the mother is 'located at the very origin of language itself';[10] yet her position there is only discovered when the 'name-of-the-father' – traditions, lore, social hierarchies, patriarchal discourses, signifying practices – is excavated. It could be surmised, therefore, that the resistance to inherited traditions, particularly literary traditions, that marks the modernist movement would engender poetics and narratives that seek a return to the mother as a means of rewriting myths and reconstructing received social and symbolic legacies. In this light, it is interesting to note that all the writers I am examining here, with the single exception of Synge, have utilized autobiographical narratives both to place themselves within the literary histories from which they grew and to announce their defiance of inherited traditions, myths and discourses.[11] Beer, in her survey of the Victorian tradition, refers to 'the dogged and dedicated search for the single...recovered origin';[12] yet what is evident within modernism is not merely an urgency to recover actual origins, but a predilection to elaborate desired origins. Ames, in describing 'modernist belatedness', refers to 'the creative rewriting...that allows the mature artist to transform the past from oppressive weight into imaginative possibility';[13] the rewriting of the mother-figure affords new possibilities in terms of both the potential subjectivity to which the child will have access and the nature of the father's name which will displace the mother when the mother–child castration is effected. The reconstruction of origins is, I argue, central to modernism, and the reconstruction of those origins cannot help but touch on the figuration of the mother. This is particularly the case where the mother – as in the Irish situation – is a central figure within the discourses which the writer both recognizes as his inheritance and seeks to resist.

'A subject,' Ragland-Sullivan notes, 'is predetermined – not entirely, of course – by the discourse of his origins.'[14] This tallies with Kristeva's notion that subjectivity must have its potential in maternal spaces, a lesson learned by the young Stephen Dedalus as he seeks the mother through whom the subjectivity he desires may be realized. Yet what Sean O'Casey's *Autobiographies* clearly shows is that it is not merely the subject who is 'predetermined by the discourse of his origins' but, more significantly in terms of the construction of the mother-figure, the discourse of the origin is also 'post-determined' by the subject. Sprengnether, in her survey of Freud, refers to ''mother'' as one's point of origin [which] can only be recovered in death, and life as a result appears at any given stage to be going backward.'[15] The child's construction of his origin – and the mother who is that origin – is directed by the subjectivity he perceives himself, or desires himself, to be. He regresses from the present to discover the mother who *should* exist at that origin, rather than the mother who does. It is a matter of speculation whether the mother who does exist can ever be found, as she will always be unveiled from the perspective of both present and future.

Space

It was Einstein who most notably theorized time and space as profoundly connected entities. The position of any body in the universe can only be determined in relation to both space and time – a change in time, for example, impacts not only on a body's position but effects a concomitant change in space.[16] This physical reality offers a useful metaphor for my discussion of subjectivity in relation to the mother. Both time and space have their origin in the 'initial singularity' posited by physicists, and this origin parallels the mother-figure through whom subjectivity originates and beyond whom the time and space in which subjectivity is realized ceases to exist. Of this dyad, it is with 'space' that the mother is most commonly associated.[17] Further, as the father's time is essentially linear – the mother's 'space' affords her access to circular time.[18] Kristeva, therefore, utilizes the time–space nexus to theorize an opposition of linearity and circularity which may be overlaid on time, history and narrative. From here, I argue, it is possible to theorize that subjectivity is determined by both the semiotic spaces of the mother and the linear history which the child accesses through the father, and any adjustment in the value of one of these entities will require a concurrent adjustment in the others. Further, there exists a tension between the linear history of the father and the circular history of the mother, a tension which threatens to overwhelm the symbolic order with the chaos and semiotic disjunctions of the maternal. While the mother possesses the child, both the linear history of the father and the child's subjectivity are vulnerable to her; when she relinquishes the child to the father's name and his history, her 'space' is rendered impotent.

Opposition

'Locked into confrontation with Britain and contestation over the motherland,' Innes argues, 'Irish literature and Irish history have created males as national subjects, women as the site of contestation.'[19]

The symbolic order privileges the concepts of culture, male, patriarchy, ritual and father; and in doing so it denies those entities which, by their very opposition to these concepts, define the symbolic order. Nature, female, matriarchy, carnival and mother exist on the underside of the symbolic; yet, while ever denied, they hold that order in place as securely as roots anchor a tree. Rewriting the cultural tradition requires a destabilization of these oppositions, and the privileging, if only temporarily, of suppressed entities.

McFarlane argues that modernism entails the 'coalescence, the fusion to the point of indistinguishability of two concepts which the structure of everyday language was designed to keep separate and distinct.'[20] From this it is possible, I suggest, to argue that the 'space' in which such fusion may be facilitated will be extensively explored by modernist writers. Concepts kept distinct by the symbolic order may be fused in the realm of the semiotic; the semiotic is figured in the mother who refuses the spaces sanctioned by the cultural tradition, and is realized in the 'phallic mother.' 'The very practice of art,' Kristeva argues, 'necessitates re-investing the maternal . . . so that it transgresses the symbolic order.'[21] This may be achieved by representing the mother-figure in spaces outside the social and symbolic order, and in which, thereby, the semiotic is privileged. Representation of this subversive mother serves to carry the writer to the 'threshold of repression'[22] – maternal space straddles this threshold, containing within its realm both the symbolic and the semiotic, moving from one to the other by alternatively possessing and relinquishing the 'phallus', all the while dissolving and (potentially) renegotiating the symbolic.

More effectively still, the maternal may be 're-invested' through the occupation of that space by a (male) writer whose inheritance is the (literary) traditions of the patriarchal culture, and who is therefore able to enter the semiotic as 'speaking subject.' And it is from this point that the modification, perhaps even the perversion, of language, of representation and of the symbolic that is the seminal characteristic of modernist texts may be traced back to the mother whose presence (or absence) initiates those texts.[23]

5
Disclosing Ritual and Challenging the Symbolic: Synge's Marginal Mothers

It's four fine plays I have though it was a hard birth I had with everyone of them and they coming to the world.

J.M. Synge in a letter to Molly Allgood[1]

Following the 1907 *Playboy* controversy, J.M. Synge wrote a letter to the Irish newspapers. Entitled 'Can We Go Back Into Our Mother's Womb? A Letter to the Gaelic League by a Hedge Schoolmaster', the letter criticized the 'senile and slobbering... doctrine of the Gaelic League',[2] which not merely denied the Irish their place within Europe (for fear of being branded 'English') but, more deleterious still, suppressed the Irish imagination. Not satisfied with the sanctioned myths and images espoused by Nationalist and Catholic discourses, Synge sought to create his drama within a locus which encompassed both the inherent value of the Irish spirit and imagination, and the artistic developments of modern Europe: Synge perceived the 'possibility of creating a European modernist art which would... draw on the Gaelic tradition – a national art which would, for all that, be international in appeal.'[3]

In asking the question 'Can we go back to our mother's womb?', Synge implicitly challenged the nexus that Nationalist discourse had constructed between the mother's nurturing role and the proliferation of an Irish cultural identity which had as its principal index the Gaelic language. This same nexus is satirized in 'Deaf Mutes for Ireland'. Here, indoctrination begins once the child has 'touched the saintly and patriotic hearts of the sweet-minded Irish mothers'.[4] Yet the incapacity of Ireland to master Gaelic – and the exclusion of English as an acceptable alternative – results, Synge asserts, in an Ireland that can do nothing other than remain speechless. Within these two texts, therefore, Synge proffers equally barren outcomes from adherence to the 'doctrine of the Gaelic League': a country infantilized; or a country without the ability to communicate, and without the ability to access, and function within, the symbolic order. Neither outcome, Synge contends, truly fosters the advancement of Irish cultural and political independence.

It is through language that the symbolic order is maintained, and it is by subverting language that the symbolic order is challenged.[5] Synge recognized that through the proliferation of Gaelic it was envisaged that a new symbolic order, organized about a distinct Irish cultural tradition, would prosper; yet he also recognized that it would be a symbolic order without foundation. In his utilization of the mother-figure to expose the basic fallacy of the Nationalist position, Synge embodied within her both the nurturing that the 'good mother' affords her child and the infantilization that comes from 'overinvestment' in her nurturing. This tendency to incorporate dual aspects of the maternal into one figure is prominent throughout Synge's work, and in this he differs markedly from those works of Irish modernism produced prior to his advent. With perhaps the sole exception of Moore's short story 'So On He Fares', dualities such as life and death generally are bifurcated into disparate 'characters' within the works; yet for Synge the amalgamation of these dualities into a single character allows an intensified exploration of both the nature of the symbolic order, and the nature of the semiotic which is repressed in order to sustain that symbolic order. His mother-figures emphasize both what is affirmed by the socio-symbolic order and what is denied – and in this Synge's mothers access a liminal space that affords them not only a degree of freedom to interact with the social and symbolic orders, but also a foothold in semiotic spaces from which resistance to those orders may be effected.

'I'll have no son left in the world'

Throughout Synge's writing there is a refusal to reinforce or even echo the image of the suffering, stoical, nurturing mother embedded within both Nationalist and Catholic discourses. While his tendency, as with his writing of women, is to distance the mother-figure from the ideal – the Widow Quin and Mary Byrne being cases in point – in *Riders to the Sea* he appropriates the mother-ideal, using her to emphasize the means by which she manipulates events in order to secure her own position. Maurya is not the passive victim of fate – she willingly orchestrates that fate. Yet, because of the subtlety with which Synge renders Maurya's actions and motivations, many critics have failed to recognize his sub-version of the suffering-mother archetype.[6]

Riders to the Sea draws on associations between the supernatural and the death of children that Synge first explored in *The Aran Islands*, and it is within that work that my reading of *Riders* has its source. In one of the tales recounted – 'A woman of Sligo had a son who was born blind...' – the mother acts as a filter between the natural and supernatural worlds. It is the mother's dream that leads to the source of her son's cure; it is her faith in the veracity of the dream that shows her the way to the well; and it is her hand that applies the miraculous water to her son's eyes: 'she kneeled down and began saying her prayers. Then she put her hand out for the water, and put it on his eyes, and the moment it touched him he called out: "O mother, look at the pretty flowers!"'[7] Through her lim-inal position in relation to both the natural and the supernatural, the mother is instrumental in affording her son access to the (visual) world. Further, she facilitates access from one realm to another, a role evident in those stories where children are stolen by faeries, or where the super-natural world intervenes in the natural order: 'Another night he had heard a voice crying out in Irish, "a mhathair, ta mé marbh" ("O mother, I'm killed"), and in the morning there was blood on the wall of his house, and a child in a house not far off was dead.'[8] The child's final plea to the mother undoubtedly adds to the poignancy of the tale. Even so, that the mother is afforded this position within the narrative serves more than a merely emotive purpose. The mother is implicated in the child's movement between one world and another:

> There was a woman went to bed at the lower village a while ago, and her child along with her... and they heard a voice and this is what it said – 'it is time to sleep from this out'. In the morning the child was dead, and indeed it is many get their death that way on the island.[9]

The sub-text here is repeated in many of the tales of children 'stolen' from the natural world: the mother has failed in her role as protectress.

In the final section of *The Aran Islands*, Synge sandwiches within the story of a mother's grief that of a mother who is herself stolen by the sidhe. The mother maintains a tenuous foothold within the natural world by 'eating no food with the fairies'. She visits the natural world both to feed herself and to feed her child:

> Then the woman they were after burying opened the door, and came into the house. She went over to the fire, and she took a stool and sat

down before the other woman. Then she put out her hand and took the child on her lap, and gave it her breast.[10]

By juxtaposing these stories within the narrative, the opposition of natural and supernatural is embedded within the structure of the text itself. 'Natural' incidents, such as the death of a child, are read as perversions of the natural order – they are able to be incorporated within the world-view of the islanders, therefore, only by first being rendered in supernatural terms. At the same time, the mother who exists primarily in the supernatural world must be bound up (by men) and brought back to her proper place. Implicit within this story is the society's concern to ensure that the child's source of nourishment, of life, exists within, and is contained by, that society. It is against this background that *Riders to the Sea* must be read. Yet such constructions – those which implicate the mother in the death of a child by supernatural causes – run counter to those readings which see *Riders* as the dramatic realization of the mother's eternal stoicism in the face of universal suffering. While in the early stages of the play there is a sense of Maurya as the stoical mother – 'You'd do right to leave that rope, Bartley, hanging by the boards. It will be wanting in this place I'm telling you, if Michael is washed up to-morrow morning . . . for it's a deep grave we'll make him, by the grace of God'[11] – questions about Maurya's own role in directing the action of the drama surface as the play progresses.

In *Riders*, the supernatural has its most resonant symbol in the sea, for it is the sea which robs the mothers of their children. It is within the superstitions of the islanders that the intentions of the supernatural are encoded. They are codes built upon irrational associations, yet they are the means by which both life and death are read and interpreted. It is, therefore, of some note that in *Riders* Bartley's fate is established by Maurya *before* these codes have been read:

MAURYA [*crying out* . . .]. He's gone now, God spare us, and we'll not see him again. He's gone now, and when the black night is falling I'll have no son left to me in the world.
CATHLEEN. Why wouldn't you give him your blessing and he looking round in the door? Isn't it sorrow enough is on every one in this house without your sending him out with an unlucky word behind him, and a hard word in his ear?[12]

Maurya does not express fear or trepidation. Her statement is one of certainty, of determination almost. It is as though, having determined

Bartley's death, her actions follow that course: it is a self-fulfilling prophecy. Even at this early point in *Riders*, Maurya has established the drama's conclusion and, from the moment of Bartley's exit, she proceeds to construct the drama, to link together incidents (which she interprets as ominous portents) in such a way that the conclusion, which sees the death of her last son, is inevitable.[13]

In terms of the opposition between the natural and the supernatural, and the mother's liminal position with respect to this opposition, Maurya uses her links to both pagan and Christian elements of the supernatural in order to construct the drama of Bartley's death and her release from the power of the sea: 'They're all gone now, and there isn't anything more the sea can do to me.'[14] The auguries of forgotten bread and failed blessing climax in Maurya's vision of the dead Michael on the grey pony. Yet it is not a vision to which the audience – neither Synge's nor Maurya's – is party. The audience learns of the vision through Maurya's narrative of events beyond the cottage, off-stage. It is Maurya who incarnates the supernatural, and through whom Michael is incarnated. By recounting this incident on-stage, by reifying the supernatural in the eyes of her audience, Maurya propels the play towards the conclusion she has determined:

> MAURYA [*a little defiantly*]. . . . Bartley came first on the red mare; and I tried to say 'God speed you', but something choked the words in my throat. He went by quickly; and 'the blessing of God on you', says he, and I could say nothing. I looked up then, and I crying, at the grey pony, and there was Michael upon it – with fine clothes on him, and new shoes on his feet.
>
> CATHLEEN [*begins to keen*]. It's destroyed we are from this day. It's destroyed surely.[15]

Almost on cue, the 'crying out by the seashore' signals the imminent arrival of Bartley's body. What is particularly interesting in the representation of the mother in this instance is that the mother becomes master of public spaces by bringing those spaces into her private world, into the home. Within private spaces, and through her narration of 'public' events, she gains control over those spaces from which – as Joyce keenly observes in 'A Mother' – she is barred. Here there is a close affiliation with Yeats's own exploration of the mother as narrator of the child's (paternal) history, constructing thereby a place for herself – as mother – within that history.

Maurya's final prayers over Bartley's body have been taken by a number of critics as evidence of the triumph of the pagan over the Christian, yet to do so ignores the essentially Christian nature of the rites Maurya performs. The principal subversion of Christian ritual results from the blessing being given by mother instead of priest. In this, it is important to remember that Synge has established through the course of the play both the impotence of the priest and the fact that he has no place within the cottage. He exists only off-stage, and his powers are rendered meaningless in the face of the sea. The young priest does not bring Michael's clothes to the cottage himself, nor does he accompany the other villagers who carry Bartley's body home. He is unwilling to stop Bartley on his journey, despite Maurya's stated belief that the word of the priest would influence Bartley's actions in a way her own words cannot:

> MAURYA [*sitting down on a stool by the fire*]. He won't go this day with the wind rising from the south and west. He won't go this day, for the young priest will stop him surely.
> NORA. He'll not stop him, mother.[16]

The young priest is either unable or unwilling to stamp his authority on society and direct Bartley's actions. He abdicates responsibility, deferring instead to the mother's word. And it is this deferral which affords Maurya much of her power in bringing the supernatural to bear:

> NORA. 'I won't stop him,' says he, 'but let you not be afraid. Herself does be saying prayers half through the night, and the Almighty God won't leave her destitute,' says he, 'with no son living.'[17]

However, the failure of 'the Almighty God' does not necessarily mean the triumph of pagan elements. Christian prayer, signs from the natural world that it is unsafe to proceed, faith that an only son will be protected: all succumb to the ineffable supernatural forces evoked by Maurya.[18]

Christian superstition is a direct challenge to the pagan superstitions that Maurya and her daughters have cited in the events leading up to Bartley's death. It is, perhaps, for this reason that the priest remains off-stage, for to allow him entry, and thereby allow him the opportunity to pit the Christian against the pagan, would undermine Maurya's authority in the reading of the signs and the construction of the drama. Despite this, it is to Christian rites that Maurya returns in her offerings over Bartley's body. Pagan elements are absorbed by the keening women and subordinated to Maurya's speech.[19] The women 'keening softly and swaying themselves with a slow movement' accompany Maurya's sprinkling of the body with Holy Water. Even so, her prayers are, for the most part, silent, and her speech is dominated by references to herself, to her own suffering and the relief from suffering that Bartley's death has brought. It is only after she renders the final blessing that the keening gains in volume, and Christian ritual is subsumed by 'pagan desperation'.[20] And it is Maurya, essentially, who has orchestrated the balance between the two.

The paradox is that, in being relieved of her suffering, Maurya is able to establish herself within a heightened archetype of suffering. This same pattern is evident in the graveside drama that is depicted in *The Aran Islands*: the power of the mourning mother to resist sanctioned rituals and symbols is highlighted. She does this by creating her own symbols, by establishing, to paraphrase Kristeva, the conditions whereby symbols are rejuvenated. And she is able to create such conditions by shifting the focus of grief from the corpse to herself:

> When a number of blackened boards and pieces of bone had been thrown up with the clay, a skull was lifted out, and placed upon a gravestone. Immediately the old woman, the mother of the dead man, took it up in her hands, and carried it away by herself. Then she sat down and put it in her lap – it was the skull of her own mother – and began keening and shrieking over it with the wildest lamentation. . . . When it was nearly deep enough the old woman got up and came back to the coffin, and began to beat on it, holding the skull in her left hand. This last moment of grief was the most terrible of all.[21]

The mother becomes the focus of the narrative and it is, to a large extent, her manipulation of events, her utilization of her own myth as suffering mother, which affords her this centre. That it is her own mother who catalyses this drama is significant. For it draws the woman within a loop of history that both unites her with her own mother and also defies the linearity of the socio-symbolic order. Having upstaged the corpse, she is now in a position to speak – through gesture and *caoin* – and to challenge the ritual of the Christian burial.

This mother's 'act' mirrors in many ways Maurya's as she constructs the conditions that will bring her her own 'peace'. In the opening of *Riders to the Sea*, before Maurya first appears, Nora and Cathleen represent their mother as vulnerable, as someone to be protected from the fact of Michael's death. Interestingly, they are content with her belief in his death, but are loathe to acknowledge its truth. Yet while the old woman who initially appears on stage matches the 'type' that Nora and Cathleen have portrayed – and in many ways directed the audience to perceive – Maurya's actions soon suggest otherwise. It becomes clear that Maurya manipulates the myth that has built up around her in order to realize her own ends. Before she requests Bartley not to venture to sea, she is careful to assume the pose of the 'poor, old mother' by 'turning round to the fire and putting her shawl over her head'.[22] She consistently reminds the audience, both in her physical appearance – Maurya 'starts, so that her shawl falls back from her head and shows her white tossed hair'[23] – and by her constant keening and muttering, of the forces which are overwhelming her. In doing so, she distracts her audience – and in many cases critics of the play – from her manipulation of events. She is able to maintain her pose as victim.

Like the distraught mother at the Aran funeral, Maurya is subject to a loop of history which disrupts linear time and undermines the symbolic order, enhancing her position on the threshold between natural and supernatural, Christian and pagan:

> There was Patch after was drowned out of a curragh that turned over. I was sitting here with Bartley, and he a baby lying on my two knees, and I seen two women, and three women, and four women coming in, and they crossing themselves and not saying a word.[24]

The old mother is reunited with the young mother through Maurya's narrative, and the rupture of linear time is emphasized by her dream-like question as Bartley's body is brought into the room: 'Is it Patch, or Michael, or what is it at all?'[25] All these elements combine to create an atmosphere within the cottage where social and symbolic bonds are severely threatened, the conditions required if the supernatural is to seem to triumph and Maurya's drama is to reach its desired resolution.[26]

'A hard birth'

In *Riders*, what Maurya encompasses is a nexus between the natural and the supernatural, between life and death: 'it was a hard birth I had with every one of them and they coming into the world – and some of them were found and some of them were not found, but they're gone now the lot of them'.[27] It is this embodiment of oppositions that figures so prominently in Synge's construction of the mother. In *The Playboy of the Western World* it is the Widow Quin who functions as the site where oppositions inherent to the play – oppositions such as protection/violation and ritual/carnival – intersect. She is offered as sentinel to Pegeen Mike (who responds 'Is it the like of that murderer?'[28]); and, crucial to the play's dramatic development, she seeks to protect Christy by forming a (sexual) alliance with him. Though not overtly stated, the sexual nature of the Widow Quin's luring of Christy is clear: 'There's a great temptation in a man did slay his da, and we'd best be going, young fellow; *so rise up and come with me.*'[29] Pegeen attempts to discredit the Widow Quin, citing her dishevelled fields and her 'leaky thatch', comments which have a distinctly sexual overtone. Further, there is the association between the Widow Quin and the Widow Casey, the woman who suckled the young Christy and with whom Mahon proposes Christy should couple in order to afford himself protection.[30] The Widow Quin has nursed a black ram, and she enters the shebeen carrying poteen at her breast, under her shawl: she is a parody of the 'good mother' and threatens to draw Christy back into a subversive, pre-symbolic world.[31] She embodies both protection and violation, for to access the protection she offers, Christy must bond with her as son to mother, a union which would see his own fledgling identity smothered.

In luring him, the Widow Quin draws associations between herself and Christy such that the essential alienation between Christy and society is emphasized. Both have 'killed', either directly or indirectly. 'I am your like,' she tells him, '... and it's for that I'm taking a fancy to you, and I with my little houseen above where there'll be myself to tend you ... and it's there yourself and me will have great times whispering and hugging.'[32] She infers an interdependence between herself and Christy that suggests the mother–child bond; yet with no father-figure available to disrupt the bond a mock-marriage between 'mother' and 'son' is effected, the 'son' taking his place on the Widow Quin's knee. Sarah Tansey presides over the union, linking the couple's arms and proclaiming gibberish vows.[33]

The world into which the Widow Quin seeks to absorb Christy is one where his own subjectivity is undifferentiated from her own. It is a carnivalesque world, where the pattern of the mother confirming the child into the Church – a pattern evident in the work of Moore and Joyce – is turned grotesquely upside-down: 'Doesn't the world know you reared a black ram at your own breast, so that the Lord Bishop of Connaught felt the elements of a Christian, and he eating it after in a kidney stew.'[34] The mother's service to the Church, rendered by her delivery of the child to the Church's authority, is made literal. What the Widow Quin emphasizes in her undermining of symbols and rituals is the disorder, particularly the shattering of the symbolic order, that Christy's slaying of the father represents. For it is within a world of symbolic disintegration that the mother is enabled and empowered. Christy must either succumb to her or re-enter society by re-establishing his relationship with his father. Christy chooses the latter, thereby acknowledging the history he and his father share; yet the order established at the conclusion of the play is, in essence, flawed. For if there is an Oedipal dynamic at work in the play it is a perverted one – the son 'slays' the father in order to *avoid* marriage with the mother (Widow Casey); he rejects a second mother in order to cleave to the father, yet it is the son who will wield authority.

Despite her desire to bond with Christy, and her emphasis on the overlap in their histories, the Widow Quin is capable of moving comfortably between her own desires as 'mother' and the demands of social authority. She moves in and out of the shebeen with ease, comfortably straddling both worlds. It is the Widow Quin who (mis)names the playboy; it is she who mediates between father and son; it is she who retreats when the son's bond to the father becomes inevitable; it is she who most clearly understands the nature of the playboy's reputation, and the impossibility of restoring that reputation merely by repeating the deed. The Widow Quin perceives the gap between the playboy and Christy Mahon, and she sees the possibility of 'picking up the pieces' where others see only the essential alienation between Christy and the playboy of their imaginations: 'Well, if worst comes in the end of all, it'll be great game to see there's none to pity him but a widow woman, the like of me, has buried her children and destroyed her man.'[35] She has been instrumental in establishing the ground upon which father and son will meet, and she has achieved this through her access to both the structures of the symbolic order, and the nature of those repressed entities which sustain it. This is a consistent theme in Synge's work: the mother-figure is used to focus opposition – Christian/pagan, material/spiritual, natural/supernatural, life/death, ritual/carnival – and to filter these oppositions in such a way that the structural relationship between them is reconstituted.[36] The Widow Quin in *The Playboy* assumes just this role, as does Mary Byrne in *The Tinker's Wedding*. Here the mother does not figure merely as the 'pagan' who operates in opposition to the 'Christian'; rather, she embodies traces of both pagan and Christian and as such her disclosure of the myths of Christianity (as practised in Ireland) establishes the irony with which the audience is to view the play's conclusion.

Mary Byrne has been able to entice the priest into the world of the tinkers.[37] She coaxes the priest across the divide, a divide which she herself (unlike Sarah Casey) comfortably straddles. Yet, significantly, it is her touch which sends him back to the world where authority is vested in him through the Church:

> MARY [*with great sympathy*]. It'd break my heart to hear you talking and sighing the like of that, your reverence. [*She pats him on the knee.*] Let you rouse up, now, if it's a poor, single man you are itself, and I'll be singing you songs until the dawn of day.
> PRIEST [*interrupting her*]. What is it I want with your songs when it'd be better for the like of you, that'll soon die, to be down on your two knees saying prayers to the Almighty God?[38]

The threat carried in her touch, the threat of complete seduction into the tinker's world, stirs him to rejection.

While Mary Byrne is prepared to subject herself to the authority of God, she questions the degree to which the priest in fact represents that authority. She warns Sarah Casey 'not to be talking whisper-talk with the like of him in the face of the Almighty God' while at the same time taunting the priest with her understanding of the Church and its hypocrisies:

> If it's prayers I want, you'd have a right to say one yourself holy father; for we don't have them at all, and I've heard tell a power of times it's that you're for. Say one now, your reverence; for I've heard a power of queer things ... but there's one thing I never heard any time, and that's a real priest saying a prayer.[39]

Mary Byrne's own peculiar faith and her simple respect for 'the Almighty God' give credence to her questioning of the priest's authority. By the conclusion of the play, she has undermined his authority so effectively that his attempt to take the moral high ground is rendered meaningless. It is Mary Byrne's capacity to read accurately the codes of both the society in which the priest has authority and that in which the tinkers exist which makes her essential to any understanding of *The Tinker's Wedding*. It is something of her insight into these codes that she seeks to explain to the priest in the final moments of the play:

> what did you want meddling with the likes of us, when it's a long time we are going our own ways – father and son, and his son

after him, or mother and daughter, and her own daughter again; and it's little need we ever had of going up into a church and swearing.[40]

The conclusion to *The Tinker's Wedding* is not an entirely successful one, and it is important that it not be read literally as the priest's victory. While such a literal reading no doubt would have satisfied the play's early audience (had it ever been performed in Synge's lifetime), Mary Byrne is used throughout the play to undermine any priestly triumph. If anything, the conclusion of the play needs to be read ironically, for the priest who triumphs is a priest who, through the course of the play, has had his authority dismantled and laid bare by Mary Byrne. She achieves this not only by functioning as the site of intersection between the Christian and the pagan, but also through her understanding and reading of the rituals that structure both societies.

It is important to note that in *The Tinker's Wedding* Mary Byrne does not enter until the moment a wedding contract between priest and couple is agreed. Her role is to dissolve this contract by undermining the rituals and symbols which afford the marriage ceremony its authority, and therefore her presence prior to this time would have been superfluous. In fulfilling this role she 'drinks' the currency – the tin can – by which marriage, and movement into the society which sanctions marriage, may be purchased. She pronounces as folly the elaborate preparations of the couple for the ceremony, the washing and re-ordering of their appearances which can be likened to a baptism. And, more significantly, she shatters the symbols by which the contract is effected by exposing the arbitrary nature of the link between symbol and meaning:

> Is it putting that ring on your finger will keep you from getting an aged woman and losing the fine face you have, or be easing your pains; when it's the grand ladies do be married in silk dresses, with rings of gold, that do pass any woman with their share of torment in the hour of birth.[41]

Mary Byrne bleeds of their meaning the very symbols that have prompted Sarah Casey's desire to marry under the auspices of the Church, and her ability to rupture signification in this way establishes her as the 'divil's scholar'.[42]

By exposing the symbols and rituals by which Sarah Casey is seeking to change her position in society, Mary Byrne establishes the basis upon which Sarah will later turn on the priest. Further, she has reinforced Sarah's position within the tinkers' world through her representations of

Sarah as one who bears in her face a rich, mythical heritage, yet who still exists outside society: she is among the 'great queens of Ireland'; she is 'a weathered heathen savage [who] quenched the flaming candles on the throne of God the time [her] shadow fell within the pillars of the chapel door'.[43]

A less subtle rendering of the mother's capacity to recast traditional symbols is seen in the early play, *When the Moon Has Set*. In this instance, symbol and meaning are not so much prised apart as transfigured. Mary Costello, the mad mother of phantom children, takes upon herself the symbols that maintain her in that space, while at the same time dissipating the threat those same symbols hold for Sister Eileen. Mary takes from Eileen the crucifix which represents the religion that has sent her into madness, while Eileen takes from Mary Costello the ring and the wedding gown which will release her from the same religion:

> May the Almighty God reward you Sister, and give you five nice children before you die.... May his blessing be on them rings, and they be going on your hand, and his blessing be on your hand and it working with the linen when the time is come.... Let you mind the words I was saying, and give no heed to the priests or the bishops or the angels of God, for it's little the like of them, I was saying, knows about women or the seven sorrows of the earth.[44]

Lacking the craft evident in his later plays, Synge does not allow this ceremony to stand on its own and has Colm Sweeny explain to the audience the significance of what has occurred. Even so, the exchange between the women is a powerful example of the association between symbol, robbed of its essential meaning, and madness.

Assaulting the symbolic from its margins

In order to reform or reconstitute the symbolic order it is imperative to undermine the links which keep that order in place. Challenging or transforming the symbols embedded within that order is a first step. Yet to replace the symbolic order with any meaningful alternative it is necessary to venture where the bonds between the sign and its meaning are fluid and far from fixed, to plunder the depths of the disorder and flux which exist beneath the symbolic surface. To this end, the mother-figure in Synge's work augments her disruption of rituals and symbols with song and *caoin* and gesture, acts which dispel the (public) silence traditionally expected of the mother. In these speech-acts 'her words fall almost always upon the deaf male ear, which hears in language only that which speaks in the masculine'.[45] By speaking in a language that is beyond 'the masculine', the mother may subvert the codes in which 'masculine speech' is engendered. Mary Byrne's drunken songs, the keening which accompanies Maurya's prayers over her son's dead body, and Mary Costello's songs and keening when 'discovered' by Colm and Eileen: all accompany a rupture in signification and a modification of meaning. Maurya projects a range of utterances to which the 'male ear' is deaf: the powerful prayers wrought over the body of Bartley; her silence, her inability to speak when she is required to offer Bartley her blessing; her lamentations by the sea; and her murmuring by the fire, 'an old woman with one thing and she saying it over'.[46] Cixous notes that 'mad-mothers, those excluded from society, are . . . promoted to function as prophets',[47] and it is this function that Maurya is afforded through her weeping and gestures. In her access to that language which exists beyond the symbolic, the mother is able to challenge society and, importantly, the coherence of those symbols which sustain that society. While Cathleen asks Maurya 'isn't it a better thing to raise your voice and tell what you've seen than to be making lamentation for a thing that's done',[48] Maurya knows that her lamentations are a powerful weapon. In terms of the dénouement of the play, and Maurya's construction of the drama in which she figures, her access to that which is beyond speech ensures that her reading of the supernatural portents is afforded full credence.

There is a suggestion that the mother's capacity to 'speak' in a way that challenges rather than maintains the existing order depends largely on the place from which she speaks. Within society, in public spaces, the mother must be silent, stoical and subordinate. Madness, drink, death and the graveyard place her on the margins of society, and of the symbolic order. Here, as Cixous writes, she has a 'dangerous symbolic mobility';[49] she has access to that 'mother-tongue' where meaning and sign are no longer inextricably bound. When Mary Byrne staggers onstage to challenge the proposed wedding of Sarah and Michael, she is drunk and singing. She has come from her ditch – metaphorically her tomb – to which she is urged to return whenever she becomes objectionable. It is from this position of insobriety and 'death' that she is able to bring into question the rituals and symbols of Christian marriage. Similarly, Mary Costello, through her madness and her association with the graveyard, is able to appropriate those symbols which bind Sister Eileen to her vows. In this, Mary Costello is central to the resolution of the play – she takes on the madness that is threatening Eileen and thereby ensures not only the marriage of Colm and Eileen, but a renewal of order:

> COLM. . . . I know you have a profound impulse for what is peculiar to women. You realize that the forces which lift women up to share in the pain and passion of the world are more holy than the vows you have made. . . . I, the male power, have overcome with worship you, the soul of credulous feeling, the reader of the saints.[50]

Eileen is contained by the patriarchal cultural tradition, and so she is doomed to perpetuate it. What the intervention of Mary Costello achieves is the displacement of one authority by another. She serves as catalyst, transmuting authority from that of the Church to that of the (secular) father.

*

At their most fundamental level, the oppositions explored in Synge's work correspond to the semiotic/symbolic divide. And it is the mother-figure who is consistently utilized to disclose, re-order and resolve these oppositions. She is the site where oppositions intersect and, through her access to the semiotic – the realm beyond language and beyond the rituals and symbols which sustain society – she is able to challenge the symbolic, rejuvenate it and facilitate the passage of the child from one realm to the other. What Synge's work highlights is the mother's capacity to bring into question the sign, the symbol, or the ritual upon which any particular order rests, and to reveal the arbitrary nature of the bond between referent and meaning. It is, therefore, primarily through the mother that social and symbolic orders may be laid bare and, to some extent, renewed. And it is this reconstitution of the social and symbolic orders, the subtle shift of meaning in the symbols and rituals underlying society, which is at the heart of Synge's work.

Rebellion and Revolution: *Couvade* and (Self-)Creation

> *In the name of God and of the dead generations from which she receives her old tradition of nationhood, Ireland, through us, summons her children to her flag and strikes for her freedom.*
>
> The Provisional Government of the Irish Republic,
> *Proclamation of the Republic*

In *Inventing Ireland*, Declan Kiberd contends that '[in] societies on the brink of revolution, the relation between fathers and sons is reversed'. The Easter Rising and the suffusion of violence that followed is painted as the bitter climax of a long-running family saga – sons rising against not merely British imperialism but also against father-figures whose own response to the 'English occupiers' was deemed to have been 'compromised'. 'The Irish father,' Kiberd argues, 'was a defeated man, whose wife frequently won the bread and usurped his domestic power, while the priest usurped his spiritual authority.'[1] This composition of the Irish home, with its dominant and domineering mother and its emotionally crippled and infantilized father, repeats itself in the literature of the period. The pattern to which Kiberd refers is rehearsed in Moore's *Celibates* and *A Drama in Muslin*; Joyce's *Dubliners* and *A Portrait of the Artist as a Young Man*; and O'Casey's Dublin trilogy, most notably *Juno and the Paycock*, which directly juxtaposes this model of the debilitated Irish family with the violence that, no longer confined to the streets, was being propelled into private spaces.

It would, of course, be naive to suggest that deeply embedded psychological factors were the sole or even the dominant issue that motivated the revolutionaries of Easter 1916: the complex of factors which led to the Easter Rising – historical, cultural, political, social and psychological – is far too entangled to allow any simple analysis. As Foster contends, while a 'clash of generations' may have been an influential factor in the Rising, whether such a clash 'led inevitably to the...Easter Rising of 1916...is another matter'.[2] Even so, in the immediate social and symbolic context of early twentieth-century Ireland, the hero who would become 'father' to the revitalized nation, and in whose name the Nationalist agenda would be realized, seemed as remote as ever: the need to reify him through revolution assumed an increasing urgency. It is just this need that Synge's *The Playboy of the Western World* so sharply satirizes.[3] However, images of revolution in terms of a struggle between fathers and sons portray an incomplete picture. For while the revolutionaries donned (whether themselves or at the hands of those who lionized them) the mantles of Christ and Cuchulain, and while the sons of Ireland fought against England in the name of an (elusive) heroic father, there remained implicitly present the figures of Christ's suffering mother, Cathleen ni Houlihan, and mother-Ireland herself. Within the discourse of revolution, these mothers played a vital role, their function to recruit the able, comfort the suffering, and define the martyrdom of the defeated.

The rhetoric of the Irish revolution, as captured by Sean O'Casey in *The Plough and the Stars*, is that of sacrifice, renewal and rebirth, those same parameters upon which the Cathleen ni Houlihan myth is founded:

> we rejoice in this terrible war. The old heart of the earth needed to be warmed with the red wine of the battlefields.... we must be ready to pour out the same red wine in the same glorious sacrifice, for without shedding of blood there is no redemption![4]

The rhetoric of Padraic Pearse, upon whom O'Casey's speaker is based, dominates the verbal landscape of the Rising – and it is language that embraces the mother-figure: as Costello notes, within Pearse's writing 'the image of his mother Ireland suffering in chains is the predominant one'.[5] It was an image widely rehearsed. As Mrs Sheehy-Skeffington protested in her response to *The Plough and the Stars*:

> Nora Clitheroe is no more 'typical of Irish womanhood' than her futile snivelling husband is of Irish manhood. The women of Easter Week, as we know them, are typified rather in the mother of Padraic Pearse, that valiant woman who gave both her sons for freedom.[6]

The image of the 'mother of martyrs' was still central to discourse, yet in the decades of war and violence that heralded the new century the dominant image was that of the martyrs themselves. For it was the martyrs who were to deliver the new nation while the mother stood back from the struggle, her iconic position within the cultural tradition secured through the death of her 'sons'. The rhetoric of sacrifice espoused by revolutionaries such as Pearse operated as a *couvade* – that (re-)enactment of the birth process in which the father assumes the mother's role. Revolution is not merely a struggle between fathers and sons – it is a form of parturition, and the rebirth effected may be social, symbolic or both. In the *couvade*, Lacan argues, 'it is...possible to see...that the function of the father and of what he contributes to the creation of the new individual is called into question. The *couvade* is located at the level of a question concerning masculine procreation.'[7] Such an assessment is immediately suggestive of Joyce's *Ulysses* – in their re-enactment of the gestation and birth of the English language, the men in 'Oxen of the Sun' occupy maternal spaces: tension is established between Mina Purefoy's labour with the physical child and their own labour with the symbolic child, language. Doubts surrounding the father's role in procreation – doubts articulated by Stephen Dedalus in 'Scylla and Charybdis' – are suppressed by the *couvade*, by masking the mother's role in birth, just as revolution masks the maternal function in social and symbolic renewal. It is something of this maternal function that I aim to recover in this chapter.

Father as origin

In 'Origin, Space, Opposition', I argued that the umbilical split not only castrates both mother and child, but allows the child access to a father's history and to a father's name. Such access positions the child as a speaking subject within the social and symbolic structures founded on the 'name-of-the-father'. The child's transit from the realm of the mother to the realm of the father not only serves to reinforce the 'de-phallicization' of the mother that is inherent to social and symbolic structures, but also ensures the consolidation of those structures. The child is brought within the confines of symbolization, finding a position from which she or he may speak; yet, ironically, it is a position which limits the child to signifying practices as determined by the father's authority and which, ultimately, fortify that authority by de-individualizing those subjects brought within its ambit.

The first step that needs to be taken in bringing the child within the social and symbolic structures governed by the father is the disruption of the mother–child bond. Separation from the mother establishes a dynamic that requires the child to either accede to the father's authority, and thereby be established within subjectivity, or to succumb to psychosis, that realm where signifier and signified are permanently dislocated: 'There can be nothing *Human* that pre-exists or exists outside the law represented by the father; there is only either denial (psychosis) or the fortunes and misfortunes ("normality" and neurosis) of its terms.' Yet, as Mitchell goes on to emphasize, 'the relation of mother and child cannot be viewed outside the structure established by the position of the father.'[8] Once the father's authority is assumed, then both the mother and the entity that was the mother–child dyad cannot be read except in terms dictated by that authority. The 'reality' of the mother, the 'reality' of the mother–child bond, no longer exist: both can only be constructed according to the processes of symbolization determined by the father's name, authority and history. The mother's presence at the origin of the child's narrative history is masked by the father; the void that was filled by the maternal body is (re)constructed by the father in order to displace the mother and assert a patrilineage.

Davis, in 'The Discourse of the Father', argues that the father must be situated 'at the origin of the text as a principle according to which narrative unfolds, his authority constituting a structural pretext'.[9] Within the Irish context, the father's 'structural pre-text' for the child's narrative is that of the British hegemony, a structure that is foreign and immediately alienating. Language and culture owe more to the oppressor than to those 'native' authorities – familial, mythological and historical – which have been suppressed as a result of British governance of Ireland. And while the cultural colonization arising out of Britain's political subjection of Ireland cannot be denied, factions within Ireland who asserted Ireland's religious, cultural and political independence, disguised – whether consciously or not – their own desire to determine the 'structural pre-text' according to which Ireland's 'children' would read and write their own subjectivities. As texts such as *A Portrait of the Artist as a Young Man, Dubliners, The Untilled Field* and O'Casey's *Autobiographies* insist, the tension between the imposed 'structural pre-text' of the father and the child's desired subjectivity was not limited to resistance of British hegemony. It extended to the demands of Catholicism and Nationalism, whose discourses were equally as oppressive in their construction of Irish history and subjectivity. The complex dynamics by which individuals moved towards or pushed against these 'pre-texts' in order to establish and assert their own identities can be mapped in the literature of the period.

The inhibitory moral standards which accompanied the founding of the Irish Free State in 1922 – and which O'Casey lamented in *Sunset and Evening Star*, and lambasted in a number of his later plays – are read by Foster as an effect of Ireland asserting its own patrilineage.[10] Yet, as Foster suggests, the 'martyrology' that emerged from the Easter Rising, and which provided the first evidence of this emerging paternal history, indicates that the patrilineage from which Ireland drew this self-definition was itself largely constructed.

His-story

History demands the mother's absence. Within the father's history, the mother is contained, and her presence is merely apparent. There she is constructed, a point Kristeva emphasizes when she writes that the woman positions herself according to pre-established 'co-ordinates' of family and patrilineage, co-ordinates which extend beyond the immediate family to the broader social and historical context in which woman is positioned. For the mother, locked within and defined by her function within the family and her role in the generation of the patrilineage, these co-ordinates fix her even more securely. Yet within these axes there exists the potential to disrupt and defy (patriarchal) history. This occurs

> if I project not the moment of my fixed, governed world, ruled by a series of inhibitions and prohibitions (ranging from rules to sexual taboos and economic, political and ideological constraints), but rather the underlying causality that shapes it, which I repress in order that I may enter the socio-symbolic order, and which is capable of blowing up the whole construct.[11]

The symbolic order, founded on the father's name, governs time, genealogy, culture, law, 'reality'; it also assigns social and symbolic space. The father is, as Kristeva asserts, 'sign and time';[12] and to maintain that position the father must suppress those elements of the social and symbolic orders which undermine that structure, and which call to mind the uncertain foundations upon which the father's authority is built. The father constructs the mother, binds her within sign and time, to effect just such a suppression. For it is in the mother and through the mother that the power to subvert the father's authority is rooted, and this power stems from the mother's 'pregnancies', her access to the child. For inherent to the maternal position is a recognition of 'the unspoken in all discourse, however Revolutionary'.[13] It is this subversive power which the father covets and seeks to contain through the *couvade* – whether through the physical re-enactment of parturition, or through the revolutionary action that seeks social regeneration. And in the same way as the *couvade* reconstructs birth by centring the father, the Irish modernists, I argue, displaced the mother and assumed her position. This allowed both the suppression of doubts concerning their own creativity while also affording them access to those creative spaces focussed in the mother and from which a symbolic revolution might be initiated.

In 'A New Type of Intellectual: the Dissident', Kristeva emphasizes the role of language in disrupting both law and the father's history – through language the father's law may be 'violated and pluralized', yet in order to achieve this language must be 'polyvalent [and] poly-logical'.[14] It must exist outside of those signifying practices determined and perpetuated by the father's name – it must have its model in that realm of the maternal where signification is fluid and capricious. Significantly, Kristeva argues that poetic language, the *avant-garde*, and other ruptures of the symbolic fabric '[accompany] crises within social structures and institutions'.[15] Such crises provide the space, the tear, through which that which is suppressed by the dominant symbolic structures may surface. Similarly, the subversion of signifying practices undermines the foundations of the symbolic structure, providing the conditions for social upheaval and even, perhaps, social renewal. For the Irish people, resisting the social and symbolic structures imposed by British political and cultural hegemony, and seeking to subvert those structures through the elaboration of a 'native' language and culture embedded in a rich and ancient mythology, the impetus towards social and symbolic revolution was extraordinary. That such subversion should realize itself in the literature of the period reflects the extent of the *couvade* – both social and symbolic – that was occurring. The social upheavals witnessed in Ireland in the early decades of the twentieth century can be linked directly to the modernism of writers such as Synge, Joyce, O'Casey and Yeats. It is not merely because the social and political revolution appropriated images of the maternal to recruit 'revolutionaries' that such a link can be forged, but that in figuring the revolution in such overt images of rebirth the revolutionaries displaced the mother and assumed her creative space. That such a space necessi-tated the destruction of so many offspring remains one of the central

ironies of the Irish experience of *couvade*. For the political revolutionaries, the effect of such a displacement enhanced the fervour with which
they participated in the national parturition. For the symbolic revolutionaries – those writers already resisting inherited cultural traditions –
the mother's displacement (as reinforced in the political revolution)
afforded ingress to the semiotic spaces within which representation
itself was challenged.

*

Within an oedipal construct of the Easter Rising, therefore, mother-
Ireland is subsumed by the English-father's name – the English-cultural
father unchallenged by the weak and incapacitated Irish-familial father
– with the child inexorably drawn into the ambit of the English-father's
authority. The child, in broad terms the Irish people, able to express
himself only in the alien language of the oppressor, reaches out for an
alternative father, an authority rooted in Catholicism and Nationalism
and accessed through mother-Ireland, mythologized as the mother-in-
chains of Pearse's rhetoric or the poor old woman of Irish legend. Yet, as
I have argued in previous chapters, passing through the mother's realm
occasions subjective death, here rendered as blood-sacrifice to land and
nation. The irony is that while such sacrifice is painted in terms of the
renewal of land and nation, personified as mother, it is not the mother
who is renewed by the sacrifice of revolution; rather it is signifying
practice, the symbolic structure itself, which is regenerated. The
mother's only opportunity for renewal comes in the nature of her construction within the regenerated symbolic order, and it is always the
dominant patriarchal cultural tradition which determines that construction. Pearse's mother is not freed from her chains through sacrifice and
revolution; she is, in fact, more trammelled than ever, particularly as the
new order has relied so heavily on constructions of her in effecting
social and symbolic change.[16] This is reflected in the displacement of
the mother from the process of the nation's rebirth as effected by the
couvade that is the revolutionary movement. The mother is an icon of
revolution, and must maintain that position if the order is to maintain
its authority and begin to tell its own history. It may be through her,
through immersion in the semiotic spaces of the maternal, that social
and symbolic renewal has its source; yet once the revolutionary – social,
political or literary – emerges from the semiotic back into the symbolic,
the mother finds that her freedom was illusory and that, in order to prop
up the father's authority, she has been reconstructed.

6

'What's Ni Houlihan to You?': Sean O'Casey's Construction of the Mother

> *We will be alright, it's the women who will suffer. The most they can do to us is kill us. But the women will have to remain behind us to rear the children.*
>
> Eamon de Valera[1]

In *Sunset and Evening Star*, Sean O'Casey's *alter-ego* asks the question: What is truth? Recognizing the 'fact' of the struggle of the Soviet people, and the 'irresistible enthusiasm of their Socialistic efforts', Sean concludes: 'we are all from the same mother.' O'Casey uses the figure of the mother to assert the essential 'brotherhood' of humanity.[2] His original question, however, remains unanswered.

Questions as to the nature of truth recur in the *Autobiographies*. They are implicit within the narrative, and arise primarily from the confusion O'Casey feels, both as child and man, in seeking to determine his political, cultural and religious self. More specifically, his search for a resolute truth sees him weighing nationalism against socialism in order to determine the road by which Ireland should progress into the twentieth century.[3] Concomitant with this search is the struggle to determine the clear and certain boundaries of his own identity, both in terms of his place in Irish politics and his place in Irish letters. This is particularly evident in the later volumes of his *Autobiographies* – more memoir than objective narrative[4] – where he rails against those who level criticism at him or his work. His bitter recollection of the Abbey's rejection of *The Silver Tassie* derives as much from his need to assert his place – self-taught and working-class as he may be – as an intellectual equal to (in particular) Yeats, as with his faith in the play itself.

Among the writers I am examining here, O'Casey is unusual in that he
is concerned primarily with defining and asserting his place within the
social order. Unlike Joyce and Yeats, who were primarily interested in
disturbing the symbolic order by which they felt bound, O'Casey's
principal focus is the social order and the means by which that order
might be subverted. It is the social against which he struggles and,
therefore, the social which he aims to disturb. Even so, he recognizes
the symbolic manifestations by which the social order is maintained. It
is clear within his writing that, for him, the key to the success of any
social revolution is the release of the Irish people from the myths and
symbols which bind them to their social position – myths and symbols
which are flouted by those who dominate discourse in order to maintain
and enhance that dominant position. This theme becomes particularly
evident in several of the later plays, most notably *Within the Gates* and
The Star Turns Red. 'There go God's own aristocracy, the poor in spirit,'[5]
the Bishop says in *Within the Gates* ; yet what is being emphasized is how
the myth of a rich and joyous after-life, cultivated by a clergy who
immerse themselves in wealth and privilege, is fed to the poor in order
to maintain the established hierarchy. In *The Star Turns Red* the effect is
more explicit: the Old Woman objects to the theft of her poverty.
Referring to the 'dignity and loveliness that priests say poverty give
the poor', she states: 'They haven't got these things themselves, and
they want to snap them from us.' It is left to Jack, in words appropriated
from Christ, to attempt to unveil the myth, showing the true face of
poverty: 'It is the peace of crying out, and no one heareth; of secret and
open hunger, and no one cometh with food; of cold and nakedness, and
no one giveth a covering: put that peace back in your bosom and go!'[6]
Red Jim is characterized almost as an icon of socialist realism, and
O'Casey's debt to this school has been emphasized by critics such as
Deane. However, Deane's argument that O'Casey was part of a 'reac-
tionary movement against the "decadence" of literary modernism'[7]
needs to be refuted. Essentially, O'Casey's modernism was expressed in
social rather than symbolic terms – he sought to rewrite myths and resist
tradition primarily in order to effect social change. It is just this manner
of resistance that is apparent in Red Jim, who seeks not to displace myth
with truth, but rather to displace one myth in order to make way for
another, an alternative myth of the Red Star rising. This myth will not
only determine the conditions for social revolution, ultimately it will
sustain a new social order. The irony of the play stems from the difficulty
of differentiating the words of Red Jim from those of the Purple Priest:
they are similar in tone and rhetorical devices, and they are words

essentially full of promise but devoid of action. It is an irony of which O'Casey, caught up in the new promise offered by a socialist workers' revolution, seems unaware, and it may be only the hindsight of one reading the play after the exposure of the excesses of Stalinism and the disintegration of the Communist bloc that makes this irony so clearly evident.[8] However, it is important to note that the myth that will displace that of the 'poor in spirit' is one that is not rendered merely in the words of Red Jim; rather it is embedded in the very imagery of the play: 'The star turned red is still the star / Of him who came as man's pure prince of peace; / And so I serve him here.'[9] Yet, in the play's closing image, the symbolic meaning of the star has been appropriated by the workers' revolution. There is a sense that the events of the play do not in themselves effect this change: as with the star leading the Wise Men to the stable, the red star represents a dramatic birth which is to take place. The star, the myth, is the cause; the birth is merely the effect.

In his overview of modern Irish drama, Maxwell argues that O'Casey was 'sceptical of and passionate against the orthodoxies of Gaelic nationalism, the Catholic puritanism of the new state, the myth and the rhetoric of violence . . . and the random suffering it inflicted'.[10] The revolution he sought was not born of violence but through a restructuring of the social order that would be effected through the reconstitution of the symbolic. On the matter of violence, however, he was equivocal, suggesting in plays such as *Within the Gates* that violence was implicit in the natural order and inherent in the process of renewal.[11] In *The Silver Tassie*, questions are raised concerning not the causes of war and violence, but the motives which see individuals participate in that violence.[12] The dynamics by which social and symbolic orders are created, maintained and dismantled affords prominent positions not only to the individual whose subjectivity will be determined by these orders, but to the relationship of the individual to a mother-figure and a father-figure within whose parameters these social and symbolic orders are able to exist; the potential for a renewal of the social and symbolic orders comes not through the father whose authority is dependent upon fixed and rigid structures, but through the mother in whom the potential for transgressions of the social and symbolic orders exists. Truth, O'Casey suggests, derives from fraternity. That fraternity is tied to a single mother. Yet how, in the establishment of truth, a new truth which would subvert the essential 'lie' upon which society was based (and a goal which he clearly believed to be possible), is the mother transcribed? In the birth of the new social order that he desires, what role does the mother play? How is the mother-figure placed in the determination of

subjectivity and in the dismantling of one social order and the construction of another? Is the mother herself mythologized as a means of fixing
the parameters and hierarchy of the existing social order? And, finally,
in what ways does O'Casey demythologize the mother in order to
release social structures. It is these questions which I will explore in
this chapter.[13]

'O Blessed Virgin, where were you ... ?'

In *Juno and the Paycock*, Johnny Boyle's superstitious insistence that the
flame on the votive light be lit in order to maintain the protective aura
of the Virgin is paralleled in his pleas to Juno when he considers himself
to be in danger: 'Sit here, sit here, mother ... between me an' the door.'[14]
In many ways, Johnny's invocation to one or other mothers foreshadows the use to which O'Casey will put the mother-figure in order to
dispel those myths he deemed to be oppressive, particularly to the Irish
working classes. The mother is structured as a place of refuge, sought
by the child as he or she attempts to flee the disintegration and
division of their social and symbolic context. The Virgin Mary, as she
functions in *Juno and the Paycock*, *Cock-a-Doodle Dandy* and *Red Roses for
Me*, embodies this sense of retreat and protection afforded by the
mother. Similarly, representations of Victoria as all-powerful mother in
I Knock at the Door offer a sense of comfort and ease amid physical and
social threats.

Durbach argues that: 'It is Juno whose comfort and protection of her
child in his emotional crises finally exposes the ineffectuality of the
Mother as religious icon.'[15] Juno herself laments the Virgin's dereliction
of duty: 'Blessed Virgin, where were you when me darlin' son was
riddled with bullets ... ?'[16] Yet in taking upon herself that same icon as
a means of expressing her suffering – 'What was the pain I suffered,
Johnny, bringin' you into the world to carry you to your cradle, to the
pains I'll suffer carryin' you out o' the world to bring you to your
grave!'[17] – Juno asserts the inevitable failure of her own proffered comfort and protection. Ultimately, there is only one conclusion that can be
drawn from O'Casey's representation of the mother as refuge, and that is
its utter futility. In *Red Roses for Me*, Our Lady of Eblana, the grit and
grime of the Dublin slums removed in an attempt to revive her splend-
our, remains impotent to improve the living conditions of those who do
her homage: she offers little more than a 'liberty of the soul that was to
leave the body and mind still in prison'.[18] In *Cock-a-Doodle Dandy* Julia's
pilgrimage to Lourdes is to no effect, except in that she now has lost not

only her health but her faith: 'she didn't cure me. . . . I've come back, without even a gloamin' thought of hope.'[19]

As symbol of suffering motherhood, the Virgin becomes the natural focus for the prayers of those whose own lives match the template proffered by the Mother of Christ. And while O'Casey's Protestant upbringing dampened any personal fidelity to the symbol of the Virgin, he was clearly aware of the power of that symbol over the minds of the Irish people and sought to unveil her myth, just as the myths of Victoria and Cathleen ni Houlihan had been unveiled for him. What he posits in his representation of the Virgin is that her cult imprisons rather than liberates. This is most critically dealt with in *Red Roses for Me*. Here the icon of the Virgin is literally sullied by the Dublin slums. The poor offer their meagre savings in an effort to restore the statue to its previous glory; and, in doing so, they deny themselves any chance of improving their own social and economic conditions. The myth of the Virgin is further ironized through the hyperbolical claims of the women – who have seen the restored statue – that a miracle has occurred. Significantly, within *Red Roses for Me*, O'Casey establishes parallels between two myths – Cathleen ni Houlihan and Virgin Mary – effectively undermining both.

However, when looking at ways in which the myth of the Virgin Mary operates in O'Casey's plays, it is difficult to go beyond *The Silver Tassie*. Within the structure of the play – which can, I suggest, be read as something of a passion play[20] – the Virgin figures prominently in the sub-text. She provides the paradigm against which the actions of Mrs Heegan may be read and her failures emphasized. Mrs Heegan is not the silent, suffering mother who disappears from view when her son realizes his glory; rather, she is the Judas-figure who betrays her son for financial rewards and in whom there is to be no respite.

Like Maurya in Synge's *Riders to the Sea*, Mrs Heegan is shown to be duplicitous in the inception and protraction of suffering:

> Remember our women, sad-hearted, proud-fac'd,
> Who've given the substance of their womb for shadows;
> Their shrivel'd empty breasts war tinselléd
> For patient gifts of graves to thee.[21]

To an extent, this echoes *Juno and the Paycock*, where there is no sense of rejuvenation as a result of sacrifice, merely waste. Juno's grief, like Mrs Tancred's before her, is centred on 'this murdherin hate';[22] the focus is not on a renewal of life through death, but on the futility of the sacrifice:

FIRST NEIGHBOUR. It's a sad journey we're goin' on, but God's good, an' the Republicans won't be always down.

MRS TANCRED. Ah, what good is that to me now? Whether they're up or down – it won't bring me darlin' boy from the grave. [23]

Yet, in *The Silver Tassie*, the mother's role in bringing her sons to sacrifice is explicitly stated. The First Soldier reminds the men:

> The padre gives a fag an' softly whispers:
> 'Your king, your country an' your muvver 'as you 'ere.'[24]

Mrs Heegan provides a potent example of the mother's complicity with the war. Her vigil in the cold watching for her son is primarily motivated by her avarice: 'an' if he misses now the tide that's waitin', he skulks behind desertion from the colours. . . . An' my government money grant would stop at once.'[25] The noble nature of the son's sacrifice is perverted by the mother: his life represents an economic investment on her part, and her interest in him is predicated upon the economic returns he brings. Any concern she shows for his well-being is undermined by her references to the allowance he – and therefore she – is receiving.

Mrs Heegan is in large part responsible for dispatching her son to a battlefield where his identity is totally dissipated and where he is unable to exist as subject. His suffering is universalized, and the attributes by which he comes to define himself are detached from him in this 'no man's land' and become free, in turn, to attach themselves to any one of his comrades. He emerges crippled, the glory he wore so easily as he went into the war now worn by his saviour, Barney Bagnal.[26] Jessie Taite is, of course, representative of this shift. The symbolic mother who oversees this scene, the stained-glass figure of the Virgin, seems almost oblivious to the pleas of her son, and in this she is indicative of many of O'Casey's mothers who maintain a psychical distance from their children, leaving them to languish in a hinterland of subjectivity where they are neither defined as mirror-image of her, nor through subjection to a father-figure.[27]

O'Casey exposes as false the premise that the mother-figure, whether she be real or metaphorical, is able to afford protection from the violence and disintegration of society: '[Cathleen ni Houlihan] galled the hearts of her children who dared to be above the ordinary, and she often slew her best ones. She had hounded Parnell to death; she had yelled and torn at Yeats, at Synge.'[28] Here, he does more than merely evoke the destroying-mother archetype, echoing – though in tones relatively subdued – Joyce's rendering in 'Circe' of the mother as 'corpse-chewer'.[29] As Yeats suggests in 'Into the Twilight', mother-Ireland's youth and beauty, while overtly relieving the decay and despair of the nation, covertly depends upon that same despair. Similarly, O'Casey emphasizes – and thereby resists – the rapacious nature of the sacrifices demanded by the Irish nation, figured as mother. By foregrounding the destruction inherent to the Cathleen ni Houlihan myth, and concomitantly subordinating those regenerative constructions of the myth that dominate discourse, O'Casey brings into question the entire symbolic structure that reveres mother-Ireland as source of strength and renewal.

' . . . a flush on her haughty cheek'

Yeats, Moore and Joyce used the symbol of mother-Ireland to explore themes of social and emotional paralysis, the power of the mythical over the literal, and the need to flee Ireland if one was to realize an individual social, psychical or artistic identity. In doing so, they proceeded to demythologize mother-Ireland by illuminating both the strings by which she was made to operate, and those social and symbolic structures whose stability and integrity were dependent upon her. O'Casey takes his demythologization of mother-Ireland – particularly in her guise of Cathleen ni Houlihan – in yet another direction.

O'Casey's own epiphany with regard to Cathleen ni Houlihan is represented in his *Autobiographies* as coming at the time of the declaration of the Irish Free State:

> [Eire's] courage broken like an old tree in a black wind; the proud step gone that was once the walk of a queen; bent now like the old Hag of Beara. . . . Turn your back on the green and gold, on the old hag that once had the walk of a queen! What's ni Houlihan to you, or you to ni Houlihan? Nothing now. . . . The little brown-backed cow was in the weeds before, and she's in the weeds again.[30]

Like Julia in *Cock-a-Doodle Dandy*, Sean has lost his faith because the mother has failed to accomplish what was promised. Ireland has not emerged from its civil unrest rejuvenated, and the sacrifices that have been made have been made for nothing. Initially, however, Sean, caught up in the fervour of the rising, does witness her transformation:

> But Cathleen, the daughter of Houlihan, walks firm now, a flush on her haughty cheek. She hears the murmur in the people's hearts. Her

lovers are gathering around her, for things are changed, changed utterly.[31]

Yet, in O'Casey's rendering, no 'terrible beauty is born'. His vision of the rejuvenated Cathleen – one which also transforms the relationship between her and the men of Ireland from that of mother to lover – offers a victorious conclusion to the third volume of autobiography, but the vision dissipates as passion dissolves and the actual outcome of events becomes clear. Even so, the seeds of disillusion are evident in *Drums Under the Window*: that the quotation 'changed, changed utterly' (from Yeats's 'Easter 1916') is not completed suggests a degree of equivocation about the transformation that has taken place. Further, having recounted Cathleen's renewed pride, Sean undercuts her celebration with an account of the sacrifices which have been made:

> A rare time for death in Ireland; and in the battle's prologue many a common man, woman and child had said goodbye to work and love and play; and many more in an hour or so would receive a terse message that life no longer needed them.[32]

These polarities eventually will be reconciled by Sean in the inversion of the Cathleen ni Houlihan image.

It is not merely the disappointed hopes of Irish resistance to British rule that colour the representation of Cathleen in the *Autobiographies*; more so, it is the effective splintering of the symbol that occurred as the Nationalist cause itself began to fragment, a phenomenon also portrayed in relation to the flag of the plough and the stars. Having been absorbed by the Nationalist cause, Sean Casside's references to Cathleen ni Houlihan are relatively traditional.[33] As personification of Ireland, the motivations and desires of the cause itself are projected onto her; as the Nationalist movement searches for relief from British dominion, so does she. The cause itself is never deserted, only Cathleen. Her way is indeed a thorny way, but primarily because of the punishment exacted on those who choose to betray her. Referring to the split in the Irish Citizen Army, Sean describes the fissure in the symbol itself:

> Now there were two Cathleen ni Houlihans running around Dublin: one, like the traditional, in green dress, shamrocks in her hair. . . . the other Cathleen coarsely dressed, hair a little tousled . . . vital and asurge with immortality.[34]

This fission in a central symbol of Irish myth is indicative of the social division which beset Ireland at the time, and which is portrayed with such tragic consequences.

A number of critics have read – and on occasion over-read – figures in O'Casey's plays as representatives of Cathleen ni Houlihan and, by extension, as personifications of Ireland.[35] In evaluating such readings, it is worthwhile to bear in mind Sean Casside's volatile relationship to symbols of mother-Ireland. For such arguments to be supported the particular character would need to provide within the structure of the play the space in which external social and familial dramas were played out. This I do not believe to be the case in any of the principal contenders for Cathleen ni Houlihan status – Mrs Breydon, Nora Clitheroe, Juno Boyle or even Mary Boyle. O'Casey's Cathleen is a vibrant, seductive, if at times disappointing figure. When rendered in terms of her failure to bring her myth to reality, she remains a rich, though ugly, incarnation. She is not stoical; nor does she move forward. This cannot be said of the women who emerge bruised, yet determined, from the conclusions of the plays. While they may, on occasion, be mercenary in their attitudes to their children's sacrifice, they are not rejuvenated by what they or their children have suffered. If they do offer allegories, of the Cathleen ni Houlihan myth, then they are weak allegories which do little more than suggest the counterfeit of the myth. I am more inclined to agree with Rollins, who argues that O'Casey's purpose in exploring the theme of renewal extends beyond the single figure of Cathleen ni Houlihan: 'O'Casey apparently laments modern man's reluctance to enter joyously into the rites of revivification which would redeem and revitalize both self and society – the sick soul and the modern wasteland.'[36] This broader reading of the renewal theme is supported by *Within the Gates*, a play which does not specifically deal with the Irish situation, yet still explores myths of death and resurrection: mother-earth renews herself in the opening scene; however, it is not until the final scene that, through the cyclical structure of the play, the audience learns that the source of renewal is the Young Woman's death. I would differ from Rollins only with respect to his use of the word 'reluctance'. While reluctance may be a factor, characters are generally prevented from entering into the renewal of self and society through an inability to determine how such a renewal may be effected without recourse to death and reckless sacrifice. The principal exception to this comes in *The Star Turns Red*, where renewal is suggested through the revitalization of a symbol – in this case that of the Christian star of Bethlehem. The mother has no part to play, represented as being caught in the past, still searching for the 'old' star, unable to see the social disintegration that is occurring around her.[37] The presence of the Woman with Baby – later named as Woman with Withering Baby – supports this reading: her opposition to Communism, and her arguments in favour of Catholicism and the nobility of the poor, are shown to be gradually taking the life of her child.

To read allegorically the powerful mother-figures of Bessie Burgess and Mrs Gogan in *The Plough and the Stars* reduces the complexity of the drama. When Bessie Burgess questions the legitimacy of Mrs Gogan's child it is not to uphold Christian morality, nor to reinforce the myth of the Virgin Mother, but it is to assert the moral weight of her own political arguments. Any reading of Bessie Burgess should be informed by recalling that the first mother-figure whose rich symbolism made an impact on the young Johnny Casside was not Cathleen ni Houlihan, but Victoria, an equally voracious mother-figure:

> Victoria is known as the Great White Mother by all the peoples under her sway, excludin' the Fenians cruelly callin' her the Famine Queen, but we'll never let the Fenians or the followers of Parnell be anything more than spouters at a meeting or two of singers of God Save Ireland.[38]

Bessie Burgess's pro-English sentiments mirror those of the Great White Mother, while Mrs Gogan, 'dipping her finger in the whiskey, and moistening with it the lips of her baby',[39] urges the Fenian cause. Even so, they personify not so much allegorical mother-figures as the political struggle represented in the play. And in allowing the mothers to compete on an equal basis, the respective politics of the Nationalists and the Loyalists are allowed to do the same: the Loyalist case is not hampered by being without a spokesperson for whom the audience will have some sympathy; and, further, the borders between the two sides of the debate are skilfully blurred. Nora Clitheroe's clash with the women at the barricade similarly challenges the premise that all mothers were prepared to offer their sons to be sacrificed: 'An' there's no woman gives a son or husband to be killed – if they say it, they're lying', lyin', against God, Nature, an' against themselves!'[40] Certainly, Nora herself shuns the role of Cathleen ni Houlihan, refusing to sanction her husband's sacrifice: to don the mantle of the maternal – as she does in terms of the play's iconography – is not necessarily to don the mantle of Cathleen. Nora's pregnancy, while suggestive of the 'terrible beauty' that is being born, proffers a child overwhelmed by the morass that is its mother's madness and disorientation. And given the general disintegration and chaos that is Dublin at the time of its birth, the child's chances of life, of achieving an independent identity, appear slim. Significantly, the chaos into which the child will be born is effected not merely in social terms – as a result of the Rising itself and the moral disintegration that ensues – but in symbolic terms, as the argument over the precise meaning of the central symbol of 'the plough and the stars' indicates.

What O'Casey essentially represents are mother-figures who, whether suffering, nurturing, drunk or offering refuge, are inherent to the social structures that exist and that are in the process of crumbling. The mother's own position in that society is itself being buried by rubble, and the role she has played is losing its relevance. To have any power to effect change in society, new myths are required and, by extension, a re-imaging of the mother-figure. Yet O'Casey does not depend on the mother-figure to bring about this symbolic 'rebirth'. Rather, he pins his faith on the transforming power of socialism to effect order from the chaos: 'The Red Star glows, and seems to grow bigger as the curtain falls.'[41]

With her or against her

It is not until late in the third volume of the *Autobiographies* that Sean Casside establishes a definite psychological break from his mother:

> She'd have to stick it, but he wouldn't. Her life was nearly over. She belonged to a different world, the world of submission, patience, resignation; he to that of discontent, resentment, resistance.... his life was away from her, and he'd have to leave her wandering in her little garden of Eden among the musk, the fuschia, and the crimson geranium.[42]

The catalyst for this disjunction between mother and son is Sean's review of his mother's life – the suffering she has experienced, her mute acceptance of the life she leads, her dreams of joy in another life – and his realization that unless he makes his break he is bound to live that same life. While he continues to live with her and to depend on her materially, Sean, through his writing and his association with various political organizations, works to establish an identity whose boundaries are a reaction not only to her life, but also to the life they shared as an interdependent unit. He represses submission in himself by over-attributing it to his mother.

Close interdependence between mother and child is most clearly evident in the *Autobiographies*. *I Knock at the Door* opens with one extended passage, broken only by semi-colons and colons, and structured on the page over seven paragraphs. It is the passage which brings the child into the world, and it may be that O'Casey is, in some way, seeking to mirror the birth process physically on the page; however, it is more likely that the opening – as Sean O'Faolain and Padraic Colum criticized with respect to a number of aspects of the texts – indicates undigested Joyce-isms.[43] While the initial image of *I Knock at the Door* centres on mother and son, and the mother's suffering in delivering the child, the principal effect of the opening is to establish the position of the mother-child dyad within a specific social context. The child may be pressed by the mother from her womb, but it is, as Krause argues, the narrator who creates that birth.[44] The child is born not to a family but to a society, encompassing literature, religion, faith and British dominion. It is a society which affords no notice to the woman in pain – the birth of the child is a marginal event. However, the opening passage, like the panoramic sweep of a film-camera, carries the reader back to the event that is the actual focus of the narrative – the birth of the hero – though the social context will be a current that continues both to buoy and to threaten the protagonist throughout the course of the six volumes. As Kenneally has noted – and as I have agued in 'Origin, Space, Opposition' – autobiography 'is primarily a process of self-definition at a given moment in time'.[45] The events of the past are selected and rendered in such a way as to give substance to that self-definition. It is in the child's relationship with the mother that the seeds of either rebellion or submission will be sown. From his first moment, Sean Casside is a rebel: 'but the round-bellied, waggle-headed, lanky-legged newborn latecomer kicked against the ambitions, needs and desires of others.'[46]

Apart from the *Autobiographies*, there is a surprising lack of intimacy between mothers and children in O'Casey's work. In *The Star Turns Red*, the Old Woman feels little more than pity for her murderer-son, Kian. Edgar, in *Oak Leaves and Lavender*, refers to his 'old, doting mother... old and dying mother', yet his reference to her merely reflects the lack of any other allegiances or meaning in his life.[47] Juno hardly understands her children and has difficulty communicating with them.[48] There is a distance between Mollser and Mrs Gogan, briefly traversed in private moments, that only Bessie Burgess makes any effective attempt to fill. The muted farewell between Harry Heegan and his mother in *The Silver Tassie* epitomizes the disinclination of mother and child to recognize the bond they once shared:

HARRY [*shyly and hurriedly kissing Mrs Heegan*]. Well, good-bye, old woman.

MRS HEEGAN. Good-bye my son.[49]

Mrs Heegan does, however, still claim possession. As I have argued above, her relationship with her son is mediated by economic concerns; and it is not until Act IV that any sense of interdependence is established. The mother's motives remain mercenary; yet, helpless and dependent, rejected by Barney and Jessie, and unable effectively to participate in the society that is represented at the Avondale Football Club, Harry seeks out a mother and a symbolic father: 'Dear God, this crippled form is still your child. [*To Mrs Heegan.*] Dear mother, this helpless thing is still your son.'[50] It remains ambiguous as to whether he is seeking his mother's assistance – recognizing that he must renegotiate the oedipal as a result of his loss of identity – or bewailing the realization of a (physical) dependence which positions him as 'child'.

In *Juno and the Paycock*, son and husband are handicapped, infantilized by their dependence on their 'mother', and on the mother's reluctance to forgo that dependence. It is perhaps not surprising that O'Casey, in his first staged work featuring a mother-figure, fell back on a paradigm that had already been widely explored by writers such as Joyce and Moore. The arguments, and general to-and-fro, between Juno and Boyle result in little more than stasis. Boyle's conversations with Joxer, as Williams argues, are indicative of men 'avoiding experience'; they are engaging in 'verbal inflation that covers [evasion]'[51] and Juno, in refusing to shake Boyle loose, contributes as much as anyone to this avoidance. As a number of critics have noted, despite an overlay of humour, Boyle is a bitter and harsh man, and the suggestion is that he suffers from the same affliction as characters such as Little Chandler, Shemus Rua, Ralph Ede and Farrington.[52] Charles Bentham's good news, a space for which is created by Juno's continual hushing of Boyle, further delays Boyle's break from Juno-as-mother: 'You won't have to trouble about a job for awhile, Jack.'[53] It is only when Juno leaves with Mary at the close of the play that, it is implied, Boyle will now be forced to assume responsibility for his own actions. Yet the conclusion of the play – or at least Juno's construction of it – suggests that failure is imminent: 'Let your father furrage for himself now; I've done all I could an' it was all no use – he'll be hopeless till the end of his days.'[54] Yet the question remains as to whether Juno leaves because she can no longer bear to support a dependent and indolent husband, or whether she refuses to accept the authority her husband has attempted to wield in insisting that Mary be banished from the house. Juno's own refuge will be amongst women, with the child who will be dependent on her as (second) mother; and, in this, it can be argued that Juno is thinking not so much of the child's well-being – there stands at the conclusion of the play the implicit suggestion that the child will be burdened with the guilt emanating from two 'suffering mothers' – but of the opportunity the child affords for her to reprise her role as central figure in the family drama.

One effect of constructing an interdependence between mother and child is that it affords an origin from which one or other – mother and/ or child – might develop their own subjective histories. The suffering mother particularly is able to anchor the individual within a social order in which they are subjugated and which, importantly, they may seek to resist. Such resistance is essential to the social revolution that O'Casey espoused. However, in moving the suffering mother away from her position of dominance, O'Casey also shifts responsibility for the paralysis and turgidity of Irish society. If the mother is no longer centred, if the child is no longer bound to her as a result of her suffering, she should no longer bear the major portion of blame for the crippled Irish society and imagination that he and other writers consistently represent. Responsibility must lie elsewhere. But where? The answer lies in the social order in which such mothers come to be constructed.

When Sean Casside observes his mother at his sister Ella's death-bed, he proffers a classic portrait of the suffering mother, and one which serves to enhance the author's own self-portrait:

> There she stood, whimpering too, and shaking with the ceaseless delicate shivering of an aspen-tree. When he looked more closely, he saw that she was breaking, that she was shivering herself into an acknowledged old age at last.[55]

Echoed here is Ayamonn Breydon's portrait of his own mother in *Red Roses for Me*, one which lavishly paints the sacrifices his mother has made on his behalf. Yet it is a portrait that is painted not so much for his mother's sake as to establish his own desired space, one whose parameters depend on her position as suffering, sacrificial mother:

> when it was dark, you always carried the sun in your hand for me; when you suffered me to starve rather than thrive towards death in an institution, you gave me life to play with as a richer child is given a coloured ball.[56]

The child embellishes the mother's suffering and sacrifice in order to construct for themselves a desired social position. The Young Woman in *Within the Gates* refuses to acknowledge any debt arising from her mother's suffering, instead using her mother to enhance her own position as object of pity; Sean Casside utilizes the symbol of the suffering mother in order to represent himself as working-class champion; Ayamonn Breydon uses the same symbol to create a position for himself as sensitive artist and working-class martyr, rehearsing the close relationship between himself and his mother, affording from that construction his own self-definition: 'I am drifting away from you, Mother, a dim shape now, in a gold canoe, dipping over a far horizon.'[57] There is a suggestion here of Stephen Dedalus's relationship with his mother, though O'Casey's rendering lacks the complexities of Joyce's *Portrait*. O'Casey renders in the relationship between Ayamonn and Mrs Breydon an almost parasitic co-dependence from which Ayamonn himself is not willing to break free completely. Ayamonn speaks explicitly of draining the mother of her strength and youth, reminiscent of Moore's description of the relationship between Esther Waters and her infant child. Yet, at the same time, Ayamonn blames his mother for his own demise, for offering all she has to her child. This is the child speaking, binding the mother to himself through his words, praising and romanticizing her sacrifices, seducing from her even greater sacrifices: 'My back can bear many a heavy burden; and my eyes, dimmer now than once they were can still see far enough.'[58] No longer is it merely the mother demanding service. This becomes clear when Mrs Breydon moves to offer her services to another in greater need, and Ayamonn objects vehemently: 'You think more of other homes than you do of your own!'[59] The sub-text of this objection substitutes 'sons' for 'homes'. It is only when a surrogate-mother arrives, in the form of Sheila, that Ayamonn releases his mother. Ironically, it is mother and mother-surrogate who are united before the rector in Act IV, not Ayamonn and Sheila as husband and wife.

The relationship of Sean and Mrs Casside should be read in terms of the relationship of Ayamonn and Mrs Breydon. One is paradigm for the other.[60] Sean constructs himself in opposition to his mother, and in order for him to play the rebel the only role available to her is that of submission. Johnny Casside, handicapped by eye disease, is unusually dependent on his mother: she feeds him, speaks for him, dresses him, helps him to sleep and function, and offers him a refuge from pain. When Johnny's father dies, she is freed to bring him up in her own faith and not that of his father. Her failure to see Johnny move within his father's authority, a fact which further binds the child to her, is evident at

Mr Casside's funeral. Mrs Casside defies both the child's duty to his father, and symbolic custom, by kissing the dead Mr Casside on her son's behalf. Both literally and metaphorically, she intervenes between father and son, between son and authority. She allows her son to shun the social and symbolic structures that kissing his father represents. Mother and son come to share an intimate, poetic world of colours and questions. As Ayling recognizes, the child's questions not only feed his imagination, but provide the basis by which he may continually question authority,[61] thereby threatening his ability to fully enter into that authority, into that symbolic order, as subject. This is exacerbated by the mother's equivocation in terms of subjecting her son to the authority of the Protestant Church, ultimately defying the dictates of the Minister by keeping her son with her at home. With his father's death, mother and son share their sorrow, just as they have shared an egg at the funeral supper; and it is this ability to empathize with sorrow which will see the young Johnny attracted to the songs and myths of the tram conductor: ' "Who was Wolfe Tone, Ma?" whispered Johnny, moved strangely by seeing tears trickling down the cheeks of the conductor as he sang.'[62] Significantly, Johnny's empathy with the tram conductor occurs when the progress of mother and son is impeded and threatened by the milling crowd, when they are stalled by social and political circumstances and the clash of ideologies. Even so, at this stage of his development, the child is unable to embrace the conductor's discourse and retreats instead into the bosom of his mother: 'Johnny shrank back and pressed close to his mother, feeling her body shudder deep as she saw.'[63]

Ultimately, however, Mrs Casside is neither able to cure Sean's afflictions nor occupy with him that space in the symbolic order in which he will realize his desired subjectivity. She affords him the space and silence in which to indulge in imaginative reveries, but not the signifying practices by which these reveries may be reified. Her own ambivalent allegiance to Church and Nation create a division and confusion in Johnny's own allegiances and in his understanding of the social milieu in which he finds himself. It is Johnny's own demand to have his curiosity satisfied that sees his mother begin to diminish in terms of her role in his development: 'he tried to share all these sights with his mother; but he saw they had but a timid and feebly-whispered message for her.'[64] He will continue to rely on her to feed him, to groom him, to house him, but he will seek answers to his questions from other sources. Beyond her threshold she will, effectively, no longer exist. Caught in a mêlée that reminds him of the night of the illuminations, he can only remember 'when he last saw such a sight he was safe on the top of a tram, warm and confident, close to his mighty mother's side'.[65] Without her as refuge, without the dim certainty of their intimacy and interdependence, and without a clear social or symbolic space in which he may exist, Sean is overwhelmed by the uncertainty of competing religious and nationalist symbols. It is a confusion Sean Casside shares with other characters in O'Casey's writing, figures for whom there is no intimate, nourishing relationship with the mother into which they may submerge themselves. Significantly, these figures are rarely offered the alternative of a strong father-figure in whose image they may begin to construct their own social and subjective histories. Charting a way through the confusion that results from these lacks and absences is the focus not only of the *Autobiographies* themselves, but of much of O'Casey's work.

'The faith me mother taught me...'

'The faith me mother taught me is the faith for the men of Maynooth':[66] this simple creed, reported with some irony in *Inishfallen, Fare Thee Well*, tallies with the representation of the mother-figure in Irish religious and nationalist discourses, and suggests the construction of the mother-figure that writers such as Joyce and Moore used in exploring the social and imaginative stasis of Ireland. However, the mothers in O'Casey's work do not take up this position: they do not place themselves between father and child with a view to bringing the child to the father and baptizing that child in its father's name. When Johnny Boyle, in romantic terms, proclaims the Irish cause – 'Ireland only half free'll never be at peace while she has a son left to pull a trigger' – his mother neither opposes him nor cheers him. Her response is both sardonic and pragmatic, undercutting the romantic imagery: 'To be sure, to be sure – no bread's a lot betther than half a loaf.'[67] In O'Casey, as in other writers I have examined here, the familial father is either weak, indolent or absent; he is in no position to assert the authority that will become the focus of social or symbolic structures. Yet, equally, he does not offer viable alternatives. The child is left in a kind of limbo, with no 'mother' with whom he shares an interdependence and with no clear authority figure in whose 'name' he will be able to construct successfully his own identity. Of course, there are examples, in plays such as *The Plough and the Stars*, *Within the Gates*, *Red Roses for Me* and *The Star Turns Red*, where 'children' have found the 'name-of-the-father' in Communist, Fascist or Labour movements, and Nationalist or British loyalties. However, in each of these plays, O'Casey consistently implies the inherent weakness of these ideologies, and their weakness stems directly from their inability to effect that social change which has, as its primary imperative, the alleviation of the oppression suffered by the working classes: 'What's th' use o' freedom, if its not economic freedom?'[68] Further, concomitant to these allegiances, there is a negation of the individual – an effect starkly evident in Act II of *The Silver Tassie* and throughout *The Star Turns Red* – a result which effectively defeats the purpose of the child's search for a 'father'.[69] It is only the Communist movement that emerges relatively unscathed, not surprising given that the 'economic freedom' of the proletariat was its stated aim: as far as Sean Casside is concerned the 'terrible beauty had been born [in the Soviet Union], and not in Ireland'.[70] He suggests nothing of the mother who brought that 'terrible beauty' to birth.

*

Sean Casside's question, What is Truth? is not answered in the context of O'Casey's plays or prose. The foundations of the social order are destroyed and the promised renewal – the renewal which would affirm truth – does not eventuate. His writing confirms the crisis of faith that was central to modernism, but is unable to offer any cogent alternative by which the fragmentation of social and symbolic structures might be induced to gel or be reintegrated within a new construction that would deliver the hope promised by these various faiths and free, not merely soul, but mind and body as well.

The social upheaval that engulfed Ireland, particularly its intensification during the first few decades of the twentieth century, is reflected in the clash of religious, political and social ideals, and the impotence of traditional symbols as a means of comprehending social chaos. In this context, the mother-figure, herself either ambivalent in her own faith or unable to see that the social order, and her traditional role in it, has collapsed, is no longer a central consideration. She stands aside while the social and symbolic orders, in which she has no power to intervene, are reconstituted. In metaphorical terms, she is made to watch while the 'names-of-the-father' battle for supremacy, the victor earning the right to command authority and institute not only the mother's new position within signification, but also the signifying practices by which their authority will be endorsed and strengthened.

The mother-figure has a role to play in the rebirth of social and symbolic orders, but it is a role which will be determined according to the needs of the new régime. This is seen most clearly in Sean Casside's own construction of his mother, which represents the mother as not merely submissive to social circumstances but to symbolic constructions; as resigned to her role as a mother struggling against poverty and surviving through her hardships. It is the part she is required to play. Mrs Casside comes to embody the daily battle of the poor against their social circumstances, their constant stoicism and good spirits. It is a romanticized portrayal, as suggested by descriptions such as 'filling the house with the incense of poverty':[71] in his effort to represent the essential nobility and worth of the working classes, O'Casey instead imbues poverty with a sweet fragrance, an exotic aura, which tends to undermine the genuine suffering he seeks to depict in both his drama and prose. In the restoration of social order – a restoration that never actually occurs within the context of the plays – it is implied that the mother-figure must subject herself to whatever construction such order demands if it is to be sustained. This suggests that it is submission to the roles constructed for her – both in her own actions and the representation of those actions – which extends the life of otherwise decrepit social and representational systems. And she must submit, for she is afforded no space from which she may offer resistance. Further, and more importantly, her submission to these roles serves to seduce her children into those same social and representational systems, binding them within a subjectivity where they are not only unable to question the authority to which they are subject, but which, in offering them an identity, serves to deny them their individuality.

The demythologization of the mother-figure that O'Casey undertakes cannot be divorced from his disappointment in Cathleen ni Houlihan's failure to deliver the promises inherent in her myth. In her moment of truth, she fails; and, in his plays, he proceeds to unveil similar myths which only serve to imprison the people in cycles of violence, wasted sacrifice and poverty. O'Casey implies that the myths which embody various mother-figures, whether those of religious lore, Irish tradition or archetypes which have served religious, Nationalist or Loyalist discourses, have locked Irish society into conditioned responses, responses which, in the scenarios he presents, are no longer effective in maintaining order and only exacerbate social disintegration. Yet, in exploding the basis of these myths and, as a consequence, in moving the mother-figure out of the focus, he is at a loss to suggest any viable alternative. The Communist faith towards which his plays increasingly move does not, at least for the present-day reader, inspire confidence. In terms of the mother-figure such a faith would construct, she is no less draped in myth, she is no less required to be submissive to society's demands, and she is not significantly different from that mother-figure O'Casey has worked so hard in his plays and prose to deconstruct. Of even greater significance, she embodies the potential to imprison the individual as securely as those mother-figures she would displace.

Part IV
Symbolic Spaces

Modernism and the Maternal: Appropriation of the Mother's Space and the Breakdown of the Symbolic

Fragmentation, splitting, crisis, rupture, flux, historical pressure, chaos, the city, the metaphoric, the self-conscious: all are terms commonly associated with modernist texts; and all can be traced to transgression of the liminal spaces which mark off the patriarchal cultural tradition from that which threatens it. It is what Marcia Ian refers to as a rejection of the symbolic, 'the breakdown of narrative conventions and their replacement by simultaneism and epiphany'.[1] Bradbury and McFarlane, in their survey of modernism, refer to the 'breaking away from familiar functions of language and conventions of form', a breakaway largely caused, in their estimation, by the 'strain' of the historical.[2] To this I would add the strain of the interpersonal, the psychological and the cultural. Wilson, tracing modernism to nineteenth-century French symbolism, emphasizes the effect on literary convention of 'metaphors detached from their subjects'.[3] Other critics cite the revivification of language and myth as one of the seminal properties of modernism, the '[refusal of] the great public mythologies of our time and . . . [the evolution of] rival myths . . . some grandiose and comprehensive, some esoteric and private, but none with any status in the world of organized scientific and historical knowledge by which the world conducts its business'.[4] Heath argues that:

> What is at stake in the work of modernism . . . is a focus on the productivity of language, its determining role in the very fact of 'reality', that recasts the understanding of language, looks at its construction of social and subjective, all the orders of meaning that are in play at any moment in the construction of our reality.[5]

In transgressing liminal spaces, in bringing within cultural tradition that which is repressed, modernism effected an essential renewal of language, myth and, more generally, representation.

Artistic expression – representation – is, as Kristeva's work insists, 'a kind of index of social stability'.[6] Texts produced by and within any particular culture will either reinforce or resist that culture; crises in representation may be mapped against social and cultural crises. Just such a correlation between social and symbolic transformation is evident in Ireland in the early decades of the twentieth century. As I indicated in 'Rebellion and Revolution', the conflicts which gripped Ireland during these years were as much a matter of seeking cultural independence as political independence. The need to overcome the English cultural and political hegemony could be read as a desire to 'slay' the British 'father' and replace 'him' with an authority whose origins were firmly anchored in Irish cultural traditions, and in whom the Irish people could just as firmly anchor their own origins. Yet to achieve this shift in patrilineage a mother, herself subject to that Irish father, herself constructed within Irish myth and fable, must first be encountered. To be subject to the desired father necessitated first dissolving subjectivity within an Irish mother, a mother-Ireland. Yet, as writers such as O'Casey, Moore and Joyce emphasize, such a transformation is doomed to defeat when there is no effective father within either Irish society or Irish lore, and when the dominant mother-figures within Irish discourse insist on the death of the child in order to preserve their own status.

Because the campaign for political independence was so firmly allied with cultural self-determination – as movements such as the Gaelic League, the Irish Literary Society and the Gaelic Athletics Association attest – it is perhaps not surprising that serious breaches in the social fabric – from Parnell's death to the Easter Rising and beyond – should be accompanied by radical incursions upon the symbolic order. And just as the sacrifice of self to a mythical mother-Ireland, affording rebirth within a new Irish political hegemony, provided the paradigm for social revolution, so too dissolution in the maternal afforded the conditions for the radicalization of the symbolic: 'In times of "rupture, renovation and revolution"... the symbolic is no longer capable of directing the semiotic energies into already coded social outlets.... The avant-garde text draws attention to its own repressed conditions.'[7] The pervasiveness and intensity of both the mother-Ireland paradigm and maternal archetypes – such as that of the suffering mother and the destroying mother – within the Irish cultural tradition is far from coincidental with the flourishing of Irish modernism. Oblation was demanded to God and to Ireland only implicitly; explicitly, sacrifice was to be made at the mother's altar. It was a model of the family dynamic from which no Irish man or woman could escape; it could, however, be eluded if it was enacted not in literal but in symbolic terms. It is such an elusion that is evident in Irish modernism and through which, with mixed success, the Irish modernists – Yeats, Synge, Joyce and O'Casey – sought to reconstitute the symbolic order and their own (creative) space within that order.

Maternal disruption of the symbolic

According to Lacan, it is only through the existence of the symbolic order, as structured by the 'name-of-the-father', that the imaginary order and indeed the mother–child dyad can actually be said to exist. The irony of this is that while the dyad suggests an inclusive world of mutual dependence, it is only able to be represented because of the existence of the very thing which will seek to intervene and destroy it.[8] In submerging their subjectivity within a maternal space, in order to access that realm where signification is disrupted and precarious, the Irish modernists had to engage with those mothers privileged by nationalist and religious discourses. At the same time, they were unable to deny the perversion of this mother-figure who prevailed within Irish society: the mother whose infantilization of both (familial) father and children muted resistance to the social and symbolic orders. Their own relationship with the mother-figure was played out within the context of not only competing discourses, but competing allegiances to Church, Nation, family and self.

What Lacan's theory also emphasizes is that the mother-child dyad can never be known in its 'reality': it will always be constructed within and by a cultural tradition; and it is as much the recognition of the absence of the 'true' mother-child relationship, as the recognition of the absence of the mother herself, from which symbolization stems. In seeking to recover the mother, and his relationship to her, the artist must infringe the interstices of the semiotic-symbolic. If, as Kristeva argues, '[language] as symbolic function constitutes itself at the cost of repressing instinctual drive and continuous relation to the mother',[9] then the subversion of language should, in a sense, recover the mother of the 'true' mother-child dyad by foregrounding her – if only fugitively – in consciousness. In finding her, the artist also finds the mirror in which his own unconstructed self is situated. And here, within a

pre-oedipal paradigm, the artist also recovers 'the presymbolic foundation of language in the rhythms, sensations and spasm of infantile
experience'.[10]

There is nothing, however, to insist that this channel between the
subversion of language and access to the pre-oedipal flows in one direction. If the disruption of the symbolic order affords access to the mother
then, equally, immersion in the mother – and particularly the search for
the 'true' mother within the constructed mother – should loosen the
framework of the symbolic order. The artist, in deconstructing the
mother privileged within the cultural tradition, discovers, I suggest, a
way into the pre-oedipal, such that he is able to access the semiotic, that
space of 'textual instability'.[11] Such a deconstruction of the privileged,
constructed mother is evident in the work of all the writers I have
examined here, with the degree of deconstruction, of demythologization and even destruction of the mother-figure tending to correlate with
the 'textual instability' of the various works. Compare, for example,
Oliver Gogarty's gentle awakening to the constraints of Catholic discourse, realized through his relationship with Nora Glynn, to Stephen
Dedalus's destruction of 'The Mother' in the 'Circe' episode of *Ulysses*. In
both cases, the response to the mother parallels the disruption to signification effected within the texts.

The later work of James Joyce figures prominently in literary criticism
as one of the principal exemplars of textual instability, and, in terms of
his perversion of literary traditions, he is probably the least 'subtle'
among the Irish modernists: that is, he so visibly – particularly within
Ulysses and *Finnegans Wake* – violates expectations in terms of language
and narrative structure that there often does not seem to be any need to
read beyond him in order to explore the tears in the symbolic through
which the semiotic bleeds. Yet what my exploration of the representation of the mother-figure suggests is that disruptions of the symbolic
occur in a much more artful way than merely through the disturbance
of form and language, as seminal as such disturbances are. It is necessary
to broaden our understanding of symbolic disturbance, particularly in
terms of how such disturbances manifest themselves. Form and language are insistent indicators; however, it is crucial to look also to
renderings of history, of personal narrative, of patrilineage and, I
argue, to the subtle shifts in the representation of figures inherent to
those myths upon which discourse draws. That Nora Clitheroe did not
mirror Padraic Pearse's mother in her actions and, importantly, her
suffering; that Stephen Dedalus addressed his *non serviam* not only to
God but to his suffering mother, epitome of the Blessed Virgin; that

Synge's *The Tinker's Wedding* could not be performed in Ireland in his lifetime; that the Mother of God, in Yeats's poem of the same name, stressed the very mediocrity upon which the miracle was bestowed: all are manifestations of profound symbolic disturbance. My reading, therefore, extends symbolic breakdown beyond the narrow confines explored, for example, by many psychoanalytic theorists, and emphasizes its exposition not only in writers such as Yeats, Synge and O'Casey, but in Joyce's *A Portrait of the Artist as a Young Man* and *Dubliners*. In drawing on constructions of the mother-figure which hold the symbolic in place, and in both exposing and resisting those constructions, the artist does not merely problematize discourse: he exposes the 'true' mother repressed by discourse, and the maternal spaces in which the potential for both symbolic disruption and regeneration lurks. It is within these spaces that the artist – most notably Yeats and Joyce – seeds his own creativity. This is the 'destructive genesis' to which Kristeva refers.[12]

Destructive genesis

Kristeva locates the splitting inherent to the semiotic in the very act of falling pregnant: 'Pregnancy seems to be experienced as the radical ordeal of the splitting of the subject: redoubling up of the body, separation and coexistence of the self and of an other, of nature and consciousness, of physiology and speech.'[13] The subsumption of the maternal space by the artist exposes him to that same splitting, a rupture that is realized not only in the artist's relationship with his art, but in the fissure of signification. And it is within this space that rebirth is predicated: 'In returning, through the event of death, towards that which produces its break; in exporting semiotic motility across the border on which the symbolic is established, the artist sketches out a kind of second birth.'[14] That is, after his immersion within the semiotic, the artist, still firmly welded to the symbolic, carries back into the symbolic order traces of that capriciousness and fluidity in signification that is inherent to the semiotic. These traces linger on the threshold between the semiotic and the symbolic, corrupting signification. It is in this way that 'destructive genesis' is realized: symbolic structures are destroyed in the passage from the symbolic to the semiotic, and reconstructed, reborn, with the act of returning.

The artist's infiltration of maternal spaces, therefore, affords him a privileged position in terms of the process of regeneration. It not only frees him, if only fleetingly, of the strictures imposed by the symbolic order, it allows him to bear himself the (repressed) 'Word': myth, history, patrilineage, figuration are (re)borne by him. And, in this, his own place within the paternal cultural tradition is refigured: 'the most intense revelation of God...is given only to a person who assumes himself as "maternal"'.[15] Writing from within his own maternal space – mother not only to his work but to a radicalized cultural tradition – the artist's investment in the (re)figuration of the mother must, I suggest, appreciate considerably.

7
Playing Her Part Too Well: the Mother and Her Construct in Yeats, 1917–39

Prior to *The Wild Swans at Coole*, Yeats's utilization of the mother-figure facilitated his exploration of processes of mythologization, and his elaboration of the means by which social and symbolic orders are both sustained and subverted. The development of his work saw a concomitant development in the subtlety of the mother-figure's operation within the text. The poems embellished a focus on the mother's social function with themes of the mother's mediation between conflicting symbolic orders, her creative function, and her weaving, and 'wearing', of those narrative structures by which her child's place may be determined. Further, Yeats's exploration and elaboration of the maternal metaphor – and, on occasion, his assumption of a maternal space – meliorated his engagement with issues of creativity.

What becomes clear in Yeats's work from *The Wild Swan at Coole* and beyond is the degree to which his engagement with the mother-figure shifted. Trends evident in the early work dissipated as the mother-figure was caught up in Yeats's broader themes of exposing the essential ambiguities inherent in Truth, the resistance of cultural constructions and the explication of Ireland's political turmoil. Developments in Yeats's representation of the mother-figure after *Responsibilities* paralleled, therefore, a change in trajectory of Yeats's own artistic concerns.

'...this flesh I purchased with my pains'

In 'Shepherd and Goatherd', the image of the suffering mother overwhelms the son's memory; memories of the son – the original focus of the poem – fade as the (living) mother's suffering is eternalized:

> How does she bear her grief? There is not a shepherd
> But grows more gentle when he speaks her name,
> . . .
> She goes about her house erect and calm
> Between the pantry and the linen-chest,
> Or else at meadow or at grazing overlooks
> Her labouring man, as though her darling lived.[1]

The paeans of the shepherd and goatherd – and the embodiment of the son contained therein – are left at the mother's door:

> To know the mountain and the valley have grieved
> May be a quiet thought to wife and mother,
> And children when they spring up shoulder high.[2]

Considerations of the nature of memory and subjectivity, of the mark an individual makes within a particular context, are embellished through the figure of the mother and the propensity of that mother to appropriate the tribute due to her dead child. Yet what is of particular significance in Yeats's rendering of the mother-figure is that it is not merely the mother's grief which centres her within the poem – she is centred because she corresponds – or is perceived to correspond – to the image of the suffering mother privileged within the cultural tradition. Essentially, this is the paradox towards which Yeats is moving: the cultural tradition is reinforced not merely because the mother acts (or reacts) according to that construction of the mother-figure reinforced by the cultural tradition, but also because those who have been inculcated by the discourses which define that cultural tradition are unable to read her in any other way. Cranly, in Joyce's *A Portrait of the Artist as a Young Man*, is a potent example of the child who can read the mother-figure only according to those codes sanctioned by Catholic discourse – he advises Stephen of the appropriate response to his mother's suffering, yet it is a reading Stephen resists. It is just this resistance which Yeats promotes through his exploration of the means by which such constructions are elaborated within discourse and myth.

The demystification of the suffering mother is acutely evident in 'The Mother of God', the title of which immediately suggests the sufferings of Mary that are enveloped within the Christian myth and which the simple phrase 'the mother of God' evokes.[3] The 'Mother of God' is allowed to speak her own experience, becoming thereby both subject and object of the poem. This is in stark contrast to other suffering mothers, most notably Mrs Dedalus, who maintains the allure of suffering through her stoical silence. Yet, in speaking herself, the 'Mother of God' reveals the ordinary considerations that influence her perception of the divine conception, and actively makes herself the centre of both this experience and, by extension, the entire experience of Christian suffering. The repetition of 'my' in the final stanza supports this point:

> What is this flesh I purchased with my pains,
> This fallen star my milk sustains,
> This love that makes my heart's blood stop[4]

The self-centredness of the speaker contrasts with the service and self-lessness with which the figure of 'the mother of God' is traditionally imbued, and our reading of that figure is, accordingly, modified.[5]

In 'Among School Children' – a poem which challenges the notion of a received Truth by establishing relativities between truths – tension exists between the suffering mother and the child who is bound to her. Within a context that sets an instinctual experience of the world against the 'long schoolroom' of a more indoctrinary mode of learning, the speaker utilizes the image of mother and child to assert that humanity opens itself to experience because it cannot foresee the pain and uncertainty that experience may bring:

> What youthful mother, a shape upon her lap
> . . .
> Would think her son, did she but see that shape
> With sixty or more winters on its head,
> A compensation for the pang of his birth,
> Of the uncertainty of his setting forth?[6]

That Yeats should choose such an image to enhance his theme suggests a recognition of the differentiation between the maternal instinct which impels the mother to bear a child and the cultural tenets by which that instinct is manipulated. The gap between the 'youthful mother' and her older incarnation parallels that between the pre-oedipal mother and that mother constructed by the paternal cultural tradition: the older incarnation has no relationship with her child bar that sanctioned by the dominant discourse, and the child, delivered to that same symbolic order, can represent mother and child in no other terms than that of the suffering mother and the guilt the child is, thereby, required to bear. Mother and child are suspended within the same cultural construction – a suspension highlighted in the structure of the stanza – and the tension within the stanza is enhanced by the dual perspectives of mother and son.[7] It is a tension which Yeats does not resolve, but one which, none the less, exposes the complexities that exist in terms of the operation of the archetype, and the impotency of merely 'setting forth' in order to escape.

'Two natures blent'

Yeats, in 'Among School Children', writes of 'two natures blent . . . / Into the yolk and white of the one shell'.[8] While ostensibly referring to the speaker's own relationship with 'Helen', the use of the adjective 'Ledaean', and the context of 'mothers' and 'children' in which the image figures, suggests the close interdependence of mother and child. The images of mother and child suggest both a peaceful coexistence, as well as the dangers inherent in such a close physical and psychical relationship. Inevitably, a tension – unresolved and, perhaps, unresolvable – develops from these two aspects of the mother–child bond.

The interdependence of the mother and child stems from the child's conception and development in the mother's womb: 'Lullaby', for example, suggests the peace which emanates from the sustenance the mother offers; and in the final stanza of 'The Mother of God' there is both the sustenance the child receives from the mother, and also the profound sense of destiny that the mother receives from the child, a destiny which has, in many ways, allowed her to position herself at the centre of the poem. 'A Nativity' offers a similar image of mother and child: 'What woman hugs her infant there?'[9] Yet there is within the poem a somewhat darker elaboration of the mother–child bond: the bond is touched by the absent father, indelibly present in the child. Within the artist's image of a nativity scene, and within the gaze of mother and child, a vital antipathy is introduced: 'Why is the woman terror-struck? / Can there be mercy in that look?'[10] In developing this image through the use of two questions, and by not answering those questions, the antipathy between mother and child is allowed to stand. In 'A Nativity' the source of the mother's terror, and the uncertainty of the (promised) mercy of the child, are not explicitly addressed, but I suggest that the only source the construction of the poem allows is their mutual gaze, as implied in the final couplet: it is the child himself who induces the mother's terror, and the mother herself who occasions questions as to the child's mercy. Yeats's rendering of the image allows mother and child to gaze one upon the other, enhancing rather than alleviating the antipathy; and it is through this gaze – at once intimate and repelling – that the ambiguity inherent in the image is emphasized. Yet it is important to realize that what the poem contends is that this ambiguity is present in constructions of the Madonna and child image. Further, it is by that *construction* that mother and child are bound, rather than by any filial bonds. Poems such as 'Among School Children' and 'A Prayer for My Son' suggest the reasons why the child's mercy is questioned, particularly in the image presented of the child struggling to escape the 'ignominy' of his dependence on his mother, and of the physical needs, demands and bonds that this dependence accentuates.[11] In addition to the 'ignominy' represented as arising from the child's dependence on the mother, there is a sense of the lack of subjectivity, of any sense of self or self-definition, that arises from the close mother– child bond. The child lacks 'articulate speech'; he is little more than a 'shape upon her lap'.[12]

Yeats's most elusive exploration of the mother–child bond comes in 'What Magic Drum?'. A poem overflowing with ambiguities – largely as a result of its use of pronouns to represent two, three or more separate figures – it has, as Bloom notes, 'been read by Ellmann as the visit of a bestial father to see his offspring by a human mother and read by Whitaker as an act of occult possession in which Ribh opens himself to a transcendental force, the offspring thus being a revelation'. Bloom himself refers to the 'trinity... of a male, Primordial Motherhood (not necessarily Eve), and the child'.[13] Various configurations of this trinity are put forward as being represented by the unidentified figures who inhabit the poem. I differ significantly from these critics in that I interpret the two stanzas as distinct, and read only two figures within the poem – Primordial Motherhood existing only as a trace within one of the two figures. There is no direct flow-on from one stanza to another; rather, one stanza comments upon the other. The first stanza is that which encapsulates the mother–child bond, and Yeats uses this bond as the paradigm for his representation of lovers.[14] There are two figures present – one identified as male, the other identified only as 'the child'. The 'him' of the first line could be read as referring to either of the pair, and the ambiguity between them corresponds with what I have argued is the basis of the mother–child bond, that of interdependence and the identification of 'self' in the other. Yet this is not an image of mother and child as such. Instead, it is lovers who take on these roles within that paradigm of love that figures in a number of the poems. 'Primordial Motherhood' governs the lovers' relationship, and is present in the trace of the mother–child bond each of the figures experienced in their own infancy. What the poem suggests is the repetition of the mother–child bond in the relationships individuals form throughout their lives, and the breaking down of the borders of self that occurs in such relationships. And it is here that there exists the potential to access the pre-symbolic.

In the second stanza of the poem a contrasting image is offered. The speaker takes us beyond civilization into a more primitive, less 'enlightened' world.[15] Here lust dominates. The relationship is bestial, sensual, base, far from that predicated by the figure of the primordial mother. What is also suggested, however, is that while one explicitly leaves desire unsatisfied, the other, implicitly, presents no such impediment to the relationship.

Structurally and thematically, the poem is dominated by unanswered questions. As in 'Among School Children', the tension between contraries is exposed and left unresolved; and in this the poem reflects an enduring strain between idealized love – reified within culture in the image of mother and child – and a more uncivilized, innate form of bond, one not explicated within culture: 'What beast has licked its young?'[16] Essentially, 'What Magic Drum?' falls within that poetic convention which sets nature against culture; yet it does not allow resolution. It holds nature and culture uneasily apart.

While 'What Magic Drum?' addresses the trace of the mother–child bond as the paradigm for mature relationships, particularly those between lovers, another important aspect of this bond is explored – the recurrence of the mother in the child, that child being, more often than not, a daughter. In 'Nineteen Hundred and Nineteen' ownership of, and responsibility for, the 'daughters' actions is attributed to Herodias. This ownership does, however, appear to be confined to those actions that are destructive or subversive, actions that occasion sterility or regression in society, and does not include those whose portents are to be felt within future generations. In these latter cases, ownership is established by the father, with the mother's trace all but banished.[17] In 'Among School Children', where there exists a degree of ambivalence in the speaker's representation of the 'Helen' figure, the mother is not entirely excluded, but exists as 'descriptor' of the daughter: 'a Ledaean body', the daughter is represented in relation to the mother, as embodying something, if not all, of her.[18] This image is extended further in 'To a Young Girl', where the mother's legacy lives, as a potential, within the daughter. While the poem is addressed to the girl, the subject of the poem is the girl's mother, and the speaker's relationship with her.[19] The speaker links mother and daughter, and the basis of this link is the effects of their 'heart beats'. The girl's course in life is predetermined by the speaker to be the same as that her mother enacted on him: the capitulation of the man to the woman's pleasure, the subjugation of the man to the woman's will. Even so, the speaker indicates his own responsibility for the effect of her 'wild thought', for it was he who did as he was bid by breaking his heart 'for her'. There is a reciprocity inherent in the relationship; yet the male, as speaker, projects blame more successfully towards the woman than towards himself. And this blame is carried through the generations of women, marking even those daughters the 'young girl' will bear. Significantly, it is only by representing the 'woman' as 'mother' that Yeats is able to achieve this sense of a recurring legacy, that legacy being woman's ability sexually to torment man.

What is also implied in 'To a Young Girl' is that the perpetuation of the mother occasions no threat to established social or symbolic orders: the relationship between man and woman remains the same because there is no distinction in time or space between mother and daughter. The mother's role in determining the child's destiny is elaborated in 'Wisdom'. The poem places the mother-figure not merely at the centre of an iconography, but as integral to the construction of that iconography.[20] Further, the symbolic structure (which provides the foundation for the iconography of the poem, and of which the child's elaborate clothing is an example) has displaced a simple history, an ordinary narrative: 'Swept the sawdust from the floor / Of that working carpenter.'[21] Through her embellishment of the child, the mother has enabled the establishment of a religious myth, a new authority and organizing principle for both society and representation. Even so, the mother herself is constructed by that very same myth: 'King Abundance got Him on / Innocence; and Wisdom He.'[22] She herself is no longer a physical, human mother, but a symbol through whom Wisdom might be generated. Simultaneously, the mother accedes to the child the 'garments' by which his place will be determined – 'garments' of Abundance which derive from the father – while she, through her very act, becomes enmeshed within that symbolic structure and is afforded the only space by which the 'desired' child may be generated, that of purity and innocence. She is, therefore, represented as being implicated in the limits – both social and symbolic – which are set for her.

The mother–child relationship, particularly the fusion of the mother and child that is occasioned by the father's absence, is a psychical space where the distinction between mother and child is problematic, and where there is sanctuary from the demands of the social and symbolic orders that the father represents. It is a space where both mother and child may be satisfied, and where each derives immediate meaning from the other. What Yeats suggests in his exploration of this relationship is the importance of the mother and child in the construction of meaning; yet it is meaning that is of questionable value because it does not enable the child to enter society in a significant way. Not merely does the mother establish the parameters of the child's potential subjectivity, she is represented as reaching actively for those threads by which she may weave a desired destiny for her child. Even so, in this she does not always succeed, and particularly where she has lost control of this process, the destiny of the child may eventually become subject to the father's authority.

What is ironic in Yeats's representations of the mother–child relationship is the implication that, by symbolically locking the child to the mother, it is possible for an external entity, whether society or the poet, to manipulate the representation of one, thereby effecting an alteration in the meaning of the other. By utilizing the fusion of the mother and child, particularly the capacity within this fused image for the construction of meaning, those external to the relationship may bind both mother and child to symbolic spaces that will enable the realization of desired political and religious ends. And in this the poet is as guilty as any propagandist.[23]

'From my mother's womb'

The image of mother and child conjoined in representation that is elaborated in 'Among School Children', 'A Nativity' and 'Wisdom' affords a pointed example of Yeats's concern with the essential ambiguities embedded in those cultural signs that are rendered within discourse as Truth. In the image of the suffering mother – an image that implicitly includes the child – Yeats suggests not only the cultural construction of that image, but the propensity of the child himself to read that image according to dominant cultural codes. The child, therefore, is implicated in the image's perpetuation. It is this same complicity which Yeats explores in relation to the dualism of destroying/nurturing mother: 'I carry from my mother's womb / A fanatic heart.' Here the use of the active voice links both mother and child in the perpetuation of Ireland's 'troubles'; just as in the line 'Out of Ireland have we come' it is implied that it is as much the entity Ireland – whether rendered in cultural or political terms – as the individual mother who has nurtured this hatred.[24] The same image informs poems such as 'His Wildness' and 'The Friends of His Youth':

> She that has been wild
> And barren as a breaking wave
> Thinks that the stone's a child.[25]

Yeats himself suggests the symbolic significance of the stone: 'some fixed idea', 'a solitary thought which has turned a portion of her mind to stone'.[26] And what poems such as 'Easter 1916' and 'Remorse for Intemperate Speech' emphasize is that it is too simple merely to conclude that 'Mother Ireland is barren ... [that] she has nursed not a living child but a nation with a heart of stone.'[27] While such a reading is no doubt present, it is important to move beyond this reading to discover what Yeats is saying about the cultural constructions that have exacerbated those 'inflexibilities' inherited from the mother. The reader needs to look not merely to the mother who has given birth, but to that mother who nurtures – and the mother who nurtures is that mother constructed and contained by the paternal cultural tradition. Those who participate in that culture are, therefore, implicated, along with the mother, in the consequences of that nurturance.

The image of the nurturing mother, the 'good mother', recurs in Yeats's work, yet it is an image which is complicated by the context in which it is figured. Two dominant themes emerge – the image of the nurturing mother subsumed in an exploration of the interdependence of lovers; or the nurturing mother within a explication of destruction. With regard to the former, the 'good mother' is proffered as paradigm for the representation of the satiation of love.[28] For example, without naming mother or child, 'Lullaby' opens with an image of a maternal scene: 'Beloved, may your sleep be sound / That have found it where you fed.'[29] However, the actual focus of the poem is the relationship of the lovers: the protection afforded by the mother's arms; the peace to be found at the mother's breast.[30] This same paradigm is used more explicitly in 'Three Things'; yet where in 'Lullaby' the mother-figure is the passive recipient of the child's needs, able to satisfy those needs without too much effort, the woman in 'Three Things', who herself speaks, actively recognizes the power she wields in terms of her satisfaction of the child's demands:

> 'A child found all a child can lack,
> Whether of abundance or of rest,
> Upon the abundance of my breast'[.][31]

While Yeats recognizes the parallel between the woman's satisfaction of the man's sexual needs and the mother's nurturing of the child, he is also aware of the concomitant threat to the male that arises from this relationship. The mother's power to alleviate the child's lack also affords her the power to deny the child. This power, as can be seen from 'A Prayer for My Son', results in a shameful dependence occasioned by the child's helpless position in relation to the mother.

Yet Yeats's most interesting delineation of the 'good mother' and her contrary comes in those poems which seek to explicate the political turmoil that dominated the early decades of the twentieth century. In 'The Tower' a parallel is established between the mother-bird building and warming her nest, and the building of dreams and memories during old age.[32] Similarly, 'The Stare's Nest at My Window' – one of the poems making up 'Meditations in Time of Civil War' – where nurturing images arising from nature are used to elicit the dreams that will replace the brutal fantasies that have led to the civil war. Further, these imaginings will bolster the crumbling house and fill its empty nests and crevices. And it is this contrast between the images of nature – the *'wild* nest' – and the constructed 'fantasies' on which the 'heart's grown brutal' (those same 'fantasies' which construct and contain mother-Ireland) which exposes the extent to which natural instincts – instincts to build, whether literally or figuratively – have been dampened through a cultural indoctrination that privileges hate: 'More substance in our enmities / Than in our love.'[33] Here the house operates as a symbol of the ageing poet – Yeats himself, therefore, seeks the nurturing and life – and thereby the 'imaginings' – which will sustain him through his physical decline. The mother-figure, he indicates, is the source of this sustenance, but, he insists, it must be a mother-figure who has not been tamed by political discourse.

In 'The Stare's Nest at My Window' the destroying mother, while not named, is present through the implied failure of the nurturing mother. In 'Nineteen Hundred and Nineteen', a poem marking the escalation of the violence which preceded the arrival of the Black and Tans, the destroying mother is also obliquely present through the representation of 'Herodias's daughters', an appellation that encompasses both (more than one) Salomé and her mother, Herodias. The figure of the destroying mother (and her daughters) is here used to illustrate the speaker's contention that 'evil gathers head':

> Herodias' daughters have returned again,
> A sudden blast of dusty wind and after
> Thunder of feet, tumult of images,
> Their purpose in the labyrinth of the wind;

And should some crazy hand dare touch a daughter
All turn with amorous cries.[34]

It is an 'evil' which threatens the promise (the prophet) that, throughout the poem, is represented as being overwhelmed by 'the labyrinth
that [man] has made / In art or politics'. Here, again, an emphasis on the
cultural construction of images which demand specific responses mod-
ifies our reading of the destroying mother. This reading is further
modified by the suffering mother who figures in an earlier movement
of the poem. Both mothers occasion feelings of horror, yet in each case
that horror emerges from a variant construction:

> the nightmare
> Rides upon sleep: a drunken soldiery
> Can leave the mother, murdered at her door,
> To crawl in her own blood, and go scot-free[.][35]

This image echoes the political propaganda which proliferated during
the First World War; and the sense of outrage provoked by this first
movement of 'Nineteen Hundred and Nineteen' emanates from the
political and social upheavals which provide the focus for the poem.
Yet, through the variant constructions employed in the poem, the
mother violated is brought into tension with the mother who violates.
Both images resonate with the poet's avowal of the turbulence that fails
to refigure the socio-symbolic order, that merely reaffirms it. Yet as the
'wind drops' and the 'dust settles' it becomes apparent that – within the
poem as in culture – both mothers have no other function but to elicit a
specific response: guilt or blame. Whether this is an ironic device on
Yeats's part, or merely – in light of the despair the period obviously
aroused in him – a failure to question cultural constructions as rigorously as he had done in other poems, it is difficult to say conclusively.
What is clear is that in this poem, as in others, Yeats refused to be
satisfied with a singular reading or representation of the mother-figure
and, by referring to both the suffering and destroying mother within the
same context, embedded her plurality, and the contradictions emanating from that plurality, within the text itself.

Womb/tomb

The concurrence of 'womb' and 'tomb' across a number of Yeats's works
is occasioned not merely by the poetic effect of this concurrence, but

also by the similarities of the spaces, and their respective associations with the limits of life: birth and death. This concurrence is evident in the later poems, but is tempered by Yeats's own philosophy. As 'A Needle's Eye' demonstrates, beyond birth and death there is an existence for which the individual will thirst throughout their 'life'.[36] The needle's eye – itself suggestive of the vagina – represents the gateway between these existences, and the encapsulation of the infinite by the finite. In 'Crazy Jane and Jack the Journeyman' this association is extended with Jane referring to 'the light lost / In my mother's womb'.[37] In this I differ from critics such as Martin, who argues that Yeats's philosophy suggests that human beings seek to return to the unity inherent in the womb 'from which they were hurled at creation'.[38] The womb, in Yeats's work, is merely a node of passage rather than a point of origin. Therefore, the choices open to Jane upon her death are to return to the light or to follow Jack; the resolution of these choices will depend upon where she is buried. Only by being buried within the tomb (metaphor for the womb) will she return to her earlier existence. Buried outside the tomb she will exist as a ghost.

Functions of (re)birth and creation are not, in Yeats's terms, explicitly the realm of the mother, and often he absents the mother-figure from these processes in order to effect a more dramatic disclosure of his philosophy. Creation and renewal proceed, very often, from a profound discord or disjunction in the natural order; creation arises from the union of opposites, a point that has been noted frequently by critics. Such a process allows for the removal of the mother-figure and her replacement by the gap between thesis and antithesis, from which space something new or reconstituted may be generated. Creation is shifted beyond the realm of the mother: the Godhead, as is indicated in 'Ribh in Ecstasy', is self-generating. In 'Fragments' Yeats utilizes the primordial paradigm for the displacement of the mother from the creative process. Creation proceeds, not from Eve, but at the hands of the father; it comes from nothing, from the void occasioned by the disintegration of order. Yet two central poems – 'Easter 1916' and 'The Second Coming' – both of which encompass an absent mother, and both of which represent birth emanating from social and symbolic chaos, suggest that the mother's absence may not necessarily arise through displacement, but rather through an inability – or unwillingness – to bring her into focus.

The 'terrible beauty' whose birth is heralded in 'Easter 1916' and the anti-Christ of 'The Second Coming' arise from chaos and upheaval. In the former, it is the Easter rising which effects the birth; in the latter, the disintegration of order: 'Things fall apart; the centre cannot hold; / Mere anarchy is loosed upon the world.'[39] It is not merely the social order which is undermined, but the symbolic also. Meaning, the certainty of meaning, is itself subverted.[40] In the face of such significant births, the mother's apparent absence is especially conspicuous. Who tends the cradle? Who delivers the 'child'? These questions may be answered by reference to other poems where Yeats has exposed the means by which the mother-figure is constructed or reconstituted for the purposes of strengthening religious or political myths. The mother is determined, to a large extent, by the 'desired' child. Prior to the birth of the 'desired' child, the mother does not exist and is, effectively, absent. The context of chaos, disorder and disintegration in which both births occur suggests a proximity to the mother – to the pre-oedipal world that exists beyond social constraints, moral authorities and representational systems – that does not allow the mother to be distinguished clearly from the disorder and disintegration that the 'child' – in this case the poet – is experiencing. Further, the mother cannot be articulated until the system within which she will be represented has been determined. This requires, first, the birth of the child within the poem, and the determination of the myth by which that child will exist: 'And what rough beast, its hour come round at last, / Slouches towards Bethlehem to be born?'[41] The question with which the poem concludes indicates that it is not yet possible to determine the symbolic order that the 'rough beast' will govern. What is clear is that, in its usurpation of elements of the Christian myth, most particularly that of the myth's birthplace, it will abnegate and refigure that myth in its own terms. The question that remains unanswered is: What would be the nature of the mother that this anti-Christian order would engender?

Sowing the seed

In 'A Prayer for My Daughter', the father does not merely contaminate or overwhelm the mother with his own lineage – he displaces her completely.[42] Placed within a implicit social and historical context, the image of father and daughter represented in the poem is one of the father deliberately positioning the child within his own history. As such, he places her as antithesis to those women through whom his mind 'has dried up of late'.[43] The daughter is placed by the father as salve to the hurt that has figured in his life at the hands of women. To achieve this, the father brings his daughter within his own history, displacing the mother and, thereby, the threat to that history that the mother embodies.

The precedence of the father's lineage, of the father's history, as it is represented in Yeats's work, is something I have discussed at length in 'Eve's Curse No More'. In assuring this precedence the mother was positioned as merely a vessel, ensuring the delivery of the father's line, untainted by her own, into the next generation. In 'A Prayer for My Daughter', the speaker bypasses the mother and himself delivers his history. However, in many instances, the father is represented as being dependent on the mother for the creation of the child, and therefore vulnerable to the possibility of her subverting or abnegating his lineage by giving precedence to her own.

One important means by which the father's lineage is assured is through the naming of the child. With the act of naming, particularly through the assumption of the 'name-of-the-father', the child is brought within the bounds of those social and symbolic orders which the father governs. Both the father, and the authority the father represents, are internalized, and the fluid, variable, disorderly realm of the preoedipal is repressed. In 'Easter 1916' naming becomes an important motif:

> our part
> To murmur name upon name,
> As a mother names her child
> When sleep at last has come
> On limbs that had run wild.[44]

Yet what is significant about this motif is that – in addition to memorializing the 'heroes' of the rebellion – the father's action of naming 'in a verse' subjects the mother's 'naming' of 'her child' to the father's. Further, while the mother's naming calms the child into a world of sleep – itself suggestive of pre-symbolic spaces – the father's naming draws the child into a patrilineage – a symbolic order – that privileges death and sacrifice, despite the fact that it is just this sacrifice which 'Can make a stone of the heart'. Again, it is not merely the 'hatred' inherited from the mother that occasions Ireland's 'fanatic heart' – it also derives from the nurturing the child receives, nurturing – while charged to the mother – that ultimately is dictated by the paternal cultural tradition.

The name given to the child by the father resonates with more than merely the patrifamilial – each repetition serves to reinforce the 'name-of-the father' and, thereby, the symbolic order from which that name derives its authority. In 'Wisdom' this resonance is realized explicitly:[45]

the child's name derives not from the natural father, but from that father whose myth the child is destined to represent. This situation is also explored in 'A Stick of Incense', where competing paternities see the natural father displaced by the supernatural father. Yet in this process of transforming the child from an element within a familial dynamic to a figure whose presence is central to a religious myth – as represented in 'Wisdom' and implied in 'A Stick of Incense' – the natural father is shifted aside, displaced by the impregnating divinity, while the natural mother remains as part of the dynamic of the new trinity. However, as I argued earlier, to enable the natural mother to bear such a child she must be resymbolized, reconstructed, in accordance with that very myth.

It is a recurrent effect: the natural father is displaced or made impotent due to the intervention of a 'superior' authority, while the mother is left to bear the symbolic burden that will enable her children to meet their 'destinies'. One possible explanation for this difference in the treatment of father and mother, particularly in terms of the generation of a child who bears some mythic or political destiny, can be found in 'Tom at Cruachan'. Through the mother, 'Eternity' is contained; it takes on a finite nature.[46] The mother-figure explicitly limits that which comes from the father; his seed is diminished by her. Yet, ironically, it is a limitation which is essential if the father's offspring is to come into existence. The mother sets boundaries on the father's attributes; however, these boundaries must be accepted by the father if his 'purpose' is, literally, to be realized. The binding of the infinite within the finite is also evident in 'The Mother of God';[47] however, the 'mother of God', as I have shown above, goes on to emphasize all that she has given to the child through her nurturing. This is the second dilemma facing the father. The generation of his seed requires the mother to 'act' as vector – thereby placing limitations on that seed – and to nurture the child, a process that entails the transmission to the child of her own sensibilities, perhaps even her own history. Placed in a position of vulnerability with respect to the mother, the father – or at least the father's myth – seeks to construct the mother in such a way that she – and her nurturing – will be brought under the control of the father.[48]

In 'Leda and the Swan', the mother is represented as wholly subject to the will of the father. Only in the title of the poem is she named; thereafter, she is referred to merely as 'staggering girl', 'her' or 'she'. Leda becomes merely object of the swan's lust:[49] there is little space left for her because of the overwhelming presence of father and daughter. The effect of the father's orgasm is not felt by the mother, but by history:

> A shudder in the loins engenders there
> The broken wall, the burning roof and tower
> And Agamemnon dead.[50]

However, blame for the disastrous realization of this history seems to rest with the mother and her inability to secure for her daughter the full extent of the father's divinity.[51] This notion of the fury and power of the father being contained, or taken on, by the mother is evident in a number of poems, including 'A Stick of Incense', 'A Nativity', 'Whence Had They Come?' and 'The Mother of God'; and what is consistent in all these poems is the sense of this power being unleashed through the child: 'What sacred drama through her body heaved / When world transforming Charlemagne was conceived?'[52] This question is central to the exploration of the theme of transmission of the father's lineage: what is the effect of the mother's filtering of the father's line? Yet it is a question to which Yeats does not proffer an answer, allowing the tension that comes from uncertainty to prevail.

In 'The Crazed Moon' the virginal moon is exalted while the mother-moon, crazed and 'over-bearing', is grasped at by an insatiable humanity. Interestingly, the movement from one state to the other is occasioned by man's touch:

> Blenched by that malicious dream
> They are spread wide that each
> May rend what comes in reach.[53]

Man's lust not only is implicated in the transition from woman to mother, but also, more particularly, the transition from a figure of adoration to one whose presence is, essentially, pathetic. This poem offers something of a reversal of the mythologization of the mother that is evident, particularly, in those poems dealing with Christian iconography. This reversal impacts on the nature of the child the mother bears, and the contrast between the supernatural father of poems such as 'Wisdom' and the rapacious human fathers presented in 'The Crazed Moon' emphasizes the mother's role in generation as merely that of distilling the father's seed. The children she bears are products both of the father and of the symbolic order to which – in their conjugation – she has been subjected.

*

Yeats's later work emphasizes the father's inability – be he supernatural or otherwise – to effect his own re-generation, and to ensure the positioning of the child according to the paternal line. It is the mother who enables this generation, and the spaces she is afforded are merely those which will facilitate this process. Yeats rarely allows the mother to exist in subversive spaces, highlighting instead her complicity in, or at least her lack of resistance to, the iconographies which decorate her social and symbolic position. What poems such as 'The Crazed Moon' and 'Wisdom' insist is that the symbolic embellishment of the mother's space, or the desire to touch and assume that space, has the effect of further restraining both mother and child.

The mother's prescribed role in the (re)production of the father's line is one of subjection to a will and power that both objectifies her and refuses to allow her to exist any longer as woman, as individual. She is subjected not merely to the male authority, but is reconstructed according to the needs of the father's lineage. Breen makes this same point in her discussion of *Purgatory*, arguing that through her role as receptacle of male production, the mother is precluded as a speaker in her own right.[54] This is generally true of the later works, where the mother figure is effectively silenced. *A Woman Young and Old* and the 'Crazy Jane' poems, texts where the woman is allowed to speak, do not include the speaking mother. One of the few exceptions comes in 'The Mother of God', where the mother's speech is used to emphasize the vulnerability of the father to the mother's interdependence with the pre-oedipal child.

The generation of the father's seed, the father's line and history, as well as the realization of his will, is represented as being tempered by the mother's humanity, and by the symbolic veiling of the mother to make her a suitable bride for the father. Alternatively, her total objectification may mean that there is no space for her in the generative narrative. Either way, the mother's transmission of the father's seed is rarely represented as having a positive impact on either the child or the societies or myths within which that child comes to exist. Yeats may recognize in his work the manipulation of the mother-figure in the development of political and religious agendas, but there still lingers a trace of mother-blame. Whether this emanates from a difficulty in disentangling himself completely from constructions of the mother-figure which surrounded him, or from an impression of the mother's complicity in her own construction, or at least the perpetuation of that construction, I am not entirely certain; yet this tension between accusation and purgation is one of the most notable aspects of his representation of the mother-figure in the later works. Despite this tension, what ultimately is clear is that Yeats's treatment of the mother-figure accorded with his overall tendency to both work with and resist traditional images in order to highlight the contraries that are repressed by various discourses in their construction of Truth.

8

'Let me be and let me live': Wresting Subjectivity from the Mother in Joyce's *Ulysses*

> *For man and for woman the loss of the mother is a biological and psychic necessity, the first step on the way to becoming autonomous.*
> Julia Kristeva, *Black Sun*

When Leopold Bloom crawls into bed beside Molly, he is neither maternal father nor womanly man: he is child. He is 'the childman weary, the manchild in the womb'.[1] He rests by Molly who is 'in the attitude of Gea-Tellus',[2] a description which, in light of 'Penelope', is surely to be read ironically. For, as Attridge perceptively argues, Molly's interior monologue reveals little in the way of maternal instinct, and her actions to ensure that she does not conceive with Blazes Boylan belie the rubric 'Gea- Tellus'.[3] Sensual, earthy woman – yes; earth-mother – almost certainly not. The metaphorical womb to which the weary Bloom retreats is that of rest, sleep. It does not belong to Molly. In 'Penelope', Molly's womb sheds its 'childbed', making it inhospitable to any child, and signalling that no child has been conceived by her in the course of the day.[4] This is no phallic mother lauded by feminist critics. The gap between Gea-Tellus and Molly widens throughout 'Penelope' to the point where Gea-Tellus is obliterated effectively by Molly's soliloquy. The symbol of maternity, in the course of a woman's unbridled thoughts, is emptied of meaning and divested of much of its potency. Molly resists the maternal icon – good mother, earth mother, virginal mother – and asserts her own (sexual) space in opposition to that space the patriarchal cultural tradition would have her occupy. And it is this resistance of the maternal icon and the reconstitution of maternal spaces – inherent to 'Penelope' – that defines the representation of the mother-figure within *Ulysses*.

Throughout *Ulysses* both Bloom and Stephen Dedalus are forced to confront images of the mother: I am concerned with the principal five – Mrs Dedalus, Mina Purefoy, Molly Bloom, mother-Ireland and the Blessed Virgin. Each embodies a symbolic potential – as good mother, earth mother, suffering mother, virgin mother – which must be challenged; and it is this challenging of symbolic potential which urges the novel forward, and which affords Stephen the opportunity to forge a subjectivity which lies outside those fashioned by religious and nationalist discourses. For the search for the father – an alternative father whose authority may counter the debilitating governance of familial and colonial fathers – is bound up with defiance of the mother. The father's authority derives from his disruption of the mother–child bond; yet where the mother refuses to forgo the privilege that comes from her possession of the child, the child must defeat her – as she exists within symbolic structures – in order to participate in representation.

Circe

The key to much of my argument lies in 'Circe'; and it is worthwhile to explore briefly those aspects of the episode which have guided my reading of the novel as a whole. Structured like a dream, 'Circe' should not be read without reference to Freud: the episode highlights incidents of 'psychic intensity' which have occurred during the course of – at least – 16 June 1904, and privileges dramatization and representation over thought and narrative.[5] Processes of condensation and displacement clearly are operating within 'Circe', and repressed elements are made manifest. Yet it is only in the structure of the episode, in the intrusion of material repressed through the course of the day, that the dream is suggested: within the novel, the action is represented as literal events and experiences occurring in nighttown. Even read as a dream, it is uncertain who the dreamer is in 'Circe' – many critics read the episode as Stephen's dream, though I consider it to be more ambiguous, with the action moving through the dream-worlds of Stephen, Bloom, the reader, and the novel itself. The dream-work, Freud argues, 'superimposes, as it were, the different components upon one another.... Ideas which are contraries are by preference expressed in dreams by one and the same element.'[6] Nighttown is a world in which both the reader and the protagonists are trapped: they are unable to escape until the contraries and conflicts inherent to the 'dream' are, if not resolved, at least refigured. Here signifier and signified, having collided, shoot off in radically different directions, re-establishing themselves in new permutations.

It is Bloom's mother who is the first of the mother-figures to appear in 'Circe', and she brings with her associations of guilt and shame. Bloom explains to his father the reason for his failure in a running race.[7] Shame shifts from the race (the Jewish race?) to Bloom's religious loyalties. Yet Ellen Bloom is far from being the stereotypical Jewish mother who suffers on behalf of her son. Rather, she is dressed as a pantomime dame. Her words are dramatically and conspicuously Irish Catholic – 'Sacred Heart of Mary, where were you at all, at all?'[8] – but they are rendered by a Jew within the context of melodrama. As such, not only the words, but the mother who recites them, and the mother encapsulated within them, are brought into question.

Bloom himself provides the next significant mother-figure within 'Circe', and this figuration in particular has tended to lead critics on a (misguided) search for the 'maternal' Bloom. First pilloried by the mob – Mother Grogan at their head – for being a 'vile hypocrite', he is then examined by Mulligan and his fellow doctors and declared to be '*virgo intacta* . . . a finished example of the new womanly man'.[9] Enveloped within these scenes is more than a parody of the new woman, and the 'womanly man' who has taken on himself what she has spurned: there is mother-Ireland, again 'eating her farrow'; there is the Roman Catholic Church, the 'scarlet woman', whom Bloom is reviled for having worshipped; and there is a satire not so much on Parnell's fall, but on the cult of the hero brought down by the mob that was extolled in the work of Yeats, Synge and Joyce himself. And, again, their representation within the dream-structure, within the carnivalesque, brings within the social and symbolic order that which the social and symbolic represses. It is in this inversion that discourses of Nationalism and Catholicism are challenged.

Shortly after this scene, Bloom gives birth to eight male children, all of whom are handsome, learned and successful, and all of whom, in their appearance '*on a redcarpeted staircase*' are suggestive of some manner of royalty. 'O, I so want to be a mother,' Bloom says;[10] yet the virgin birth of royal children that brings first awe and veneration soon leads to the sacrifice of Bloom by his disciples. 'Forgive him his trespasses,' Brother Buzz says,[11] drawing an association with the central prayer of the Christian Church and the words given by Christ when teaching his disciples how to pray.[12] Here, however, it is Bloom who is about to be put to death: the swirling associations of the Circean 'dream' have seen Bloom progress from Virgin Mother to Christ. That there is a confusion between the Virgin Mother and Christ, that there is a bleeding of signification between the 'saviour' (as both sacrifice and priest) and his mother, is evident in the lament of the Daughters of Erin.[13] The banal events of Bloom's day are combined and confused with Christian icons – saviour and priest – the liturgy of the Virgin Mary and a touch of Irish history, emphasizing the processes of condensation and displacement inherent in the dream. However, two aspects of the events of Bloom's virgin birth and sacrificial death are especially pertinent: the usurpation of the place reserved for the 'Son' within Catholic dogma by the 'Mother'; and Bloom's comic challenge to the singularity and solemnity of the virgin birth. And, in this, it is apparent that Bloom's apparition has little to do with his own desire to 'mother' (a desire which would necessitate 'Circe' to be entirely Bloom's dream, a reading which, I suggest, cannot be sustained). Rather, the association between Bloom and the maternal is a device for disclosing the means by which the mother-figure has come to operate in Irish culture. This is further explicated through the figure of Mina Purefoy: the mother on whose labour Bloom's thoughts have turned throughout the day is herself sacrificed amid scenes suggestive of the final resurrection prefigured in the Book of Revelations.[14] It is important to note Mrs Purefoy's fettered state: bound to the altar of discourse with no choice but to participate in the sacrifice. Yet, concomitant to this, the sacrifice of Calvary, re-enacted in the mass, is transformed into the sacrifice and, thereby, veneration of the Mother, here in the guise of Mina Purefoy. Mother usurps Son, unbalancing the trinity of Father, Mother and Son.[15]

Significantly, it is between these two sequences of 'Circe' that Stephen Dedalus confronts his mother, referred to in the text as 'the mother'. Stephen's dancing – an activity he first shared with his mother[16] – is interrupted by his father.[17] Simon Dedalus here appears in his own guise, having previously been 'condensed' with the mythical father Stephen had adopted in *A Portrait of the Artist as a Young Man*.[18] The success of Stephen's flight in *A Portrait* – both in terms of his exile and the soaring of his artistic self – is brought into question by the uncertain flight of his father, and the image reinforces Stephen's difficulty in divorcing himself completely from the structures – both familial and social – into which he has been born. Within this image, Joyce presses doubts as to Stephen's exile, his 'bird-girl' epiphany, his place in society, the father he claims to have found, and his art. And the seed of these doubts is his mother's ghost, her spectral intrusion into his life and consciousness. Stephen is unable either to repress or dismiss his mother, and the events of the day, eliciting associations with her, provoke her repeated appearance.

In 'Circe', where the unconscious is reified, the mother's realm is virtually without limit. Stephen's dancing halts when she appears 'emaciated...in leper grey with a wreath of faded orange blossoms and a torn bridal veil, her face worn and noseless, green with grave mould'. She names herself as the 'once...beautiful May Goulding. I am dead.' Even so, Stephen does not recognize her immediately, perhaps an attempt to keep her from him, or perhaps because prior to this she has merely been evoked by association.[19] Here she is both bride and corpse, an amalgam of beauty and horror, life and death, a dramatic representation of the myriad thoughts Stephen has had of her throughout the day. It is Stephen's confrontation with his mother which brings 'Circe' to its climax; and to fully understand the encounter between Stephen and The Mother it is important not only to be conscious of the two sequences in 'Circe' where the mother is deified, but also the mother-figure's penetration of the text prior to this point.

Mother and son, ghost and guilt

In the opening pages of *Ulysses*, Joyce positions the text within the constructs of both the Catholic mass – the significance of which becomes clear in 'Circe' – and Shakespeare's *Hamlet*: Stephen Dedalus is immediately framed by sacrifice and guilt. Stephen and Buck Mulligan stand on the parapet of the Martello tower in which they live, paying homage to their 'great, sweet mother', the sea.[20] Having drawn the association between the sea and the mother, Buck Mulligan is prompted by the vista to accuse Stephen of killing his mother.[21] In doing so, Mulligan functions in a similar way to Horatio and Marcellus in *Hamlet*, drawing Stephen's attention to the presence of the ghost and introducing the question of responsibility for the death that has occurred. Where the narratives differ significantly is that the father's ghost incites revenge, while the mother's ghost instils guilt.

The ghost of Stephen's mother does not call upon her son to find her murderer, but to recognize that murderer in himself. His only response is retreat; he cannot confront her, and he cannot acquiesce. Yet, for the whole day, he is preoccupied – whether consciously or not – with reconciling his relationship to her and dealing with the implications – for father and son – of that relationship.[22] Mulligan's accusation – implicating Stephen in his mother's death – wounds Stephen, a wound 'that was not yet the pain of love': 'But to think of your mother begging you with her last breath to kneel down and pray for her. And you refused.'[23] Stephen has denied his mother. He has chosen instead the *non serviam* he professed in *A Portrait*. And he takes Mulligan's references to his mother's death not as an insult to her memory, but as a personal affront.[24]

The death of Mrs Dedalus has left a profound imprint on Stephen's psyche. Lacan refers to the psychic knot or impasse that results from a moment 'in a person's life history which conscious knowledge does not account for, but which leaves its imprint anyway'. The knots in Joyce's texts, Lacan suggests, 'have to do with the metonymical signifying chains surrounding the Name of the Father'.[25] In *A Portrait* these metonymic chains led Stephen from his mother to the physical father, to the authority of the Church and, finally, to the mythical father, Daedalus. Ultimately, the mythical father affords Stephen an identity which allows him to take flight from mother, Ireland and Church. Yet in *Ulysses*, he has returned, and it is for his mother that he has made this journey.[26] Stephen finds himself bound to the mother – and it is the conflict between his own desired position as saviour – a position which requires a mother beyond death, who is immortalized as symbol – and his mother's mortality that secures this bond. Stephen desires a virgin birth, one that will foster his own creativity; yet he cannot escape the sordidness of his conception: 'all there is of her but her woman's unclean loins, of man's flesh made not in God's likeness, the serpent's prey.'[27] The symbol – whether mourning mother or virgin mother – insists on his service, his submission, and as such threatens his subjectivity. Yet without it, his own claim to the role of artistic saviour is constrained. It is this paradox which affords substance to May Dedalus's ghost.

It is not until 'Circe', where the repressed surfaces, that Joyce allows the ghost to speak. Yet, through the associations which frame her appearance in the preceding episodes of the novel, and the thoughts which bring her into being and, in turn, dispel her, the silent bond between son and mother is afforded some voice. She is first called into consciousness by Mulligan's reveries over the sea, and in the silence bred of Mulligan's shaving Stephen's thoughts turn to her: 'Silently, in a dream she had come to him after death...he saw the sea hailed as a great sweet mother.'[28] Stephen's dream is filled with sensuous impressions of her deathbed, these impressions shifting metonymically to become essential elements of her: candle wax and ashes, aspects possibly of her final unction, the scent of rosewood from the furniture of her room. Even the scene on which he gazes is appropriated by the ghost, the 'green mass of liquid' that is the sea becoming elemental to his memory of her.[29] Stephen is unable to differentiate May Dedalus from his barely conscious perceptions of the moments of her death. The objects scattered around the death-room, its scents, have been stripped of their essential meaning, and with his own guilt and refusal they have condensed and combined, allowing her presence to be felt in the myriad aspects of Stephen's life.

In *A Portrait*, Stephen's *non serviam* was linked with both his recognition of the mourning mother's power to bind him within 'nets' of religion and nationality, and his desire to realize himself in artistic terms. Yet, in *Ulysses*, it becomes clear that Stephen has not succeeded in his efforts to create. In 'Wandering Rocks', Mulligan gives his own assessment of Stephen's art, determining that Stephen will never be the artist he desires to be.[30] It is an assessment which will be brought fully into focus in 'Oxen of the Sun', where Stephen's failure to create will align him not with Mina Purefoy, mother to an enormous brood, but with Leopold Bloom whose own son – the progenitor of his line – has also died. Stephen's art is stillborn; he has been unable to take on the function of the mother, conceiving and bearing the child of his imagination. As Beja argues, the 'basic point is that Stephen is, on June 16th, an unfulfilled artist, frustrated by his failure to create any art of genuine significance.'[31] His identification with the mother as creator and with the mythical father of flight that defined the final 'portrait of the artist as a young man' has foundered in the face of his own mother's death. Yet it is important to recognize the difficulty in identifying cause and effect: is it his mother's death that has impacted on his ability to create; or has his failure to create imbued his mother's death with greater resonance that it might otherwise have had?

By holding up to him a cracked mirror, Buck Mulligan draws attention to the split that has developed in Stephen's self-image. While much has been made of Stephen's epigram – 'a symbol of Irish art. The cracked lookingglass of the servant'[32] – his witticism is little more than an effort to divert attention – his companion's and his own – from his face. As I have argued with respect to *A Portrait*, the mirror in his mother's room was an important metaphor for Stephen's developing sense of self, and it was to this mirror that Stephen retreated to view himself after he had written his first poem. Yet, at the moment of her death, he is denied access both to the gaze that is self-affirming and to the mirror in which his own fledgling identity coalesced. It is not coincidental that Mulligan links the mirror and the sea by a line of reflected light before holding it to Stephen, emphasizing the link between Stephen, his mother, his self-image and his art. The ambiguity of Mulligan's use of the word 'dreadful' also serves to undermine this particular 'portrait of the artist' – a dishevelled, shattered and bitter image of what others see but what Stephen himself has not envisaged. This, I suggest, is the true nature of the crack: the gap between the 'face' he desires and the 'face' he presents to the world. And, as will be reiterated throughout the novel, because Stephen has his mother's face – 'Face reminds me of his poor mother'[33] – the image which reminds Stephen of his failure, ostensibly, is that of his mother.

The ghost who haunts Stephen is also fed, therefore, by his failure to create:

> Creation from nothing. . . . A misbirth with a trailing navelcord . . . Wombed in sin darkness I was too, made not begotten. By them, the man with my voice and my eyes and a ghostwoman with ashes on her breath. Is that then the divine substance wherein Father and Son are consubstantial?[34]

The 'misbirth' is Stephen's art and its 'trailing navelcord' is the imprint of the mother who has, metonymically, infiltrated Stephen's consciousness. The 'creation from nothing' is the power of the (virgin) mother that Stephen desires – recall that in *A Portrait* he figured himself within the construct of the Annunciation – and the Father with whom Stephen will be consubstantial is he for whom Stephen still searches. For it is in the union of father and son that the mother may be banished and the trinity of mother, father and son become instead that of father, son and spirit.

Throughout the 'Telemachia', Stephen's self-image slowly unravels. Every trailing moment of his history leads him to his mother. Stephen faces his dying mother 'silent with awe and pity' unable to speak the words she demands.[35] Now that she is dead, he is unable literally to bury her: he substitutes the word 'grandmother' for that of 'mother' in the riddle he poses for the schoolboys.[36] The boys seated before him drag Stephen back into his own 'ugly and futile' youth and, inevitably, into the realm of the mother: 'His mother's prostrate body the fiery Columbanus in holy zeal bestrode.'[37] Here he experiences the guilt triggered by the image of the suffering mother, a reflex almost, but a reflex deeply embedded in Stephen's (and the Irish) psyche. It is impossible not to speculate how much guilt would be felt had the zeal of Columbanus not dissipated; yet, ultimately, what this emphasizes is that for Stephen the prophet's fire has been doused by the mother. The traces of Stephen's childhood feed the memories of his mother, drawing the threads of Stephen's history inextricably back to her: 'Secrets, silent, stony sit in the dark palaces of both our hearts: secrets weary of their tyranny: tyrants willing to be dethroned.'[38] In 'Telemachia', Mrs Dedalus reifies the sense of failure that haunts Stephen. His inability to create is made manifest in her power to destroy: 'Ghoul! Chewer of corpses! No mother. Let me be and let me live.'[39] Conflicts of birth and death, creation and destruction, subjectivity and the collapse of self are apparent in Stephen's memories and dreams of his mother. Further, his history has become knotted at the moment of her death, such that the past has no meaning except in relation to her. Stephen is unable to progress, to move into the future, until these conflicts are resolved. Unresolved, he is bound to the mother, and she will persist in dragging him back to her. To move forward he must bury her, and in order to bury her he must first unpack her of meaning. It is only then that he will be able to find the father who is worthy of his allegiance and who will 'ground him in a representational lineage, thereby giving him a way to subsist in language as a coherent subject'.[40] While the mother exists outside the bounds of the social and the symbolic, receptacle of Stephen's own projected conflicts, meaning is concentrated in her. The paradox is that the more Stephen searches for meaning in the world around him – as a means of combating her – the more he is led back to her and his own past.

'...the wife should live and the babe to die'

It is to matters of birth and death that the attention of both Bloom and Stephen are drawn throughout 16 June 1904. Images of his mother's death are never far from Stephen's consciousness; Bloom makes his way to Paddy Dignam's funeral, there to muse, like Stephen, on the causes and consequences of life and death. Both are dressed in mourning; Stephen, as Mulligan points out, rather hypocritically so.[41] The funeral draws from Bloom's subconscious memories of several deaths: his son's, Mrs Dedalus's, his mother's, and his father's suicide. But it is the deaths of father and son that give him most pause.[42] It is in the course of 'Lestrygonians' that Bloom, accidently, learns of the plight of Mina Purefoy and her 'stiff birth'. Spurred by Mrs Purefoy's predicament, Bloom imagines the worst of childbirth,[43] horrors that echo much later in 'Oxen of the Sun' and, later still, in 'Penelope'.[44] In particular, Bloom's vision of the son trapped by the mother's womb recalls Stephen's own plight, and Bloom's empathy with this image foreshadows the rapport he and Stephen will later develop in the context of the Purefoy birth and their joint entrapment in Nighttown.

Mother and child are united in birth and in death: 'Only a mother and deadborn child ever buried in the one coffin.'[45] Womb and tomb are conflated, weaving through the thoughts of both Stephen and Bloom: 'One born every second somewhere. Other dying every second.'[46] The capacity of the mother to afford both life and death is explicit in *Ulysses*: it is acknowledged and ruminated upon at length. She may bury the child interminably in her womb or she may bear it into the world – her volition is consistently implied.

'Our mighty mother' the sea is also a basin of death: 'the dead sea: no fish, weedless, sunk deep in the earth. . . . Dead: an old woman's: the grey sunken cunt of the world.'[47] In this sea, children may drown[48] – Stephen identifies with the man who drowns in 'our mighty mother'. At the same time, he laments his failure as Saviour: he was unable to save his mother, to protect her life. This lament is reiterated later in 'Scylla and Charybdis', where Stephen refers to the woman who 'saw the artist into and out of the world' and recalls the reversal of that image in his own case. It is he who sees his mother from the world:

> Mother's deathbed. Candle. The sheeted mirror. Who brought me into this world lies there, bronzelidded, under few cheap flowers. *Liliata rutilantium.*
> I wept alone.[49]

It is Stephen's *non serviam* which has prevented him from 'saving' his mother, if not in literal at least in metaphorical terms. For he has refused to be confirmed within that faith which would have seen her revered and perpetuated among the mothers of the faithful. The debate in 'Oxen of the Sun' foregrounds the question that underlies Stephen's torment: When both mother and child are unable to survive, whose life should be privileged? With the travails of Mina Purefoy marginalized by the men's 'wassailing' and camaraderie, this question is put and answered: 'but all cried with one acclaim nay, by our Virgin Mother, the wife should live and the babe to die.'[50] Importantly, it is Stephen, for whom the dilemma is immediate (bearing as it does on his own battle to escape from his mother's womb-tomb), who eludes the question, highlighting instead the potential for creation that is wasted through lust. He sets 'holy mother' against 'earthly mother', highlighting the Church's demand for souls, a demand that may occasion the mother's physical demise: it was for this the Church was established – and for the same reason the Church, he insists, has 'foundered' in its mission.[51] For Stephen, the question of whose life should be privileged – mother's or child's – not only focuses his own creative failure, but also the struggle he has faced in pronouncing his *non serviam*. His own creative subjectivity is brought into direct conflict with the principal purpose of his mother's life – the delivery of his soul and self to the Church.

' . . . so does the artist weave and unweave his image'

In 'Oxen of the Sun', Stephen's artistic failures are brought sharply into focus: 'He could not leave his mother an orphan. The young man's face grew dark. All could see how hard it was for him to be reminded of his promise and of his recent loss.'[52] The correlation between his mother's death and the stillbirth of his art is explicitly stated, and affects Stephen deeply. Yet what it is important to recognize is that in this episode Stephen's failure and loss are framed by Mina Purefoy's creative success and Leopold Bloom's own loss. This framing is reinforced by the linguistic evolution that takes place in the episode – an evolution which, as Moore had done in *Hail and Farewell,* represents the development of English in terms of the foetus.[53] Further, it emphasizes for both the reader and Stephen that he shares his creative impulse with Leopold Bloom – father to a dead son – rather than the mother, who spawns children at an alarming rate, and whose (creative) space he covets.[54]

It is in 'Proteus' that Stephen muses on the 'creation from nothing' that he represents – the son made, not begotten. As I have argued in relation to *A Portrait*, Stephen's sense of his own creativity is closely aligned with maternal images – he would receive the seed of creativity much as the Virgin received the word of God at the annunciation. Yet, in this, he has failed. And, as I have suggested, his failure feeds the mother who haunts him. It is a vicious circle, for her dilatant potency and presence further incapacitates him. Lawrence argues that 'Stephen's theory of creation . . . pre-empts the role of the mother and leaves the male artist self-sufficient, free to create a world';[55] yet Mina Purefoy's parturition and May Dedalus's ghost crowd this space, allowing Stephen no ground in which to seed his own creativity. His urge to banish the mother, therefore, proceeds on two allied fronts: that of his own desire to create, and that of his desire to be positioned as saviour.[56] It is in 'Scylla and Charybdis' that Stephen attempts to intellectualize himself into these positions and, thereby, displace the mother.[57]

Constructing his argument that Shakespeare's ghost is Hamlet's grandfather, Stephen extends the association between mother and creativity. In *A Portrait* and 'Proteus', it is within the metaphor of conception and birth that he finds his model for the artistic process. Such a model is parodied by Mulligan as he delivers his 'brainchild'.[58] Here, however,

Stephen emphasizes the subjective breakdown, anchored by the father, from which creativity stems:

> – As we, or mother Dana, weave and unweave our bodies, Stephen said, from day to day, their molecules shuttled to and fro, so does the artist weave and unweave his image. And as the mole on my right breast is where it was when I was born, though all my body has been woven of new stuff time after time, so through the ghost of the unquiet father the image of the unliving son looks forth.[59]

Yet there are several significant difficulties with this image: it is not the unquiet father but the unquiet mother who dominates Stephen's self-image. And while Stephen's subjectivity has been gradually 'unweaving' through the course of the novel, he lacks that fixed point, that mole, which both fosters and secures the (re)weaving of the self.[60] And it is, as I have argued in 'Modernism and the Maternal', the ability to reconstitute, to (re)weave the self after subjective breakdown, that enables the artist to bear 'the word'. Stephen, without that paternal anchor, and dominated by the 'unquiet mother', will continue to be frustrated in his efforts to create.

In 'Oxen of the Sun', until reminded otherwise, Stephen, emboldened by drink, maintains the façade he developed in 'Scylla and Charybdis' as artist and intellectual, even if, as Beja points out, this means that he lies about the source of his money.[61] The absence of his spectral mother during both these episodes is significant: again this absence correlates with his bravado, but it is impossible to determine what is cause and what is effect. In line with his arguments in 'Scylla and Charybdis', Stephen represents his own power as extending beyond the mother; he represents the mother as merely providing the physical stepping stone to his own spiritual creation and creativity. Yet it is a transient representation, there again being no anchor to hold his own faint substance to reality. He belies the mother intellectually, but he cannot dismiss her essence which he must encounter whenever he seeks to realize his creativity through the unweaving and weaving of his image. His only recourse is to divorce that essence from the ghost of his own mother. And he can only displace his own mother by reducing her from icon to benign trace.

Patriarchal fictions

In 'Scylla and Charybdis', Stephen articulates the core of his conflict with his mother: '*Amor matris*, subjective and objective genitive, may be the only true thing in life. Paternity may be a legal fiction. Who is the father of any son that any son would love him or he any son?'[62] In seeking the source of consubstantiality between father and son, Stephen alludes to that which blocks his own progress to the father. For in the Dublin that is portrayed in *Ulysses*, it is the mystery of the mother which defines the social and symbolic orders. The apostolic succession of father to son, the begetting of the son by the father on the mother, is disrupted by the strength of the myth of the mother – suffering, virginal, distanced from the familial or literal father. The mother dominates the Blessed Trinity, preventing the (post-oedipal) transformation of that trinity to father, son and spirit.[63] It is in terms of the mother – of a spurious matrilineage – that the child is placed within history and society: she is the 'foremother'.[64] In referring to Eve, Stephen also emphasizes the mother as progenitor of the line.[65] In *Ulysses*, few mothers are presented in anything other than mythical or archetypal terms: the ministering angel, the suffering mother, the primordial mother, the virgin mother, the destroying mother.[66] And for Stephen, though not necessarily articulated as such, they all bleed one into the other, realizing themselves, I suggest, in the figure of May Dedalus.[67]

It is the mothers prevalent within religious and nationalist discourses who are manifest in the figure of the spectral May Dedalus, and which, in 'Circe', alternatively merge with and split off from the literal mother. In this context, it is of note that mother-Ireland makes her first appearance in 'Telemachus' shortly after the apparition of Stephen's mother first appears. 'Old Mother Grogan' with her 'old shrunken paps' brings milk which is praised for its goodness, for the beneficence it affords to individual and nation: 'If we could only live on good food like that ... we wouldn't have the country full of rotten teeth and rotten guts.'[68] Stephen's own poor teeth suggest both the paucity of the nurturing he has received from Ireland and his refusal to partake of her 'nourishment'. Even so, he is compelled to construct about the milk-woman a mythical context in which he deems her to exist.[69] That Stephen's construction of the old woman as messenger from a mythical Ireland is inaccurate obviously picques him; however, the significance of the episode lies in the power of the old woman immediately to be submerged in myth and, thereby, afforded meaning far beyond that which is borne by a simple milkwoman. And it is imbued with such meaning that she is able – in the guise of Old Gummy Granny – to incite Stephen to kill Private Carr, an English soldier, so that 'Ireland will be free'.[70]

Yet the importance of Old Gummy Granny and Mother Grogan to the conflict that haunts Stephen during the course of *Ulysses* is that she corresponds to that paradigm of the mother who – through her mythologization – usurps the rightful place of the son. In the case of mother-Ireland, it is Parnell and others, who have sacrificed themselves in her name, who have been usurped by her myth. They have promoted her cause and given themselves to it.[71] Dead sons are used to feed her myth; and mother-Ireland lives on, rejuvenated, while Parnell remains dead: 'Parnell will never come again, he said.'[72] It is just such a paradigm of the mother usurping the place of the son and father that Stephen reads in Catholicism, and this reading is starkly dramatized in 'Circe'. Further, the dissemination of the Virgin's myth is pervasive enough, and insidious enough, that Joyce figures her as one of the sirens calling men to their doom.[73] In *A Portrait*, Stephen Dedalus had been just so seduced. As 'God' she takes the place of the father; and, in the sorrow she bears for sin, she displaces the son.[74] It is this positioning of mother as martyr that is made manifest in Mina Purefoy's sacrifice in 'Circe', and which is foreshadowed in 'Sirens'.[75] The mother moves between the father's space and the son's space, inevitably playing one off against the other.

It is in 'Nausicaa', however, that the true potency of the Blessed Virgin becomes clear. It is a potency not inherent, but embodied within her construction. Joyce uses the adoration of Mary as part of the context in which the incidents of the episode are played out: the men at a temperance retreat venerate the Virgin, their prayers weaving in and out of the narration.[76] She is virgin 'most powerful', offering protection to those who seek her, refusing to abandon them, and 'fitly is she too a haven of refuge for the afflicted because of the seven dolours which transpierced her own heart'.[77] Yet Joyce challenges the Virgin's benefactions by paralleling them with those of the young 'mothers' on the beach: 'It was all no use soothering him...but Ciss...gave him in his mouth the teat of the suckingbottle and the young heathen was quickly appeased.'[78] The Virgin's potency is resisted by the parody of the narrative. And this comic representation of the spiritual mother appeasing her sons signals the means by which Stephen Dedalus – through and within the parody that is nighttown – may confront and banish the mother who haunts him.

Circe again

Stephen's desire to bear his own artistic creation, to afford it life, is paralleled by his desire for consubstantiality with the father: 'a pregnancy without joy, he said, a birth without pangs, a body without blemish, a belly without bigness.'[79] The death of Stephen's mother blocks his progress towards this goal because, in her embodiment of life and death, creation and destruction, she reifies the conflict against which Stephen struggles in order to create, that of weaving and unweaving his own image. The spectral mother impedes Stephen's access to the father, to that authority by which the (re)weaving of his image may be secured. And her ability to block the father has its source not merely in the peculiar dynamics of the Dedalus family, but the prevalence within Irish nationalist and religious discourses of the mother who has become over-privileged in representation and who is thus able to displace both father and son and impede their union. It is this disruption to the consubstantiality of father and son which threatens the son's subjective self.

In order to be and to live, Stephen must confront this spectral mother and divest her of meaning.[80] And it is in the inchoate world of night-town-dreamtown – where signification is 'naturally' corrupted – that this confrontation occurs. Accompanied by a choir of virgins and confessors 'The Mother' enters 'Circe'. Stephen pleads with her to divulge her secret: 'Tell me the word, mother, if you know now. The word known to all men.'[81] Is the word love, the 'word made flesh', the secret to creation, a seminal word whose articulation will unravel the signification through which the mother draws her potency? It must remain a matter of speculation, for the mother does not answer. She merely reiterates the suffering her son has caused her and the guilt he must bear for his denial of her.[82] She calls for repentance; he reviles her. His accusations – 'the corpsechewer! Raw head and bloody bones!'[83] – resist her myth, but they are not sufficient to dispel her. He renews his vows – *'Ah non, par example! The intellectual imagination! With me or not at all. Non serviam!'*[84] – words which wound her, leaving her wringing her hands and invoking the Sacred Heart of Jesus. Stephen claims mastery: 'No! No! No! Break my spirit all of you if you can! I'll bring you all to heel!'[85] But she is still to claim her triumph over him: 'Inexpressible was my anguish when expiring with love, grief and agony on Mount Calvary.'[86] The mother asserts her place as Christ and saviour.

The Mother's words make explicit the paradigm of the mother's usurpation of the son, and are the culmination of her mythologization. Made explicit, articulated by the mother herself, the mother's position becomes vulnerable: the mother's usurpation of the son may be recognized and dismantled with the wielding of a single word: *'Nothung!'*[87]

*

The effect of the rich symbology of the mother-figure – whether spiritual mother, earth mother, mythical mother or otherwise – is to paralyse both the father and the son as they search fruitlessly for the place wherein they may be united – that place where she is absent and that place where she is, essentially, meaningless. In the post-climactic 'Nostos', father and son are afforded their best opportunity. That Stephen is no longer haunted by his mother is evident from 'Ithaca'. Watching Bloom light the fire, his memories skim over a number of incidents in his life, incidents portrayed in *A Portrait* and *Dubliners*. His mother is present within his memory, but she is contained there, merely a trace among other traces.[88]

Bloom and Stephen are calm and easy in each other's company, but to what extent have they positioned themselves as father and son? Not at all, I suggest.[89] In 'Oxen of the Sun', Bloom positions himself as father to all the young men gathered in the room, but he does so in a moment of whimsy.[90] Further, to claim as critics such as Perreault does that 'Leopold Bloom, unwittingly, undergoes the female experience of pregnancy and childbirth, mystically bearing Stephen to an emotional and spiritual rebirth'[91] is to misread the novel. Stephen and Bloom, in their final encounter in the novel, urinate together, an event more suggestive of a general level of male bonding than the establishment of a mystical tie between father and son (or 'mother' and son).[92] Stephen departs soon after and the reader is no longer privy to his thoughts. Bloom's own thoughts meander as he makes his way to bed. His recollection of the day does not touch directly on his alleged newfound son.[93] Stephen is only mentioned in the context of Bloom's 'narration' to the 'somnolent' Molly.[94] Neither Bloom nor the reader is led to a point of revelation where a new trinity – whether father, son, spirit, or son, paternal mother, maternal father – is established. Equally, Molly is no mother to Stephen, nor, as 'Penelope' reinforces, is she interested in becoming so. The relationship she figures with Stephen is not maternal but carnal.

In the course of 'Ithaca', Bloom notes: 'From infancy to maturity he had resembled his maternal procreatrix. From maturity to senility he would increasingly resemble his paternal procreator.'[95] The note serves almost as a coda to *Ulysses*. Undoubtedly, there is a sense that Stephen, in bleeding the mother of meaning, has reached the nadir of maturity and is moving, in the image and shadow of the father, towards the fullness of this maturity. Yet Bloom is not the father in whose shadow Stephen will develop. What is clear from 'Eumaeus' and 'Ithaca' is that Stephen now possesses the capacity to form some manner of union with a father-figure, but the question as to who that father-figure will be

cannot be answered within the boundaries of *Ulysses*. What the conclusion to *Ulysses* emphasizes is the void created by the mother's absence
and the lack of a father who will effectively fill this void. Lacan refers to
artistic practice as '[adorning] the void' created by the mother's
absence,[96] and it is this potential for creation that hovers over the
final pages of the novel. It is a potential for which Stephen Dedalus
has been searching since his departure from Ireland at the conclusion of
A Portrait. Yet how he will fill the void created by the shattering of the
mother's image in 'Circe' is a matter about which it is possible to do no
more than speculate.

Part V
Conclusion

'sad and weary I go back to you, my cold father'

Yes, you're changing, sonhusband, and you're turning, I can feel you, for a daughterwife from the hills again.

James Joyce, *Finnegans Wake*

The reader of *Finnegans Wake* may feel very much like one of the leaves that Anna Livia Plurabelle[1] has carried on her back, coursing from mountain to ocean, subject to the tumult, the calm, the meandering of her journey from birth to death.[2] After a turbulent, perambulating and often disorienting odyssey,[3] the reader is swept up by Anna Livia's 'final' soliloquy and carried to the eventual peace and calm that comes from the acceptance of death and her passage into the 'arms' of her oceanic progenitor. It is a peace that comes not merely from the rest that death, at last, heralds, but from the sense of rebirth that is figured both in the structure of the novel – enticing the reader from its final page back to its beginning – and in the imagery utilized in the soliloquy:

> May I be wrong! For she'll be sweet for you as I was sweet when I came down out of me mother. My great blue bedroom, the air so quiet, scarce a cloud. In peace and silence. I could have stayed up there for always only. It's something fails us. First we feel. Then we fall. And let her rain now if she likes. Gently or strongly as she likes. Anyway let her rain for my time is come.[4]

Yet the mother who runs from her source in the mountains when the novel resumes is at once a (re)newed mother – (reborn in her daughter), revitalized by her passage from ocean to stream – and the same mother, an eternal, immutable figure.[5] She is, like so many other mothers I have discussed, self-perpetuating, giving way to the father's name, if only to

183

prepare the ground for her own resurgence. Joyce structures the novel around the mythical figure of Finn MacCumhall, 'lying in death beside the river Liffey and watching the history of Ireland and the world – past and future – flow through his mind like flotsam on the river of life';[6] and it is this mythical figure that Anna Livia calls from sleep.[7] Worship of the mother, 'norvena', is over, but at the mother's own behest. The father is allowed again his prominence, but only to ensure her regeneration. She calls him from sleep – Finn wakes and Finn again wakes. It is a call she has made before, and a call she will make again; the novel's *ricorso* ensures that he again will sleep and the 'norvena' will resume. For, despite the defeat of the mother that Joyce figured in the 'Circe' episode of *Ulysses*, the mother's threat to the father's progenitive dominance – articulated within both 'Scylla and Charybdis' and 'Oxen of the Sun', and a predominant concern of Yeats's later poems – remains. The repression of the mother, within the 'dream-world' of the *Wake*, is inverted. The father is subjected in sleep to the meandering of the mother – his dream dictated and, in effect, governed by her currents – unable to wake until she sacrifices herself to the paternal ocean.

'Fatimiliafamilias'

In George Moore's *The Lake*, Oliver Gogarty immerses himself in the lake – metaphorically realized in Nora Glynn – and emerges free of the constraints of the Catholic tradition. In the final section of *Finnegans Wake*, 'most blessed Kevin' immerses himself in a bathtub: 'recluse, he meditated continuously with seraphic ardour the primal sacrament of baptism or the regeneration of all men by affusion of water. Yee.'[8] Both baptismal rituals present an acute comparison with the promise of life embodied in Anna Livia Plurabelle:

> and slipping sly, by Sallynoggin, as happy as the day is wet, babbling, bubbling, chattering to herself, deloothering the fields on their elbows leaning with the sloothering slide of her, giddygaddy, granny-ma, gossipaceaous Anna Livia.[9]

Her waters not only cleanse and refresh; they sluice the flotsam and jetsam of history, such that history itself is regenerated, shaping the banks within which that history is contained and layering (like silt) narrative upon narrative each time she traverses from mountain to sea. She is, like Bertha in *Exiles*, figured as the fecund[10] sexual mother whom Joyce sought to encounter in order to realize his creativity.[11]

Anna Livia's 'untitled mamafesta' begins with a prayer – 'In the name of Annah the Allmaziful, the Everliving, the Bringer of Plurabilities, haloed be her eve, her singtime sung, her rill be run, unhemmed as it is uneven.'[12] In Joyce's rich parody of Christian prayer, it becomes evident that there lingers in Anna Livia the same threat inherent to the venerated mother that figures in the work of Yeats, O'Casey and Moore, and in Joyce's own *Ulysses* and *A Portrait of the Artist as a Young Man*. However, it still sees the usurpation of the father's place: reverence is afforded not to 'Our Father' but to 'Our Mother'. Christian tradition may be resisted; yet it is a resistance which effects the enthronement of the mother. She is 'Mother of us all!... My Lourde! My Lourde!',[13] her apparitions figuring her in the place of the saviour, that same place from which Stephen Dedalus sought to banish her with his '*Nothung!*' In this, again, the mother is figured as self-perpetuating: 'for teaching the Fatima Woman history of the Fatimiliafamilias, repeating herself, on which purposeth of the spirit of nature as definely developed in time.'[14] The myth is not only 'handmade' – the handmaiden herself a construct – it encompasses and overwhelms the father's line – the 'familias' – within the mother's shrine; the 'Word', domain of the patriarchy, is realized and uttered by the matriarchy.[15]

More powerful than the parody he employs, Joyce resists the icon of the Virgin Mother through a maternal sexuality that consistently is foregrounded: 'and knew her fleshly when with all my bawdy did I her worship.'[16] It is through her sexuality that the mother may (seem to) be possessed and contained;[17] yet it is a union – figured in terms of the bond between England and Ireland – which ostensibly may be dissolved.[18] Even so, the 'bonds of schismacy' remain impenetrable, foreshadowing the eventual immersion of the mother–wife–daughter in the son–husband–father ocean:

> she who will not rast from her running to seek him till, with the help of the okeamic, some such time that she shall have been after hiding the crumbends of his enormousness in the areyou looking for Pearlfar sea . . . stood forth.[19]

Anna Livia Plurabelle longs for the father – 'The river felt she wanted salt'[20] – yet her longing signals her own desire for regeneration rather than her subjection to the paternal authority. Throughout *Finnegans Wake*, the father's line is resisted, and this resistance emanates from the mother's essential carriage of events, of the histories and narratives that the novel encompasses. Inherent to the mother is the potential for the erasure of the father's name:

> her wife, Langley, the prophet ... disappeared ... from the sourface of this earth, the austral plain he had transmaried himself to, so entirely spootlessly (the mother of the book with a dustwhisk tabularasing his obliteration done upon her involucrum) as to tickle the speculative to all but opine.[21]

Not only is the father threatened, but the 'mother of the book' emphasizes the creative capacity of the female at the expense of the male.

In essence, *Finnegans Wake* posits a mother-figure who encompasses the same threat to son and father that is represented in Joyce's earlier work, yet that threat is never realized. Conversely, it operates to engender life rather than death; to foster and nurture the imagination rather than choke it. Why? The answer lies, I argue, in the mother's willingness to sacrifice herself rather than her children, and to recognize the centrality of her immersion in a 'male principle',[22] here figured as a father ocean, in order to occasion her own regeneration and in order to access the 'seed' that can come only from the father:

> Life, he himself said once ... is a wake, livit or krikit, and on the bunk of our breadwinning lies to cropse of our seedfather, a phrase which the establisher of the world by law might pretinately write across the chestfront of all manorwomanborn. The scene, refreshed, reroused, was never to be forgotten.[23]

In her very 'plurability', Anna Livia operates differently from the ghost of May Dedalus who focused representation within herself, functioning for Stephen as a singularity towards which all signification moved and within which meaning converged. In Anna Livia (paralleling the entire *Wake* and those who 'attend' it) meaning is uncertain: it radiates from her and constantly shifts: 'Her untitled mamafesta memorialising the Mosthighest has gone by many names at disjointed times.'[24] She can be contained by neither time nor space – 'Anna was, Livia is, Plurabelle's to be'[25] – yet she recognizes and heeds the paternal creator who seeds her eternity: 'The eversower of the seeds of light to cowld owld sowls ... – speaketh.'[26] Her renewal, and the words and histories that she bears, are dependent not on a spurious promise of privilege in return for the service of herself and her children, but on a cycle of birth, death and rebirth which has its source in the father not of law but of creation:

'Creator he has created for his creatured ones a creation.'[27] In my reading of the 'creative act' Joyce has realized in *Finnegans Wake*, I differ from those critics who seek within the text an *écriture feminine* or the representation of female desire.[28] Rather than claiming, as Lawrence does, that Anna Livia's ' "untitled mamafesta" might be a figure for the wayward path of the writing of desire',[29] I suggest Joyce interfuses *Finnegans Wake* with both maternal and paternal creation – maternal 'writing' and paternal 'writing' – which results in the unique structure and narrative of the novel. Further, 'maternal desire' does not subvert the 'law and language of the father', as Henke argues.[30] The maternal river carries the encoded law and language of the father towards a finality where – through immersion in the father or even through critical explication – it will be deciphered and rendered according to the father's name. This encoding and deciphering of language parallels, I suggest, death and rebirth.

In accessing this cycle of death and rebirth, Joyce realized the 'post-creation'; he traversed the maternal spaces that foster the disruption of signification and seeded himself the (re)creation of signifying practices that characterizes *Finnegans Wake*. 'Leave the letter that never begins to go find the latter that never comes to end, written in smoke and blurred by mist and signed of solitude, sealed at night':[31] Joyce has forsaken the Annunciation – the Virgin waiting passively for the seed – as his image of creation and turned instead to a more primitive, a more mythical paradigm encompassing cycles of creation and destruction, cycles realized in the mother yet, despite the threat to patrilineage that maternal regeneration entails, sustained ultimately by the father.

Step by step to matricide

In *Finnegans Wake*, Joyce engages many of the same themes that concerned him in his earlier works, and in terms of the representation of the mother-figure, Anna Livia Plurabelle again affords the opportunity for not merely the exploration of the mother's place in society, but her symbolic presence and the competition – here between mother and father – for creative space. As I emphasized above, here the mother gives way – albeit tenuously – to a paternal creation, one that both incorporates the male author and diminishes the threat to patrilineage that creativity centred wholly in the mother occasions. Yet the transition from the mother-figure who sought regeneration through the destruction of her own children and the denial of the familial father to one who recognized her dependence on the generative father was an arduous one (not without its casualties). And this figuration of the mother who realizes her rebirth through her own sacrificial death could only be accomplished through a thorough dismantling of the mother's social role as precursor to the deconstruction of her symbolic position, specifically the reification of Church, Nation and sacrifice in her purged and idealized corpus. It is just such a transition that the work of Moore, Joyce, Yeats, Synge and O'Casey evince.

When he began writing in the 1880s, George Moore was working within a largely realist literary tradition, enhancing that tradition with his own experiments in naturalism, impressionism and decadence. He lived the greater part of his working life in a social and political climate that was defined – as the conclusion of *Esther Waters* and *A Drama in Muslin* suggest – by 'smug optimism . . . [and] materialism',[32] and dominated by the oppressive morality and comfortable stability that marked Victoria's reign. It was a climate remarkable for its durability; yet, at the same time, it was subject to an insidious decay which emanated from its inherent stagnation. However, in Ireland, the country of his birth and the country in which his pre-eminent works are set, social and political stagnation was giving way to a desire for self-realization, both economically and politically, and an emerging search for a cultural identity, distinct from England, and wrought from the myths and legends of an heroic Ireland. This was the climate in which Irish modernism was born, and while Moore – somewhat like Moses – led the way, he himself was unable to 'enter'. Moore's achievement was, nevertheless, fundamental to the development of Anglo-Irish literature, and *The Lake* remains, I suggest, the prototypical work of Irish modernism.

When Oliver Gogarty swims across the lake towards his rebirth, he anticipates Stephen Dedalus, Christy Mahon, Sean Casside, and he foreshadows Yeats's 'Wisdom', 'A Song from "The Player Queen"' and 'On Woman', and the paternal history borne by Anna Livia Plurabelle: immersion in the maternal principle fosters the collapse of an inherited, ill-fitting subjectivity and the emergence in its place of that desired self who is pre-figured in the mother. Yet Moore himself came to this position primarily through an engagement with the mother in her social aspect – she was, after all, defined within culture according to her social function – representing the mother as protecting her social position either through the deliverance of her children to Church and Nation, or to that stagnant cycle of marriage, generation and death which served to enhance and perpetuate the mother's position. In this, Moore worked directly with the figuration of the mother within Catholic and Nationalist discourses, and the function attributed to the mother by those discourses. It was just this mother that Moore personally encountered in his autobiographical works and who he, ultimately, condemned for the parasitic service she demanded of her children and the psychically contorted and constrained individuals that Ireland produced as a result. Ireland's own stagnation and its debilitating emigration could be traced, Moore's work suggests, not merely to priest and church, but to the mother whose allegiance to celibate rather than generative 'fathers' bolstered a decrepit social system.

While the representation of the mother in Moore's work diverged on occasion from this central paradigm, it is this interrelationship between mother, child and church which dominates. Moore's only answer to the mother's procurement of children to religious service was its exposure and, eventually, a self-imposed exile. His work encapsulated the life and death struggle between mother and child that he had inherited from the Irish literary tradition; yet, while utilizing this struggle metaphorically, he was only able to resolve it in social terms. The single exception is *The Lake*, where a physical transition mirrored a psychological journey, and Moore was able to achieve this by refiguring the mother and exploring not her potential for destruction but her potential for (re)creation.

The social realization of the mother–child–church dynamic was taken up by Joyce in *Dubliners*; however, the rich symbolical palimpsest underlying the stories afforded him the scope to move beyond exposition and towards resolution. Such resolution was not to be effected until *Finnegans Wake*, and its operation not even wholly understood until *Ulysses*, but Joyce was able to see within the mother-figure her essential duality, the creation–destruction binarism which, his work suggests, defined her. He condemned the manipulation of this binarism by church, state and the mother herself, before exploiting that binarism to realize his own creativity. The mother, certainly in the early social realism of *Dubliners*, was equated with entrapment, and Ireland's paralysis stemmed from the covert power she wielded in infantilizing men and seducing men and children to the service of church and state. Yet, while this image of the mother was still dominant in *A Portrait of the Artist as a Young Man*, Joyce opposed it with a mother-figure in whom rebirth is centred – that mother in whom subjectivity is pre-figured and who, importantly, is seeded by the father in whom a desired subjectivity is realized. Yet, while *A Portrait* identifies these two aspects of the mother, Stephen centred his creative self in an icon – that of the Annunciation – which owed more to the former than the latter, and it is this identification which presages Stephen's creative failure. Even so, in terms of Joyce's artistic achievement in *A Portrait*, the prevarication that is evident in the figuration of the mother, particularly the tension that exists between the mother through whom creation is possible and the mother who 'seeks' the subjective destruction of her children, realizes itself in the novel's narrative structure. The refusal of various paternal histories – be they familial, historical or religious – is mirrored in the tentative breakdown of a linear narrative that seems to resolve itself only when Stephen accepts a mythical father – Daedalus – and attains through that father a place as speaking subject. This place – realized in Stephen's diaries – sits uneasily with the creative space he has fashioned for himself, that of virgin mother within a religious icon; and such an icon is acutely at odds with the sexual mother in whom creativity, Joyce insists in his letters and in works such as *Exiles*, resides. It is only in *Finnegans Wake* – having dispatched the destructive mother in *Ulysses* – that Joyce merged both aspects of the mother into a life-enforcing, regenerating entity.

Among the Irish modernists it was primarily Synge who dealt with the mother-figure at the level of her dualities, and in this his work encompassed her in both social and symbolic spheres. Paralleling a semiotic/symbolic divide, and embodied in the mother – in crude terms – on the basis of her possession or loss of the child, Synge represented the mother in terms of a number of core binarisms: ritual/carnival, protection/violation, life/death. The mother's liminal position in relation to these binarisms afforded her a unique perspective on social and symbolic structures, and on that which was repressed in order to maintain those structures. In this, Synge was able to merge those aspects of the mother which representation had largely kept separate – creation and destruction. While Moore, and Joyce and Yeats in their earlier works, had tended to figure this binarism by bifurcating the mother into distinct figurations, Synge emphasized the mother's liminality, and thereby, the essential contiguity of birth and death, creation and destruction. He achieved this structurally by positioning the mother-figure within marginal social spaces – the graveyard and the roadside ditch; and by alienating her from society – as mad or drunk. From this liminal position the mother disclosed the tenuous foundations of the social and symbolic orders, thereby occasioning the opportunity either to resist those orders or manipulate them.

It is just such a maternal dualism that Yeats figured in his later work; as his work developed, and as he came to explore more deeply his own creativity, one prevailing theme came to dominate his representation of the mother-figure: her role in the establishment of iconographies and myths and the threat to patrilineage that this role occasioned. Yeats's suggestion that the mother was instrumental in her own symbolization emphasized both the means by which symbolic networks proliferated and, ironically, the poet's role in constructing the mother in order to realize or enhance his own (creative) subjectivity.

Such a construction of the mother had its epitome in O'Casey's *Auto-biographies*, the explicit nature of O'Casey's construction illuminating the more subtle shades in which Joyce and Yeats painted their own portraits of the mother. For O'Casey, the search for the 'desired' mother, in whom subjectivity was prefigured, was displaced by the *construction* of that mother-figure who would stand in opposition to the child's desired subjectivity. It was through resistance to this figure that the child's subjectivity might be defined. What O'Casey's work emphasized was the need for social revolution, and the importance of the subversion of the symbolic order as a means of effecting just such a revolution. However, what comes of this subversion is not the replacement of myth with truth, but rather the replacement of myth with an alternative myth. The demythologization of the mother-figure was an important device in effecting social change; yet what O'Casey was unable to challenge was the remythologization of the mother which any victorious hegemony would undoubtedly foster.

It is through representation, Kristeva suggests, that the mother is most effectively 'murdered' and a space vacated for the development of the child's subjectivity. That the Anglo-Irish modernists effectively murdered the mother should not be contested: she became the focus of blame for the stagnation and inertia of Irish society, for seducing Ireland's 'children' into the service of timeworn authorities, and for the destruction and 'disappearance' of Ireland's greatest source of potential renewal – her 'sons'. Yet it must be remembered that in so constructing the mother, the writers were responding to – and in many senses doing little more than exposing and deconstructing – a figuration of the mother that was, effectively, a social and cultural reality. While it is difficult to blame the 'Irish mother' for attaining a spurious privilege through the only means available to her – absolute service to religious and nationalist causes – it is also difficult to condemn those writers who accused the mother for her participation in a moribund cycle that appropriated identity and abnegated individuality. While this culturally sanctioned figure of the Irish mother was murdered through representation, it is important to weigh this symbolic 'matricide' against the creative vigour that it effected.

*

The deconstruction of those mother-figures privileged within the Irish cultural tradition – her murder through representation – served both to deny the cultural tradition and discourses in which she figured, and to create the conditions whereby maternal spaces could be appropriated and utilized in fostering not only creativity, but the reconstruction and renewal of signification. And this is precisely what occurred in Anglo-Irish literature in the late nineteenth and early twentieth centuries. The question is: why at this time, and why with such intensity in Ireland? The answer, I argue, is to be found in the seminal nature of the mother-figure in the Irish cultural tradition out of which these writers developed (and which itself was at its most intense in this period) and the profound social and political shifts that Ireland was experiencing at the time. Coupled with the more generic effects of the *fin-de-siècle*, the Great War and literary movements pervading Europe, the conditions were established for a concentration of symbolic disruption and representational 'crises' not previously experienced.

To forge their own traditions – literary, cultural and historical – and to subvert social and moral edicts which limited their personal and sexual freedoms,[33] Anglo-Irish writers needed not only to rewrite those traditions but to encounter the mother-figure inherent in them. Such an encounter, while figured in social and symbolic terms, could not be wholly divorced from the personal and the psychological; the mother encountered was not merely the figure constructed by the patriarchal cultural tradition, but the pre-oedipal mother in whom the potential for subversion of the symbolic rested. In accessing that mother, and in chancing the subjective dissolution that submergence in the pre-oedipal dyad occasioned, the writer penetrated not only a fount of creativity but a source of profound symbolic renewal. It is precisely this that Moore realizes in *The Lake*, and that Joyce and Yeats exploit in challenging signification, in resisting and refiguring myth and tradition, and in confronting the social and symbolic structures by which such traditions are maintained. That it was almost impossible in this period to engage with the Irish cultural tradition without engaging with sanctified and pervasive mother-figures (mother-Ireland and mother-Church specifically) facilitated the exploitation of a maternal principle in realizing creative subjectivities. While certainly not the only catalyst of Irish modernism, resistance of these mother-figures manifested itself not only in shifts in the representation of the mother-figure, but moreover in a regeneration of signification occasioned by the writers' incursions – however transient they might have been – into maternal spaces.

Yet it was not merely the pervasive nature of the mother-figure within these discourses which impacted on the literature of the period but, more importantly, the subjective death which these mother-figures demanded of their 'children'. To elude this 'death', it was necessary to deconstruct the mother-figure, a process which almost inexorably led to the search for either the 'true' mother, who existed beyond the culturally constructed mother, or that mother in whom a 'desired' subjectivity was prefigured. It was here, as a corollary of this search, that the writer gained access to presymbolic maternal spaces and the potential therein for profoundly disrupting representational practices. And this, coupled with the social and political ferment impacting on Ireland during the early decades of the twentieth century – disturbances which themselves effected ruptures in the socio-symbolic order – afforded these writers the means of effecting the symbolic subversion integral to modernism.

Notes

Mother-Ireland calls me

1 *Irish Homestead*, 4 July 1914. Quoted in Bourke (1994).
2 J. Joyce, *Exiles, The Essential James Joyce*, H. Levin, ed. (London: Jonathan Cape, 1948) 430.
3 Joyce, *Exiles*, 439. J. Joyce, Letter to Nora Barnacle Joyce, 5 September 1909, *Letters of James Joyce, Volume II*, R. Ellmann, ed. (London: Faber & Faber, 1966) 248. See also, Ellmann (1982) 293, and Henke (1990) 105.
4 R.F. Foster, *Modern Ireland, 1600–1972* (London: Allen Lane, 1988) 433.
5 Luddy (1992) in her review of the relevant research dealing with the period 1800–1900 emphasizes that one area where the research is particularly scant is that investigating the role and function of motherhood in Irish society: 'Did a cult of motherhood exist within Irish society? If so, when did it develop, and how strong a role did the churches play in its implementation? How did couples regulate their families?' (28).
6 A.J. Wiemers, 'Rural Irishwomen: Their Changing Role, Status, and Condition', *Eire-Ireland* 29.1 (1994): 76–91, 77.
7 H.L. Wood, 'Women in Myths and Early Depictions', *Irish Women: Image and Achievement*, E. Ni Chuilleanain, ed. (Dublin: Arlen House, 1985) 16. See also MacCana (1980).
8 A.-M. Fyfe, 'Women and Mother Ireland', *Image and Power: Women in Fiction in the Twentieth Century*, S. Sceats and G. Cunningham, eds (London: Longman, 1996) 184.
9 R. Sawyer, *'We are but Women': Women in Ireland's History* (London & New York: Routledge, 1993) 1–2.
10 J. Bourke, *Husbandry to Housewifery: Women, Economic Change amd Housework in Ireland, 1890–1914* (Oxford: Clarendon Press, 1993) 262.
11 Taken from 'Household Hints', *Irish Homestead*, 4 March 1899. Quoted in Bourke (1993) 224.
12 F. O'Brien, *The Poor Mouth (An Béal Bocht)* (London: Flamingo, 1993) 14.
13 See, for example, Sawyer (1993) 81, Bourke (1993) 268, Foster (1988) 412, and Innes (1993).
14 Howes (1996), for example, writes: 'women could best embody and safeguard the national character by staying home and becoming mothers, and in this context female emigration, women working outside the home, and resistance to tradtional gender roles were all linked as threats to the national being' (137).
15 *The Leader*, 15 September 1900. Quoted in Hywel ('Elise and the Great Queens of Ireland: Femininity as Constructed by *Sinn Fein* and the Abbey Theatre', in O'Brien Johnson and Cairns, 1991) 25.
16 Bourke (1993) quotes from a Lenten pastoral letter distributed by the Bishop of Clyne in 1911: 'inside the house, the floor is brushed and unspotted, the walls are decorated with suitable prints, the simple household furniture is

neatly kept and arranged, and the mother of the home, proud queen of her own little realm, is surrounded by healthy, happy children. It is a blessed change, hopeful of the future of our country' (210–11).

17 M. Howes, *Yeats's Nations: Gender, Class and Irishness* (Cambridge: Cambridge University Press, 1996) 137.

18 D. Cairns and S. Richards, *Writing Ireland: Colonialism, Nationalism and Culture* (Manchester: Manchester University Press, 1988) 79.

19 Cardinal J.H. Newman, 'The Glories of Mary for the Sake of Her Son', *Discourses Addressed to Mixed Congregations* (London: Longmans Green & Co., 1902) 344.

20 Newman, 'The Glories of Mary for the Sake of Her Son', 349.

21 Such disquiet is evident in Bram Stoker's *Dracula*, where Jonathan Harker is given a rosary and crucifix for protection: 'as an English Churchman, I have been taught to regard such things as in some measure idolatrous.' The old woman pleads with him to take the rosary 'For your mother's sake' (1983) 5. See also Sawyer (1993) 14. With regard to the figure of the *pietà*, I read it as an image not so much of sacrifice but of suffering, and, as such, it encapsulates what was happening to Irish Catholicism through mariolatry. Here, the mother threatens to overwhelm the son, centring herself as figure of suffering and thereby responsible for limiting or marginalizing her son's presence. In this, she has much in common with mother-Ireland.

22 See Cairns and Richards, 'Tropes and Traps: Aspects of 'Woman' and Nationality in Twentieth-Century Irish Drama', in O'Brien Johnson and Cairns, 1991.

23 T. Brown, *Ireland: A Social and Cultural History, 1922–1985* (London: Fontana, 1981) 80.

24 G.B. Shaw, *John Bull's Other Island, John Bull's Other Island and Major Barbara: Also How He Lied to Her Husband* (London: Archibald Constable & Co., 1907) 18. Later in the play, Doyle says: 'Is Ireland never to have a chance? First she was given to the rich; and now that they have gorged on her flesh, her bones are to be flung to the poor, that can do nothing but suck the marrow out of her' (65).

25 W.J. McCormack, 'Nightmares of History: James Joyce and the Phenomenon of Anglo-Irish Literature', *James Joyce and Modern Literature*, W.J. McCormack and A. Stead, eds (London: Routledge & Kegan Paul, 1982).

26 S. Deane, *Celtic Revivals: Essays in Modern Irish Literature, 1880–1980* (London: Faber & Faber, 1985) 103; S. Deane, *A Short History of Irish Literature* (London: Hutchison, 1986) 179. In determining what writers to examine in this work, I have been guided by literary historians and the broad consensus that exists with regard to the central writers of the period. Oscar Wilde and G.B. Shaw are the obvious omissions, and work on these authors would no doubt provide an interesting perspective on my research.

27 T. Eagleton, *Heathcliff and the Great Hunger: Studies in Irish Culture* (London: Verso, 1995) 154.

28 D. Kiberd, *Inventing Ireland* (London: Jonathan Cape, 1995). See also, Innes (1994) who argues that figures such as Mother Ireland '[seemed] to be a product not so much of colonialism and dispossession itself as the consequent anti- colonialist and nationalist movements' (10).

29 M. Bradbury and J. McFarlane, 'The Name and Nature of Modernism', *Modernism: 1890–1930*, M. Bradbury and J. McFarlane, eds (London: Penguin, 1976) 47.

30 M. Ian, *Remembering the Phallic Mother: Psychoanalysis, Modernism and the Fetish* (Ithaca, NY & London: Cornell University Press, 1993) 87.

31 J. Kristeva, 'Semiotics', *The Kristeva Reader*, T. Moi, ed. (Oxford: Blackwell, 1986) 86. In a similar vein, Wollaeger (1993) refers to the distance between the narrative event and the narrative discourse that is evident in modernism.

32 F. Kermode, *The Sense of an Ending: Studies in the Theory of Fiction* (New York: Oxford University Press, 1967).

33 D. Sidorsky, 'Modernism and the Emancipation of Literature from Morality: Teleology and Vocation in Joyce, Ford and Proust', *New Literary History* 15.1 (1983): 137–53, 143.

34 See, for example, Gilbert and Gubar (1988), Showalter ('Syphilus, Sexuality, and the Fiction of the *Fin de Siecle*', in Yeazell, 1986) and Gilbert and Gubar (1989).

35 G.B. Shaw, Preface to Politicians', *John Bull's Other Island*, v.

36 Foster, *Modern Ireland, 1600–1972*, 451.

37 F.S.L. Lyons, *Ireland Since the Famine* (London: Fontana, 1973), 234.

38 Kiberd, *Inventing Ireland*, 99–100. Kiberd ('The Perils of Nostaligia: A Critique of the Revival', in Connolly (1982)) also refers to the 'syndicated wisecrack that a literary revival occurred because five or six people lived in the same town and hated one another cordially' (1).

39 See Foster (1988), Hall (1980), Lyons (1973), and Maxwell (1984).

40 Shaw, *John Bull's Other Island*, 14.

41 S.M. Watt, 'Boucicault and Whitbread: The Dublin Stage at the End of the Nineteenth Century', *Eire-Ireland* 18.3 (1983): 23–53, 25.

42 Watt, 'Boucicault and Whitbread', 23.

43 W.B. Yeats, *Dramatis Personae, Autobiographies* (London: Macmillan, 1961) 398.

44 D.E.S. Maxwell, *A Critical History of Modern Irish Drama, 1891–1980* (Cambridge: Cambridge University Press, 1984) 7.

45 See, for example, 'Revolution in Poetic Language', *The Kristeva Reader*.

46 L. Gauthier, 'Desire for Origin/Original Desire: Luce Irigaray on Maternity, Sexuality and Language', *Canadian Fiction Magazine* 57 (1986): 41–6. Kristeva (1986) makes a related point in 'Stabat Mater': 'a woman seldom (although not necessarily) experiences her passion (love and hatred) for another woman without having taken her own mother's place – without having herself become a mother, and especially without slowly learning to differentiate between same beings – as being face to face with her daughter forces her to do' (184).

47 M. Sprengnether, *The Spectral Mother: Freud, Feminism and Psychoanalysis* (Ithaca, NY & London: Cornell University Press, 1990) 153.

48 Cairns and Richards (1987), Cixous (1976), Cullingford (1993), Gallagher (1983), Henke (1990), Henke and Unkeless (1982), Howes (1996), Innes (1993), Keane (1988), Kline (1983), O'Brien Johnson and Cairns (1991), and Scott (1984).

49 G.C. Kline, *The Last Courtly Lover: Yeats and the Idea of Woman* (Ann Arbor: UMI Research Press, 1983) 2.

50 B. Webster, *Yeats: A Psychoanalytic Study* (London: Macmillan, 1973) 42.

51 T.M. Dipasquale, 'Seraphic Seduction in *Portrait of the Artist* and *Ulysses*', *Studies in the Novel* 19.4 (1987): 475–85, 478.

52 E.B. Gose, 'Joyce's Goddess of Generation', *James Joyce: The Centennial Symposium*, M. Beja, et al., eds (Urbana & Chicago: University of Illinois Press, 1986) 163.

53 S.A. Henke, 'James Joyce and Women: The Matriarchal Muse', *Work in Progress: Joyce Centenary Essays*, R.F. Peterson, A.M. Cohn and E.L. Epstein, eds (Carbondale: Southern Illinois University Press, 1983) 118.

54 S.A. Henke, *James Joyce and the Politics of Desire* (London: Routledge, 1990) 3.

55 B.K. Scott, 'Emma Clery in *Stephen Hero*: A Young Woman Walking Proudly through the Decayed City', *Women in Joyce*, S. Henke and E. Unkeless eds (Urbana, Chicago: University of Illinois Press, 1982) 57.

56 See, for example, Ellmann (1982), Henke (1983), Henke (1990), Henke and Unkeless (1982), Knowles (1986), Leonard (1993), Levitt (1989), Keane (1988), Morrison (1993), Norris (1987), Obed (1985) and Scott (1984). 'In Joycean psychology,' Norris insists, 'being the good child means being the dead child' (16).

57 A. O'Connor, *Child Murderess and Dead Child Traditions: A Comparative Study* (Helsinki: Suomalainen Tiedeakatemia, 1991) 94–5.

58 See, for example, Sheridan le Fanu's *The House by the Churchyard* and Bram Stoker's *Dracula*. In the latter, the good mother/destroying mother binarism is figured in the characters of Mina Harker and Lucy Westernra respectively.

59 E.B. Cullingford, *Gender and History in Yeats's Love Poetry* (New York: Cambridge University Press, 1993) 7.

60 See Ellmann (1964), Ellmann (1987), Kuch (1989) and Levine (1983).

Home and hearth

1 E. Grosz, *Sexual Subversions: Three French Feminists* (Sydney: Allen & Unwin, 1989) 121.

2 T. Brennan, *The Interpretation of the Flesh: Freud and Femininity* (London & New York: Routledge, 1992) 226.

3 G. Moore, *A Drama in Muslin* (Gerrards Cross: Colin Smythe, 1981) 325.

4 W.E. Houghton, *The Victorian Frame of Mind, 1830–1870* (New Haven & London: Yale University Press, 1957) 341.

5 N. Auerbach, *Woman and the Demon: The Life of a Victorian Myth* (Cambridge, Mass.: Harvard University Press, 1982) 72. Cullingford (1993) similarly refers to the 'angel' being 'entombed and sanctified' (46).

6 M. Luddy, *Women and Philanthropy in Nineteenth Century Ireland* (Cambridge: Cambridge University Press, 1995) 2.

7 E. Grosz, *Volatile Bodies: Towards a Corporeal Feminism* (Sydney: Allen & Unwin, 1994) 15.

8 See, for example, Laquer (1987).

9 M. Poovey, *Uneven Developments: The Ideological Work of Gender in mid-Victorian England* (Chicago: University of Chicago Press, 1988) 77. For extensive discussions of women both as commodities within the political economy

and as suppressed by that same economy, see, for example, de Beauvoir (1972), Millet (1972), Manheimer (1979), Kaplan (1992) and Poovey (1988). See also Grosz (1989) for a useful discussion of Irigaray's work in this area.

10 See, for example, Lee, 'Women and the Church Since the Famine', in Mac-Curtain and O Corrain, 1978, and Lubbers (1985).

11 Grosz, *Volatile Bodies*, 19.

12 Poovey, *Uneven Developments*, 78.

13 M. Sprengnether, *The Spectral Mother: Freud, Feminism and Psychoanalysis* (Ithaca, NY & London: Cornell University Press, 1990) 215.

14 Brennan, *The Interpretation of the Flesh*, 225.

15 P.J. Keane, *Terrible Beauty: Yeats, Joyce, Ireland and the Myth of the Devouring Female* (Columbia: University of Missouri Press, 1988) 18.

16 J. Manheimer, 'Murderous Mothers: The Problem of Parenting in the Victorian Novel', *Feminist Studies* 5.3 (1979): 530–46, 545.

17 Sprengnether (1990) theorizes that the pre-oedipal mother – that mother who is not subject to social and symbolic authorities – is '[allied]...with hostile or threatening forces' (117). Of particular relevance to my argument is her contention that the significant psychical moment – in terms of the establishment of the social and symbolic orders – is not the resolution of the Oedipus complex, but is instead centred in the mother-child split that begins at 'birth'. This argument is also put forward by Ian (1993).

18 J. Kristeva, *Black Sun: Depression and Melancholia* (New York: Columbia University Press, 1989) 28.

19 Kristeva, *Black Sun*, 28.

20 Cullingford's (1993) suggestion that representations within the *fin-de-siècle* of women as monsters was a response to the growing assertiveness of women does not entirely unravel the source of this trope. It is, I argue, more fear of the sexual and maternal 'power' that would be unleashed should women be granted greater social and political freedoms that led to the proliferation of the trope than fear of losing (patriarchal) political and social power should those freedoms be granted.

The mother's procurement of the child in George Moore

1 J. Hone, *The Life of George Moore* (London: Gollancz, 1936) 219.

2 G. Moore, *Hail and Farewell: Ave, Salve, Vale: Ave* (Gerrards Cross: Colin Smythe, 1976) 213.

3 S. Deane, *A Short History of Irish Literature* (London: Hutchison, 1986) 145. Moore himself, in *Confessions of a Young Man*, records: 'Two dominant notes in my character – an original hatred of my native country, and a brutal loathing of the religion I was brought up in' (76).

4 G. Moore, *Esther Waters* (Oxford: Oxford University Press, 1983) 394.

5 Moore, *Esther Waters*, 227.

6 N. Auerbach, *Woman and the Demon: The Life of a Victorian Myth* (Cambridge, Mass.: Harvard University Press, 1982) 7.

7 Watt (1984) argues quite persuasively that Esther's choice of husband is determined as much on the basis of a comparison of their physical strengths and weaknesses as any other. This argument does not conflict with my own,

and in fact supports my reading of Esther's struggle against society – as represented by Moore – as being profoundly influenced by social Darwinism and an obvious legacy of Moore's earlier compact with naturalism. Esther chooses a 'mate' who will enable her and her offspring to succeed in the struggle for survival. While William's apparent physical superiority – a significant factor in her early attraction to him – is an important element of that choice, given the situation in which she finds herself, a union which will bestow social respectability on her child is a significant advantage to both her and Jackie. More recently, Grubgeld (1994) has also emphasized that Jackie's survival is paramount, and Esther's choices are prioritized on that basis.

8   Moore, *Esther Waters*, 151.

9   G. Moore, *A Mummer's Wife* (London: William Heinemann, 1918) 4. It is important to note that on the principal occasion that Ralph 'rules' his mother's will – that is, whether they should let out a room to the mummers – he unwittingly provides the catalyst for the breakdown of his already weak marriage.

10 Moore, *A Mummer's Wife*, 125.

11 Moore, *Hail and Farewell: Salve*, 275.

12 G. Moore, *A Drama in Muslin* (Gerrards Cross: Colin Smythe, 1981) 68–9. See also Cave ('George Moore and His Irish Novels', in Martin, 1985).

13 Moore, *A Drama in Muslin*, 127. Moynahan (1995) makes the interesting point that the lack of reference to political and social causes in the latter stages of the novel is due to historical necessity: that is, at this time, various legislative measures had 'defused the main issues of contention between the landowners and the tenants and brought the Land War to a close for at least the next few years' (156–7). This defusion of conflict is, of course, reflected in the novel as Alice and Dr Reed make their way out of Ireland.

14 Moore, *A Drama in Muslin*, 202.

15 Moore, *A Drama in Muslin*, 132.

16 Moore, *A Drama in Muslin*, 328.

17 Moore, *A Drama in Muslin*, 324.

18 Moore, *A Drama in Muslin*, 315.

19 Moore, *Hail and Farewell: Vale*, 608.

20 The paucity of life and vibrancy is also reflected in the title of the volume. As Carens ('In Quest of a New Impulse: George Moore's *The Untilled Field* and James Joyce's *Dubliners*', in Kilroy (1984)), for example, notes: 'The title [*The Untilled Field*] for which Moore settled implies both the economic state of the country and the rejection of sexual opportunity' (48). Costello (1977) similarly notes that the title 'suggests not only the unploughed acres of Irish fiction, but also the uncultivated Irish heart' (51). Gilbert and Gubar (1989) argue that in *The Untilled Field* Moore used 'an artful combination of surface and symbol' (98) that would evolve thoroughly in the work of Joyce, most notably in *Dubliners* and *Ulysses*. Moore's utilization of surface and symbol is most readily seen in his commentary – implict and explicit – on the Catholic Church and the priesthood. In the context of the mother's alliance with the priest in the securing of children for Catholicism, the story 'A Letter to Rome' offers an interesting twist – Father MacTurnan seeks to shift the relationship between priest and mother from a symbolic to a literal one.

21 Moore, *Hail and Farewell: Salve*, 383.

22 Moore, *Hail and Farewell: Ave*, 187.
23 Moore, *Hail and Farewell: Salve*, 349.
24 'Some Parishioners', 'Patchwork' and 'The Wedding Feast'.
25 G. Moore, 'The Wedding Feast', *The Untilled Field* (Gerrards Cross: Colin Smythe, 1976) 96. Significantly, it is the priest who speaks for Peter in engaging Peter and Kate. Mother and priest, therefore, apparently conspire in effecting the marriage and its conjugation. The generally disastrous nature of the marriages in which Father Tom is involved should not pass without comment.
26 This theme of Irish emigration – particularly the emigration of the young – is one of the strongest themes in *The Untilled Field*. The volume explores both the reasons for the emigration – mother and Church being both heavily implicated – and its impact upon the country.
27 Moore, 'The Wedding Feast', 100. As she makes clear, Mrs Connex's material wealth affords her the right to choose her own daughter-in-law, and she will choose the daughter-in-law who, unlike Kate Kavanagh, will perpetuate the social order in which the mother's position is secure.
28 Moore, *Hail and Farewell: Salve*, 402–3.
29 G. Moore, *A Mere Accident* (London: Vizetelly & Co., 1887) 20.
30 Moore, *A Drama in Muslin*, 119.
31 Moore, *A Drama in Muslin* 156.
32 Moore, *A Drama in Muslin*, 313.
33 Moore, *A Drama in Muslin*, 263.
34 Moore, *A Drama in Muslin*, 327
35 Moore, *A Drama in Muslin*, 187. Bensyl (1994) argues that Cecilia is also used by Moore to comment on Irish Catholicism: 'Moore uses Cecilia's lesbian tendencies both to contrast the Catholic peasantry's obvious dysfunction, as expressed in their large families, and to mirror grotesquely the Catholic gentry's displays of sexuality' (74). While I concur with Bensyl that Cecilia does allow Moore to comment on Catholicism, it is only one role – and far from being the principal role – she takes within the overall structure of the novel. Moore's commentary on Catholicism in *A Drama in Muslin* serves as a specific example of the 'type' of commentary that occurs regularly in Moore's work. Moore's criticism of orthodoxies in *A Drama in Muslin* – whether they be religious or social – cannot be fully appreciated if Cecilia is read as the principal model of that criticism.
36 Very few critics have noted this parallel between Cecilia Cullen and John Norton. One who has is Fernando (1977) who notes with regard to Cecilia's 'deviant' personality that: 'It is a major irony that no English novelist, except Moore (in 'John Norton' and *The Brook Kerith*), cared to represent corresponding deviations in men although there was at least equal justification for such a theme' (96).
37 G. Moore, 'John Norton', *Celibates*, 320–1. It is interesting to note the degree to which Moore developed this aspect of John Norton's aversion to Thornby Place in the almost twenty years between the appearance of 'John Norton' and the story's original incarnation in *A Mere Accident*. In *A Mere Accident*, for example, Moore couches John's abhorrence of his mother's furnishings in the following – less loaded – terms: 'Personally I cannot bear upholstery; I cannot conceive anything more hideous than a padded arm-chair. Stuffing is a

vicious excuse for the absence of design' (75). While this description is also included in 'John Norton', it is not developed beyond this point. The use of words such as 'conceive' and 'stuffing' tempts a crude Freudian reading; yet, I think it is clear that Moore's portrayal of John's aversion was much more subtlely rendered in 'John Norton'. However, what that story does lack is the degree of effort John devotes to changing that environment. This, again, is tempered in 'John Norton', while in *A Mere Accident* John's efforts to rebuild Thornby are much more central to the text. With regard to 'John Norton', it is important to note that John's seeking after 'hard lines' parallels his spiritual search. That is, his near-obsessive devotion to medieval theology would provide representations of women which would reinforce his inherent aversion.

38 A. Anderson, *Tainted Souls and Painted Faces: The Rhetoric of Fallenness in Victorian Culture* (Ithaca, NY & London: Cornell University Press, 1993) 36.
39 Moore, *Esther Waters*, 89.
40 Auerbach, *Woman and the Demon*, 158.
41 R.A. Cave, *A Study of the Novels of George Moore* (New York: Barnes & Noble, 1978) 86.
42 G. Moore, *The Brook Kerith: A Syrian Story* (Edinburgh: T. Werner Laurie, 1916) 136.
43 Moore, *The Brook Kerith*, 185.
44 Moore, *Hail and Farewell: Ave*, 159.
45 G. Moore, 'Agnes Lahens', *Celibates*, 487.
46 Moore, 'Agnes Lahens', 554.
47 G. Watt, *The Fallen Woman in the Nineteenth-Century English Novel* (London & Canberra: Croom Helm, 1984) 182.
48 Moore, *A Drama in Muslin*, 317–18.
49 Moore's 'Albert Nobbs' (*Celibate Lives*) provides an interesting example of the ambivalence of Moore's attitude to female sexuality and maternal instincts. While both Albert and Hubert Price defy female sex-roles by living as men, neither are presented as sexual creatures. Neither seek sexual congress, but rather a manner of idealized companionship or romantic love they imagine is only possible with another woman. As Gilbert and Gubar (1989) point out, despite the radical role reversals employed by Moore, 'Albert Nobbs' does not question the silence surrounding lesbianism, nor does it revoke the sense of sin attached to women who deny their heterosexuality and their maternal instincts. Moore explicitly denies the women a sexual nature – they possess 'nothing' where their sexual centre should be – they remain symbolically castrated even in the garb of men. Moore's ambivalence is reinforced when he has Hubert Price return to her husband on the death of her companion, ensuring that despite a flirtation with patriarchal and moral subversion, the patriarchy is re-established in the guise of the re-formed family.
50 J. Kristeva, 'Stabat Mater', *The Kristeva Reader*, T. Moi, ed. (Oxford: Blackwell, 1986) 169.
51 Moore, *Esther Waters*, 126.
52 Moore, *Esther Waters*, 135; 138. The burden on the mother who is destined to constant child-bearing – whether as a result of doctrines such as Catholicism, or the lack of viable alternatives – was something with which Moore seems to have had a great deal of sympathy. This is particularly

evident in the character of Esther's mother, who is so drained by her child-bearing, and the constant demands (sexual and material) of her husband, that she dies in childbirth, the latter years of her life having been lived in abject misery.

53 Moore, *A Mummer's Wife*, 92–3.

54 Moore, *A Mummer's Wife*, 169–70.

55 Moore, *A Mummer's Wife*, 361.

56 Moore, *A Mummer's Wife*, 352.

57 Moore, *A Mummer's Wife*, 356.

58 Moore, *A Mummer's Wife*, 477. It is worth noting that parallels exist in terms of the effect upon Kate of motherhood, romantic novels and alcohol. All three tend to allow Kate to secede from consciousness and, thereby, the social order in which she has placed herself and with which she is clearly unable to cope. In addition, all three model the pre-oedipal semiotic. Having tasted (again) this psychic state, Kate is unable to relinquish it. Mitchell (1986) notes that Kate's 'romantic dreaminess' serves to '[increase] Kate's distance from the narrator, from the reader, and ultimately from herself' (73). Similarly, Farrow (1978) argues that '[Kate's] drinking is constitutive in that it allows her to reach the alienated world from which she has been debarred by the limitations of an unsatisfying experience' (48). Even so, it is clearly alcohol which best facilitates Kate's passage from the symbolic to the semiotic: 'Without getting absolutely drunk, she rapidly sank into the sensations of numbness, in which all distinctions are blurred, and thoughts trickled and slipped away like the soothing singing of a brook' (356–7).

59 In this, I am surprised that more is not made of *The Lake* in terms of Moore's impact on Anglo-Irish modernists such as Joyce. Costello (1994) notes that Joyce read *The Lake* during his period in Rome sometime around August 1906, during which time Joyce was working on both *Dubliners* and *A Portrait of the Artist as a Young Man*. Ellmann (1982) includes a letter from Joyce to his Aunt Josephine (4 December 1905) in which Joyce requests a copy of any critiques of *The Lake* which have appeared in the Dublin papers. Ellmann notes Joyce's later mocking of the novel's 'symbolism', but concludes that Joyce 'remembered the ending when he came to write the visionary scene at the end of the fourth chapter of *A Portrait of the Artist as a Young Man*; there Stephen, like Father Gogarty, undergoes a rite of secular baptism, and Joyce's water and bird imagery, while he has made it altogether his own, seems to owe something to Moore's symbolism of lake, stagnant pool, and fluttering curlew. Joyce winnowed Moore of the preposterous; he found him a good man to improve upon' (234).

60 J. Malkan, 'George Moore's *The Lake*: Repetition, Narcissism and Exile', *English Literature in Transition* 32.2 (1989): 159–69, 162–3. See also J.S. O'Leary, 'Father Bovary', in Welch (1982).

61 G. Moore, *The Lake* (Gerrards Cross: Colin Smythe, 1980) 99–100.

62 Moore, *The Lake*, 93.

63 'What father Peter did not like about the girl was her independent mind.... Her independence betrayed itself in her voice... her independent mind informed every sentence, even the smallest, and that was why she was going to be dismissed from her post' (Moore, *The Lake*, 18–19).

64 Moore, *The Lake*, 175.

65   Moore, *The Lake*, 134.

66   Moore,*The Lake*, 35.

67   In discarding his priestly garb, Gogarty of course echoes Moore's own sentiments when he refers to the 'thought of every brave-hearted boy... to cry,
Now, off with my coat that I may earn five pounds to take me out of this
country.'*Hail and Farewell: Salve*, 349.

68   In Moore's attitude to mother-Ireland, I see parallels with the 'mothers'
present in 'So On He Fares' from *The Untilled Field*. In this story, it is not the
mother-image which is split into good and bad components, but the child
whose self-image is split, as realized in the two Ulricks. The schism in the
child – one warranting the good mother, and the other the bad mother –
seems to me evident in the Irish exile. Prior to exile, the child engages solely
with the 'bad' mother. The child who returns encounters the mother is her
ideal aspect, mothering the 'new' child – in actuality another aspect of
himself – as the 'good mother'. It is the ideal mother-Ireland to which the
child returns, but it is only a matter of time before she resumes her previous
guise when she discovers she is face-to-face with the child who has run away
from her and disobeyed her dictates.

69   G. Moore, 'The Wild Goose', *The Untilled Field*, 243.

70   Moore, 'The Wild Goose', 254.

71   Moore, 'The Wild Goose', 278.

72   Moore, *Hail and Farewell: Salve*, 291.

73   Moore, *Hail and Farewell: Salve*, 278–9.

74   Moore, *Hail and Farewell: Salve*, 343–4. Moore rehearses this argument in
Confessions of a Young Man: 'the language of English fiction is stagnant. But
if the realists should catch favour in England the English tongue may be
saved, for with new subjects they would introduce new forms of language
would arise' (149).

75   Moore, *Hail and Farewell: Salve*, 350. This is echoed in Hone (1936): 'One
night Martyn, who had just come back from Ireland, spoke of the Gaelic
League and of his dear wish to write plays in Irish, Moore was in a receptive
mood – "A new language to enwomb new thought"' (199).

76   Moore, *Hail and Farewell: Salve*, 355.

77   One of the few examples of Moore's exploration of the creative process
within his fictional work reinforces this point: 'The artist, like the mother,
has to undergo the throes and labour of child-bearing, long months of
solitude and suffering; whilst the amateur, like the father, unweighed by
the struggling infant in the womb, is free to explain and criticize at ease' (*A
Modern Lover*, 68). Something of an aberration, coming as it does in Moore's
first novel, the image is not developed in Moore's later works. He comes close
in *Ave* when, referring to AE, he writes: 'He has helped all and sundry through
the labours of parturition with the single exception of Lady Gregory, who
delivers herself, and very easily, of her own plays and stories' (xii). It is,
however, a position he seems unable to assume in relation to his own work.
Moore's polemic on circulating libraries also uses maternal images, but again
maternal images where 'mother' does not encounter the child within the
semiotic realm: for example, 'What it disapproves of comes into the world, as
it were, stillborn...' (*Literature at Nurse, or Circulating Morals*, P. Coustillas, ed.
[Hassocks, Sussex: Harvester, 1976] 28). That Moore did not have a great deal

of insight into his own use of the maternal metaphor is evident in his shift of the maternal image from the author to the circulating libraries themselves.

78 G. Moore, *Confessions of a Young Man* (London: William Heinemann, 1952) 98.
79 Grubgeld's (1994) discussion of Moore's process of self- creation is relevant here. However, despite her extensive analysis, Grubgeld doesn't posit what the relationship between Moore and maternal spaces might be, or how Moore positions himself in relation to those spaces. She doesn't examine Moore's representation of mother-figures, though she does make the important point that, for Moore, both language and nationality serve as wombs to self-creation.
80 This image of Moore being chased from Ireland by a voracious mother is, of course, tempered by a secondary reason for his departure. This reason, while not 'played up' as much as the Cathleen ni Houlihan image, stems from his realization that he was not the Messiah for whom Ireland waited. He shares with Stephen Dedalus this desire to be the Messiah, yet, unlike Stephen, he is able to acknowledge his own failure (as muted an acknowledgement as that might be): 'And, feeling that I was not the predestined hero whom Cathleen ni Houlihan had been waiting for through the centuries, I fell to sighing, not for Cathleen ni Houlihan's sake, but my own . . . ' (*Ave*, 29).

Yeats's displacement of the mother

1 See, for example, Hough ('The Modernist Lyric', in Bradbury and McFarlane, 1976) 318.
2 P. Kuch, *Yeats and AE: 'The antagonism that unites dear friends'* (Gerrards Cross: Colin Smythe, 1986) 90–1.
3 D. Toomey, 'Labyrinths: Yeats and Maud Gonne', *Yeats Annual, No. 9*, D. Toomey, ed. (London: Macmillan, 1992) 107.
4 J. Moynahan, *Anglo-Irish: The Literary Imagination in a Hyphenated Culture* (Princeton: Princeton University Press, 1995).
5 W.B. Yeats, *Cathleen ni Houlihan, The Variorum Edition of the Plays of W.B. Yeats* [Hereafter *V.Plays*] R.K. Alspach, ed. (London: Macmillan, 1966) 218, ll. 71–2. See also Harris (1996) who argues that, in *Cathleen ni Houlihan*, Yeats '[complicates a] double vision of woman as either a supernatural force propelling man toward heroic self- immolation or a wife/mother intent on trapping him in materialism' (476).
6 Yeats, *Cathleen ni Houlihan*, 222–3, ll. 161–3, 165, 170, 172.
7 The 'reading' of the audience when the play was first played, and the degree to which it did, in fact, send out young men to be shot, is, as many critics have recognized, worthy of its own discussion
8 Yeats, *Cathleen ni Houlihan*, 216, ll.28–32.

PATRICK. . . . Do you remember what Winny of the Cross Roads was saying the other night about the strange woman that goes through the country whatever time there's war or trouble coming?
BRIDGET. Don't be bothering us about Winny's talk.

9 R. Barthes, 'Myth Today', *Mythologies* (London: Paladin, 1973) 134.

10   E.B. Cullingford, 'Yeats and Women: *Michael Robartes and the Dancer*', *Yeats Annual, No. 4*, W. Gould, ed. (London: Macmillan, 1986) 37. In this respect, Yeats's own words in 'J.M. Synge and the Ireland of His Time' seem relevant: 'Thomas Davis, whose life had the moral simplicity which can give to actions the lasting influence that style alone can give to words, had understood that a country which has no national institutions must show its young men images for the affections, although they may be but diagrams of what should be or may be' (*The Cutting of an Agate, Essays* [London: Macmillan & Co., 1924] 387).

11   Yeats, *Cathleen ni Houlihan*, 229, ll.313–22. Kristeva theorizes the mother as embodying within her only the potential for a finite number of subjectivities. A child who desires a subjectivity that is not embodied within his or her mother must then search for the 'mother' through whom he or she may be born into their 'desired' subjectivity. For further discussion of this point see the chapter 'Mothers and Martyrs'.

12   'But pity Moll Magee', 'The Ballad of Moll Magee' (*Crossways*, 1889) *The Variorum Edition of the Poems of W.B. Yeats* [Hereafter *VP.*] P. Allt and R.K. Alspach, eds (New York: Macmillan, 1957) 16, l. 4.

13   Cullingford (1993) argues: 'Yeats's crossing of the *aisling* with the Marian hymn is puritanical: the image of Kathleen stills the beating of worldly, passionate hearts, and purifies bodies' (66). This appropriation of Catholic iconography within Nationalist discourse is highlighted in Yeats's essay 'Poetry and Tradition': 'Miss Maud Gonne could still gather great crowds out of the slums by her beauty and sincerity, and speak to them of "Mother Ireland with the crown of stars about her head"' (*The Cutting of an Agate, Essays*, 308). Such appropriation is also evident in O'Casey's work (see chapter 6, 'What's ni Houlihan to you?').

14   R.F. Foster, *W.B. Yeats: A Life, I: The Apprentice Mage, 1865–1914* (London & New York: Oxford University Press, 1997) 176. Foster makes this point with respect to the period 1897–8, during which time Yeats was working on one of several drafts of *The Speckled Bird*. Here, Michael Hearne has a vision of the Virgin with 'trellises of roses behind her... and little flowers under her feet' (16–17). See also Toomey (1992) 104, and Toomey (1993) 15.

15   Yeats's use of Catholic iconography is, then, far from coincidental. Relevant here is Kristeva's (1986) argument in 'Stabat Mater' regarding the 'self-sacrifice involved in becoming anonymous in order to pass on the social norm, which one might repudiate for one's own sake but within which *one must* include the child in order to educate it along the chain of generations' (183). The greater the mother's suffering and self-sacrifice, the tighter the bond between mother and child. The more passive she is, the greater her power to effect the transition of the child to the symbolic order in which she is venerated. In this, the 'good mother' or the 'suffering mother' becomes exactly what Auerbach (1982) charges her with being: 'a monster of ego... she is militant rather than nurturing, displacing the God she pretends to serve... she becomes the source of all shaping and creative power, dropping her mask of humility as she forecasts apocalyptic new orders' (185). The Countess Cathleen, in the elegaic poem 'The Countess Cathleen in Paradise', operates in a similar way. She has no function other than as vessel for grief and mourning. In recognizing her deeds, in recognizing and venerating her

suffering, the child, the reader and the penitent are all drawn into service of that symbolic order which has thus mythologized her.

16 W.B. Yeats, 'Two Years Later' (*Responsibilities*, 1914) *VP.* 139, ll. 9–10.
17 R. Ellmann, *The Identity of Yeats* (London: Faber & Faber, 1964) 229.
18 W.B. Yeats, 'A Song from "The Player Queen"' (*Responsibilities*, 1914) *VP.* 133, ll. 17–20.
19 Yeats, 'A Song from "The Player Queen"', ll. 5–8.
20 W. Johnsen, 'Textual/Sexual Politics in Yeats's "Leda and the Swan"', *Yeats and Postmodernism*, L. Orr, ed. (Syracuse: Syracuse University Press, 1991) 88. Johnsen makes this comment in relation to 'Leda and the Swan', a poem I discuss at length in chapter 7.
21 W.B. Yeats, 'The Magi' (*Responsibilities*, 1914) *VP.* 146, l. 8.
22 Ellmann, *The Identity of Yeats*, 181.
23 The inability of humanity to understand the mysteries and miracles they encounter is also canvassed by Yeats in the earlier story 'The Adoration of the Magi' (1897). The 'mother' is explicitly present in this story: 'and a strange voice spoke through him, and bid them set out for Paris, where a dying woman would give them secret names and thereby so transform the world that another Leda would open her knees to the swan, and another Achilles beleaguer Troy' (Yeats, *Mythologies*, 310). The mother dominates the myth and the father is absented – a reversal of the later poem – and the mystery or vision is one from which 'the Magi' seek protection. I suggest that this seeking after protection is a response to the mother's dominance over the father. The Magi seek a more comforting narrative – a Christian narrative – as protection from the strange vision before them.
24 W.B. Yeats, *Deirdre*, *V.Plays*, 346, ll. 13–16.
25 W.B. Yeats, 'The Sorrow of Love' (*The Rose*, 1893) *VP.* 28, ll. 5–8.
26 The mother determined by the apparel she dons is explored by Yeats in an early story 'Our Lady of the Hills' (1893). A 'young Protestant girl, who was both pretty herself and prettily dressed in blue and white' is mistaken by a group of children for the Blessed Virgin. Wearing 'a plain black dress' she is not recognized. (W.B. Yeats, *Writings on Irish Folklore, Legend and Myth* [London: Penguin, 1993] 98–9). What this story suggests is that recognition of the mother is dependent on surface rather than substance: the signs we read are superficial, but they are signs impressed upon us by the nature of the myths in which those signs appear.
27 I read the 'red-rose-bordered hem' as a mother- figure, rather than merely a female personification, because of her role in generation: 'The measure of her flying feet / Made Ireland's heart begin to beat' (ll. 11–12). Of course, it is also possible to read this as a woman who has excited those who watch her dancing, and I acknowledge that an ambiguity is present. Read either way, I do not consider it diminishes my argument as to the means by which poet and myth are mutually constructed. I find Cullingford's (1992) reading of the poem particularly relevant. She argues that the 'poet situates himself on the margins, the borders of the hegemonic political and lyrical traditions. Woven into the hem of the Irish rose is the subversive narrative of the oppressed; its cloth is not the cloth of heaven but of history' (53). This positioning of the poet on the border between various discourses is one that is central to my argument.

28   Yeats, 'To Ireland in the Coming Times', l. 29; ll. 47–8.
29   Barthes, 'Myth Today', 140; 155.
30   W.B. Yeats, 'Into the Twilight' (*The Wind Among the Reeds*, 1899) *VP.* 48, ll. 5–6.
31   R. Kearney, 'Myth and Motherland', Field Day Theatre Company, *Ireland's Field Day* (London: Hutchison, 1985) 70. Yeats himself writes in 'Poetry and Tradition', referring to the poems of Johnson: 'Ireland . . . speaks to him with the voice of the great poets, and in *Ireland's Dead* she is still mother of perfect heroism, but there comes doubt too' (*The Cutting of an Agate*, 319).
32   W.B. Yeats, 'Pardon, old fathers . . .' (*Responsibilities*, 1914) *VP.* 118, ll.19–22. Yeats utilizes a similar construct in 'Reconciliation' in exploring the loss of, and reconciliation with, his muse: 'But, dear, cling close to me; since you were gone, / My barren thoughts have chilled me to the bone' (*From 'The Green Helmut' and Other Poems*, 1910) *VP.* 101, ll. 11–12).
33   Cullingford, 'Yeats and Women: *Michael Robartes and the Dancer*', 40.
34   B.S. Webster, *Yeats: A Psychoanalytic Study* (London: Macmillan, 1973) 139.
35   W.B. Yeats, *The Countess Cathleen*, V. *Plays*, 123, ll. 637–9.
36   W.B. Yeats, 'A Cradle Song' (*The Rose*, 1893) *VP.* 26, ll. 11–12.
37   W.B. Yeats, 'The Song of the Old Mother' (*The Wind Among the Reeds*, 1899) *VP.* 50, ll. 2, 10.
38   W.B. Yeats, 'Adam's Curse' (*In the Seven Woods*, 1904) *VP.* 86, ll. 4–6.
39   Yeats, 'Adam's Curse', ll. 18–20.
40   Yeats, 'Adam's Curse', ll. 21–2.
41   K. Carriker, 'The Doll as Icon: The Semiotics of the Subject in Yeats's Poem "The Dolls"', Orr, *Yeats and Postmodernism*, 141.
42   W.B. Yeats, 'The Dolls' (*Responsibilities*, 1914) *VP.* 147, ll. 14–15.
43   Yeats, 'The Dolls', ll. 19–20.

Mothers and martyrs

1   *United Irishman*, 22 March 1902. Quoted in Lyons (1973), 239.
2   *The Daily Telegraph*, 14 October 1891. Quoted in Hall (1980), 28.
3   J. Joyce, 'The Shade of Parnell' (1912), *The Critical Writings of James Joyce*, E. Mason and R. Ellmann, eds (London: Faber & Faber, 1959) 227.
4   F.S.L. Lyons, *Ireland Since the Famine* (London: Fontana, 1973) 201.
5   J. Hone, *W.B. Yeats, 1865–1939* (London: Macmillan, 1962) 89.
6   Joyce, 'The Shade of Parnell', 228.
7   'The modern literature of Ireland . . . and indeed all that stir of thought that prepared for the Anglo-Irish war, began when Parnell fell from power in 1891. A disillusioned and embittered Ireland turned from Parliamentary politics; an event was conceived; and the race began, as I think, to be troubled by that event's long gestation.' W.B. Yeats, 'The Irish Dramatic Movement', *Dramatis Personae, Autobiographies* (London: Macmillan & Co.,1936) 177.
8   See, for example, Costello (1977), Foster (1988), Foster (1993), Kelly (1976) and Moynahan (1995).
9   S. Deane, *Celtic Revivals: Essays in Modern Irish Literature* (London: Hutchison, 1986) 53.
10 R. Kearney, 'Myth and Motherland', Field Day Theatre Company, *Ireland's Field Day* (London: Hutchison, 1985) 66.

11   J. Kristeva, 'Stabat Mater', *The Kristeva Reader*, T. Moi, ed. (Oxford: Blackwell, 1986) 175.

12   J. Chadwick, 'Family Romance as National Allegory in Yeats's *Cathleen ni Houlihan* and *The Dreaming of the Bones*', *Twentieth Century Literature* 32.2 (1986) 155–68.

13   S. de Beauvoir, *The Second Sex* (Harmondsworth: Penguin, 1972) 204.

14   J. Lacan, 'From Interpretation to the Transference', *The Four Fundamental Concepts of Psycho- Analysis*, J.-A. Miller, ed. (London: Penguin, 1979) 257.

15   Mitchell and Rose (1982) make the important point that the focus within psychoanalytic theory on the mother–child relationship often has the effect of denying the symbolic structure in which that relationship exists and is represented. This argument seems pertinent here. The symbolic order which is dominant here insists that the mother 'forms' the child in accordance with that order. The mother is, therefore, required to exist within strictly delineated parameters which will reflect the order that the child is required to absorb as its subjectivity develops. Within psychoanalytic theory, the image the child draws from the mother is paramount, while the image the mother draws from the child is neglected.

16   M. Sprengenether, *The Spectral Mother: Freud, Feminism and Psychoanalysis* (Ithaca, NY & London: Cornell University Press, 1990) 220.

17   J. Gallop, 'The American Other', *The Purloined Poe: Lacan, Derrida & Psychoanalytic Reading*, J.P. Muller and W.J. Richardson, eds (Baltimore & London: Johns Hopkins University Press, 1988) 272.

18   Kristeva, 'Stabat Mater', 174–5.

19   M. Warner, *Alone of All her Sex: The Myth and the Cult of the Virgin Mary* (London: Weidenfeld and Nicolson, 1976) 183.

20   C.L. Innes, *Woman and Nation in Irish Literature and Society, 1880–1935* (Athens: University of Georgia Press, 1993) 191. Both Innes and Kearney (1985) theorize the rise in Irish mariolatry in terms of doctrinal developments during the nineteenth century which 'advanced' Mary's position within the Catholic Church. Theorists such as Kristeva would argue that such 'advances' bound the Virgin Mother's power more fully, pinioning her more completely within the symbolic order on which the Catholic Church's power was – and is – founded. MacCurtain (1980) offers an alternative – though complementary – explanation, suggesting that with the Great Famine '[men], women and children were confronted with an act of God so terrible in its manifestation that a society which had been increasingly involved in the liberating processes of self- improvement, searched providence for an answer. It was given at Knock, Co. Mayo in 1879 with an apparition of Mary' (542).

21   Innes (1993) rightly argues that both mother-Church and mother-Ireland 'are dependent upon their children to make them whole and glorious ... [and] are instruments of their children's redemption' (41). Innes also points to the parallels between Christ's sacrifice and the redemption that ensues, and the overlaying of this myth on the Irish context of sons offering their lives for their 'mother' land (47).

22   de Beauvoir, *The Second Sex*, 530.

23   Kearney, 'Myth and Motherland', 77.

Denying the mother in James Joyce

1   J. Joyce, *A Portrait of the Artist as a Young Man, The Essential James Joyce*, H. Levin, ed. (London: Jonathan Cape, 1948) 367.

2   Cixous (1976) writes that 'Absent from *Dubliners*, scarcely present in *Portrait*, [the mother] has become a ghost in *Ulysses*, as though Joyce were carrying out some kind of conscious relegation. The reduction of the mother and her role shows that she constitutes a threat to James as artist, by the paralysing force she represents' (37). While I am not inclined to engage with Cixous's analysis of Joyce himself based on the texts, I feel her point is relevant in terms of my argument regarding Stephen's bond with his mother. For it is the effective absence of Mrs Dedalus, her passivity, her silence and her non-existence beyond the home which feeds her hold on her son. Such service is, for Joyce, the source of paralysis. Yet, in embedding the suffering mother in the very act of his escape from her, Stephen fails to fully reject that paralysis.

3   G. Moore, 'The Wild Goose', *The Untilled Field* (Gerrards Cross: Colin Smythe, 1976) 79–80.

4   See, for example, Carens ('In Quest of a New Impulse: George Moore's *The Untilled Field* and James Joyce's *Dubliners*', in Kilroy, 1984) 67, Costello (1994) 172, and Ellmann (1982) 98.

5   P.A. McCarthy, 'The Moore-Joyce Nexus: An Irish Literary Comedy', *George Moore in Perspective*, J.E. Dunleavy, ed. (Gerrards Cross: Colin Smythe, 1983) 104.

6   G. Moore, *The Lake* (Gerrards Cross: Colin Smythe, 1980) 159.

7   McCarthy, 'The Moore–Joyce Nexus', 107.

8   Joyce, *A Portrait of the Artist as a Young Man*, 327.

9   P. Costello, *James Joyce: The Years of Growth, 1882–1915* (London: Papermac, 1994) 221–2.

10   J. Joyce, 'A Mother', *Dubliners, The Essential James Joyce*, 111.

11   J.E. Miller, ' "O, she's a nice lady!" ': A rereading of "A Mother" ', *James Joyce Quarterly* 28.2 (1991): 407–26, 413.

12   That Mrs Kearney is well aware of where exactly her place is cannot be disputed: 'But she knew that it would not be ladylike to do that: so she was silent' (114).

13   Joyce, 'A Mother', 110–11.

14   Joyce, 'A Mother', 112.

15   Joyce, *A Portrait of the Artist as a Young Man*, 181.

16   Joyce, *A Portrait of the Artist as a Young Man*, 176–8.

17   Joyce, *A Portrait of the Artist as a Young Man*, 246; 192–202.

18   Joyce, *A Portrait of the Artist as a Young Man*, 194–5.

19   Joyce, *A Portrait of the Artist as a Young Man*, 202.

20   Joyce, *A Portrait of the Artist as a Young Man*, 197; 201.

21   Joyce, *A Portrait of the Artist as a Young Man*, 200.

22   Joyce, *A Portrait of the Artist as a Young Man*, 247–8.

23   Joyce, *A Portrait of the Artist as a Young Man*, 241.

24   R. Ellmann, *James Joyce* (New York: Oxford University Press, 1982) 297.

25   Joyce, *A Portrait of the Artist as a Young Man*, 176.

26   See, for example, Lyons (1973), 226.

27 So complete is Stephen's break with his father in the final structure of *A Portrait* that the admonition of Simon Daedalus to Mrs Daedalus in *Stephen Hero* would be both superfluous and meaningless, except as evidence of the delusion of the Irish father in terms of his influence over his children: 'You needn't interfere between me and my son. We understand each other.' J. Joyce, *Stephen Hero* (New York: New Directions, 1963) 216.

28 J. Joyce, 'Eveline', *Dubliners*, 41.

29 J. Joyce, 'Grace', *Dubliners*, 125.

30 J. Kristeva, 'About Chinese Women', *The Kristeva Reader*, T. Moi, ed. (Oxford: Blackwell, 1986) 146.

31 'He wondered whether he could write a poem to express his idea.... he was not sure what idea he wished to express but the thought that a poetic moment had touched him took life within him like an infant hope.' *Dubliners*, 66.

32 J. Joyce, 'A Little Cloud', *Dubliners*, 73.

33 Joyce, 'A Little Cloud', 73.

34 Joyce, 'A Little Cloud', 73–4.

35 H. Cixous, *The Exile of James Joyce*, Trans. S.A.J. Purcell (London: John Calder, 1976) 96.

36 Joyce, 'A Little Cloud', 74.

37 J. Joyce, *Exiles*, *The Essential James Joyce*, 439. (This edition is used for all textual references. When referring to the author's notes, I have used the 1991 Paladin edition.) What Richard seeks in Bertha, he has sought, unsuccessfully, in his own mother: 'I waited too, not for her death but for some understanding of me, her own son, her own flesh and blood' (376). Their conflict over their son reflects, therefore, a tension in which Richard seeks both his wife's subjection to him and a position in relation to her that will see him as 'son' to her 'mother'. While I am not as confident as Henke (1990) that 'at the conclusion of *Exiles*, Bertha, the mother/muse of Joyce's drama, has successfully given birth to the artistic hero who will return to her in the role of primordial lover', the final episode of the play does suggest Bertha's capacity to renew or reclaim his creativity (105).

38 Joyce, 'Grace', 125.

39 A notable exception is Mrs Sinico in 'A Painful Case'. The story also suggests something of the extent to which Joyce's work resisted and even challenged Moore's. Mrs Sinico's story is essentially the stuff of a naturalist novel, such as Moore told in *A Mummer's Wife*. Yet, Joyce shifts the focus from the 'naturalist' story, concentrating instead on the story of one of the lives whose Mrs Sinico's own life touched.

40 See also French, 'Women in Joyce's Dublin', in Benstock, 1988, 270, and Walzl, '*Dubliners*: Women in Irish Society', in Henke and Unkeless, 1982, 46–7.

41 'She watched the pair and kept her own counsel'; 'but still her mother's persistent silence could not be misunderstood'; 'still Mrs Mooney did not intervene'; 'At last, when she judged it to be the right moment, Mrs Mooney intervened.' *Dubliners*, 59. In this, I differ from Leonard (1993) who contends that men are entrapped not so much by women as by a self-constructed subjectivity. Leonard acknowledges the importance of mother and daughter's 'silent partnership', yet he seems keen to deflect responsibility for Bob Doran's dilemma away from them. Ironically, his reading of the fate of Bob

Doran and Little Chandler tends to reinforce those same codes that have allowed Mrs Mooney and her daughter to manipulate events according to their own will. Given the social, political, religious and psychological context in which the men in *Dubliners* are represented, it is difficult, I suggest, simply to argue that men are bound by a subjectivity they have created for themselves.

42   J. Joyce, 'The Boarding House', *Dubliners*, 60.

43   Joyce, 'The Boarding House', 60. Levin, his introduction to *The Essential James Joyce*, notes; 'Joyce's women tend to be either mothers or daughters' (18). The reason for this, I argue, is that the daughter virtually moves straight from that position to the mother's position, barely lingering in the position of 'sexual woman'. This is not a simple matter of volition, but a factor of the social and religious context in which these women exist.

44   Joyce, *A Portrait of the Artist as a Young Man*, 262.

45   J. Joyce, *Exiles* (London: Paladin, 1991) 170.

46   J. Joyce, 'An Encounter', *Dubliners*, 29.

47   Joyce, 'Grace', 126.

48   Joyce, *Stephen Hero*, 54–6.

49   Joyce, *Stephen Hero*, 127.

50   J. Joyce, 'Epiphany 19', *Poems and Shorter Writings* (London: Faber & Faber, 1991) 179; Joyce, *Stephen Hero*, 163.

51   Joyce, *Stephen Hero*, 165. The cutting of Isabel's death from *A Portrait* largely correlates with the overall removal of much of Stephen's family from the narrative. Even so, in *Stephen Hero* Isabel is linked with Stephen fulfilling his Easter duties, a link which deflects from Stephen's refusal. The more simple and effective structure of *A Portrait* allows Stephen's *Non serviam* full focus. His debt to his mother and his own dissatisfaction with the service demanded by the Church are, thereby, also emphasized.

52   Joyce, *Stephen Hero*, 209.

53   Joyce, *Stephen Hero*, 131–5.

54   Joyce, *A Portrait of the Artist as a Young Man*, 294.

55   Joyce, *Stephen Hero*, 84–6. Scott (1990) refers to 'the surprising view of a woman who has been hungry for intellectual stimulation and who momentarily takes action against her chief suppressor, the patriarch Mr Daedalus' (200–1). See also, Lawrence, 'Joyce and Feminism', in Attridge (1990).

56   This shift is echoed in the relatively minor part played by the Blessed Virgin Mary in *Stephen Hero*. Here, Stephen's attraction to the Church is not centred on the iconography of the Virgin but on the rituals of Catholicism.

57   Joyce, *A Portrait of the Artist as a Young Man*, 357.

58   Joyce, *A Portrait of the Artist as a Young Man*, 358.

59   Joyce, *A Portrait of the Artist as a Young Man*, 298.

60   Joyce, *A Portrait of the Artist as a Young Man*, 360.

61   J. Joyce, 'A Portrait of the Artist', *Poems and Shorter Writings*, 214.

62   Joyce, *Stephen Hero*, 64.

63   Joyce, *Stephen Hero*, 146.

64   Joyce, 'A Portrait of the Artist', 218.

65   Joyce, *Stephen Hero*, 247–8.

66   Joyce, *A Portrait of the Artist as a Young Man*, 355; 262.

67 Joyce, *A Portrait of the Artist as a Young Man*, 328. Joyce does not engage to any significant extent with mother- Ireland in his early work. While some critics read (variations on) mother-Ireland into a number of figures in *Dubliners* and *A Portrait* – see, for example, Cowart (1989), Grayson (1982) and O'Grady (1990) – such arguments cannot, on the whole, be sustained. It is particularly notable that Joyce, in his critical writings on Irish politics, does not refer to mother-Ireland, nor does he personify the nation to any significant extent (and only then as woman, not as mother). It is in this that Stephen Dedalus differs most markedly from Moore's protagonists – at one stage Stephen refers to Ireland as 'fatherland' (362) – and from O'Casey's observations of the Irish political context. It is only in *Stephen Hero* and the critical works that Joyce really engages with Ireland as nation.

68 Joyce, *A Portrait of the Artist as a Young Man*, 327.

69 S Henke, 'James Joyce and Women: the Matriarchal Muse', *Work in Progress: Joyce Centenary Essays*, R.F. Peterson, A.M. Cohn, and E.L. Epstein, eds. (Carbondale: Southern Illinois University Press, 1983) 117; S. Henke, 'Stephen Dedalus and Women: a Portrait of the Artist as a Young Misogynist', *Women in Joyce*, S. Henke, and E. Unkeless, eds. (Urbana, Chicago: University of Illinois Press, 1982) 87.

70 J. Joyce, 'Epiphany 7', *Poems and Shorter Writings*, 167.

71 J. Joyce, 'Epiphany 37', *Poems and Shorter Writings*, 197; 194.

72 Joyce, *A Portrait of the Artist as a Young Man*, 252.

73 Ellmann, *James Joyce*, 294.

74 Joyce, *A Portrait of the Artist as a Young Man*, 296. Significantly, the meeting with his mother which will follow soon after, and in which he senses 'a first noiseless sundering of their lives' uses similar images: 'silence', 'coldly', 'dimly', 'silence' (298).

75 Joyce, *A Portrait of the Artist as a Young Man*, 226.

76 J. Kristeva, 'Revolution in Poetic Language', *The Kristeva Reader*, 95.

77 Joyce, *A Portrait of the Artist as a Young Man*, 244.

78 Joyce, *A Portrait of the Artist as a Young Man*, 243. In this I am in opposition with Maud Ellmann ('Polytropic Man: Paternity, Identity and Naming in *The Odyssey* and *A Portrait of the Artist as a Young Man*', in MacCabe, 1982) who contends that there is no explanation within the text for Stephen's reaction to the word 'foetus'. I do, however, agree with her that the word links Stephen with a maternal rather than paternal principle: 'A navel, where the mother's namelessness engraves itself upon the flesh before the father ever carved his signature' (96).

79 Joyce *A Portrait of the Artist as a Young Man*, 301.

80 Joyce, *A Portrait of the Artist as a Young Man*, 344–5. My emphasis.

81 J. Kristeva, 'Stabat Mater', *The Kristeva Reader*, 162.

82 Joyce, *A Portrait of the Artist as a Young Man*, 287.

83 Joyce, *Exiles*, 409.

84 G.M. Leonard, 'Joyce and Lacan: "The Woman" as a Symptom of "Masculinity" in "The Dead"', *James Joyce Quarterly* 28.2 (1991): 451–72.

85 J. Joyce, 'The Dead', *Dubliners*, 147.

86 Joyce, *Exiles*, 376.

87 Joyce, *Exiles*, 439.

88 Joyce, *Exiles*, 377.

89   G.M. Leonard, 'Wondering Where All the Dust Comes From: *Jouissance* in "Eveline"', *James Joyce Quarterly* 29.1 (1991): 23–43.

90   J. Joyce, 'Eveline', *Dubliners*, 43.

91   Joyce, 'Eveline', 44.

92   J. Joyce, 'The Day of the Rabblement', *The Critical Writings of James Joyce*, E. Mason and R. Ellmann, eds (London: Faber & Faber, 1959) 71.

93   J. Kristeva, 'Word, Dialogue and Novel', *The Kristeva Reader*, 55.

94   Kristeva, 'Stabat Mater', 183.

Origin, space, opposition

1   W.B. Yeats, *Reveries Over Childhood and Youth, Autobiographies* (London: Macmillan & Co., 1961) 5.

2   Yeats, *Reveries Over Childhood and Youth*, 27. Toomey (1993) also notes Yeats's delay in introducing his mother into his autobiography: 'Susan Yeats . . . enters the narrative with death, again a most unusual presentation in autobiographical writing' (6). She goes on to speculate that Yeats's re-figures his relationship with his mother in his early novel, *John Sherman*.

3   Yeats, *Reveries over Childhood and Youth*, 61.

4   R.F. Foster, *Yeats: A Life. I: The Apprentice Mage, 1865–1914* (Oxford: Oxford University Press, 1997) 530.

5   This point is taken up by a number of critics. See, for example, Ellmann (1987), Foster (1993), Foster (1997), Kuch (1986), O'Connor (1988) and Ronsley (1968).

6   Yeats, *Reveries Over Childhood and Youth*, 31.

7   J. Kristeva, 'Motherhood According to Bellini', *Desire in Language: A Semiotic Approach to Literature and Art* (Oxford: Blackwell, 1982) 238.

8   Kristeva, 'Motherhood According to Bellini', 238.

9   J. Rose, 'Introduction – II', *Feminine Sexuality: Jacques Lacan and the* école freudienne, J. Mitchell and J. Rose, eds (London: Macmillan, 1982) 54.

10   J. Doane, and D. Hodges, *From Klein to Kristeva: Psychoanalytic Feminism and the Search for the 'Good Enough' Mother* (Ann Arbor: University of Michigan Press, 1992) 77.

11   Synge did not write an *Autobiography* as such, and what has been labelled as 'Autobiography' is an amalgamation of early writings and notes. Importantly, these were written prior to his embarking on a literary career and this, along with his early death, may explain something of his difference from Yeats, Joyce, Moore and O'Casey in this respect.

12   G. Beer, 'Origins and Oblivion in Victorian Narrative', *Sex, Politics and Science in the Nineteenth- Century Novel*, R.B. Yeazell, ed. (Baltimore & London: Johns Hopkins University Press, 1986) 76.

13   C. Ames, 'The Modernist Canon Narrative: Woolf's *Between the Acts* and Joyce's "Oxen of the Sun"', *Twentieth Century Literature* 37.4 (1991): 390–404, 399.

14   E. Ragland-Sullivan, 'Lacan's Seminars on James Joyce: Writing as Symptom and "Singular Solution"', *Psychoanalysis and . . .* R. Feldstein and H. Sussman, eds. (New York & London: Routledge, 1990) 75. Maud Ellmann ('Polytropic Man: Paternity, Identity and Naming in *The Odyssey* and *A Portrait of the Artist*

as a Young Man', in MacCabe, 1982) makes a similar point with respect to *A Portrait of the Artist as a Young Man*, arguing that 'The autobiographer cannot escape his autobiographies. Instead, identity consists of tales it spins about itself in the attempt to recover its own origins' (80).

15 M. Sprengnether, *The Spectral Mother: Freud, Feminism and Psychoanalysis* (Ithaca, NY & London: Cornell University Press, 1990) 28.

16 For accessible discussions of the space-time continuum see, for example, Feynmann (1995) and Davies (1984): 'Space is inextricably linked to time, and as space stretches and shrinks so does time. Just as the big bang represents the creation of space, so it represents the creation of time' (18). The impact of a number of scientific advances on models of the world is, of course, one of the determining factors of modernism, and Einstein's postulation of the time-space continuum is no exception. As Bullock ('The Double Image', in Bradbury and McFarlane, 1976) notes: 'in 1915 [Einstein] produced his *General Principles of Relativity* with its model of a non- Euclidean four-dimensional space–time continuum. Thus, in twenty years between 1895 and 1915 the whole picture of the physical universe, which had appeared not only the most impressive but also the most secure achievement of scientific thought, was brought into question and the first bold attempts made to replace it by a new model' (66).

17 J. Kristeva, 'Woman's Time', *The Kristeva Reader*, T. Moi, ed. (Oxford: Blackwell, 1986) 191. Joyce makes just this distinction in *Finnegans Wake*, aligning the Father with time and the Mother with space (599–600).

18 Kristeva (1986) draws on Nietzsche for this differentiation: 'we confront two temporal dimensions: the time of linear history, or *cursive time* ... and the time of another history, thus another time, *monumental time* ... which englobes these supra-national, socio-cultural ensembles within even larger entities' (189).

19 C.L. Innes, *Woman and Nation in Irish Literature and Society, 1880–1935* (Athens: University of Georgia Press, 1993) 3.

20 J. McFarlane, 'The Mind of Modernism', *Modernism: 1890–1930*, M. Bradbury and J. McFarlane, eds. (London: Penguin, 1976) 72.

21 J. Kristeva, 'Revolution in Poetic Language', *The Kristeva Reader*, 115.

22 Kristeva, 'Motherhood According to Bellini', 249.

23 While theorists such as Kristeva tend to suggest a cause-and-effect relationship between access to the semiotic and the production of poetic language, even a revolution in such language, I prefer to read a correlation, thereby encapsulating an uncertainty as to which way the dynamic may be moving at any particular time.

Synge's marginal mothers

1 Quoted in Greene and Stephens (1989) 257.

2 D.H. Greene and E.M. Stephens, *J.M. Synge: 1871–1909*, revised edn (New York & London: New York University Press, 1989) 282. The letter was never sent.

3 D. Kiberd, *Synge and the Irish Language* (London: Macmillan, 1993) 13.

4 J.M. Synge, 'Deaf Mutes for Ireland', *Collected Works: Volume III* (London: Oxford University Press, 1968) 218–19. As Synge notes in *The Aran Islands*

'the women are the great conservative force in this matter of the language', *The Aran Islands, Collected Works: Volume I*, 115.

5   J. Kristeva, 'From One Identity to Another', *Desire in Language: A Semiotic Approach to Literature and Art* (Oxford: Blackwell, 1982) 134.

6   For example, Deane (1985) argues that 'Maurya is the voice of humanity uttering its resignation to an incurable human plight' (60–1). See also, Deane (1986) 153. Innes (1993) makes a similar point arguing that 'Maurya accepts the power of nature' (150). Durbach (1972) comes closer to my reading of Maurya's role within the play. He argues against reading Maurya as passive witness to her son's destruction and attempts 'to demonstrate...Maurya's implication in the death of her sons which converts pathos into a tragic vision of existence' (365). Even so, in arguing that Maurya is implicated because she is the bearer of life and recognizes 'death as an inextricable element in the whole cycle of life' (369), Durbach still affords Maurya a largely passive role. My argument asserts not merely implication on Maurya's part, but an element of volition

7   J.M Synge, *The Aran Islands, Collected Works: Vol. II*, 57.

8   Synge, *The Aran Islands*, 80.

9   Synge, *The Aran Islands*, 160.

10   Synge, *The Aran Islands*, 159. It is interesting to note that the story explicitly differentiates between the actual mother and the foster mother through the source of the milk they give to the child: the former comes from a breast, the latter from a cup.

11   J.M. Synge, *Riders to the Sea, Collected Works: Volume III*, 9.

12   Synge, *Riders to the Sea*, 11.

13   It is central to any understanding of *Riders* to realize the extent to which Maurya herself constructs the drama occurring around her. Critics, however, differ on this point. Templeton (1985), for example, refers to Maurya's 'total helplessness' (153); Durbach ('Synge's Tragic Vision of the Old Mother and the Sea', in Ayling, 1992) writes that Maurya embodies within her maternal function that universal principle of destruction suggested through the persuasive symbolism of the sea' (83).

14   Synge, *Riders to the Sea*, 23. Deane (1986) reads this moment as that of Maurya '[resigning] her motherhood' (153). This suggests a certain degree of volition on Maurya's part, and in this respect I am in agreement with Deane's assessment. However, I take the argument a step further in that I suggest that Maurya resigns her *actual* motherhood precisely in order to take on fully the mantle of suffering mother.

15   Synge, *Riders to the Sea*, 19.

16   Synge, *Riders to the Sea*, 7.

17   Synge, *Riders to the Sea*, 5.

18   In this regard it is important to bear in mind that Bartley does not in fact set sail. Ironically, it is on account of an accident on land, an accident already encoded with islander superstitions, that causes Bartley's drowning.

19   The paradox inherent to keening and burial is noted by Synge: 'Before they covered the coffin an old man kneeled down by the grave and repeated a simple prayer for the dead. There was an irony in these words of atonement and Catholic belief spoken by voices that were still hoarse with the cries of pagan desperation.' *The Aran Islands*, 75.

20 Synge, *Riders to the Sea*, 24–6; Synge, *The Aran Islands*, 75.

21 Synge, *The Aran Islands*, 161.

22 Synge, *Riders to the Sea*, 11.

23 Synge, *Riders to the Sea*, 19.

24 Synge, *Riders to the Sea*, 21.

25 Synge, *Riders to the Sea*, 21.

26 I cannot wholly agree with Williams ('John Millington Synge: Transforming Myths of Ireland', in Garton, 1985) when he refers to the close of the play as a final reconciliation of the natural and the supernatural. While the tension between the two is moving back into some kind of balance, I do not believe it is possible to talk of any reconciliation being accomplished. Further, despite the fact that Maurya's final prayers emphasize the vulnerability of humanity to the will of gods, it is important to bear in mind that Maurya is anything but vulnerable in the final moments of the play. Even so, what can be said about the fact that Maurya has forgotten the nails of the coffin? Does this suggest that while she has assembled all the materials for the conclusion of the drama, she is, ultimately, unable to hold them together? Can she re-assemble the social and symbolic order – re-establish linear time – but not provide the bond with which to hold them in place?

27 Synge, *Riders to the Sea*, 21.

28 J.M Synge, *The Playboy of the Western World, Collected Works: Vol. IV*, 61.

29 Synge, *The Playboy of the Western World*, 89. My emphasis.

30 Synge, *The Playboy of the Western World*, 89, 101–3.

31 Synge, *The Playboy of the Western World*, 89, 135–7.

32 Synge, *The Playboy of the Western World*, 127.

33 Synge, *The Playboy of the Western World*, 105.

34 Synge, *The Playboy of the Western World*, 89.

35 Synge, *The Playboy of the Western World*, 131.

36 Deane ('Synge's Poetic Use of Language', in Casey, 1994) writes with respect to *The Playboy*: 'the oppositions...do not remain static. As the play progresses we begin to see the opposition resolved; and then after an intermediate resolution branch out again, but now with a renewed power and a different meaning' (33). Deane doesn't, however, foreground the role of the mother-figure in resolving these oppositions.

37 J.M. Synge, *The Tinker's Wedding, Collected Works: Volume IV*, 17–19.

38 Synge, *The Tinker's Wedding*, 19–21.

39 Synge, *The Tinker's Wedding*, 21.

40 Synge, *The Tinker's Wedding*, 47.

41 Synge, *The Tinker's Wedding*, 37.

42 Synge, *The Tinker's Wedding*, 29. Sarah Casey tells Mary: 'I'll be married now in a short while; and from this day there will be no one has a right to call me a dirty name' (35). Brown (1995) argues that the 'desire Sarah confuses, Mary clarifies.... she presents the essential difference between the two weddings through a process of comic reversal' (130). Further, Brown refers to to Mary's 'transforming power' (156), a power I directly relate to the translation of rituals and symbols.

43 Synge, *The Tinker's Wedding*, 25, 33.

44 J.M. Synge, *When the Moon Has Set, Collected Works: Volume III*, 173.

45 H. Cixous, 'The Laugh of the Medusa', *New French Feminisms: An Anthology*, E. Marks, and I. de Courtivron, eds (Amherst: University of Massachusetts Press, 1980) 251. In *The Aran Islands*, Synge writes: 'The grief of the keen...seems to contain the whole passionate rage that lurks somewhere in every native of the island. In this cry of pain the inner consciousness of the people seems to lay itself bare for an instant....They are usually silent, but in the presence of death all outward show of indifference or patience is forgotten, and they shriek with pitiable despair before the horror of the fate to which they are all doomed' (75).

46 Synge, *Riders to the Sea*, 11. Maurya says to Bartley: 'Isn't it a hard and cruel man won't hear a word from an old woman and she holding him from the sea?' (11).

47 H. Cixous, 'The Guilty One', *The Newly Born Woman*, H. Cixous and C. Clement (Minneapolis: University of Minnesota Press, 1986) 25.

48 Synge, *Riders to the Sea*, 17.

49 Cixous & Clements, *The Newly Born Woman*, 7.

50 Synge, *When the Moon Has Set*, 175, 177. The importance of motherhood to Eileen's fate is suggested by draft versions of the play: 'COLM: Far down in below the level of your creed you know that motherhood, the privilege that lifts women up to share in the pain and passion of the earth, is more holy that the vows you've made' (172). In the final version, this suggestion of motherhood comes with Mary Costello's many dead children and the implication that in taking up the position of wife that Mary offers to Eileen through the exchange of symbols, she will also take on the position of mother, bearing the children that Mary had been unable to (successfully) bear: 'There are five children, five children that wanted to live, God help them, if the nuns and priests with them had let me be' (173). Her grievance with the Church may explain the motivation for her 'conversion' of authority within the play.

Rebellion and revolution

1 D. Kiberd, *Inventing Ireland* (London: Jonathan Cape, 1995) 380. See also Innes (1994), who notes that such a construction 'allows no role for women except as passive victims of the quarrel between fathers and sons' (13). I differ somewhat from Innes in that I suggest women – at least particular constructs of woman – have an implicit role to play.

2 R.F. Foster, *Modern Ireland, 1600–1972* (London: Allen Lane, 1988) 432.

3 See also, Kiberd ('The Perils of Nostalgia: A Critique of the Revival', in Connolly, 1982).

4 S. O'Casey, *The Plough and the Stars*, *Collected Plays: Volume I* (London: Macmillan, 1950) 195–6.

5 P. Costello, *The Heart Grown Brutal: The Irish Revolution in Literature from Parnell to the Death of Yeats, 1891–1939* (Dublin: Gill & Macmillan, 1977) 73. Costello goes on to analyse Pearse's actions and writings in terms suggestive of the oedipal construct that Kiberd also identifies and, more extensively, analyses: 'perhaps the emotional confusion due to an unnaturally strong affection for his mother was only to be sublimated in a bloody gesture of

revolt; the Rising was a political expression of his desire to murder his English father for the love of his mother' (79). Foster (1988) emphasizes the degree to which Pearse's rhetoric of 'messianic and sacrificial' death heralding the rebirth of the nation struck a cord with his 'brothers' (477).

6 Quoted in G. O'Connor, *Sean O'Casey: A Life* (London: Hodder & Stoughton, 1988) 201.

7 J. Lacan, 'The Hysterics Question (II): *What is a woman?' The Psychoses: The Seminar of Jacques Lacan, Book III, 1955–1956*, J.-A. Miller, ed. (London: Routledge, 1993) 179. It is possible to argue that in their re-enactment of the gestation and birth of the English language, the men in 'Oxen of the Sun' also participate in a form of *couvade*. In this regard, see also Walkley (1980) who argues that, within *Ulysses*, the *couvade* operates to effect a shift in the novel from 'matriarchy to patriarchy'. While much of Walkley's argument hinges on the acceptance of Bloom as 'womanly man', a position with which I am in some disagreement, it nevertheless provides a useful insight into the novel's birth metaphors.

8 J. Mitchell, 'Introduction – I', *Feminine Sexuality: Jacques Lacan and the* école freudienne, J. Mitchell and J. Rose, eds (London: Macmillan, 1982) 23.

9 R.C. Davis, 'The Discourse of the Father: A Critical Introduction', R.C. Davis, ed., *The Fictional Father: Lacanian Readings of the Text* (Amherst: University of Massachusetts Press, 1981) 12–13.

10 Foster, *Modern Ireland, 1600–1972*, 516.

11 J. Kristeva, 'About Chinese Women', *The Kristeva Reader*, T. Moi, ed. (Oxford: Blackwell, 1986) 153.

12 Kristeva, 'About Chinese Women', 153.

13 Kristeva, 'About Chinese Women', 156.

14 J. Kristeva, 'A New Type of Intellectual: The Dissident', *The Kristeva Reader*, 295.

15 J. Kristeva, 'From One Identity to An Other', *Desire in Language: A Semiotic Approach to Literature and Art* (Oxford: Blackwell, 1982) 125.

16 Kearney's observatons ('Myth and Terror (Excerpt)' in Allison, 1996) are particularly relevant in this regard: '[Pearse] included a poem entitled "A Mother Speaks" in which he patently identifies himself with the sacrificed Christ "who had gone forth to die for men" and compares his mother's faith in his powers of renewal with Mary's faith in the resurrection. ... In the months following the Rising numerous posters with the caption "All is Changed" were to be seen in Dublin depicting the martyred Pearse in a *pietà* position supported by the mythic figure of Mother Ireland.' My own reflections on the image of the *pietà* (chapter 1, note 21) could as well be applied to Pearse's 'mother'.

Sean O'Casey's construction of the mother

1 Spoken to one of de Valera's officers on Holy Saturday, 1916. Quoted in Costello (1977), 108.

2 S. O'Casey, *Sunset and Evening Star, Autobiographies: Volume II* (London: Macmillan and Co., 1963) 539–40.

3 Newsinger (1985) argues that O'Casey was initially opposed to socialism as a way forward, and saw the Republic as the priority. The Dublin lock-out,

however, made O'Casey 'receptive to socialism as espoused by Larkin and Shaw' (226). Regarding O'Casey's resignation from the Irish Republican Brotherhood (IRB), Newsinger asserts that: 'it is sometimes assumed that O'Casey rejected Irish nationalism. In fact, what he now argued was that the interests of the working class had to be central to Irish nationalism, and he rejected those, like the IRB, who could not accept this' (229).

4   For an interesting discussion of this transition in O'Casey's *Autobiographies*, see Kenneally (1982).

5   S. O'Casey, *Within the Gates, Collected Plays: Volume II* (London: Macmillan and Co., 1950) 196. Also note Mrs Gogan's words: '"Many a good one," says I, "was reared in a tenement house."' *The Plough and the Stars, Collected Plays: Volume I* (London: Macmillan and Co., 1950) 165.

6   S. O'Casey, *The Star Turns Red, Collected Plays: Volume II*, 313; 318. Lyons (1973) describes James Larkin's speeches – James Larkin providing the model for Red Jim – in the following terms: 'Larkin's speeches were larger the life because Larkin himself was larger than life. Physically a very powerful man, he had a big presence and an even bigger voice which allowed him to dominate vast meetings even in the open air' (276). Arthur Griffith claimed that Larkin's policies would result in 'workless fathers, mourning mothers, hungry children and broken homes. . . . the curses of women are being poured on this man's head' (quoted in O'Connor, 1988, 63). The image of the suffering mother was applicable to almost any cause.

7   S. Deane, *Celtic Revivals: Essays in Modern Irish Literature, 1880–1980* (London: Faber & Faber, 1985) 121.

8   In this regard, it is useful to note in the *Autobiographies* O'Casey's determined rejection of the testimony of a woman who details the worst excesses of the Soviet concentration camps. As late as the 1950s, his faith in Soviet Communism remained strong. 'The Dree Dames', *Sunset and Evening Star.*

9   O'Casey, *The Star Turns Red*, 351.

10 D.E.S. Maxwell, *A Critical History of Modern Irish Drama, 1891–1980* (Cambridge: Cambridge University Press, 1984) 96.

11 Deane (1986) writes in this regard: 'the so-called pacifism of O'Casey's plays is bogus. He is opposed to useless violence, but sees no escape from the futile illusions which promote it and the bibulous eloquence which seems to be its natural counterpart' (164).

12 This is particularly evident in Act II of *The Silver Tassie*, where the soldiers do not contemplate the philosophy of war, but try to understand how they came to be there. The only answer they come up with is 'We're here because we're here because we're here because we're here!' (*Collected Works, Volume II*, 39).

13 Much is made in O'Casey criticism of the disjunction in his life and writing that occurred when he moved into exile in England, and it has been vigorously debated whether this physical movement can also be read as a dividing line between realism and expressionism in the drama, and even between genius and mediocrity: see, for example, O'Connor (1988), Deane (1986), de Baun ('O'Casey and the Road to Expressionism', in Ayling, 1985), Innes (1990) and O'Connor (1988). For my purposes, the most significant assertion is that he was now viewing Ireland – and his life and experiences there – from a vastly altered position. This physical and psychical distance enhanced his historical perspective. Whether this impacted on his representation of the

mother-figure is another matter, though, as I argue, it did allow him to recognize mother-Ireland's failure to fulfil her promise. For me, there are four plays which, in conjunction with the *Autobiographies*, form the essential corpus of his achievement: the Dublin trilogy and *The Silver Tassie*. However, the remainder, though of uneven quality, do provide an important source of commentary on this corpus: most notably any reading of the *Autobiographies* would suffer, I think, from an ignorance of *Red Roses for Me* and, to a lesser extent, *The Star Turns Red*. In terms of the mother- figure, it would seem to me that O'Casey's representation did not alter dramatically over the course of his writing career, and those alterations which did occur were largely the result of his experimentation with different dramatic forms, rather than a modification of the mother's function within the text.

14 S. O'Casey, *Juno and the Paycock*, *Collected Plays*, *Vol. I*, 46.

15 E. Durbach, 'Peacocks and Mothers: Theme and Dramatic Metaphor', *O'Casey: The Dublin Trilogy*, R. Ayling, ed. (London: Macmillan, 1985) 116.

16 O'Casey, *Juno and the Paycock*, 87.

17 O'Casey, *Juno and the Paycock*, 87.

18 S. O'Casey, *Inishfallen, Fare Thee Well*, *Autobiographies: Volume II*, 9.

19 S. O'Casey, *Cock-a-Doodle Dandy*, *Collected Plays: Volume IV* (London: Macmillan, 1964) 220. O'Casey dwells at some length on the Lourdes phenomenon in *Inishfallen, Fare Thee Well*. He writes: 'Lourdes, where hope is swallowed down by misery to be vomited up again, more miserable, and lost. Where Lazarus is offered a crumb, but can never crawl near enough to get it' (239).

20 Act I: the last supper; Act II: the crucifixion; Act III: the three days in the tomb; and, Act IV: the resurrection. Harry Heegan's progress through this passion sequence is, of course, thwarted, there being no resurrection as a result of the sacrifice. He is also a poor and unsympathetic version of the Christ-figure. In 'Barney's' crucifixion on the gun-wheel there is also the suggestion that the action has been displaced from the genuine figure representing Christ's sacrifice. Through the symbol of the daffodil cross in *Red Roses for Me*, O'Casey makes a similar comment upon Ayamonn's sacrifice.

21 O'Casey, *The Silver Tassie*, 55. It is important to note that in the next verse the mother is sprinkled with the blood of sacrifice, as though it were holy water.

22 O'Casey, *Juno and the Paycock*, 87.

23 O'Casey, *Juno and the Paycock*, 53.

24 O'Casey, *The Silver Tassie*, 39. In *The Plough and the Stars*, Mrs Gogan foreshadows this complicity: 'there's a power o' women that's handed over sons an' husbands to take a runnin' risk in th' fight they're wagin!' (220).

25 O'Casey, *The Silver Tassie*, 18. With regard to Mrs Heegan, I am at odds with Ayling ('"Two Words for Woman": A Reassessment of O'Casey's Heroines', in Gallagher, 1983) who argues that Mrs Heegan 'has been, and is seen to be... destroyed by her environment' (99). While O'Casey reflects a social reality in the economic relationship between mother and son, the relationship is constructed deliberately to emphasize the mother's advancement at her son's (literal) expense. The mercenary nature of mothers in war is also evident in Mrs Gogan's and Bessie Burgess's enthusiastic participation in the looting of Dublin, though it must be said that this enthusiasm is not confined to the mothers in the play. Similarly, Mrs Breydon is the one who, in the crucial moment, encourages her son to fight: 'Go on your way,

my son, an' win. We'll welcome another inch of the world's welfare' (S. O'Casey, *Red Roses for Me, Collected Plays, Vol. III* [London: Macmillan & Co., 1950–51] 213).

26   As Fussell (1975) notes: 'The sacrificial theme, in which each soldier becomes a type of the crucified Christ, is at the heart of countless Great War poems' (117–19).

27   Zeiss (1984) in her reading of the stage-imagery of Act II of *The Silver Tassie* argues: 'The detached arm [of the crucified Christ] pointing to the image of the Virgin, conveys a plea for the human bonds of kinship and love that existed between Christ and Mary in their earthly relations' (172). While this interpretation does not contradict my own, I argue that it is significantly more than kinship that the sacrificed son seeks from his mother.

28   O'Casey, *Inishfallen, Fare Thee Well*, 150.

29   J. Joyce, *Ulysses* (New York: Random House, 1961) 581.

30   O'Casey, *Inishfallen, Fare Thee Well*, 124. Unlike Stephen Dedalus in *A Portrait of the Artist as a Young Man*, Sean does not find the symbol drained of all its symbolic richness. Rather, it is seen in its mirror-image, though still rich with colour and meaning. It is useful to note that Ireland in this guise Sean first learned to recognize through Shaw (*Drums Under the Windows*, 559). The transformation of Cathleen is also noted by Seamus Shields in *The Shadow of a Gunman*: 'she's a ragin' divil now, an' if you only look crooked at her you're sure of a punch in th' eye' (*Collected Plays: Volume I*, 132).

31   S. O'Casey, *Drums Under the Window, Autobiographies, Vol. I*, 665–6. In this she is very like the 'shadow-dhreams of th' past leppin' to life in th' bodies of livin' men that show, if we were without a titther o' courage for centuries, we're vice versa now!' (*The Plough and the Stars*, 195); and the same process of de-mythologization that O'Casey experiences and, in turn, reinforces, is repeated in his undermining of nationalist myths in *The Plough and the Stars*.

32   O'Casey, *Drums Under the Window*, 661. Sean is, of course, also disillusioned by Cathleen ni Houlihan because of her un-reasoned opposition to *The Playboy of the Western World*. Seeking a reason for the extreme reaction which the play has provoked, Sean asks the Poor Old Woman why she is joining in with the general outrage. Her reply: 'An if I am aself, what signifies? D'ye want me to be th' one odd outa th' many?' (*Drums Under the Window*, 509).

33   They are not, however, exclusively in terms of Cathleen as mother in relation to the sons of Ireland. Often, she is represented primarily as woman: for example, *The Seamless Coat of Kathleen* and *Kathleen Listens In*. It is amusing to note that while he is not immune from indulging in the rhetoric of Cathleen ni Houlihan, he recognizes that she can be a woman 'of immemorial moaning, so that a fellow turned aside and longed for a tale of bawdry' (*Drums Under the Window*, 475).

34   O'Casey, *Drums Under the Window*. 608–9. This split is foreshadowed by O'Casey in *The Story of the Irish Citizen Army*. At the time of writing this piece, O'Casey still subscribed to the symbolism of renewal through sacrifice: 'The breath of Death which had swept over poor Dublin carried with it the seeds of a new life . . .' (S. O'Casey, *The Story of the Irish Citizen Army, Feathers from the Green Crow: Sean O'Casey, 1905–1925*, R. Hogan, ed. [London: Mac-

millan, 1963] 235). Cathleen's 'thorny way' is referred to in both *The Shadow of a Gunman* and the *Autobiographies*.

35 See, for example, Corballis (1985), Innes (1994), Kleiman (1982), Kosok (*'Juno and the Paycock'*, in Bloom, 1987), Thompson ('Easter 1916: O'Casey's Naturalistic Image', in Ayling, 1985) and Thomson (1986).

36 R.G. Rollins, 'From Ritual to Romance in *Within the Gates* and *Cock-a-Doodle Dandy'*, H. Bloom, ed., *Sean O'Casey* (New York: Chelsea House, 1987) 22.

37 The Old Woman's statement explaining the dangers of Communism is the best example of this: 'The quiet loveliness and grand quality of family life would go forever' (*The Star Turns Red*, 267). She is oblivious to the fact that this has already occurred.

38 S. O'Casey, *I Knock at the Door, Autobiographies, Vol. I*, 65. Kuch (1986) refers to an article written by Yeats for the *'United Irishman* and entitled "Noble and Ignoble Loyalties", [which] was directed at those who had cheered the Queen, reminding them that her three previous visits, in 1849, 1853 and 1861, had "commonly foreshadowed a fierce and sudden shaking of English power in Ireland", and asking them to contrast the ignoble "self-applauding egotism" of loyalty to Queen Victoria with the noble, enduring, self-sacrifice of loyalty to Kathleen ny Houlihan' (186).

39 O'Casey, *The Plough and the Stars*, 202.

40 O'Casey *The Plough and the Stars*, 220.

41 O'Casey, *The Star Turns Red*, 354. O'Connor's (1988) observation offers some perspective on this point: 'Both [Shaw and O'Casey] kept a photograph of Uncle Joe [Stalin] on the mantelpiece of his inner sanctum – like devout Irish peasants with their postcards of the Virgin Mary' (322).

42 O'Casey, *Drums Under the Window*, 594.

43 O'Faolain's and Colum's criticisms of the *Autobiographies* are quoted in O'Connor (1988), 349–50. O'Connor argues that O'Casey's representation of the birth indicates just how little he knew about actual childbirth at the time he was writing the book: 'O'Casey's birth in 1880 he describes in terms similar to animal parturition, which shocked people in 1939 when he published the first volume of his autobiography' (14).

44 D. Krause, 'On Fabrications and Epiphanies in O'Casey's Autobiography', *Essays on Sean O'Casey's Autobiographies*, R.G. Lowery, ed. (London: Macmillan, 1981) 202.

45 M. Kenneally, 'Joyce, O'Casey and the Genre of Autobiography', *O'Casey Annual, No. 3*, R.G. Lowery, ed. (London: Macmillan, 1984) 125.

46 O'Casey, *I Knock at the Door*, 5. It is useful to compare O'Casey's description of his mother's labour with that of his wife's: 'A young girl inexperienced, just beginning to realize and comprehend the seriousness of her own life and the lives budding from her; so sensitive that she shuddered at the thought of any child in pain' (*Sunset and Evening Star*, 481). Such a comparison supports my argument, and that of Krause, that the narrator himself is instrumental in his own birth – the narrator creates himself through the representation of his birth (whether metaphorical or literal).

47 S. O'Casey, *Oak Leaves and Lavender, Collected Plays: Volume IV*, 28.

48 Ayling's argument ('"Two Words for Woman"': A Reassessment of O'Casey's Heroines', in Gallagher, 1983) is relevant here. He writes that Juno 'does not

seem to recognize *any* ethical validity in the social or political views of her children' (96).

49 O'Casey, *The Silver Tassie*, 33.

50 O'Casey, *The Silver Tassie*, 101.

51 R. Williams, 'The Endless Fantasy of Irish Talk', Bloom, *Sean O'Casey*, 16. Schrank (1986) makes a similar point, referring to the 'intrinsic emptiness of much of the characters' discourse' (290).

52 In 'A Little Cloud', *Dubliners*; *The Countess Cathleen*; *A Mummer's Wife*; and 'Counterparts', *Dubliners*. See, for example, Thomson (1986) and Durbach ('Peacocks and Mothers: Theme and Dramatic Metaphor' in Ayling, 1985).

53 O'Casey, *Juno and the Paycock*, 33.

54 O'Casey, *Juno and the Paycock*, 86.

55 O'Casey, *Drums Under the Window*, 486. The power of the suffering-mother archetype is such that it is able to transform antipathetic women into sympathetic mothers. Note, for example, O'Casey's reference in *Rose and Crown* to a 'vulgar woman' who, because of her tears for her dead son, is said to have 'the immovable pearl of sorrow in her breast' (*Autobiographies, Volume II*, 438).

56 O'Casey, *Red Roses for Me*, 135.

57 O'Casey, *Red Roses for Me*, 135.

58 O'Casey, *Red Roses for Me*, 135.

59 O'Casey, *Red Roses for Me*, 138.

60 Both examples were written late in O'Casey's career. An early version of the paradigm is evident in the relationship of Jack Rocliffe and his mother in *The Harvest Festival* (1920).

61 R. Ayling, 'Colonialism and Rebellion in the Childhood Autobiographies of Sean O'Casey and Wole Soyinka', *Anglo-Irish and Irish Literature: Aspects of Language and Culture*, B. Bramsback and M. Croghan, eds (Uppsala: Uppsala University Press, 1988) 133.

62 O'Casey, *I Knock at the Door*, 163.

63 O'Casey, *I Knock at the Door*, 170.

64 S. O'Casey, *Pictures in the Hallway, Autobiographies, Vol. I*, 388.

65 O'Casey, *Pictures in the Hallway*, 366.

66 O'Casey, *Inishfallen, Fare Thee Well*, 210. Fluther Good's statement that he was 'taught at his mother's knee to be faithful to th' Shan Van Vok!' is also relevant here (*The Plough and the Stars*, 208).

67 O'Casey, *Juno and the Paycock*, 31. The romanticizing of the Irish cause is, of course, the central theme of O'Casey's previous play *The Shadow of a Gunman*, and its disastrous consequences on those who are seduced by this romance are seen in the fate of Minnie Powell.

68 O'Casey, *The Plough and the Stars*, 197. See also Cairns and Richards (1988) who argue that, in *The Plough and the Stars*, O'Casey highlights the lack of a socialist voice adequate enough to counter Nationalist rhetoric (128).

69 Kosok ('*Juno and the Paycock*', in Bloom, 1987) makes a similar point when he refers to the patriot 'who is inclined to undervalue the existence of the individual' (159). In fact, such movements as O'Casey portrays depend upon the de-individuation of those who 'sign-up'.

70 O'Casey, *Inishfallen, Fare Thee Well*, 138.

71 O'Casey, *Pictures in the Hallway*, 310.

Modernism and the maternal

1 M. Ian, *Remembering the Phallic Mother: Psychoanalysis, Modernism and the Fetish* (Ithaca, NY & London: Cornell University Press, 1993) 161.
2 M. Bradbury and J. McFarlane, 'The Name and Nature of Modernism', *Modernism: 1890–1930*, M. Bradbury and J. McFarlane, eds (London: Penguin, 1976) 24.
3 E. Wilson, *Axel's Castle: A Study in the Imaginative Literature of 1870–1930* ([London]: Fontana, 1961) 24.
4 G. Hough, 'The Modernist Lyric', Bradbury and MacFarlane, *Modernism: 1890–1930*, 318.
5 S. Heath, 'Realism, Modernism and "Language- Consciousness"', *Realism in European Literature*, N. Boyle and M. Swales, eds (Cambridge: Cambridge University Press, 1986) 116.
6 E. Grosz, *Sexual Subversions: Three French Feminists* (Sydney: Allen & Unwin, 1989) 54.
7 E. Grosz, *Jacques Lacan: A Feminist Introduction* (Sydney: Allen & Unwin, 1990) 154.
8 J. Mitchell and J. Rose, eds, *Feminine Sexuality: Jacques Lacan and the* école freudienne (London: Macmillan, 1982). See, in particular, Mitchell's and Rose's introductions to Lacan's work.
9 J. Kristeva, 'From One Identity to An Other', *Desire in Language: A Semiotic Approach to Literature and Art* (Oxford: Blackwell, 1982) 136.
10 G.M. Schwab, 'Mother's Body, Father's Tongue: Mediation and the Symbolic Order', *Engaging with Irigaray: Feminist Philosophy and Modern European Thought*, C. Burke, N. Schor and M. Whitford, eds (New York: Columbia University Press, 1994) 353.
11 M. Sprengnether, *The Spectral Mother: Freud, Feminism and Psychoanalysis* (Ithaca, NY & London: Cornell University Press, 1990) 143.
12 J. Kristeva, 'Word, Dialogue, Novel', *Desire in Language*, 77.
13 J. Kristeva, 'Women's Time', *The Kristeva Reader*, T. Moi, ed. (Oxford: Blackwell, 1986) 206.
14 J. Kristeva, 'Revolution in Poetic Language', *The Kristeva Reader*, 120.
15 J. Kristeva, 'Stabat Mater', *The Kristeva Reader*, 162.

The mother and her construct in Yeats

1 W.B. Yeats, 'Shepherd and Goatherd' (*The Wild Swans at Coole*, 1919) *The Variorum Edition of the Poems of W.B. Yeats* [Hereafter *VP.*] P. Allt and R.K. Alspach, eds (New York: Macmillan, 1957) 163, ll. 28–9; 35–8.
2 Yeats, 'Shepherd and Goatherd', ll. 117–19.
3 The prophecy to Mary that, because of the child she is to bear, a sword will pierce her heart provides one of the principal seeds from which the image of the suffering mother of Christ has grown. This prophecy haunts the gospel stories, such that no account of Mary's actions can be given without it being read in the light of the prophecy. Gerty MacDowell in the 'Nausicaa' episode of *Ulysses* also sets out the 'value' of Mary's suffering.

4 W.B. Yeats, 'The Mother of God' (*The Winding Stair and Other Poems*, 1933) *VP.*
   269, ll. 11–13. It is possible to see similarities here between 'The Mother of
   God' and *Ulysses*. In 'Circe' in particular Stephen's principal battle is to
   unlock the link that the mother has established between herself and suffering, a link which centres the mother within Christian myth thereby displacing the Christ-figure. The mother's domination of the 'child' can only be
   subverted through the subversion of the symbolic structures which hold the
   mother in place at the centre of experience. See chapter 8 for a more detailed
   discussion of this point.

5 Reflected in this shift is, I suspect, the fact that Yeats's own period of mariolatry had well and truly passed (see chapter 3, note 17).

6 W.B. Yeats, 'Among School Children' (*The Tower*, 1928)*VP.* 230, ll. 33–40.

7 Innes (1993) draws particular attention to icons of the Blessed Virgin where
   the 'infant Jesus...is rather precariously perched on her right arm, thus
   emphasizing her motherhood, while at the same time asserting the dominance of the child rather than the mother, and distancing it from reliance on
   the nurture of her breast' (40).

8 Yeats, 'Among School Children', ll. 13–16.

9 W.B. Yeats, 'A Nativity' (*Last Poems*, 1936–39) *VP.* 377, l. 1.

10 Yeats, 'A Nativity', ll. 11–12.

11 W.B. Yeats, 'A Prayer for My Son' (*The Tower*, 1928) *VP.* 224, ll. 23. Note
    particularly:

    > You have lacked articulate speech
    > To tell Your simplest want, and known,
    > Wailing upon a woman's knee,
    > All of that worst ignominy
    > Of flesh and bone.
    >   (*VP.* 224, ll. 20–4)

    Keane (1987), referring to stanza V of 'Among School Children' suggests:
    'The result is...an intoxicating concoction that seduces potential mothers
    into coition and so betrays infants into the world of generation'(131).

12 Yeats, 'A Prayer for My Son', l. 20; 'Among School Children', l. 33.

13 H. Bloom, *Yeats* (New York: Oxford University Press, 1970) 415. Cullingford
    (1993) also refers to a 'nursing male' which Yeats uses to trouble gender
    categories (183). In reading the poem I cannot help but be reminded of a
    letter written to Yeats by his father on the occasion of the birth of Yeats's first
    child: 'I could not bear to see you lying on [the nurse's] knees. I was for the
    first time – I suppose – pure animal.' Quoted in Foster (1997) 15.

14 W.B. Yeats, 'What Magic Drum?' (*From 'A Full Moon in March'*, 1935) *VP.* 324,
    ll. 1–3. That there is a homo-erotic quality to the poem is also suggested.

15 Yeats, 'What Magic Drum?' l. 4.

16 Yeats, 'What Magic Drum?' l. 6.

17 See, for example, 'Leda and the Swan', 'My Descendants', 'Whence Had They
    Come?' and 'A Prayer for My Daughter'.

18 Yeats, 'Among School Children', l. 9

19 W.B. Yeats, 'To a Young Girl' (*The Wild Swans at Coole*, 1919) *VP.* 160, ll. 4–6.

20 W.B. Yeats, 'Wisdom' (*The Tower*, 1928) *VP.* 227, ll. 11–13.

21 Yeats, 'Wisdom', ll. 6–7.

22 Yeats, 'Wisdom', ll. 16–17.

23 Cullingford (1992) makes a similar point with respect to the representation of women in Western love poetry: 'In telling women that they are beautiful, mysterious and spiritual, but also incapable of voice, agency or logical thought, the poet contributes to their social oppression even as he pretends to abase himself before "The eternal feminine"' (32). What I am suggesting is that there are more than just the mother and child who have a vested interest in the perpetuation of the image of the fused mother and child. Joyce's comments regarding the Roman Catholic Church in his notes to *Exiles* are particularly relevant here (see chapter 4).

24 W.B. Yeats, 'Remorse for Intemperate Speech' (*The Winding Stair and Other Poems*, 1933) *VP*. 274, ll. 11–15.

25 W.B. Yeats, 'The Friends of His Youth' (*The Tower*, 1928) *VP*. 240, ll. 10–12.

26 W.B. Yeats, 'J.M. Synge and the Ireland of His Time', *The Cutting of an Agate, Essays* (London: Macmillan & Co., 1924) 389.

27 E.B. Cullingford, *Gender and History in Yeats's Love Poetry* (New York: Cambridge University Press, 1993) 180–1. Cullingford argues that what Madge nurses is, essentially, 'political inflexibility' and 'obsessive political commitment'.

28 Cullingford (1993) also notes the extensive use of the maternal metaphor in Yeats's love poetry, particularly the 'parallels [between] the lover's satisfaction with that of the child at the mother's breast' (217).

29 W.B. Yeats, 'Lullaby' (*The Winding Stair and Other Poems*, 1933) *VP*. 291, ll. 1–2. However, it should be noted that the use of the word 'may' in the first verse suggests an ambiguity; that the child may, in fact, find it difficult to attain peace in his mother's arms. 'Chosen' (*VP*. 306, ll. 4–7) and 'The Wild Old Wicked Man' (*VP*. 351, ll. 61–2) also suggest the figure of the mother in relation to the lovers' satiation.

30 The nature of the protection afforded by the mother is also suggested in 'The Wild Old Wicked Man', where the mother's womb is one among many refuges that 'men' seek in order to escape from human suffering. (*VP*. 351, ll. 46–53).

31 W.B. Yeats, 'Three Things' (*The Winding Stair and Other Poems*, 1933) *VP*. 290, ll. 3–5.

32 W.B. Yeats, 'The Tower' (*The Tower*, 1928) *VP*. 212, ll. 160–72. Bloom (1970) notes: '*The Tower* is primarily a poem about an excess of imagination, or perhaps an imagination in excess of its historical stimuli' (350).

33 Yeats, 'The Stare's Nest by My Window', ll. 18–19.

34 W.B. Yeats, 'Nineteen Hundred and Nineteen' (*The Tower*, 1928) *VP*. 220, ll. 118–23.

35 Yeats, 'Nineteen Hundred and Nineteen', ll. 25–8.

36 W.B. Yeats, 'A Needle's Eye' (*From 'A Full Moon in March'*, 1935) *VP*. 328, ll. 3–4. Other texts where the womb–tomb association is drawn include *The Herne's Egg* and 'A Stick of Incense'. With regard to the latter, Ellmann (1964) makes the interesting point that 'Christianity is shown to have substituted a virgin womb and an empty tomb for the almost inclusive phallicism of earlier religions' (181).

37 W.B. Yeats, 'Crazy Jane and Jack the Journeyman' (*Words for Music Perhaps*) *VP*. 279, ll. 11–12.

38 H.C. Martin, *W.B. Yeats: Metaphysician as Dramatist* (Waterloo, Ont.: Wilfred Laurier University Press, 1986) 65.

39 W.B. Yeats, 'The Second Coming' (*Michael Robartes and the Dancer*, 1921) *VP.* 207, ll. 3–4.

40 Yeats, 'The Second Coming', ll. 5–8.

41 Yeats, 'The Second Coming', ll. 21–2.

42 This point is also made by Perloff (1990) 40.

43 W.B. Yeats, 'A Prayer for my Daughter' (*Michael Robartes and the Dancer*, 1921) *VP.* 208, ll. 49–56.

44 W.B. Yeats, 'Easter 1916' (*Michael Robartes and the Dancer*, 1921) *VP.* 200, ll. 74–6; 60–4. Cullingford (1993) also comments on the issue of naming in 'Easter 1916' referring to the 'psychological empowerment that the rebels must have felt in naming themselves the "children" of Mother Ireland, and that Yeats reflects in mourning them as such' (129). While not incompatible with my own reading, Cullingford takes her reading further than I'm prepared to go.

45 Yeats, 'Wisdom', ll. 16–20. That Yeats often uses 'wild' in relation to 'divinity' is an important point, and in this Blake's influence is apparent. I am particularly thinking of Blake's illustrations, etc. which seem to represent divine energy, both in kinesis and as a potential. See, for example, Blake's designs for Dante's *Divine Comedy*, and illustrations for his own work including 'The Marriage of Heaven and Hell', 'Jerusalem', 'Urizen' and *Europe: A Prophecy*.

46 W.B. Yeats, 'Tom at Cruachan' (*The Winding Stair and Other Poems*, 1933) *VP.* 298, ll.4–6.

47 Yeats, 'The Mother of God', ll. 4–5.

48 Here, it is possible to see the development of this theme from the early to the later poems. While in the earlier texts the emphasis was on the importance of an untainted transmission of the father's seed, here there is greater recognition of the necessity of the mother's taint if the child is to be 'realized', and the father's line assured ongoing generation. My reading of the mother's role differs somewhat from Webster's (1973) who argues that the womb for Yeats is a place where 'one receives magical powers, both sexual and poetic' (15–16). Webster intimates the source of these powers is the mother; my argument is that these powers come through the father, and are merely limited and 'realized' by the mother.

49 W.B. Yeats, 'Leda and the Swan' (*The Tower*, 1928) *VP.* 228, ll. 2–4. This representation of divine conception corresponds closely with that in 'The Mother of God' and, to a lesser extent, 'A Stick of Incense'.

50 Yeats, 'Leda and the Swan', ll. 9–11. Johnsen's reading of the poem ('Textual/ Sexual Politics in Yeats's "Leda and the Swan"', in Orr, 1991) corresponds with my own, particularly in his suggestion of Leda's complicity, as represented by Yeats: Leda 'serves as an expression of Zeus's history, a complicit or commensurate symbol of Zeus's refutation of her own culture' (84).

51 Yeats, 'Leda and the Swan', ll. 13–14. There is an obvious parallel here with the 'terrible beauty' born in 'Easter 1916'. Using texts such as 'Leda and the Swan', 'A Stick of Incense', 'The Mother of God', 'Whence Had They Come?' and 'A Nativity' as a guide, it is possible to argue that the 'terrible' aspect of the child born of the Easter rising is generated from the father's line. The mother's role in this generation is not explicitly stated in the poem, but, as I have argued, she is implicated (through her naming and renaming of the

child) in the placement of the child within that symbolic order governed by the mythical-herioc father. The parallel is also evident in the destructive outcomes of the child's birth, suggesting the mother in 'Easter 1916', whoever she may be, has put on the father's power and fury, but not his knowledge. In this I differ from Eagleton (1985) who argues that Yeats's 'terrible beauty' refers to not just the Easter Rising but woman in general: 'She is at once impossible, anarchy and order, carnal and ideal, dis-solution and a reassuring refuge from it' (138).

52 W.B. Yeats, 'Whence Had They Come?' (*From 'A Full Moon in March'*, 1935) *VP*. 325, ll. 11–12.

53 W.B. Yeats, 'The Crazed Moon' (*The Winding Stair and Other Poems*, 1933) *VP*. 260, ll. 16–18.

54 M.S. Breen, 'The Female Position of Auditor in Yeats's *Purgatory*', *Colby Library Quarterly* 25:1 (1989): 42–54.

Wresting subjectivity from the mother in *Ulysses*

1 J. Joyce, *Ulysses* (New York: Random House, 1961) 737. The notion of Leopold Bloom as 'womanly man' is one widely discussed among critics. See, in particular, Kiberd (1986), 188–97. See also Dipasquale (1987), Innes (1993), Keane (1988), Unkeless (1976) and Walkley (1980). I disagree with arguments such as Innes's (1993) that: 'Joyce pairs the "womanly" male, Bloom, who "mothers" Molly, Milly and Stephen, and the "manly" female, Molly, who imagines herself a man' (73–4). Arguments such as this, I suggest, carry an allusion within *Ulysses* much further than is warranted. To do so, subjects Bloom to abstract (and often spurious) notions of femininity and/or maternity, rather than to those constructs of maternity figured by Joyce not only in *Ulysses*, but throughout his *oeuvre*.

2 Joyce, *Ulysses*, 737.

3 D. Attridge, 'Molly's Flow: The Writing of "Penelope" and the Question of Woman's Language', *Modern Fiction Studies* 35.3 (1989): 543–65. Arguments that Molly functions within the novel as archetypal mother – see, for example Scott (1987) – are also challenged by a recognition of Molly's resistance of maternity within 'Penelope'. Molly touches maternal spaces only briefly in her consideration of Milly and Rudy, and her interest in Stephen is far from a mother's. It is worth considering Henderson's (1989) argument with regard to Joyce's 'encoding' of Molly's soliloquy with the defeat of the mother: 'The impulse to order and control the m/other could hardly be more blatant. Woman signifies womb. Mother-Earth and the world's four corners are reduced to a sex object, and the verbal artist literally fucks Nature when she says "yes". Molly's words are Joyce's ironic code' (520). This is interesting in that Molly as mother is so often read according to the linguistic and semantic construction of 'Penelope'. The defeat of the mother, I suggest, comes not through any implicit linguistic code, but in the word-thoughts of a woman who no longer desires that space. Molly's place in society is determined by her art and her sexuality and, like her soliloquy, she is unbound by the structures and strictures that the mother, who no longer possesses her child, must bear.

4 Joyce, *Ulysses*, 769.
5 S. Freud, 'On Dreams', *The Standard Edition of the Complete Psychological Works of Sigmund Freud, Volume V*, J. Strachey, ed. (London: Hogarth Press, 1953–66). Ellmann (1982) notes: 'Joyce was close to the new psychoanalysis at so many points that he always disavowed any interest in it.... But he partly belied himself by the keen interest he took in the notebook [Frank] Budgen kept to record his dreams; Joyce's interpretations showed the influence of Freud' (436).
6 Freud, 'On Dreams', 649, 661.
7 Joyce, *Ulysses*, 438.
8 Joyce, *Ulysses*, 438.
9 Joyce, *Ulysses*, 492–3.
10 Joyce, *Ulysses*, 494.
11 Joyce, *Ulysses*, 498.
12 Matthew 6: 9–13; Luke 11: 2–4.
13 Joyce, *Ulysses*, 498–9.
14 Joyce, *Ulysses*, 598–9.
15 See also, Deane (1985) 81 for a discussion of Joyce's parody in *Ulysses* of the family unit, particularly as portrayed in the nineteenth-century English novel.
16 This is described in the first chapter of *A Portrait of the Artist as a Young Man*. Also, see my discussion in chapter 4.
17 Joyce, *Ulysses*, 579.
18 Joyce, *Ulysses*, 572.
19 Joyce, *Ulysses*, 579–80.
20 Joyce, *Ulysses*, 5.
21 Joyce, *Ulysses*, 5.
22 Lawrence ('Joyce and Feminism', in Attridge, 1990) argues: 'Throughout *Ulysses*, Stephen wrestles with the nightmare of his own history, especially its origin in the maternal body, his conception, the result of what he calls "an instant of blind rut". Indeed, Stephen's theory of literary creation in "Scylla and Charybdis" and patriarchal literary culture itself in "Oxen of the Sun" neutralize the power of the mother by effacing her role in culture' (249). As I will argue, while these episodes prepare the ground for her effacement, it is only Stephen's action in 'Circe' that will dispel the mother and allow the father and son their proper place.
23 Joyce, *Ulysses*, 5.
24 Joyce, *Ulysses*, 8–9.
25 E. Ragland-Sullivan, 'Lacan's Seminars on James Joyce: Writing as Symptom and "Singular Solution" ', *Psychoanalysis and...* R. Feldstein and H. Sussman, eds (New York: Routledge, 1990) 67.
26 Joyce, *Ulysses*, 42.
27 Joyce, *Ulysses*, 14.
28 Joyce, *Ulysses*, 5.
29 Joyce, *Ulysses*, 5.
30 Joyce, *Ulysses*, 249.
31 M. Beja, 'A Poor Trait of the Artless: The Artist Manqué in James Joyce', *James Joyce Quarterly* 26.1 (1988): 89–104, 94. Deane (1985) similarly argues that 'Stephen in *Ulysses* is not a writer at all' (80).

32 Joyce, *Ulysses*, 6.
33 Joyce, *Ulysses*, 609. Stephen's resemblance to his mother is also remarked upon in 'Eumaeus' and 'Penelope'.
34 Joyce, *Ulysses*, 37–8. Morrison (1993) suggests that in 'Proteus', 'Stephen's mind wanders to an idea of a connection backward through time, via the umbilical cords of all humanity, to the original mother, Eve in Eden' (350). While I agree that the mother acts in relation to Stephen as something of a 'black hole' drawing all signification towards it and into it, there is for Stephen no other mother than May Dedalus. Eve, mother-Ireland, the Virgin Mary are all drawn into her and she comes to represent the whole gamut of maternity in both its life-affirming and life-denying aspects.
35 Joyce, *Ulysses*, 9.
36 Joyce, *Ulysses*, 27. See Johnson's notes to the Oxford edition of *Ulysses* (1993).
37 Joyce, *Ulysses*, 27–8.
38 Joyce, *Ulysses*, 28.
39 Joyce, *Ulysses*, 10.
40 Ragland-Sullivan, 'Lacan's Seminars on James Joyce', 73.
41 Joyce, *Ulysses*, 6.
42 Joyce, *Ulysses*, 96.
43 Joyce, *Ulysses*, 161.
44 Joyce, *Ulysses*, 742.
45 Joyce, *Ulysses*, 110.
46 Joyce, *Ulysses*, 164. See also 'Aeolus' (138); 'Proteus' (48); 'Oxen of the Sun' (386); and, 'Oxen of the Sun' (390).
47 Joyce, *Ulysses*, 61.
48 Joyce, *Ulysses*, 45–6.
49 Joyce, *Ulysses*, 190.
50 Joyce, *Ulysses*, 389. Mina Purefoy's marginalization by the 'patriarchy' is noted by a number of critics. Lawrence ('Joyce and Feminism', in Attridge, 1990) argues that the paradox of 'Oxen of the Sun' is that the womb of the mother as source of the discussion is 'borrowed by male writers who are pregnant with the word'. But Mrs Purefoy is physically removed from the space in which those discussions occur, she is 'excluded from cultural production' (250).
51 Joyce, *Ulysses*, 390.
52 Joyce, *Ulysses*, 415.
53 Moore, of course, merely states the metaphor; Joyce dramatizes it and embeds it within the narrative as a structural device.
54 Joyce, *Ulysses*, 390.
55 K. Lawrence, 'Joyce and Feminism', *The Cambridge Companion to James Joyce*, D. Attridge, ed. (Cambridge: Cambridge University Press, 1990) 249.
56 Note Druff's (1982) argument that Stephen 'celebrates pregnancy not as a life-process... but rather as an exclusively artistic metaphor, whereby he can draw support for his constant references to himself as the Christ; by blaspheming the religious mystery and supplanting it with an artistic one he hopes to legitimize himself as the Messiah of the Word' (311).
57 Many critics have discussed the privileging of the father and the displacement of the mother that occurs in *Ulysses* and particularly in 'Scylla and Charybdis'. For example, Rabaté ('A Clown's Inquest into Paternity: Fathers,

Dead or Alive, in *Ulysses* and *Finnegans Wake'*, in Davis, 1981) argues that 'Stephen's paradox lies precisely in the fact that he needs to present Shakespeare in the midst of family rivalries, usurpations, and treacheries in order to free paternity as creation from the power of the mother' (81). See also, Deane (1986), Gilbert and Gubar (1988) and Morrison (1993).

58 Joyce, *Ulysses*, 208.

59 Joyce, *Ulysses*, 194.

60 Johnsen ('"Beyond the Veil"': *Ulysses*, Feminism and the Figure of Woman', in van Boheeman, 1989) makes the important point that 'in choosing [the mole, Stephen] ignores the navel, that fleshy scar which signifies his maternal connection' (217). This image of 'weaving' and 'unweaving' offers an interesting comparison with the expanding and contracting of subjectivity that Stephen experienced in *A Portrait* as he reads forwards and then backwards the fly-leaf of his geography book.

61 Joyce, *Ulysses*, 391; Beja, 'A Poor Trait of the Artless'.

62 Joyce, *Ulysses*, 207.

63 The traditional strength of the mother's figuration within religious discourse is highlighted by Sawyer (1993) who recalls that St Oengus (Aengus) referred to Christ as 'Jesus McMary so great was the mariolatry he practised' (15).

64 Bloom refers to his foremother in 'Lestrygonians' (167).

65 Joyce, *Ulysses*, 391. This point is also noted by Scott (1987) who writes that Stephen is encouraged 'to think of the female generative function as an essential linking back of humanity. The ultimate mythical figure in this scheme is the first mother, Eve, whose fructive form is in great contrast to Stephen's deathly view of woman' (90). Yet, all mothers are, for Stephen, conflated in Mrs Dedalus, and most meaning is invested in her – she is that which is 'signified' by so many of the 'signifiers' Stephen encounters during the day, whether that be the sea or Eve – she monopolizes signification, and it is this monopoly that Stephen must defeat if he is to emerge from *Ulysses* with any sense of his own subjectivity.

66 The mother's self-perpetuation is assured by her sons' unchallenged allegiance to the authority which affords her a privileged, if constructed, position, and by her regeneration of daughters. This paradigm is evident in *Ulysses* in the figure of Gerty MacDowell (355). The dark side of that portrait comes in the guise of Polly Mooney and her mother, first seen in *Dubliners* but referred to in 'Cyclops' (302–3). The mother's responsibility for holding the home together is also evident in *Ulysses* (151). While such figurations of the mother are aligned with those I have discussed in 'Social Spaces', I am more concerned here with those figurations which resonate in the symbolic order.

67 McKnight (1977) makes a similar point, arguing that for Stephen there is 'the threat of losing his sense of himself as a separate being by having his identity submerged into any of the institutions or people he experiences as mothers' (422). It is with regard to this point that I differ from critics such as Fitzpatrick (1974), who refers to the 'maternal triad' from which Stephen must 'dissociate' himself. In my reading, the mothers Fitzpatrick refers to – 'May Dedalus, Ireland/Dublin and the Church' (124) – are subsumed into the single figure of May Dedalus.

68 Joyce, *Ulysses*, 14.

69 Joyce, *Ulysses*, 13–14. Wollaeger (1993) argues that Joyce uses the peasant woman to ironize the figure of the traditional Irish peasant. This irony comes, I suggest, through Stephen's response to her. Further, she offers a marked contrast to the 'milkwoman' who figures in *A Portrait of the Artist of a Young Man*, trying to seduce Davin into her cottage.

70 Joyce, *Ulysses*, 600. Ellmann's (1967) assessment of Old Gummy Granny is an interesting one. He argues that Joyce is essentially parodying Yeats's *Cathleen ni Houlihan*: 'While Joyce's attitude is not without occasional ambiguities, essentially the "poor old woman" is admissible only as a comic fury' (40). Cranly's reference to 'Gap-toothed Kathleen, her four beautiful green fields' (184) and 'the auric egg of Russell . . . [for whom] the earth is not an exploitable ground but the living mother' (186–7) would seem to support this. Deane's (1985) argument is also useful here: 'Joyce did not repudiate Irish nationalism. Instead he understood it as a potent example of a rhetoric which imagined as true structures that did not and were never to exist outside language' (107).

71 Joyce, *Ulysses*, 640.

72 Joyce, *Ulysses*, 112–13.

73 Joyce, *Ulysses*, 259–60.

74 Joyce, *Ulysses*, 284.

75 Joyce, *Ulysses*, 286.

76 Joyce, *Ulysses*, 346.

77 Joyce, *Ulysses*, 358.

78 Joyce, *Ulysses*, 357.

79 Joyce, *Ulysses*, 391–2.

80 In this I go further than critics who read Stephen's confrontation with his mother in terms of his need to 'repress' his mother's 'selfhood' – see, for example, Hill (1993) – or to eliminate the barrier to the 'union of father and son' which the mother represents – see, for example, Ferrer ('Circe, Regret and Regression', in Attridge and Ferrer, 1984).

81 Joyce, *Ulysses*, 581.

82 Joyce, *Ulysses*, 581. Here The Mother echoes the words of the mother in Epiphany 34, yet she offers a stark contrast to the 'imaginative influence in the hearts of my children' (Joyce, 1991) 194.

83 Joyce, *Ulysses*, 581.

84 Joyce, *Ulysses*, 582.

85 Joyce, *Ulysses*, 582.

86 Joyce, *Ulysses*, 582.

87 Joyce, *Ulysses*, 583. That Stephen's dismissal of his mother has allowed him to move towards the saviour's role which he covets is suggested in 'Eumaeus' where Stephen refers to one of his 'betrayers' as 'Judas' (615). In this, I suggest, Stephen's 'murder' of The Mother – and that she is represented as a generic mother supports my arguments regarding May Dedalus embodying all mother-figures – is more than simply an effort to retain his individuality. I go further, therefore, than Norris (1987), for example, who argues: 'That his mother's love is contingent on behavior that will kill his emerging individuality, his growth into personhood and adulthood, creates the murderous dilemma that ends in Stephen's matricidal triumph' (16).

88 Joyce, *Ulysses*, 670.

89 See, for example, Benstock (1977), Deane (1985) and Rabaté ('A Clown's Inquest into Paternity: Fathers, Dead or Alive, in *Ulysses* and *Finnegans Wake*', in Davis, 1981) who also differ from those many critics who argue that Bloom and Stephen are, in effect, 'father and son' at the conclusion of the novel.

90 Joyce, *Ulysses*, 413. In 'Circe', asked by Zoe whether he is Stephen's father, Bloom replies 'Not I!' (475).

91 J. Perreault, 'Male Maternity in *Ulysses*', *English Studies in Canada* 13.3 (1987): 304–14. There is a preoccupation among critics to identify Stephen's 'new' parents, with both Bloom and Molly being figured among the contenders. See, for example, Bormanis (1992), Gilbert and Gubar (1989), Keane (1988), Obed (1985) and Restuccia (1989).

92 See also Miller (1993) whose discussion of 'Ithaca' argues for a relevance to the episode that goes muich further than the 'celebrated...locus of Bloom and Stephen's long awaited mystical union' (210).

93 Joyce, *Ulysses*, 728–9.

94 Joyce, *Ulysses*, 735–6.

95 Joyce, *Ulysses*, 708.

96 Ragland-Sullivan, 'Lacan's Seminars on James Joyce', 74.

'sad and weary I go back to you, my cold father'

1 Benstock (1965) reminds readers that 'the full appellation of "Anna Livia Plurabelle" is not to be found as such in the final text' (8). For convenience, I use the full appellation throughout the chapter, though I recognize the very plurablity inherent to ALP.

2 J. Joyce, *Finnegans Wake* (London: Minerva, 1992) 628.

3 It is too much, I suggest, to refer (as do Campbell and Robinson [1944]) to *Finnegans Wake* as an 'amniotic fluid' (293). I prefer Joyce's own description, merged within the *Wake*'s narrative (*Finnegans Wake*, 117; 120).

4 Joyce, *Finnegans Wake*, 627.

5 Ellmann (1982) refers to her as 'eternally constant in spite of inconstancies' (713).

6 R. Ellmann, *James Joyce* (Oxford: Oxford University Press, 1982) 544.

7 Joyce, *Finnegans Wake*, 619.

8 Joyce, *Finnegans Wake*, 606.

9 Joyce, *Finnegans Wake*, 195.

10 Joyce, *Finnegans Wake*, 210; 101.

11 Joyce, *Finnegans Wake*, 139.

12 Joyce, *Finnegans Wake*, 104. The same prayer – central to the Christian tradition – is parodied by Brother Buzz in the 'Circe' episode of *Ulysses*. Joyce's resistance of Christian tradition, and the place of the mother within that tradition – is evident throughout *Finnegans Wake*. Yet, beneath the parody, there still lingers the threat of the icon of the Virgin Mother – Joyce fails to convince me that he has nullifed completely her 'siren' call.

13 Joyce, *Finnegans Wake*, 299. In this I am in some disagreement with Burgess (1965) who argues that while she is 'hymned...as if she were God the

Father... she reflects the eternal father, she bore his sons, she is the custodian of the truth about him' (209).

14 Joyce, *Finnegans Wake*, 389.
15 Joyce, *Finnegans Wake*, 561.
16 Joyce, *Finnegans Wake*, 547.
17 Joyce, *Finnegans Wake*, 548.
18 Joyce, *Finnegans Wake*, 585.
19 Joyce, *Finnegans Wake*, 101–2.
20 Joyce, *Finnegans Wake*, 110.
21 Joyce, *Finnegans Wake*, 50.
22 I have borrowed this usage from Ellmann (1982) 713.
23 Joyce, *Finnegans Wake*, 55. While I acknowledge Hart's (1962) argument – an argument further developed by Devlin ('ALP's Final Monologue in *Finnegans Wake*: The Dialectical Logic of Joyce's Dream Text', in Beja and Benstock, 1989) that the conclusion to *Finnegans Wake* echoes Joyce's earlier story 'Eveline', I suggest that ALP's cycle ultimately is much more life-affirming than Eveline's. Ellmann (1982) emphasizes the reciprocity of life and death that figures so prominently in Joyce's work, and that has its finest realization in *Finnegans Wake*: 'Joyce's greatest triumph in asserting the intimacy of living and dead was to be the close of *Finnegans Wake*. Here Anna Livia Plurabelle, the river of life, flows towards the sea, which is death: the fresh water passes into the salt, a bitter ending. Yet it is also a return to her father, the sea, that produces the cloud that makes the river, and her father is also her husband, to whom she gives herself as a bride to her groom' (253).
24 Joyce, *Finnegans Wake*, 104. Benstock (1965) writes: 'Time after time in the *Wake* a single name opens two or more possibilities' (23).
25 Joyce, *Finnegans Wake*, 215. In this I agree, to a point, with Norris (1987), who argues that the last chapter of *Finnegans Wake* 'demonstrates how dying can also be rejuvenation, how male is also female, and female, male, and how time and space are versions of one another' (11). However, I cannot concur with her conclusion that this chapter also 'dramatizes Stephen Dedalus's *rapprochement* with his mother' and the return of the son to the mother's womb.
26 Joyce, *Finnegans Wake*, 593.
27 Joyce, *Finnegans Wake*, 29.
28 For varying perspectives on this point see, for example, Cixous (1976), Gilbert and Gubar (1988), Henke (1990), Lawrence ('Joyce and Feminism', in Attridge, 1990), MacCabe (1978) and Scott (1984).
29 K. Lawrence, 'Joyce and Feminism', *The Cambridge Companion to James Joyce*, D. Attridge, ed. (Cambridge: Cambridge University Press, 1990) 254.
30 S. Henke, *James Joyce and the Politics of Desire* (London: Faber, 1990) 210.
31 Joyce, *Finnegans Wake*, 337.
32 G. Moore, *A Drama in Muslin* (Gerrards Cross: Colin Smythe, 1981) 325.
33 Cairns and Richards (1988) argue that an essential element of the maintenance of Nationalist discourse was ensuring that the proliferation of the cause remained 'pure and unsullied'. This ran counter to the desire of writers such as Moore and Joyce to assert not merely a personal freedom but a sexual one (74–7).

Bibliography

Allison, J. ed. *Yeats's Political Identities: Selected Essays* (Ann Arbor: University of Michigan Press, 1996).

Ames, C. 'The Modernist Canon Narrative: Woolf's *Between the Acts* and Joyce's "Oxen of the Sun" ', *Twentieth Century Literature* 37.4 (1991): 390–404.

Anderson, A. *Tainted Souls and Painted Faces: The Rhetoric of Fallenness in Victorian Culture* (Ithaca, NY & London: Cornell University Press, 1993).

Attridge, D., ed. *The Cambridge Companion to James Joyce* (Cambridge: Cambridge University Press, 1990).

Attridge, D. 'Molly's Flow: The Writing of "Penelope" and the Question of Woman's Language', *Modern Fiction Studies* 35: 3 (1989): 543–65.

Attridge, D. and D. Ferrer, eds, *Post-structuralist Joyce: Essays from the French* (Cambridge: Cambridge University Press, 1984).

Auerbach, N. *Woman and the Demon: The Life of a Victorian Myth* (Cambridge, Mass.: Harvard University Press, 1982).

Ayling, R., ed. *J.M. Synge: Four Plays* (Basingstoke: Macmillan, 1992).

Ayling, R., ed. *O'Casey: The Dublin Trilogy* (London: Macmillan, 1985).

Barthes, R. *Mythologies* (London: Paladin, 1973 [1957]).

Beja, M. 'A Poor Trait of the Artless: The Artist Manqué in James Joyce', *James Joyce Quarterly* 26.1 (1988): 89–104.

Beja, M. and S. Benstock, eds, *Coping with Joyce: Essays from the Copenhagen Symposium* (Columbus: Ohio State University Press, 1989).

Beja, M. et al., eds. *James Joyce: The Centennial Symposium* (Urbana & Chicago: University of Illinois Press, 1986).

Benstock, B., ed. *James Joyce: The Augmented Ninth*, Proceedings of the Ninth International James Joyce Symposium (New York: Syracuse University Press, 1988).

Benstock, B. *James Joyce: The Undiscover'd Country* (Dublin: Gill & Macmillan, 1977).

Benstock, B. *Joyce-Again's Wake: An Analysis of* Finnegans Wake (Seattle & London: University of Washington Press, 1965).

Bensyl, S.L. 'Cecilia: Irish Catholicism in George Moore's *A Drama in Muslin*, 1886', *Eire-Ireland* 29.2 (1994): 65–76.

Bloom, H., ed. *Sean O'Casey* (New York: Chelsea House, 1987).

Bloom, H. *Yeats* (New York: Oxford University Press, 1970).

Bormanis, J. ' "in the first bloom of her new motherhood": The Appropriation of the Maternal and the Representation of Mothering in *Ulysses*', *James Joyce Quarterly* 29.3 (1992): 593–606.

Bourke, J. *Husbandry to Housewifery: Women, Economic Change and Housework in Ireland, 1890–1914* (Oxford: Clarendon Press, 1993).

Boyle, N. and M. Swales, eds, *Realism in European Literature* (Cambridge: Cambridge University Press, 1986).

Bradbury, M. and J. McFarlane, eds, *Modernism: 1890–1930* (London: Penguin, 1976).

Bramsback, B. and M. Croghan, eds, *Anglo-Irish and Irish Literature: Aspects of Language and Culture* (Uppsala: Uppsala University Press, 1988).

Breen, M.S. 'The Female Position of Auditor in Yeats's *Purgatory*', *Colby Library Quarterly* 25.1 (1989): 42–54.

Brennan, T. *The Interpretation of the Flesh: Freud and Femininity* (London & New York: Routledge, 1992).

Brivic, S. *Joyce Between Freud and Jung* (New York, Kennikat, 1980).

Brown, M.R.F. ' "An angle of experience": Tragic and Comic Aspects of the Plays of John Millington Synge', PhD Thesis (University of New South Wales, 1995).

Brown, T. *Ireland: A Social and Cultural History, 1922–1985* (London: Fontana, 1981).

Burgess, A. *Here Comes Everybody: An Introduction to James Joyce for the Ordinary Reader* (London: Faber & Faber, 1965).

Burke, C., N. Schor and M. Whitford, eds, *Engaging with Irigaray: Feminist Philosophy and Modern European Thought* (New York: Columbia University Press, 1994).

Cairns, D. and S. Richards, 'Reading a Riot: The "Reading Formation" of Synge's Abbey Audience', *Literature & History*, 13 (1987): 219–37.

Cairns, D. and S. Richards, *Writing Ireland: Colonialism, Nationalism and Culture* (Manchester: Manchester University Press, 1988).

Campbell, J. and H.M. Robinson, *A Skeleton Key to* Finnegans Wake (London: Faber & Faber, [1944]).

Casey, D.J., ed. *Critical Essays on John Millington Synge* (New York: G.K. Hall, 1994).

Cave, R.A. *A Study of the Novels of George Moore* (New York: Barnes & Noble, 1978).

Chadwick, J. 'Family Romance as National Allegory in Yeats's *Cathleen ni Houlihan* and *The Dreaming of the Bones*', *Twentieth Century Literature* 32.2 (1986): 155–68.

Cixous, H. *The Exile of James Joyce*, Trans. S.A.J. Purcell (London: John Calder, 1976).

Cixous, H. and C. Clement, *The Newly Born Woman* (Minneapolis: University of Minnesota Press, 1986).

Connolly, P. ed. *Literature and the Changing Ireland* (Gerrards Cross: Colin Smythe, 1982).

Corballis, R. 'The Allegorical Basis of O'Casey's Early Plays', *O'Casey Annual, No. 4*, R.G. Lowery, ed. (London: Macmillan, 1985).

Costello, P. *The Heart Grown Brutal: The Irish Revolution in Literature from Parnell to the Death of Yeats, 1891–1939* (Dublin: Gill & Macmillan, 1977).

Costello, P. *James Joyce: The Years of Growth, 1882–1915* (London: Papermac, 1994).

Cowart, D. 'From Nun's Island to Monkstown: Celibacy, Concupscience and Sterility in "The Dead" ', *James Joyce Quarterly* 26.4 (1989): 499–504.

Cullingford, E.B. 'At the Feet of the Goddess: Yeats's Love Poetry and the Feminist Occult', *Yeats Annual, No. 9*, D. Toomey, ed. (London: Macmillan, 1992).

Cullingford, E.B. *Gender and History in Yeats's Love Poetry* (New York: Cambridge University Press, 1993).

Cullingford, E.B. 'Yeats and Women: *Michael Robartes and the Dancer*', *Yeats Annual, No. 4*, W. Gould, ed. (London: Macmillan, 1986).

Davies, P. *God and the New Physics* (Harmondsworth: Penguin, 1984 [1983]).

Davis, R.C., ed. *The Fictional Father: Lacanian Readings of the Text* (Amherst: University of Massachusetts Press, 1981).

Deane, S. *Celtic Revivals: Essays in Modern Irish Literature, 1880–1980* (London: Faber & Faber, 1985).

Deane, S. *A Short History of Irish Literature* (London: Hutchison, 1986).

de Beauvoir, S. *The Second Sex* (Harmondsworth: Penguin, 1972 [1953]).

Dipasquale, T.M. 'Seraphic Seduction in *Portrait of the Artist* and *Ulysses*', *Studies in the Novel* 19.4 (1987): 475–85.

Doane, J. and D. Hodges, *From Klein to Kristeva: Psychoanalytic Feminism and the Search for the 'Good Enough' Mother* (Ann Arbor: University of Michigan Press, 1992).

Druff, J.H. 'History vs the Word: The Metaphor of Childbirth in Stephen's Aesthetics', *James Joyce Quarterly* 19.3 (1982): 303–14.

Dunleavy, J.E. ed. *George Moore in Perpsective* (Gerrards Cross: Colin Smythe, 1983).

Durbach, E. 'Synge's Tragic Vision of the Old Mother and the Sea', *Modern Drama* 14.4 (1972): 363–72.

Eagleton, T. *Heathcliff and the Great Hunger: Studies in Irish Culture* (London: Verso, 1995).

Eagleton, T. 'Politics and Sexuality in W.B. Yeats', *The Crane Bag* 9.2 (1985): 138–42.

Ellmann, R. *Eminent Domain: Yeats among Wilde, Joyce, Pound, Eliot and Auden* (New York: Oxford University Press, 1967).

Ellmann, R. *The Identity of Yeats* (London: Faber & Faber, 1964).

Ellmann, R. *James Joyce* (New York: Oxford University Press, 1982).

Ellmann, R. *Yeats: The Man and the Masks* (London: Penguin, 1987 [1979]).

Farrow, A. *George Moore* (Boston: Twayne, 1978).

Feldstein, R. and H. Sussman, eds, *Psychoanalysis and . . .* (New York & London: Routledge, 1990).

Fernando, L. 'Moore: Realism, Art, and the Subjection of Women', *'New Women' in the Late Victorian Novel* (University Park & London: Pennsylvania State University Press, 1977).

Feynman, R.P. *Six Easy Pieces* (Reading, Mass.: Helix Books, 1995 [1963]).

Fitzpatrick, W.P. 'The Myth of Creation: Joyce, Jung and *Ulysses*', *James Joyce Quarterly* 11.2 (1974): 123–44.

Foster, R.F. *Modern Ireland, 1600–1972* (London: Allen Lane, 1988).

Foster, R.F. *Paddy and Mr Punch: Connections in Irish and English History* (London: Allen Lane, the Penguin Press, 1993).

Foster, R.F. *W.B. Yeats: A Life, I: The Apprenctice Mage, 1865–1914* (Oxford & New York: Oxford University Press, 1997).

Freud, S. *The Standard Edition of the Complete Psychological Works of Sigmund Freud*, J. Strachey, ed. (London: Hogarth Press, 1953–66).

Fussell, P. *The Great War and Modern Memory* (London: Oxford University Press, 1975).

Gallagher, S.F., ed. *Women in Irish Legend, Life and Literature* (Gerrards Cross: Colin Smythe, 1983).

Garton, J., ed. *Facets of European Modernism* (Norwich: University of East Anglia Press, 1985).

Gauthier, L. 'Desire for Origin/Original Desire: Luce Irigaray on Maternity, Sexuality and Language', *Canadian Fiction Magazine* 57 (1986): 41–6.

Gilbert, S.M. and S. Gubar, *No Man's Land: The Place of the Woman Writer in the Twentieth Century, Vol. 1: The War of Words* (New Haven & London: Yale

University Press, 1988) *Vol. 2: Sexchanges*. (New Haven & London: Yale University Press, 1989).

Grayson, J. ' "Do You Kiss Your Mother?": Stephen Dedalus' Sovereignty of Ireland', *James Joyce Quarterly* 19.2 (1982): 119–26.

Greene, D.N. and E.M. Stephens, *J.M. Synge, 1871–1909*, revised edn (New York & London: New York University Press, 1989).

Grosz, E. *Jacques Lacan: A Feminist Introduction* (Sydney: Allen & Unwin, 1990).

Grosz, E. *Sexual Subversions: Three French Feminists* (Sydney: Allen & Unwin, 1989).

Grosz, E. *Volatile Bodies: Towards a Corporeal Feminism* (Sydney: Allen & Unwin, 1994).

Grubgeld, E. *George Moore and the Autogenous Self: The Autobiographies and Fiction* (Syracuse: Syracuse University Press, 1994).

Hall, W.E. *Shadowy Heroes: Irish Literature of the 1890s* (Syracuse, NY: Syracuse University Press, 1980).

Harris, S.C. ' "Blow the Witches Out": Gender Construction and the Subversion of Nationalism in Yeats's *Cathleen ni Houlihan* and *On Baile's Strand*', *Modern Drama* 39 (1996): 475–89.

Hart, C. *Structure and Motif in* Finnegans Wake (London: Faber & Faber, 1962).

Henderson, D.E. 'Joyce's Modernist Woman: Whose Last Word?', *Modern Fiction Studies* 35.3 (1989): 517–28.

Henke, S. *James Joyce and the Politics of Desire* (London: Faber, 1990).

Henke, S. and E. Unkeless, eds, *Women in Joyce* (Chicago: University of Illinois Press, 1982).

Hill, M. ' "*Amor Matris*": Mother and Self in the Telemachiad Episode of *Ulysses*', *Twentieth Century Literature* 39.3 (1993): 329–43.

Hone, J. *The Life of George Moore* (London: Gollancz, 1936).

Hone, J. *W.B. Yeats, 1865–1939* (London: Macmillan & Co., 1962).

Houghton, W.E. *The Victorian Frame of Mind, 1830–1870* (New Haven & London: Yale University Press, 1957).

Howes, M. *Yeats's Nations: Gender, Class and Irishness* (Cambridge: Cambridge University Press, 1996).

Ian, M. *Remembering the Phallic Mother: Psychoanalysis, Modernism and the Fetish* (Ithaca, NY & London: Cornell University Press, 1993).

Innes, C. 'The Essential Continuity of Sean O'Casey', *Modern Drama* 33.3 (1990): 419–33.

Innes, C.L. 'Virgin Territories and Motherlands: Colonial and Nationlist Representations of Africa and Ireland', *Feminist Review* 47 (1994): 1–14.

Innes, C.L. *Woman and Nation in Irish Literature and Society, 1880–1935* (Athens: University of Georgia Press, 1993).

Joyce, J. *The Critical Writings of James Joyce*, E. Mason and R. Ellmann, eds. (London: Faber & Faber, 1959).

Joyce, J. *The Essential James Joyce*, H. Levin, ed. (London: Jonathan Cape, 1948).

Joyce, J. *Exiles* (London: Paladin, 1991 [1916]).

Joyce, J. *Finnegans Wake* (London: Minerva, 1992 [1939]).

Joyce, J. *Poems and Shorter Writings*, R. Ellmann, A. Walton Litz and J. Whittier-Ferguson, eds (London: Faber & Faber, 1991).

Joyce, J. *Letters of James Joyce, Volume II*, R. Ellmann, ed. (London: Faber & Faber, 1966).

Joyce, J. *Stephen Hero* (New York: New Directions, 1963 [1944]).

Joyce, J. *Ulysses* (New York: Random House, 1961 [1922]).

Joyce, J. *Ulysses* (Oxford: Oxford University Press, 1993 [1922]).

Kaplan, E.A. *Motherhood and Representation: The Mother in Popular Culture and Melodrama* (London: Routledge, 1992).

Keane, P.J. *Terrible Beauty: Yeats, Joyce, Ireland and the Myth of the Devouring Female* (Columbia: University of Missouri Press, 1988).

Keane, P.J. *Yeats's Interaction with Tradition* (Columbia: University of Missouri Press, 1987).

Kearney, R. 'Myth and Motherland', Field Day Theatre Company, *Ireland's Field Day* (London: Hutchinson, 1985).

Kelly, J.S. 'The Fall of Parnell and the Rise of Irish Literature', *Anglo-Irish Studies* 2 (1976): 1–23.

Kenneally, M. 'The Changing Contents of O'Casey's Autobiography', *O'Casey Annual, No. 1.*, R.G. Lowery, ed. (London: Macmillan, 1982).

Kenneally, M. 'Joyce, O'Casey and the Genre of Autobiography', *O'Casey Annual, No. 3*, R.G. Lowery, ed. (London: Macmillan, 1984).

Kermode, F. *The Sense of an Ending: Studies in the Theory of Fiction* (New York: Oxford University Press, 1967).

Kiberd, D. *Inventing Ireland* (London: Jonathan Cape, 1995).

Kiberd, D. *Men and Feminism in Modern Literature* (London: Macmillan, 1986).

Kiberd, D. *Synge and the Irish Language*, revised edn (London, Macmillan, 1993 [1979]).

Kilroy, J.F., ed. *The Irish Short Story: A Critical History* (Boston: Twayne, 1984).

Kleiman, C. *Sean O'Casey's Bridge of Vision: Four Essays on Structure and Perspective* (Toronto: University of Toronto Press, 1982).

Kline, G.C. *The Last Courtly Lover: Yeats and the Idea of Woman* (Ann Arbor: UMI Research Press, 1983).

Knowles, S. 'The Substructure of "Sirens": Molly as *nexus omnia ligans'*, *James Joyce Quarterly* 23.4 (1986): 447–63.

Kristeva, J. *Black Sun: Depression and Melancholia* (New York: Columbia University Press, 1989).

Kristeva, J. *Desire in Language: A Semiotic Approach to Literature and Art* (Oxford: Blackwell, 1982).

Kristeva, J. *The Kristeva Reader*, T. Moi, ed. (Oxford: Blackwell, 1986).

Kuch, P. 'What Can I But Enumerate Old Themes''', *Omnium Gatherum: Essays for Richard Ellmann*, S. Dick, et al., eds. (Gerrards Cross: Colin Smythe, 1989).

Kuch, P. *Yeats and A.E.: 'The antagonism that unites dear friends'* (Gerrards Cross: Colin Smythe, 1986).

Lacan, J. *The Four Fundamental Concepts of Psycho-Analysis*, J.-A. Miller, ed. (London: Penguin, 1979).

Lacan J. *The Psychoses: The Seminar of Jacques Lacan, Book III, 1955–1956*, J.-A. Miller, ed. (London: Routledge, 1993).

Laqueur, T. 'Orgasm, Generation and the Politics of Reproductive Biology', *The Making of the Modern Body: Sexuality and Society in the Nineteenth Century*, C. Gallagher and T. Laqueur, eds. (Berkeley: University of California Press, 1987).

le Fanu, S. *The House by the Churchyard* (Belfast: Appletree, 1992 [1886]).

Leonard, G.M. 'Joyce and Lacan: "The Woman" as a Symptom of "Masculinity" in "The Dead"', *James Joyce Quarterly* 28.2 (1991): 451–72.

Leonard, G.M. *Reading* Dubliners *Again: A Lacanian Perspective* (Syracuse, NY: Syracuse University Press, 1993).

Leonard, G.M. 'Wondering Where All the Dust Comes From: *Jouissance* in "Eveline"', *James Joyce Quarterly* 29.1 (1991): 23–43.

Levine, H.J. *Yeats's Daimonic Renewal* (Ann Arbor: UMI Research Press, 1983).

Levitt, A.S. 'The Pattern Out of the Wallpaper: Luce Irigaray and Molly Bloom', *Modern Fiction Studies* 35.3 (1989): 507–16.

Lowery, R.G., ed. *Essays on Sean O'Casey's Autobiographies* (London: Macmillan, 1981).

Lubbers, K. 'Irish Fiction: A Mirror for Specifics', *Eire-Ireland* 20.2 (1985): 90–104.

Luddy, M. 'An Agenda for Women's History, 1800–1900', *Irish Historical Studies* 28.109 (1992): 19–37.

Luddy, M. *Women and Philanthropy in Nineteenth-Century Ireland* (Cambridge: Cambridge University Press, 1995).

Lyons, F.S.L. *Ireland Since the Famine* (London: Fontana, 1973).

MacCabe, C. *James Joyce and the Revolution of the Word* (London: Macmillan, 1978).

MacCabe, C. ed. *James Joyce: New Perspectives* (Brighton: Harvester, 1982).

MacCana, P. 'Women in Irish Mythology', *The Crane Bag Book of Irish Studies* 4.1 (1980): 520–4.

MacCurtain, M. 'Towards an Appraisal of the Religious Image of Women', *The Crane Bag Book of Irish Studies* 4.1 (1980): 539–43.

MacCurtain, M. and D. O Corrain, eds, *Women in Irish Society: The Historical Dimension* (Dublin: Arlen House, 1978).

Malkan, J. 'George Moore's *The Lake*: Repetition, Narcissism and Exile', *English Literature in Transition* 32.2 (1989): 159–69.

Manhiemer, J. 'Murderous Mothers: The Problem of Parenting in the Victorian Novel', *Feminist Studies* 5.3 (1979): 530–46.

Marks, E. and I. de Courtivron, eds *New French Feminisms: An Anthology* (Amherst: University of Massachusetts Press, 1980).

Martin, A., ed. *The Genius of Irish Prose* (Dublin: Mercier Press, 1985).

Martin, H.C. *W.B. Yeats: Metaphysician as Dramatist* (Waterloo, Ont.: Wilfred Laurier University Press, 1986).

Maxwell, D.E.S. *A Critical History of Modern Irish Drama, 1891–1980* (Cambridge: Cambridge University Press, 1984).

McCormack, W.J. *From Burke to Beckett: Ascendancy, Tradition and Betrayal in Literary History* (Cork: Cork University Press, 1994).

McCormack, W.J. and A. Stead, eds. *James Joyce and Modern Literature* (London: Routledge & Kegan Paul, 1982).

McKnight, J. 'Unlocking the Word-Hoard: Madness, Identity and Creativity in James Joyce', *James Joyce Quarterly* 14.4 (1977): 420–35.

Miller, J.E. ' "O, she's a nice lady!" ': A Rereading of "A Mother" ', *James Joyce Quarterly* 28.2 (1991): 407–26.

Miller, N.A. 'Beyond Recognition: Reading the Unconscious in the "Ithaca" Episode of *Ulysses*', *James Joyce Quarterly* 30.2 (1993): 209–18.

Millet, K. *Sexual Politics* (London: Sphere, 1972).

Mitchell, J. '*A Drama in Muslin*: George Moore's Victorian Novel', *English Literature in Transition* 25.4 (1982): 211–24.

Mitchell, J. 'George Moore's Kate Ede', *English Studies in Canada* 12.1 (1986): 69–78.

Mitchell, J. and J. Rose, eds, *Feminine Sexuality: Jacques Lacan and the* école freudienne (London: Macmillan, 1982).

Moore, G. *The Brook Kerith: A Syrian Story* (Edinburgh: T. Werner Laurie, 1916).

Moore, G. *Celibate Lives* (London: Chatto & Windus, 1968 [1927]).

Moore, G. *Celibates* (London: Walter Scott, 1895).

Moore, G. *Confessions of a Young Man* (London: William Heinemann, 1952 [1888]).

Moore, G. *A Drama in Muslin* (Gerrards Cross: Colin Smythe, 1981 [1887]).

Moore, G. *Esther Waters* (Oxford: Oxford University Press, 1983 [1894]).

Moore, G. *Hail and Farewell: Ave, Salve, Vale* (Gerrards Cross: Colin Smythe, 1976 [1911–14]).

Moore, G. *The Lake* (Gerrards Cross: Colin Smythe, 1980 [1905]).

Moore, G. *Literature at Nurse, or Circulating Morals: A Polemic on Victorian Censorship*, P. Coustillas, ed. (Hassocks, Sussex: Harvester, 1976 [1885]).

Moore, G. *A Mere Accident* (London: Vizetelly & Co., 1887).

Moore, G. *Mike Fletcher* (London: Ward & Downey, [n.d] [1889]).

Moore, G. *A Modern Lover* (London: Vizetelly, 1885 [1883]).

Moore, G. *A Mummer's Wife* (London: Heinemann, 1918 [1885]).

Moore, G. *The Untilled Field* (Gerrards Cross: Colin Smythe, 1976 [1903]).

Morrison, M. 'Stephen Dedalus and the Ghost of the Mother', *Modern Fiction Studies* 39.2 (1993): 345–68.

Moynahan, J. *Anglo-Irish: The Literary Imagination in a Hyphenated Culture* (Princeton: Princeton University Press, 1995).

Muller, J.P. and W.J. Richardson, eds. *The Purloined Poe: Lacan, Derrida & Psychoanalytic Reading* (Baltimore & London: Johns Hopkins University Press, 1988).

Newman, J.H. Cardinal. 'The Glories of Mary for the Sake of Her Son', *Discourses Addressed to Mixed Congregations* (London: Longmans Green & Co., 1902).

Newsinger, J. ' "In the Hunger-Cry of the Nation's Poor is Heard the Voice of Ireland": Sean O'Casey and Politics, 1908–1916', *Journal of Contemporary History* 20 (1985): 221–40.

Ni Chuilleanain, E., ed. *Irish Women: Image and Achievement* (Dublin: Arlen House, 1985).

Norris, M. 'The Last Chapter of *Finnegans Wake*: Stephen Finds His Mother', *James Joyce Quarterly* 25.1 (1987): 11–30.

Obed, B. 'The Maternal Ghost in Joyce', *Modern Language Studies* 15.4 (1985): 40–7.

O'Brien, F. *The Poor Mouth (An Béal Bocht)* (London: Flamingo, 1993 [1941]).

O'Brien Johnson, T. and D. Cairns, eds, *Gender in Irish Writing* (Milton Keynes: Oxford University Press, 1991).

O'Casey, S. *Autobiographies, Volume I–II* (London: Macmillan, 1963).

O'Casey, S. *Collected Plays, Volumes I–III* (London: Macmillan & Co., 1950–51).

O'Casey, S. *Collected Plays, Volume IV* (London: Macmillan, 1964).

O'Casey, S. *Feathers from the Green Crow: Sean O'Casey, 1905–1925*, R. Hogan, ed. (London: Macmillan, 1963).

O'Connor, A. *Child Murderess and Dead Child Traditions: A Comparative Study* (Helsinki: Suomalainen Tiedeakatemia, 1991).

O'Connor, G. *Sean O'Casey: A Life* (London: Hodder & Stoughton, 1988).

O'Grady, T.B. 'Conception, Gestation and Reproduction: Stephen's Dream of Parnell', *James Joyce Quarterly* 27.2. (1990): 293–302.

Omidsalar, M. 'W.B. Yeats' "Cuchulain's Fight with the Sea'", *American Imago* 42.3 (1985): 315–33.

Orr, L., ed. *Yeats and Postmodernism* (Syracuse: Syracuse University Press, 1991).

Perloff, M. 'Between Hatred and Desire: Sexuality and Subterfuge in "A Prayer for my Daughter'", *Yeats Annual, No. 7*, W. Gould, ed. (London: Macmillan, 1990).

Perreault, J. 'Male Maternity in *Ulysses*', *English Studies in Canada* 13.3 (1987): 307–14.

Peterson, R.F., A.M. Cohn and E.L. Epstein, eds. *Work in Progress: Joyce Centenary Essays* (Carbondale: Southern Illinois University Press, 1983).

Poovey, M. *Uneven Developments: The Ideological Work of Gender in mid-Victorian England* (Chicago: University of Chicago Press, 1988).

Restuccia, F.L. *Joyce and the Law of the Father* (London: Yale University Press, 1989).

Ronsley, J. *Yeats's* Autobiography: *Life as Symbolic Pattern* (Cambridge, Mass.: Harvard University Press, 1968).

Sawyer, R. *'We Are But Women': Women in Ireland's History* (London & New York: Routledge, 1993).

Sceats, S. and G. Cunningham, eds, *Image and Power: Women in Fiction in the Twentieth Century* (London: Longman, 1996).

Schrank, B. 'Language and Silence in *The Plough and the Stars*', *Moderna Sprak* 80.4 (1986): 289–96.

Scott, B.K., ed. *The Gender of Modernism: A Critical Anthology* (Bloomington & Indiana: Indiana University Press, 1990).

Scott, B.K. *James Joyce* (Brighton: Harvester, 1987).

Scott, B.K. *Joyce and Feminism* (Bloomington: Indiana University Press, 1984).

Shaw, G.B. *John Bull's Other Island and Major Barbara: Also How He Lied to Her Husband* (London: Archibald Constable & Co., 1907).

Sidorsky, D. 'Modernism and the Emancipation of Literature from Morality: Teleology and Vocation in Joyce, Ford and Proust', *New Literary History* 15.1 (1983): 137–53.

Sprengnether, M. *The Spectral Mother: Freud, Feminism and Psychoanalysis* (Ithaca & London: Cornell University Press, 1990).

Stoker, B. *Dracula* (Oxford: Oxford University Press, 1983 [1897]).

Synge, J.M. *Collected Works: Volumes I–IV* (London: Oxford University Press, 1968).

Templeton, J. 'The Bed and the Hearth: Synge's Redeemed Ireland', *Drama, Sex and Politics*, J. Redmond, ed. (Cambridge: Cambridge University Press, 1985).

Thomson, L. 'Opening the Eyes of the Audience: Visual and Verbal Imagery in *Juno and the Paycock*', *Modern Drama* 29.4 (1986): 556–66.

Toomey, D. '"Away'", *Yeats Annual, No. 10*, W. Gould, ed. (London: Macmillan, 1993).

Toomey, D. 'Labyrinths: Yeats and Maud Gonne' *Yeats Annual, No. 9*, D. Toomey, ed. (London: Macmillan, 1992).

Unkeless, E.R. 'Leopold Bloom as Womanly Man', *Modernist Studies: Literature and Culture, 1920–1940* 2.1 (1976): 35–44.

van Boheeman, C. *Joyce, Modernity and its Mediation* (Amsterdam: Rodopi, 1989).

van Boheeman, C. *The Novel as Family Romance: Language, Gender and Authority from Fielding to Joyce* (Ithaca, NY & London: Cornell University Press, 1987).

Walkley, R.B. 'The Bloom of Motherhood: Couvade as a Structural Device in *Ulysses*', *James Joyce Quarterly* 18.1 (1980): 55–67.

Warner, M. *Alone of All Her Sex: The Myth and the Cult of the Virgin Mary* (London: Weidenfeld and Nicolson, 1976).

Watt, G. *The Fallen Woman in the Nineteenth-Century English Novel* (London & Canberra: Croom Helm, 1984).

Watt, S.M. 'Boucicault and Whitbread: The Dublin Stage at the End of the Nineteenth-Century', *Eire-Ireland* 18.3 (1983): 23–53.

Webster, B.S. *Yeats: A Psychoanalytic Study* (London: Macmillan, 1973).

Welch, R., ed. *The Way Back: George Moore's* The Untilled Field *and* The Lake (Dublin: Wolfhound Press, 1982).

Wiemers, A.J. 'Rural Irishwomen: Their Changing Role, Status, and Condition', *Eire-Ireland* 29.10 (1994): 76–91.

Wilson, E. *Axel's Castle: A Study of the Imaginative Literature of 1870–1930* ([London]: Fontana, 1961 [1931]).

Wollaeger, M.A. 'Posters, Modernism, Cosmopolitanism: *Ulysses* and World War I Recruiting Posters in Ireland', *The Yale Journal of Criticism* 6 (1993): 87–131.

Yeats, W.B. *Autobiographies* (London: Macmillan & Co., 1961).

Yeats, W.B. *Essays* (London: Macmillan & Co., 1924).

Yeats, W.B. *John Sherman* and *Dhoya*, R.J. Finneran, ed. (Detroit: Wayne State University Press, 1969).

Yeats, W.B. *Mythologies* (London: Macmillan & Co., 1959).

Yeats, W.B. *The Speckled Bird*, W.H. O'Donnell, ed. (London: McClelland & Stewart, 1976)

Yeats, W.B. *The Variorum Edition of the Plays of W.B. Yeats*, R.K. Alspach, ed. (London: Macmillan, 1966).

Yeats, W.B. *The Variorum Edition of the Poems of W.B. Yeats*, P. Allt and R.K. Alspach, eds (New York: Macmillan, 1957).

Yeats, W.B. *Writing on Irish Folklore, Legend and Myth* (London: Penguin, 1993).

Yeazell, R.B., ed. *Sex, Politics and Science in the Nineteenth-Century Novel* (Baltimore & London: Johns Hopkins University Press, 1986).

Zeiss, C. 'Liturgy and Epiphany: Religious Experiences as Dramatic Form in Two of O'Casey's Symbolic Plays', *O'Casey Annual, No. 3*, R.G. Lowery, ed. (London: Macmillan, 1984).

Index